THE

AREMAC

PROJECT

THE AREMAC PROJECT

GERALD M. WEINBERG

Little West Press

a division of
DORSET HOUSE PUBLISHING
353 WEST 12TH STREET
NEW YORK, NEW YORK 10014

Library of Congress Cataloging-in-Publication Data

Weinberg, Gerald M.
  The Aremac project / Gerald M. Weinberg.
     p. cm.
  ISBN-13: 978-0-932633-70-5 (pbk. : alk. paper)
  ISBN-10: 0-932633-70-6 (pbk. : alk. paper)
  1. United States. Federal Bureau of Investigation--
Fiction. 2. Nanotechnology--Fiction. 3. Terrorists--
Fiction. I. Title.
  PS3573.E3917A88 2007
  813'.6--dc22

                                              2006039574

Quantity discounts are available from the publisher. Call (800) 342-6657 or (212) 620-4053 or e-mail littlewest@dorsethouse.com. Contact same for examination copy requirements and permissions. To photocopy passages for academic use, obtain permission from the Copyright Clearance Center: (978) 750-8400 or www.copyright.com.

This novel is a work of fiction. Any references to historical events; to real people, living or dead; or to real locales are intended only to give the fiction a setting in historic reality. Other names, characters, places, and incidents either are the product of the author's imagination or are used fictitiously, and their resemblance, if any, to real-life counterparts is entirely coincidental.

Trademark credits: All trade and product names are either trademarks, registered trademarks, or service marks of their respective companies, and are the property of their respective holders and should be treated as such.

Cover Design and Illustration: Brandon Swann, Swann Design Studio, http://www.swanndesignstudio.com

Distributed in the English language in Singapore, the Philippines, and Southeast Asia by Alkem Company (S) Pte. Ltd., Singapore; and in the English language in India, Bangladesh, Sri Lanka, Nepal, and Mauritius by Prism Books Pvt., Ltd., Bangalore, India.

Printed in the United States of America

Library of Congress Catalog Number: 2006039574

ISBN-10: 0-932633-70-6
ISBN-13: 978-0-932633-70-5

                          12 11 10 9 8 7 6 5 4 3 2 1

God gave us memory so that we might have roses in December. —J.M. BARRIE

It's a poor sort of memory that only works backward. —LEWIS CARROLL

THE AREMAC PROJECT

1

A scientist would call it chaos—one of those unlikely phenomena in which the flutter of a butterfly wing stirs a hurricane half a world away. And make no mistake, had Tesla Bell Myers failed to seduce the young genius, Roger Wahid Fixman, that balmy spring in Ann Arbor, the Aremac's hurricane effects would never have saved the city of Chicago from terrorist extortion. Though the hyacinths spread *fragrance d'amour* over the entire campus, it was still an improbable romance—the merest flick of a butterfly wing—until Roger held up the campus bank and Tess accidentally lost her body.

As it was, save for the war on terror, Tess's plan to marry young Roger might never have gotten off the ground. Though Tess generally accomplished anything she set her brilliant mind to, that same brilliant mind had always placed a stumbling block in the way of her matrimonial plans. She admired brains, and all through her life, she'd waited for a man with brains to match hers.

She didn't count Mel Myers—fathers don't count, except to mothers. At twenty-two, Tess was already four years older than her mother, Leonora Myers, had been when she snagged herself a genius husband. At age eight, Tess had understood that Leonora's Mel was already taken. She vowed to catch a genius of her own.

When she was twelve and the other girls' mothers were warning them about sex and babies, Leonora told her, "Be sure he knows how to apply for a patent, test his inventions, and read a royalty statement."

Tess agreed those were minimal essentials, but she and her genius would share much more. They would not be sidetracked by money, like her mother, or mean-spirited and conservative, like her father. United by love and idealism, they would change the world.

At fourteen, she learned she could easily attract any boy who met her standards—but none did. She tried to settle for sex, but soon realized that good sex required an intelligent partner. So, a genius would certainly be the hottest mate she could find. Science was much more interesting than dating dull boys, and she was so much better at it. She gave up dating and breezed through high school in three lonely years, finishing at the top of her class. Heading for college, scholarship in hand, she dreamed of better luck. On campus, though, she was quickly disappointed. Even the smartest undergraduates were driven away by her superior brain. She was lonelier than ever, but she refused to play dumb.

At twenty-two, almost finished with graduate school in Michigan, she had pretty much resigned herself to the single life— which would at least be better than boring matrimony. Tess wanted desperately to make a difference in the world through science, but she was going to have to go it alone.

But then she found her man—a boy, really—sitting quietly in the back row of her advanced circuit theory class. It was Roger.

At first, like all the other girls, she noticed he was tall, half-Arab, and handsome, but Tess dismissed him as just another brainless pretty face. All he ever did in class was stare vacantly at his laptop. Or his fingernails. Had she known he was controlling his laptop with brainwaves sent through the air by one of his inventions, embedded in the back of his hand—had she even seen on the screen the next invention he hoped would one day save the world—she would have dragged him off to City Hall and married him on the spot.

But as the semester wore on and test scores were posted, Tess began to realize that Roger did have a brain worthy of her love. Scrap by scrap, she researched her target. He lived alone. He never dated. He was at the top of every class, way beyond all the others. He was definitely a prodigy, only seventeen—well, eighteen by the time of the final exam. He had already published half a dozen important inventions in electronics, but he hadn't applied for any patents and had no royalty statements to read. Clearly, he needed guidance.

His Valentino profile proved to be a small, titillating bonus, and their age difference didn't bother her at all. Genius was genius, regardless of age or form. But if genius was going to make an impact on the world, genius needed a guide, someone more worldly, with a will to succeed. Someone like her mother had been for her father. Someone like Tess.

She made up her mind to meet Roger, but all her attempts to corner the shy boy failed. Ever since the Chicago bombings, the other students seemed to be shunning the Arab students, only deepening his shyness. After each class, Roger disappeared before Tess could pack up her notes and turn around. She didn't want to look too obvious, but she was running out of time. Come summer, the genius might be gone forever. She was going to have to make a frontal assault. She would accost him when they emerged from their final exam. That would certainly give them something in common to talk about.

But, on final exam day, Roger didn't show up.

2

Don Capitol usually enjoyed the drive from Chicago through the wet, winding streets of Inverness, with the clean fragrance of newly mown grass and the reverent silence of the empty sidewalks. Not today. Today, in spite of his agency's best efforts, and in the face of multiple security-service placards conspicuously set in each manicured lawn, this sacrosanct neighborhood had felt the mournful caress of a terrorist bomb.

In Don's five years as agent-in-charge, the Chicago FBI office had never investigated a crime scene in such an exclusive neighborhood. Its residents—including members of the United States Congress—surely ought to be immune from acts of terrorism. In such an elegant neighborhood, nobody should be bombed. Heck, it shouldn't even be raining here. But it was raining. Hard. And definitely bombed—making it his case, regardless of when, where, or weather.

He stopped checking addresses as soon as he saw the crowd up ahead. He slowed his government-issue blue Ford—first to a crawl, then to a dead stop. His salary grade entitled him to a limo and driver, but he preferred the less-conspicuous vehicle when on field work. His status-conscious superiors in Washington had already reprimanded him twice for not using the limo. Luckily, they wouldn't allow themselves to become involved in a scene like this.

Until this recent wave of bombings, he'd been spending too much time in the limo. He loved fieldwork. It was an acquired taste, like his grandmother's *kielbasa*, but he'd had twenty-some years to learn to savor it.

He rolled down his window, taking in the outside air. Out here, even with the rain coming in, the air was a thousand times better than in the office. He should never have taken the promotion. He ought to be a bit grateful to the bombers for getting him back outside, since this was too big a situation to be delegated to anyone else in the office.

But he was too angry to be grateful, and too frustrated with the lack of leads. This was not a situation he could allow to escalate. It had gone too far already. Nobody had been killed yet, but it wouldn't be long.

On the drive here, as the array of passing homes grew more palatial, he realized that the limo would not have been conspicuous. Certainly, the posh neighborhood was a plum target for burglaries, but the FBI never dirtied its hands on mere burglaries. Not unless the ransacked home had *Masha'allah*—God's will— written in Arabic on a wall. Maybe it had been written on one of the walls at the address in question, but according to the call-in, there wasn't a single wall of the million-dollar chateau left standing.

As it was later revealed, *Masha'allah* had been spray-painted on the driveway but hidden by rubble from the explosion. After some of the rubble had been swept away, the local cops—none of whom read Arabic or even recognized it as writing—figured it was teenage graffiti. Don wasn't called in until a Lebanese doctor, passing by, pointed out the writing and translated it for the cops. Until then, the prevailing theory (totally naive) was that the cause was a natural gas explosion. A shattered family portrait hung from the limb of a red maple on the neighbor's lawn—a lawn covered with glass that likely burst from the neighbor's windows, now open to the elements and seeming to support the natural gas hypothesis.

Three orange-and-white gas company vans were parked just outside the ring of cops' blue-and-whites. Perhaps the cops hadn't given up on the gas explosion theory, or maybe the vans were just there to repair the gas mains. Either way, with debris found more than five hundred feet from the scene, Don already knew this had been no residential gas accident.

Part of the crime scene was already hopelessly ruined by the mass of drenched spectators inside that five-hundred foot perimeter. Don's first job was to persuade the locals to move everyone back. Then he noticed that the spectators had formed their own ragged perimeter, avoiding the dismembered parts of a dog's body. Or maybe it was two dogs. It was hard to tell. He remembered something about the congressman's wife breeding dogs—Golden Retrievers or something. One of the big breeds.

Taking in the scene as a whole, he automatically estimated the size of the bomb, further indicating the work of *Yom alKhamis*—the self-named Thursday Group. *Probably plastic-bonded explosives,* Don surmised. He hoped the cell hadn't yet learned how to make the PBX itself, making it feasible for the forensics lab to use DMNB—2,3 dimethyl 2,3 dinitrobutane—to identify the ordnance factory that produced it. Not that the identification would help locate *alKhamis* any better than it had in the four previous bombings. Those explosives went missing two years earlier from Fort Benning in Georgia, and nobody in the Army or FBI had the slightest idea who had taken them.

But these thoughts were premature, and speculative. He stacked them in the back of his mind while he introduced himself to the local police. They seemed to be expecting him—a mystery until he saw the cropped, straw-colored hair atop Lucinda Dukes as she strode between two tall local officers. As usual, the efficient LD had reached the scene ahead of him and briefed the locals. She and the cops were discussing the unattached head of what appeared to have been a Golden Retriever. It was lying on the zoysia grass with a hunk of aluminum window frame sticking out of its left eye.

"Hello, Don. Grisly enough for you? It's worse inside—or what used to be inside. There was a kennel on the grounds, but not anymore. And I'm dying for a cigarette, but the utility boys say that's a no-no. They've got the line capped, but they have to finish their checking. When they talk, I listen, but I sure could use some nicotine."

Lucinda didn't usually babble. She'd seen lots of dead bodies in the Middle East, but the decapitated dog must have touched some sensitive spot. "And hello to you, LD," he smiled. "Why don't you walk down the block and take a break. I can cover here for five minutes. Dead dogs are bad, but at least it's not people who were hurt."

"Didn't you hear? They found a survivor."

He shivered, though the rain was warm. This was new. All the previous *alKhamis* bombings had occurred in empty buildings. Don quickly resurveyed the scattered remains of the house—antique bricks blown two hundred feet, twisted and sheared duct work, unidentifiable electronic parts. "From inside the house? I don't believe in miracles."

"They don't know where he was." She pointed to the remains of the attached garage, which he identified by the smoldering ruins of two cars. "They found him buried over there. He might have been outside, but there's no way to tell."

"Identity?"

"Nada. His clothes were burned or blown off, and they say his face won't ever be the same again, unless he's a stand-in for Frankenstein."

"So, male. Adult. You see anything else?"

"I never even saw him. They carted him off before I arrived. He's at Suburban now." She glanced at her cell phone. "As of fifteen minutes ago, still alive. That's why I can't take a break. Now that you're here, I'm going over there in case he wakes up."

"I won't keep you, but is it the congressman?"

"We don't think so. None of his cars are here. But it's hard to be sure until I've talked to the victim."

"If it is, this *alKhamis* has just escalated to a new level."

3

By now, the whole country believed the war on terror was endless and irresolvable. The bombing in Inverness was only one more example. Volunteers for the armed services had dried up, and the draft had been reactivated. So, on Roger's eighteenth birthday, he had to go back home, to Chicago, for his draft board physical. It was the same day as his circuit theory final.

Roger had no car, so he took the bus from Ann Arbor. He had arranged to return by five o'clock, to take the make-up exam in Professor Wyatt's office. By that time, all the other students had gathered in the hallway—Wyatt was notoriously slow at posting grades online.

Wyatt's exams were killers—designed to humiliate the students rather than measure their knowledge. Tess had the highest grade—seventy-one. Wyatt was prepared to scale everyone to Tess's grade by adding twenty-eight points, giving Tess a sterling ninety-nine. She would have had one hundred, but Wyatt didn't believe anyone besides himself could be perfect. Even with the added twenty-eight points, only about half the class was going to pass.

Then, Roger, in just thirty minutes, still in his bus-rumpled gray suit, turned in his perfect paper. Wyatt nitpicked him out of two points, but it really had been perfect. Wyatt was a sharp dresser, especially among professors, but Roger was the Beau Brummell of electronics. Even so, young Roger didn't know much about arguing with egotistical professors.

So, Roger's raw score was ninety-eight, certain to earn an A in the course. But if Wyatt used Roger's score, he would have to scale down all the other grades, and Roger, if he had thought about it, would have been upset that only five students passed the course, but he had assumed that everyone would pass such a trivial exam. It didn't really call for problem-solving skills, just memorization of the material.

Roger lingered in Wyatt's office, studying the glass-framed circuit boards and gold-sealed award certificates lining the wall, while Wyatt posted the grades in the hall and quickly returned. As students crowded and fought to check the posting, a moan arose in response to their grades. A few feet behind the crush of students— totally confident of her grade—stood Tess Myers.

When Roger took his eyes off Wyatt's trophies and realized that the crowd had virtually trapped him behind the door with Wyatt, he was surprised to see Tess pushing herself through the fray and into the office. Big as Roger was—six-four to her four-eleven—he couldn't have pushed his way through. So, he sat down and watched—jaw slack—while this tiny creature with apricot-colored hair persuaded Wyatt to set aside Roger's ninety-eight and use her grade for scaling the rest of the class. That accomplished, she persuaded Wyatt to add ten more points, so that almost eighty percent of the class passed. Though Roger heard every word she said, he had no clue how she had done it. Girls were not his strongest subject. Especially girls in tight wool sweaters.

Roger watched Tess finish with Wyatt, return to the hall, command the crowd's attention, and announce the new scaling. The students cheered and thanked Tess for several minutes. They gradually streamed out of the building, toward the dining hall, taking a somewhat baffled Professor Wyatt with them. Roger had his eyes wide open all the time, staring. He'd never seen anything like what Tess had just accomplished.

He was still pondering Tess's actions when she really astonished him by returning to Wyatt's office and speaking to him. "You're Roger Wahid Fixman, aren't you?" She stumbled over his

Arabic middle name. "I got your name from the grade list. Do you call yourself Roger? Or Wahid?"

He croaked something that sounded like yes. All of his brain power was struggling to process the unfamiliar feelings induced by the smell of lilacs and the sight of her eyes, those two huge brown eyes staring up at him. He bent his back so he could get a better look at her luminous brown eyes, but he only succeeded in making himself feel even more awkward.

"That was really gracious of you, Roger," she said, assuming that his croak indicated his American name. He had absolutely no idea what she was talking about.

"Huh? What?"

"Don't be so modest, Roger. I'm Tess. Tesla, really, after the inventor—you know, magnetic flux density? I was born on his birthday. But you should call me Tess." She held out her right hand.

He gawked at it, wondering what it was doing sticking out there in space like a soft pink cantilever. She looked at his right hand, then shifted her eyes to her own hand. Aha! She wanted to shake hands.

He was puzzled by how cool her hand felt, though somehow it was warm, too, probably because his was cold with sweat. He didn't know how he was supposed to shake hands with a girl, but she rescued him with a firm grip. When she pulled her hand away, his was left suspended in space, but she was polite enough not to look at it again.

Instead, she looked directly into his eyes. "It wasn't really fair to you, Roger, that we all got our grades scaled up. You could have insisted that Wyatt give you credit for an outstanding job. I mean, you could still complain to the dean or something. You'd be perfectly within your rights."

She paused, but he couldn't think of anything to say, so she continued. "But if you do, I would get a C. Or worse. And that would be the end of my post-doc chances."

"Oh," he sputtered, thinking the last thing he wanted was for her to leave campus. "Are you a grad student?" Not too profound—Electronics 451 was only open to grad students—but it was all he could muster.

"Neurophysiology."

He relaxed a notch. The nervous system was one of those circuits that fascinated him. "Are you going to be a doctor?"

"Not a medical doctor, though someday I hope to help Third World kids—like Albert Schweitzer did."

"Oh, yeah," he said, wondering who this Schweitzer was.

She rescued him again. "I'm sure you know more about his medical mission in Lambarene than I do."

"Oh, yeah. Sure. That Albert Schweitzer." Roger disliked not knowing facts. He would look it up tonight.

She touched his arm, wresting his mind back to the here-and-now. "Someday, if I get my post-doc, I'm going to save people's lives, and they will owe it all to your generosity. Little children will live because of you."

He deeply wanted to save little children, but couldn't quite understand how anyone would live because of him. She could have stuffed an apple in his gaping mouth, but she just gripped his hand—which was still hanging out there in space—shook it, and said, "I've got to get to the lab now. I'd like to buy you a Coke sometime. How about tonight at the Student Union?"

"Tonight?"

"Oh, sorry, you've probably got a date. You pick a better time."

Actually, Roger had never had a real date in his life, as long as you didn't count chatting online. "Uh, no. I mean, yes. That's okay. I'm not doing anything tonight. I mean I'm not doing anything important. I mean, more important . . ."

She nodded, "Shall we make it seven o'clock? In the coffee shop?"

"Seven? Uh, sure. Seven o'clock."

"In the coffee shop. Okay?"

"Coffee shop?"

"You know, The Grille? At the Student Union?"

"Yeah. Okay."

Now she smiled. It was the first time he noticed her mouth as something other than the source of beautiful words.

Her lips started to move again, sensuously. "And, um, could I have my hand back, please?"

And then she was gone, leaving only the lilacs.

4

Chicago's Merchandise Mart is one of the largest buildings in the world, and certainly one of the busiest. Fifteen stories high, occupying an entire city block on the Chicago riverfront, the Merchandise Mart holds more than a thousand different shops and diverse eateries. It was the perfect place to hold secret meetings, especially during a crowded spring show. Into the milling crowd, the four leaders of *Yom alKhamis* entered, one by one, from all directions, converging by different routes to a windowless room on an upper floor.

Qaaf, the only female, arrived first. Looking every bit the pudgy, middle-aged suburban housewife in her light-blue pants suit, carrying a shopping bag from the latest upscale shopping pavilion. To passersby, she appeared to be shopping, but she was actually ever-vigilant for any hint of possible detection.

Alif, with the compact frame and waddling gait of a body-builder, arrived next, from the opposite direction, dressed as a laborer. Upon close examination, his hair would have looked a bit too thick and black, but nobody looked so closely at such an anonymous worker.

A few minutes later, Zay strolled in from yet another entrance. Tall but not hefty, in a not-too-expensive, gray three-piece suit, he was just another older businessman, perhaps a minor executive. He carried an old brown leather briefcase as if it had hung from his hand for two or three decades.

Jiim arrived in the building last, as was his habit, though he had been first on the scene, watching the outside crowd from the riverfront. His telephone serviceman's uniform and toolbox looked innocuous, but had anyone examined him closely, his steel-gray eyes—and the contents of the toolbox—would have revealed him as the most dangerous of the four.

The room on which they converged was concealed behind the stockroom of three seemingly unrelated permanent showrooms—a lighting company, an importer of Oriental rugs, and a distributor of fine chocolates. Curiously, the three stores' surveillance cameras were always scheduled for preventive maintenance on Thursday afternoons, leaving no record of who entered or left for a period of two hours.

The Thursday Group's watchword was anonymity. The members' external appearances were disguises, altered every week, and only Zay knew the identities of the others. During their meetings, they addressed each other only by code names—letters of the Arabic alphabet. Each led a subsidiary cell of four, but none knew anything about the others' subordinates, who, in turn, may have led cells of their own. Not even Zay knew the full extent of the organization, and therefore, no cell could betray the others.

Qaaf, obviously wigged and heavily made-up, did not accept the anonymity passively, and over time, she had winnowed some ideas about the others' identities. At the very least, she knew their motives were quite different from hers. Zay, clearly, wanted the money; he had organized the group and set up their offshore accounts. She guessed that he'd been, or still was, in some high financial position.

Jiim, though too quiet to get a good read on, was quite likely a religious fanatic—or maybe he just liked mayhem and destruction. Tough guy Alif, on the other hand, never hesitated to remind them that he was seeking revenge against the government, or Cook County in particular. Qaaf's own revenge was aimed in quite a different direction.

This Thursday, she gave her status report in a voice she disguised so that it might, in fact, have been male. "He's still alive." Everyone knew she was referring to the wounded man found at the explosion site, the man they referred to as Dhal. Though he had not been a member of their group, they did not want to risk saying his real name aloud.

Alif was first in the alphabet and indisputably the alpha male—in his mind, at least, judging from the way he tried to control the meetings. He spit on the floor, then used the sole of his shoe to rub the spittle into the concrete. "Why wasn't Dhal terminated?"

Qaaf averted her eyes from Alif's disgusting habit. "They found him unconscious at the site. At present, he is so severely disabled, he can't leave his bed."

"And your group? Why haven't they terminated him?" Alif spit again. A roach scuttled out of the way of his spittle. "Why haven't you taken steps personally?"

"At first, he wasn't expected to live. The plan was that he would die naturally. But he didn't. Now he's heavily guarded, but hanging on by a thread."

She waited for Alif to interrupt, but he simply stared at her. After waiting for thirty seconds, she continued. "If I do anything overt, they'll know there's a mole in their organization. And if I kill him, they'll know he isn't really one of ours."

"Not necessarily. They may think he's one of ours, but we're ready to sacrifice him to keep him quiet."

"That's problematic. And it will still expose my existence."

"Has he spoken?"

"Dhal knows the consequences of speaking. He has spoken to me, in private, and devoutly wishes we will keep our promise. I am sure he has not spoken to anyone else."

"Can they break him?" Jiim asked.

"Perhaps, but they're weak. They won't use effective methods. Dhal could withstand their pathetic interrogation forever, but they're developing a new machine that may take information from him in spite of his utmost dedication to his family."

Alif punched his palm. "Then you know what you must do."

"I know, but I have to plan carefully."

"I agree," said Zay, who had been silent until now. "It cost a lot to establish you in your position. We wouldn't like to lose you. But if this machine of theirs will break Dhal, you have to do your job. If he's so badly injured, I'm sure you can think of something subtle. In the meantime, though, since we are about to send our first money demand, I have an alternative plan."

As far as Qaaf could recall, in all the *Yom alKhamis* meetings, nobody had ever spoken after Zay pronounced his last words. Today was no different, and one by one, the Thursday Group dissolved among the oblivious shoppers at the Merchandise Mart.

5

When Tess arrived two minutes early at The Grille, in the Student Union, she found Roger already sitting in a corner booth. His sneakers were untied, and he was paging through *On the Edge of the Primeval Forest* and *More from the Primeval Forest*, highlighting Schweitzer quotes, trying not to let his suffering show on his face. She noticed anyway. "Have you been waiting long?"

"Not too long." He tried to act casual.

She nodded at the six empty Coke bottles on the table. "The service in here isn't that great," she said, as if she didn't understand the implication of the bottles. "I guess they forgot to clear the booth before you sat down."

She snagged one of the waiters and, with a smile and a gesture, induced him to remove the bottles and even wipe down the sticky tabletop. When he finished, the waiter asked if she'd like to order anything, making it perfectly clear that she could occupy the booth for as long as she liked—even if she never spent a penny.

"I'll have a Coke," she said. "Roger, would you like something? Did you have supper?"

"Well, actually not. But that's—"

"Waiter, would you bring Roger a menu, please? I think he's hungry, and it's my treat."

"Sure thing," he said, tossing Roger a nasty glance.

When the waiter disappeared, Tess turned her attention back to her date. "You look uncomfortable, Roger. Do you need to use the bathroom?"

"Well, yes," he muttered through pressed lips. "Can you hold the booth? I'll be right back." Without waiting for her answer, he shot down the aisle, stumbling over the outstretched leg of a lanky undergraduate in a basketball jacket. Somehow, he reached the men's room in time.

Once he had returned and was fed a fried shrimp platter, they talked for hours. They started with Albert Schweitzer. Roger didn't understand much, but he did listen avidly to Tess's explanations. Then Roger described some of his experiments in graph theory and the mathematical theory of statistics. And he threw in some parallels he was working on between the physics of tripartite alloys and the three-body problem in celestial mechanics. She could tell he was trying to impress her, and he succeeded—with both his genius and his ignorance.

The whole time, she carefully kept her penetrating brown eyes focused on his, and, from time to time, she asked a question. Nothing stupid. Maybe ignorant of some of the details, but always penetrating. She knew she had to impress him, too, and she sensed that she was succeeding. The genius was taken with her.

She decided it was time to ask a more intimate question. "Roger, you seem to be hiding your left hand. Is there something wrong with it?"

He looked down to where his hand was hidden under the table. "Well, it's just an invention of mine."

"An invention?" She didn't have to fake her excitement. "Let me see."

"It's, uh, not working too well." He kept his hand under the table.

She extended her hand. "Then let me see. Maybe I can help."

Shyly, his hand emerged, palm up, from its hiding place. "I don't see anything," she said. She took his hand and turned it over. Then dropped it.

"My God, Roger. What did you do to your hand? Did something bite you?"

"I had to do a little surgery."

"On yourself? Whatever for?"

"I had a wireless interface embedded in contact with my nerves. So I could operate the computer with my mind."

Her eyes widened. "What happened? Didn't it work?"

"Oh, it worked okay. Once I trained myself to it."

"But you took it out. . . ."

"I couldn't control the infection. It was a dumb idea. It's dangerous to embed things in a living person. So, I'm working on a more sensitive interface, one that I can just lay on the surface. And probably not on the hand. Right on the skull would be best." He explained that the new model would involve Khinchin's concept of entropy in probability theory and Shannon's first and second theorems in information theory, using autocorrelation computations on data picked up by nanosensors. And that was only the beginning.

Roger would have rattled on all night if the Union wasn't closing at eleven. When the fifteen-minute warning was called, Tess reached across the table and beckoned for his wounded hand by wiggling her fingers. He seemed to have no other thought than to give her his hand, or anything else she wanted. She squeezed the hand gently in hers, careful to avoid the open wound. To her surprise, it seemed to her as if his hand had always belonged there.

"Roger," she whispered, leaning forward. For the last half hour, she had planned this move carefully. "You are absolutely the most boring person I've ever met. I think I'm in love with you."

He started to say something, but she held her finger to her lush lips. "You are so boring that sex with you would probably put me to sleep. So just put that out of your mind. But someday, I'm going to marry you." His eyes told her that until she mentioned sex, it never consciously crossed his mind. But now he was blushing from his neck up.

"I won't sleep with you," she continued, "until you learn not to be boring. If you're going to change the world with your inventions, you've got to learn about initiative. Among other things."

Of course, she didn't know then that he would hold up the Student Union Bank. He would never have done so but for the draft. So, in the end, the fallout from Roger's bold act would be felt by the Thursday Group and by millions of others. The butterfly's wings were beginning to stir.

6

When Don reached the silent white monolith of Suburban Hospital, his ears were still ringing from the mayor's rebuke. The sour-faced chief of police had read the terrorist demand for fifty million to stop the bombings, and Don—having grown up on the South Side—couldn't resist saying it sounded like business as usual in the Windy City.

The mayor wasn't Don's boss and had no real authority over him, but maintaining sweet relationships with the locals was part of his job as branch office chief. God, he hated these political maneuvers. He was sure the FBI chief in Washington had already heard from the mayor. At least the mayor would learn that Don was absolutely correct about federal policy—not one penny to terrorists, even if the continued bombings cost the mayor his job.

The note hadn't mentioned the survivor—their John Doe—and Lucinda still hadn't been able to interview him. After a week of extensive skin grafts and other surgeries, the man was still neither awake nor identified. He wasn't a member of the congressman's family, his fingerprints were burned off, and the Bureau's DNA records had yielded nothing. Lucinda's theory was that their John Doe was one of the terrorists. Don wasn't convinced, but he hoped it was true. If true, it was their only solid lead.

21

Don and Lucinda identified themselves to the plainclothes guard outside the patient's private room. Then they stood watching him breathe for twenty minutes before deciding they would learn more from interviewing his doctors.

The lead physician took them into a small, windowless examining room. "We haven't been able to communicate with him in any way. His mouth is badly burned. He can't talk. He may not even be aware."

The doctor suggested they wait another week, but Don pressed for more information. "Can't talk? Or won't? He shows no signs of awareness? Nothing at all?"

"We think there's a person in there somewhere, but we can't really prove it. He could be in shock. I would be, after what he's gone through. He swallows what's spooned into his mouth, but even broth and gelatin are difficult because of the wounds. Most of his nourishment and meds are given intravenously, but we'll keep trying oral feeding so his throat muscles will stay in practice."

"We'll want to bring in our forensic anthropologist to examine his bone structure for ethnic clues," Don noted.

"Not without my supervision," the doctor asserted. "His grafts could still be rejected quite easily."

"I'll want to be there," said Lucinda.

Over the next few days, they learned that John Doe had no tattoos or distinguishing scars or birthmarks on the small amount of unburned skin remaining. If he had marks anywhere else, they were gone. They estimated his height and weight, but since he could not be moved, the measurements were probably off by a few inches and ten or more pounds. He had no prosthetic devices implanted in his body. However, there were a few slight clues.

His dental work suggested it had been done outside North America, or at least not by a North American-trained dentist. When examining him, the dentist discovered a false tooth and carefully removed it. Lab analysis hadn't returned yet, but Don suspected it would turn out to hold a poison pill of a type often used by Middle Eastern terror groups.

At Lucinda's request, John Doe's DNA genotype was profiled for alleles that might indicate subpopulation origin. Don thought that was a long shot, but the report showed a pattern of alleles suggestive of a Middle East background. Don was impressed.

Before Lucinda left the hospital for an appointment with the explosives laboratory, she spoke with Don, who in turn spoke with the lead physician in his private office. "Agent Dukes had a hunch, and I want to try an experiment—with your permission, of course." He explained what he had in mind, and after some hesitation, the doctor agreed.

Don left the hospital and drove to a small barbecue joint he'd noticed a few blocks from the hospital. He wolfed down a brisket sandwich while his special order was being packed, then gave the cook a rather large tip and left with his plain white paper sack.

At the hospital entrance, a uniformed security guard tried to stop him from bringing in food, but his FBI identification got him through. Since John Doe had to be fed by hand, Don needed to wait thirty-five minutes until a nurse brought in the lunch tray. All that time, he studied Doe for any sign of voluntary movement. Nothing. Either he wasn't aware or he was an excellent actor.

The nurse had been informed of the experiment and allowed Don to replace the meat on the tray. She diced it into tiny chunks, then put one in John Doe's mouth. An instant later, the cube of pork flew over the nurse's shoulder and across the room, landing at Don's feet.

Don picked up the meat in a tissue. "Thank you, Nurse." He deposited the folded tissue in the wastebasket. "Agent Dukes was right. That's all I need. You may feed him his regular meal now."

As he walked out of the room, he whispered to the attending physician. "Your patient seems to have some awareness after all. He's been faking. Please prepare him to be moved."

"Moved?" The doctor shook his head. "No way. He's in no condition to be moved."

"The Agency will take responsibility for his condition. Don't worry. We have every incentive to keep him alive."

"Sorry, but you can't do that without a court order."

Clearly, the doctor was accustomed to being in total command here, but Don knew otherwise. "That won't be a problem. A court order will be faxed here in a few minutes."

The doctor's shoulders sagged. "But where are you taking him?"

"To our own hospital."

"Which one?"

"You've never heard of it."

"Where, then?"

"I'm sorry, but you don't need to know that."

"But why? Is there something wrong with our care?"

"No, your care has been more than we expected. You kept him alive. Thank you."

"Then why are you moving him?"

"Because he doesn't like pork."

7

It wasn't that Roger left the Student Union that night with the intention of holding up a bank, or anything else so dumb, but Tess had laid down a challenge. A challenge of a new kind, and Roger could never resist a challenge. It's just that he hadn't the slightest idea of how to go about meeting it.

As a start, he looked up *boring* in the dictionary, but the definition—"tending to cause boredom or tedium"—was itself an example of something boring. He spent almost a week trying to make a mathematical model of boring, reporting his progress to a bored Tess every day in the Union—sometimes in the evening, sometimes in the afternoon, depending on their schedules. He kept that up until the day he chanced to meet her at the drugstore checkout counter. She visually inventoried the toiletries he had laid on the counter. "You even use boring soap and boring shaving cream."

"But I'm working on a new theory of boring based on stochastic information theory. You should find it very interesting."

As they carried their purchases back to campus, Roger expounded on the outline of his theory. When they reached the Union, she stopped and asked him to sit with her on the green wooden bench at the bus stop.

"Roger, you're making progress—in the wrong direction. Not only are you boring, but now you're meta-boring. Boring about boring."

"I know what meta means," he said, hurt. He didn't mind being called meta-boring, but he didn't want her to think he didn't know his scientific Greek roots.

"I think you need less mental activity and something more physical."

"Like what?" He knew she didn't mean the s-word.

"I don't know. Perhaps you could learn how to keep your shoes tied. But if I choose for you, that's even more boring. Just go out somewhere and do something."

Roger looked down, noticing his shoes for the first time that day, but not understanding why tying them would be so interesting. "I don't have a car."

"Are you so boring you can't think of any other way to go somewhere?"

He pondered that question, which seemed far more profound than the derivation of Fisher's F-test. She waited patiently for a few minutes, then stood up to leave. "I'm sure you'll think of something."

Making notes in his head, Roger began to see a few possibilities. He could take a taxi. He could take a bus. He had never taken a city bus in Ann Arbor, but he was vaguely aware that they existed. Then he realized he was sitting on the bus bench, which confirmed his bus theory. He liked that.

He wasn't so sure about taxis, but he figured it would be good to have some money either way. He checked his pockets and found three quarters, a dime, and four pennies—probably not enough. He did know a lot about money. He'd learned about saving from his uncles, and he'd studied actuarial mathematics when he was twelve. He had a modest savings account drawing interest at the Student Union Bank. He decided he would make a withdrawal.

When he reached the bank, there were lines all the way back to the student lounge. He checked his watch and calculated that he couldn't make too much of an excursion if he stood in line for very long. Having mastered queueing theory, he decided to analyze the service times and queue discipline to see if he could estimate the wait time.

He asked the last person in line to hold his place and wiggled his way toward the tellers' cages, apologizing to the others that he wasn't trying to break into the line. As it turned out, he didn't need anything so sophisticated as queueing theory to understand the delay. All three tellers, plus the branch manager, were behind the bulletproof glass partition in one cage handling a single agitated student. Roger noticed that the student looked rather scruffy, which, if Roger noticed, was really saying something.

The student turned out to be as strident as he was scruffy. "Why can't you just tell me how much I have in my account?"

The branch manager adjusted his striped tie and tried to sound patient. "What's your account number?"

"I don't know my stupid account number. You're the bank. You should know it."

"If we don't have your number, we have to look it up by your name. That will take longer. Our computer is down—again—and we have to use backup printouts."

Reluctantly, the student gave his name. The line grew longer.

"We'll have to see your student ID," the manager said.

The student fished around in his filthy gray book bag for several minutes and finally retrieved a battered ID card. The teller confirmed his claimed identity and turned around to check a card file, presumably containing the account-holders' names and signa-tures in alphabetical order. The other two tellers and the branch manager just stood there watching. The line grew longer.

Eventually, the teller retrieved the student's account number, wrote it on a slip of paper, and took it over to a huge printout, presumably the accounts file. After a tedious search, she copied a number off one of the pages in the middle of the stack and returned to the window, where the student, the tellers, and the manager still waited patiently. "Your balance is twenty-seven cents," she announced.

"Then I want to write a check."

"Do you have your checkbook?"

"No, I forgot it."

"All right," the teller sighed, taking a counter check from a slot in the cage. "I'll write it on this check for you. How much should I write the check for?"

"Twenty-five cents."

The teller looked up and exchanged glances with the manager and the other two tellers. The manager nodded to her. "You can't do that," she said.

"Why not?"

"Because you'd be overdrawn."

"But you said I had twenty-seven cents."

"Yes, but there's a ten-cent charge for the check, and that would cause you to be overdrawn. You could write a check for seventeen cents."

"But I need twenty-five."

"I'm sorry, you can't do that."

The student scratched his ratty brown hair. Grayish flakes spewed out, driving the students behind him backward. "Okay," he said, "then I'll close my account. Would that give me twenty-five?"

"Actually, it will give you twenty-seven, but you'll have to fill out some forms to close the account." She motioned to the manager, who reached back and fetched a sheaf that looked five pages thick. Roger could see that the line was now about twice as long as when he'd arrived. He wasn't going to get to go on his excursion. Tess was going to think he was even more boring. When he saw the student begin to fill out the first page, with all four employees watching, something snapped.

He rushed out to the men's room and emptied his shopping bag into his backpack, all but a can of Gillette shaving cream. Then he used his Swiss Army knife to cut three holes in the bag. He put away his knife and placed the bag over his head, checking the eyehole alignment in the mirror. He turned his jacket inside-out and stuck the Gillette canister in one pocket, where it made an intimidating bulge. Looking armed and dangerous, he left the men's room and marched into the bank.

"This is a stickup," he said in his best Humphrey Bogart voice. "Put your hands on the counter where I can see them. If you don't do anything stupid, nobody will get hurt."

"W-we don't keep much c-cash here," the manager stuttered, his hands quivering on the counter.

"I don't want cash," Roger growled. "I just want you to obey my orders. Explicitly. Do you understand?"

"Yes. We u-understand. Girls, do what he says." He turned to Roger, pleading. "Just don't h-hurt them."

"I'm not going to hurt anybody. I want each of you to get to your own cage, and you, manager, you go to the fourth cage and open it, too."

They moved with quick steps to their assigned positions. He could practically smell their fear. "Okay. Now you, with the forms."

The scruffy student looked more offended than surprised. "Me?"

"Yes, you. Here's a quarter. Take those forms and chuck 'em. And get out of the way." Roger wiggled the Gillette can in his pocket. The student stopped objecting and moved as directed.

"All right. Now, the rest of you form four lines. If you don't know your account number, or if you don't have a slip already made out for a withdrawal, get in line at the manager's window. The rest of you take these three windows."

Then he turned to the tellers. "I'll be watching you, so no funny stuff. Just move these people through the lines as quickly as possible."

The first girl in the second line started to fill out a deposit slip. Roger put one hand on her arm and shifted the Gillette can in his pocket with the other. "No good, girlie. You should have done that while you were waiting. Go over there to the counter and fill it out while the next person gets served. When you're finished, go to the end of the line."

Trembling, she grabbed her purse and skittered to the counter, where the scruffy student was still standing. "And you . . ." Roger poked his index finger in the student's ribs, thinking he would have to wash his hands later. "Yes, you. Grab some deposit and withdrawal slips and pass them out to everyone in line who needs them." Then he announced to the lines, "If your slip isn't filled out by the time you reach the window, you'll have to go back to the end of the line. So get cracking."

With four windows operating in parallel, the lines began to dissolve rather quickly. But Roger hadn't thought about what he would do next. He realized that even at the speed the lines were going, he wouldn't have time to get any money. And that would have meant revealing his identity. So, before the lines disappeared completely, he slipped out a side door. Snatching off the bag and his jacket, he rounded the nearest corner and entered the student lounge. Students were reading or playing chess, and nobody looked up when he walked in. Taking an armchair near the fireplace, he tossed the bag into the flames. He caught his breath, turned his jacket right-side-out, and rose casually to walk around the lounge.

He took a seat between two chess matches and sized up the players at each board, waiting for a chance to make some quick money off one of the winners. He had a reputation among the

Union's regular chess players, but winners were always confident. After a game, he could usually persuade the winner to accept only a pawn, or at most a knight, as a handicap. This time it was a knight, but the player was a *putzer*, so Roger took his dollar in twenty-two swift moves. He knew he would remember every move, years later, just as he could replay every game he'd every played, but in the exhilaration of what had just happened, that dollar was unforgettable.

After three games of lightning chess, he had three more dollars, but it was too late for an adventure. He should have thought of this sooner. He still had no adventure to report to Tess that night. He shuffled directly to The Grille and waited for his punishment. When she arrived, he was halfway through his third Coke. He opened the conversation with his excuse for spending another boring day. "I needed money for the bus ride, and the lines were so long at the bank, I couldn't get it in time."

Her maple-sugar eyes lit with excitement. "So, you saw the bag bandit?"

"How did you know about that?"

"It's all over campus. Tell me about it. Was he really scary?"

He scratched his upper lip. His mustache needed shaving every four days, but not every three, and that evening, it was three-and-a-half. "I have a confession to make," he said at last.

"Oh, no. You didn't really see him? Were you doing equations in your head or something? You never notice *anything*." She took a sip of her Coke.

"Actually, my head was inside the bag."

"What?" she asked, her lips still on the straw.

"I was the bandit."

Tess coughed up her mouthful of Coke, splattering the table and adding a few more stains to his shirt. Laughing, she pulled a couple of napkins from the holder and reached across to dab at his chest. He knew right away he would always remember how nice it felt. While she wiped the table, she tried to recover. "Roger, that was very good. I don't think you've ever made a real joke before."

"It's not a joke, Tess. It was really me under the bag."

She held her finger to her lips. "No, Roger. When you make a joke, you have to learn when enough is enough. It was good, but if you push it too far, it's not funny anymore. It's just boring."

"But it really was me. I used the bag from the drugstore." He opened his backpack and showed her the toiletries on top. "I put everything in here. No, wait a minute. I still have my gun in my pocket."

"Your *gun*?"

"Like this." He showed her the can of Gillette, then turned the jacket back and showed her how it looked when he held the can in his pocket.

She still looked dubious. "Where's the bag now?"

"I burned it. In the fireplace in the lounge. I didn't want to leave fingerprints."

"That was clever. I'm beginning to believe you. Tell me all the details, from the beginning. And you'd better not be fooling."

He had never seen her so animated in his presence. He suggested they find a corner of the lounge so they wouldn't be overheard. While they sat on a small couch to one side of the fireplace, holding hands, he whispered the whole story. She was hungry for every detail, and when he finished, she kissed him on the cheek. Just a little peck, but it burned like a brand. He wondered what was so fascinating about his being a bank robber. How could it be more exciting than being an inventor?

8

Adara Halabi, Roger Fixman's first cousin and Nazim Halabi's eldest daughter, desperately needed distraction from her distressing circumstances. But no one in her huge family even knew she was in Cook County Hospital. Alone, injured, frightened, and hardly a terrorist, she resolved to be tougher than she'd ever had to be. She was determined not to give the slightest satisfaction to those whose irrational actions had placed her in the emergency room. Later, she would try to understand such people, as was her nature. For now, she had to survive.

Adopting the protective shield and professional eye of a fresh rehabilitation-nurse graduate, she surveyed Cook County Hospital's X-ray room, comparing it to all the X-ray facilities in which she had worked. She willed herself to be oblivious to the cold X-ray film frame pressed against her naked back, the pain radiating from her dislocated shoulder, and the largely ineffective morphine drip needled into her left wrist. Functionally, the room was adequate to its specialized task—lead-lined gloves and aprons, step stools with chrome handrails, and even a baby-blue modesty panel, though that had been pushed callously aside by the all-too-male technician.

No, it wasn't the familiar equipment that was lacking; it was the staff. The janitors had overlooked a used cotton wipe—its blood-spotted corner peeked out from under the maroon wheel of an instrument cart. Maintenance had left one large square ceiling tile half open, revealing a dark, foil-lined cavity crisscrossed by cables draped with cobwebs. Her nose told her that, somewhere nearby, a lab technician had spilled pungent acetone and failed to remove it properly. The room's decorators had provided three presumably cheering art posters, but two were placed so that the stark ceiling lights reflected off the glass, making them indiscernible. The other poster was blocked from patient view by a carelessly placed IV rack hung with a lab jacket, two blood pressure cuffs, her rented stars-and-stripes Uncle Sam costume, and her bra.

The female nurse who had wheeled Addie into X-ray was friendly enough, but had disappeared on some errand, violating hospital policy and leaving Addie's voluptuous femininity exposed to the leering eyes of the technician. Though Addie was a modern, freethinking Muslim woman who didn't believe in covering her face in the presence of men, she drew the line at exposing her breasts. Having been manhandled into Cook County Hospital by the police, she wasn't given much choice. Everyone was trying to humiliate her. Why? Simply for daring to participate in a demonstration of Arab-Americans for America?

As far as she knew, the police hadn't even detained the skinhead who had ripped away her "MUSLIMS ARE CITIZENS TOO" sign, mangling her elbow and shoulder in the process. Now that the entire city was in an uproar over the *alKhamis* bombings, any Arab seemed fair game, which was why she had been demonstrating in the first place. Right now, though, she would much rather be in her own hospital, helping needy patients. Not being one.

Still, the violence, the humiliation, the slovenliness of this historic hospital—all were nothing compared with the scolding Uncle Qasim would administer when she arrived at his Merchandise Mart emporium. How would she explain that she couldn't drive herself home because her arm was in a sling?

9

Sitting in Harvey Wyatt's pretentious full-professor's office as he tried to recruit her, Tess couldn't resist comparing him with Roger. *Is this the kind of arrogant bastard Roger will turn into when he's forty-three? Wyatt's worse than Mel. Will Roger be half-bald, with a beer belly? I can't do anything about the hair, but once we're married, I'll see that he doesn't grow that belly. God, is that what boring becomes when it grows unchecked?*

For the past half-hour, Tess had been listening to Wyatt brag about his many grants and publications. She had to admit she was interested in the grant for biological instrumentation, but as for the rest, she was growing tired of playacting the fascinated grad student. *He could still place some roadblock against my career, so I'd better be careful. He's definitely the vindictive type.*

He invited her to sit next to him to watch a PowerPoint show of a grant application on his giant wall monitor—the latest, greatest, and most expensive tech toy he had. "Like the screen?" he asked. "Paid for by grants. You've practically got your degree, now, haven't you?"

She was close enough to smell his deodorant. *Honest sweat would be better.* "If all goes well, I should be finished by the end of the first summer session. It's really just formalities now."

"Then you'll need an experienced mentor. Someone to teach you . . . how to win grants."

He touched her bare forearm, and she struggled mightily to resist jerking her arm away. *I shouldn't have laid it on so thick about the test scores. Now he's coming on to me. Is that how you apply for grants?*

He waved his arm, indicating the degrees and awards in matched gold frames covering all the wall space around his bookshelves. "Someone who knows how to make things happen."

She seized the excuse to stand up. Easing away from his touch, she walked over to inspect the awards. "It's an impressive array." He moved in her direction, but she backed toward the door before he could block her path.

"Are you leaving already?" He sounded like a pimply date who wanted a goodnight kiss.

"Was there something else you wanted to talk to me about, Professor Wyatt?"

"Why don't you call me Harvey? I asked you here to offer you a post on one of my grants. We would be working closely together." He moved closer.

Tess was revolted by the idea of working closely with Harvey Wyatt, but she was curious about the grant. "Which project, Professor?" *Better keep it formal.*

He frowned at her refusal to use his given name. "The bio-instrumentation. It's hard to find a biology person who understands circuits, and you were the best in the class."

"Second best, actually," she reminded him. "Roger Fixman was head and shoulders above me. Above everybody. And when he publishes his thesis, it's going to revolutionize bio-instrumentation."

"Yes, I'll admit he's a clever boy." He emphasized the last word. "But I like my assistants to be more . . . *mature*," he said, focusing on her chest in a way that made her squirm and wish she'd worn a bra. "He's a baby. Bright, but out of control. Can you imagine that he tried to tell me that his answer on one of the test questions was superior to mine?" He blew a small raspberry through his dry lips. "No respect."

"Was his answer superior?" *Oh, I shouldn't have asked that.*

He hesitated, thinking of the right words. "Let's say it was a matter of real-world judgment. He's memorized a lot of facts, but like all the self-educated, he has gaping holes in his knowledge."

She saw her opportunity. "You're right about that. He didn't even know who Albert Schweitzer was—can you imagine?"

Wyatt's eyes rolled up, trying to access some information. Tess knew what that meant. *You don't know, either, do you?*

He covered himself quickly. "Yes, that's the kind of thing I mean. So, you see why he's not a suitable candidate."

"That's too bad, Professor Wyatt. I thought that he and I would make a good working team in biotech—covering each other's weaknesses. I can't touch his knack for circuits, but I've got more experience with signal-processing software. So, I'm looking for a job where we can work together. He is very bright, you do have to give him that." She took a step toward the door. "Well, I guess I'll just have to keep looking."

He placed his hand on her bare forearm again, restraining her. His hand was cold and soft as dough, but she resisted the impulse to yank it away. "Maybe I *can* use him, if my granting agency will allow it."

"Why wouldn't they?" She snaked her hand away, pretending to scratch her nose.

"If you have a few minutes, let me show you something." He moved to the computer on his desk and typed a few commands. He stepped back and offered her his own chair so she could watch the screen. "This was my presentation that won the grant," he said, self-importance dripping from his words. Leaning over her, he touched a key that started an automatic slide show, narrating each slide as if he were seeking the grant. She watched in morbid fascination as a slide showed a simulated interrogation—a rear view of a handcuffed prisoner in a plain room, wearing an instrumented skullcap. *I hope that's not drawn from life.*

The next slide was labeled EARLIER—a rather lifelike drawing of two sinister men with Middle Eastern features inside a tent. One man was holding some kind of machine gun, listening to the other—above whose head was a cartoon balloon filled with what looked to Tess like Arabic writing. Roger popped into her mind. He would know what it said.

The third slide showed the detainee from the original slide, now seen in profile. She could see now that he was the man who held the machine gun in the EARLIER slide. This view was expanded to reveal the electronic rack connected to the skullcap's wires. Mounted in the rack was a loudspeaker emitting another cartoon balloon filled with Arabic letters. Tess thought they looked the same as in the second slide.

Before he could explain, Tess, horrified, blurted out, "It's a mind-reading machine."

He leaned over her, his chest against her back, and blanked the screen. "Clever, eh?" He spoke in conspiratorial tones, directly into her ear. His breath tickled the hairs on her neck, and she shuddered.

He continued as if the shudder meant she was impressed with the display. "I call it the mind recorder. Of course, it doesn't precisely read minds, but we will be able to, uh, . . . induce people to play back memories of heard speech. A lot of people would like to have one of these babies."

There was no way she could stand up without bumping into him. She stood anyway, as forcefully as her tiny frame would allow, knocking him backward against the window. "Who gave you the grant? Homeland Security?"

"Yes. And that's why I probably can't hire Roger."

"Why on earth not?"

"He's an Arab."

"He's an American, at least as much as you or I."

"He doesn't look American."

"And just how do Americans look? Like that?" She pointed past his shoulder out the window. A rainbow host of students were out in the courtyard. "Maybe you can point out the Americans for me."

"You know that's not the point."

"It's *precisely* the point. If it's instrumentation you want, Roger is the best person on this campus. Possibly the best in the world, once his thesis is published. He's not some sort of Arab terrorist." He started to interrupt, but she held up her hand and pointed between his eyes. "Besides, if spying on terrorists was the only application, I don't think Roger would work on the project. And neither would I."

Wyatt babbled as she withdrew her finger. "Are you saying you won't accept? You might not get another offer like—"

"Don't threaten me," she said, interrupting him. "I didn't say I wouldn't accept. It's a fascinating project, and I already have some ideas about the software you'll need."

His face brightened. "Then you will work with me on it?"

"Only if Roger comes on board . . . and only if we can develop some of the obvious peaceful applications."

"Yes, well, there are those, of course. That's not what Homeland Security is paying for, but what will they know? All right, I'll agree to that. You can develop those applications on your own time—"

"Only if Roger comes along. I don't think I could contribute without him."

"All right, I'll see what I can do when I'm in Washington tomorrow."

He took a step toward her, but she was out the door before he could close the gap between them.

10

As she watched Zay arguing with Alif over their next target, the smoke from Jiim's chain-smoked Gauloise irritated Qaaf's nose. There was no relief, because the tiny, secret storage room had been walled off from the shops it served. The only ventilation came from leaks around the locked door. Qaaf did not want to sneeze. She pinched her nose, enduring her discomfort in hopes that Alif would sneeze first, throwing his hairpiece further out of place. From a previous slippage, she was certain the real Alif was as bald as a rutabaga—valuable information should she ever need to identify her compatriots.

She needed these men, but they weren't a trustworthy bunch. Two weeks ago, someone had tried to change the password on the offshore account Zay had opened for her share of the payoff. Not being stupid, she had beaten them to it, setting up flags to notify her of any attempted intrusion. It had to have been Zay. Alif and Jiim, unless they were better actors than she'd seen so far, didn't have the computer savvy. Maybe it was just a test, but in that case, why hadn't Zay said anything about it afterward?

"They aren't taking our demands seriously yet." Zay always had a theory of why things weren't going well. "We need targets with more symbolic impact. Something like Wrigley Field."

Alif shook his head. "Symbols don't mean shit. Somebody has to get hurt. Then they'll pay."

She watched the hairpiece budge a quarter-inch, but this wasn't funny. "No killing. That was my condition."

"That was then. This is now. Now we know they're not responding, and they won't as long as nobody's life is at stake." Alif was growing excited, and louder.

Zay cupped his hand over his ear to remind Alif of people in the stores who might hear him. "That's why Wrigley would be a good choice. The bomb goes off at game time on an off day. There won't be anybody there, but they'll get the message about what *could* have happened with a packed house."

"No good," she said. "There's always somebody at Wrigley, cleaning up or repairing or—"

"All the better," said Alif, brushing his hands together. "If a few are hurt, they won't need to use their imagination—something our city fathers are short on. I agree with Zay. Let's do Wrigley."

She lifted her leather purse from the floor, signaling she was ready to leave. "If there's going to be killing, then I'm out."

"Why so squeamish? What about Dhal?"

"Dhal's a different case. That's one Arab who's getting what he deserves. I'll say it one more time. No killing."

"So we'll do Wrigley and we'll be careful." Alif's voice sounded conciliatory, but his smile didn't quite match his eyes.

"He has a point," Jiim suggested through a cloud of noxious smoke. "If we think of everything that could go wrong, we can bomb the ballpark without the risk of killing anyone."

Qaaf sighed, "If. The problem with that kind of planning is that nothing you think of ever happens. Only things you don't think of."

"Then," said Zay, "we'll just have to think harder. Jiim, I want a plan for Wrigley at our next meeting." He nodded to Qaaf. "Make sure it's detailed enough to satisfy Qaaf. There's no reason we can't give her what she wants. All right?"

It was not really a question, but only a marker that a decision had been made and this Thursday's meeting was over.

11

Harvey Wyatt enjoyed most of his trips to Washington. The restaurants were vastly superior to Ann Arbor's plebeian offerings—and the bills could be charged to his grants. The hotel staff treated him with the quality of respect to which he believed himself entitled, however seldom he received it from students. And then there were the escort services—lots of "respect," but unfortunately not chargeable to any of his grants.

Yes, Harvey Wyatt enjoyed most of his trips to Washington, but at the moment he wasn't enjoying this one. His Homeland Security grant supervisor, Dr. Inga Steinman, was chewing his butt, and obviously enjoying every bite. "It was a mistake to show her your slides. Assistants have no need to know . . ."

She paused for effect, but Wyatt knew better than to interrupt this aggressive bitch. She wanted him to look into her piercing eyes, but he stared at the inconsequential reward plaques and degrees arrayed on the walls of her excessively decorated office. He knew she was trying to impress him with her Doctorate in Educational Administration, but he had a real Ph.D. He didn't allow himself to be impressed.

". . . to know what we intend to use it for." Her pudgy hand slapped the glass top on her enormous walnut desk, which was bigger than Wyatt's. "Are you listening to me?"

41

"I'm listening," he said, but still didn't look at her.

"So tell me what's so good about these particular post-docs that makes them worth breaking security for?"

Wyatt related Tess's and Roger's intellectual assets in terms they would have been astonished to hear—terms he would never use in their presence because he didn't want them to become swell-headed. "And this kid—he's just a boy—could be in line for a Nobel . . . if he gets the right guidance."

"From you, of course?"

Wyatt nodded, trying to look humble. No point antagonizing someone who could terminate his funding.

"And you think that justifies breaching security? Hiring an Arab?"

"He's only half Arab."

"You can't believe that makes any difference?" She stood up from behind the shield of her mammoth desk, her many bracelets making tinny sounds. She strode to the window, thumbs hooked behind her rump. "Yes, I suppose you can, or you wouldn't even have told me. All right, I'll have to create a cover for the project. I'll have it transferred to Mental Health—that should satisfy their idealistic young minds. You tell them that Homeland Security dropped you."

"They may not believe it."

"I'll get you documentation to show them. Tell them you never finalized the contract from us, but Mental Health heard about it and showered you with cash. Talk to a few psychologists. Read an article or two in *Psychology Today*. Make up a mental health slide show. You're good at that sort of thing. You certainly don't know squat about security."

He endured her insults in silence by studying a photograph on her desk. She was pictured in the foyer of the White House, shaking hands with the Vice President. Wyatt tried to appear as if he were appreciating her political power—so he wouldn't show his fear of it. While she droned on with her plans, he turned his mind to what he would do with the escort he'd lined up for tonight.

Soon Steinman was finished chewing on Wyatt, so she saw him off in a cab in front of the Georgian brick building that housed her office within the Homeland Security complex. When the cab was out of sight, she stepped to the smokers' plaza, lit a cigarette, and dialed a number on her disposable non-government cell phone.

She spoke a name into the phone, then scanned the magnificent panorama of the District while waiting for a response. When the person at the other end identified himself, she said, "Yes, I think he may be onto something that would interest you."

Listening to the instructions that followed, she had time for three deep drags on her Marlboro. Finally, the voice paused long enough for her to reply. "I understand. I'll stay on top of it and keep you informed. I'll let you know when I need you to take action."

She snapped the phone closed, took one last long drag, coughed as she exhaled, then ground the butt under one pump, bringing her full weight down upon it. Satisfied, she returned to her office to resume her role as a trusted government executive.

12

After the holdup, Tess discretely checked around campus, but nobody who'd been in the bank could identify the Bag Bandit. There seemed to be something about the presence of a gun—even a reputed gun concealed in a pocket—that distracted people from looking at anything else. Some of them did give Tess descriptions, but all the descriptions were wildly different. Tess was satisfied that Roger was in no danger.

But the best part of the Bag Bandit's holdup—other than that it showed her that Roger had the courage to be an entrepreneur—was the way the bank changed its procedures, which told her how effective he might be at translating theory into action. A week later, she took Roger to the bank to deposit some of his chess winnings. Though the first summer session had barely started, the two active windows were engaged. Immediately, the teller in the back dropped what she was doing and opened the third window for them. While they were making the deposit, another student came in. Without hesitation, the manager opened the fourth window.

On the way out, Tess whispered, "Congratulations, Roger. It looks like the Bag Bandit had a lasting effect. For the better."

"Oh, I'm sure they would have figured it out for themselves, eventually."

She poked him with her elbow, which came up to his hip. "Modesty is boring, Roger. If you don't take credit for your actions, then you're not likely to repeat them."

"I hope I don't have to repeat *that* one. If I'm ever caught, they'll throw me out of school and I'll never get a job and—"

She stopped, turned to him, and clasped his ears in both hands. She did this when she wanted him to really listen to what she said, and she wanted to see if he would be assertive enough with her to say he heard better when his ears weren't covered. But he heard her well enough this time.

"Jobs are boring, Roger. You don't ever want to have a job. I could never marry a man who had a job."

She was ready to take him to the next step. By design, this was the first time she'd mentioned marriage in a long while. She was giving him the message that if he carried out his previous life plans and didn't follow her lead, she'd never marry him.

"But how can I live," he squeaked, "without a job?"

"I could support you," she said, removing her hands from his ears.

Roger's eyes widened. "I could never allow that."

You would, she thought, but this was not the time to bring up his cultural shortcomings. She pursed her lips and stamped her foot, hard enough so the chess players looked up. "Don't be stupid. If you're stupid, I definitely won't marry you."

"But I don't understand what you're saying."

"That's because you're too boring to imagine anything in between being a bank teller and a bank robber." She rapped his forehead with her delicate knuckles. "Think, Roger. Think."

"A bank messenger?"

"Boring. Think harder." She took his hand and led him into the Union's game room.

"A bank manager?"

"Warmer, but not very warm. This bank already has a manager. Besides, before the robbery, they were still running a stupid business that didn't serve their customers."

"True. So what?"

"So, what was missing? What changed them into an intelligent business that does serve their customers?"

"I guess the holdup awakened them to what they were doing."

"And why is that?"

"I don't know."

"It's because most people eventually become boring. They find some pattern that sort of gets them by, and they stick to it like gumbo to a plow blade. Like Wyatt, as soon as he got tenure."

"I love it when you talk like a farmer's daughter. How does it go? 'She was only the farmer's daughter, but all the horsemen knew'er.'"

She threw him a teasing slap on the cheek, though she thought his addiction to bad puns was cute. "I know that one. And don't change the subject. It's boring when you won't stick to a topic just because you don't understand something. Wyatt does that. Don't be like Wyatt."

"But how can you be interested in something you don't understand?"

She replaced her hands on his ears. "That's the only thing that *is* interesting. So, tell me what you just learned."

"That people trap themselves in inefficient patterns and aren't likely to change unless something drastic happens to them?"

She let go of his ears, patting his cheek before she dropped her hands. "Good boy. So, if you land a job, do you think you'll be exempt from this boring behavior?"

He felt cornered, and he had to admit it. "No, I guess I'd get just as stupid as those tellers. But that happens to everybody."

"It did happen to Wyatt. Once upon a time, he must have been pretty clever. But he lost his nerve. It won't happen to me, Buster. And if you let it happen to you, you'll never get me in the sack."

He looked around to see if any of the chess players heard her. "Shhh. Somebody might hear you."

"You mean somebody might see your ears turning red. Come on, Roger, I know about the cows and the horses. Do you want to screw me or not?"

"Tess!" He lowered his voice. "Could we talk about this somewhere else? Or maybe change the—"

"What boring thing were you going to say?"

"Nothing. But let's go sit in that corner. I play chess with some of these guys."

He chose vinyl-covered seats as far from the chess tables as possible. If he hoped she would change the subject (although perhaps he secretly hoped she wouldn't), he need not have worried. Pit bull that she was, she never let anyone change the subject on her.

"Okay, so we were talking about what you're going to have to do if you want to screw me. You're going to have to find a way to make a living without getting sucked into a job. Any job. And you can't do it robbing banks. Not anything stupid like that. And bank manager is just another stupid job. You have special talents, genius talents, and I'm not going to let you waste them."

"I'm not wasting them. I'm an inventor. I'm inventing things."

"In your dreams, Roger." She shook her head slowly from side to side, disapproval on her face, and then took his hand. "In my dreams, too. That's what I dream of for you, cutie pie, that you'll become an inventor. But today, no, you're no inventor. You're just a hacker. You're just hacking."

Roger pulled his hand out of hers and fisted both hands. "I've never broken into anything in my life."

"Breaking into things is cracking, not hacking. Hacking is just sort of messing around, patching this and that, until you get something that sort of works. That's you to a T."

"I'm not like that."

"Yes, you are. I've seen the way you work, and it's totally limiting. Your code is crap spaghetti, and your hardware is no better."

"Now, wait a minute. You may be more experienced at software, but you don't know squat about hardware."

She stared out the window in frustration, then fixed his eyes with her stare. "I know that when you plug wires in your hand and get a terrible infection, you're hacking."

"I had to get access to brain waves. What was I supposed to do?" Absentmindedly, he touched the sore spot on his hand.

"You could have done better than that. If you had some discipline, you could build something that could access brain waves without cutting. With no risk of infection at all." She pulled his hand away from the wound.

He looked shaken, but was defiant. "That's easy for you to say."

"Yes, it is easier for me to say, because I may not be as smart as you are, but I'm not a hacker. I set goals and limits before I start a project, and I work within them. I'll accomplish something, but you never will unless you acquire some discipline."

"Well, if that's what's required, I just don't work that way. It destroys my creativity."

"Of course you would think that, because you don't know how to be disciplined. You think discipline means wearing a uniform and marching in step."

"It's not?"

He looked befuddled, and Tess knew she was finally penetrating his defenses. "Of course it's not. That's just what stupid, boring people think. Which is why you need to harness your creativity, not hack around with it. But, you said it. You aren't likely to change unless something drastic happens to you. And I'm something as drastic as you're ever going to meet."

Roger looked desperately around as if to find some escape, but his eyes kept coming back to Tess's. He said nothing.

"So, are you going to do it?" She questioned him with those big brown eyes and opened her palms, waiting.

He seemed to know the answer she was looking for, but he still said nothing. He realized that his whole life hung in the balance.

"Well?" The brown eyes grew even bigger.

"You want me to put myself in your hands?" he said meekly.

"Is that an answer, or another boring question?"

"Okay, yes," he said, but immediately followed with a question that drained half the strength of his assertion. "But how am I going to earn my living if I lose my creativity?"

"Oh, darling," she sighed, and it was the first time she'd called him *darling*. "That's the business end of things. You leave that to me. I'll be your business manager."

"My business manager?"

"Of course. Every genius needs a business manager."

He blushed again. "But I know about finance."

"No, you don't. You just know about the math. Real finance is about *people*. Like everything else that's real," she tapped him on the forehead, "unlike the stuff you've got up here."

"But the math—"

"Forget that math crap. I can hire any mathematician I want for a hundred thou a year. Listen, Mr. Boring. Mozart needed a business manager. Einstein needed a business manager. Bobby Fischer needed a business manager, but he fired his, and look what happened to him."

She had no idea whether Einstein really had a business manager, but the Bobby Fischer argument seemed to make a big impression on Roger. "I suppose you're right."

"You're damn right I am. From now on, you do the smarts, I'll teach you the discipline you need, and I'll figure out how to make it pay. I'll also have to keep teaching you some of the social graces."

"What social graces?"

She winked, with a sly smile on her face. "Well, we'll start with kissing lessons—if you earn them."

Roger's face brightened, but Tess quickly doused that flame. "But we'll take it slow. You may have a goal in mind, but you'll have to practice patience. Just like my goal. We're going to build a company, our own high-tech start-up, but the first thing you're going to do is work with me on one of Professor Wyatt's research projects. We need capital, so we're going to work hard and bank most of our pay."

"But isn't that a job?"

"Not the way we're going to do it."

13

Addie's worst fears were not being realized, as she should have anticipated. Released from the hospital and police custody, she went straight to Uncle Qasim's shop, still dressed as Uncle Sam. Qasim—short, dark, and handsome like all the Halabi brothers, though the only one with a mustache—was her favorite among her four uncles. Marid, Zahid, and Suhayb also spoiled her, but of them all, only Qasim, second-oldest to her father, took her career aspirations seriously.

When Qasim saw the state she was in, he immediately tore open a case of her favorite chocolate-covered coconut cookies, closed his shop, and gently escorted her down to the parking area. He helped her into the passenger seat of his gray Lexus, buckled her in, and headed north on a circuitous route home, giving her lots of time to comfort herself with cookies, settle down, and tell her story.

By the time they could see the WIN flag fluttering over Wrigley Field, he had heard the entire tale, punctuated by sobs and gasps. To her relief, he wasn't commenting on her emotional state. Nor was he chewing her out. But he was offering a successful businessman's advice on her recent behavior—advice she didn't want right now.

"If you want to be a professional nurse—"

"Rehabilitation nurse, Uncle."

"Rehabilitation nurse, then. All the better. If you want to be a rehabilitation nurse, a real professional, you can't display yourself out on the street at political demonstrations."

"This is America, Uncle Qas, not Syria. I'm just exercising my American citizen's right of free speech."

"Adara, my sweet, maybe you can dress in short skirts and leave your face uncovered, but they still won't think you're an American." He glanced over at her outrageous costume. "Not even if you dress yourself like Uncle Sam."

"Why not? I was born in Chicago—at a Jewish hospital, no less—"

"Ah. So you think these Christians consider the Jews Americans? Some of them even financed the American Revolution, but it didn't help. And what difference has two hundred years made for them?" He caressed his bushy mustache and laughed, "Unless they give money to politicians, of course."

"But why should these European-Americans hate us—"

"There's the bombings—"

"Yes, they're terrible, but *I'm* not bombing anyone. And what about the Christians who bomb federal buildings, Black churches, and abortion clinics?"

"You're asking for logic, my little gazelle, and logic does not apply to these matters. If it did, the Crusades would be over—and would never have started in the first place."

Qasim stopped his lecture to maneuver around a triple-parked Goose Island Beer Company truck, giving his niece time to think about the Crusades. Once he cleared the truck, he stopped at the Middle Eastern grocery on Lunt to pick up fresh radishes and pine nuts for his wife—something Addie's so-traditional father, Nazim, had never done. She wondered if Qasim ran errands for women when he was a young antigovernment radical growing up in Syria. Probably. Apparently, men were free to violate tradition whenever they chose. And just as apparently, women weren't.

After Qasim came back with his paper bags and they started driving again, heading west, she picked up that line of questioning. "Bart doesn't have this kind of trouble." Bart—Barakah—was the oldest of Qasim's three boys.

"Boys are different. But not that different. Barakah knows how to keep his head down. You won't find him marching around holding hands with Christian girls."

She blushed, then recovered quickly by remembering she had seen Bart doing exactly that. "What about Roger? Roger has a Christian girlfriend."

"Roger's father was a Christian. It's his mother who broke the traditions."

"Kamilah's your older sister. How could she date an American, even back in the old country?"

"Kamilah was always a strong-minded woman. Who could stop her from doing what she chose?" He shrugged, momentarily taking his hands off the wheel. "It's because of her that we're all safe in America."

"We're not so safe." She unconsciously touched her sling. She could smell the radishes in the paper bag. "And I want to be a strong-minded woman, too."

Qasim raised his eyebrows. "I won't stand in your way. Just don't let your father catch you with an American boyfriend."

"Anything Roger can do, I can do. I'm older."

"Roger is a boy—and a down-to-earth boy. He'd never be so wild and foolish as you, his cousin, strutting around in public in a costume."

14

As Tess had predicted, once Roger had access to the expensive equipment in Wyatt's lab, his creativity blossomed. Tess was delighted, but she paid a price. Seeing her in the lab every day, Wyatt intensified his unwelcome pressure for her to "get closer." She knew Wyatt would react badly to her relationship with Roger, but she couldn't keep him in the dark forever. To be free, they had to develop other sources of income—sources that were off Wyatt's radar, since their post-doctoral fellowships prohibited moon-lighting.

Tess had a stack of ideas, but she believed that the most imme-diate way to supplement their meager stipends was to take advan-tage of Roger's chess prowess. She saw that the Middle Eastern boys from the business school were part of a male culture constitu-tionally unable to refuse a challenge—and they had lots of ready cash. Roger established contacts by speaking Arabic, and Tess took charge of promoting his matches.

She first raised Roger's usual friendly dollar stakes to a more lucrative twenty dollars. Whenever he won too easily, she would allow his opponent to handicap Roger and play double-or-nothing. A pawn handicap cost an extra five dollars, a knight or a bishop cost an additional twenty. The weakest players were encouraged to purchase rooks, and one hapless Saudi prince was allowed to start by removing Roger's queen—for an extra hundred dollars.

Part of Tess's original strategy was to have Roger lose once in a while, to encourage his opponents to raise the stakes, but Roger simply couldn't lose on purpose. So, Tess needed another idea. Since the campus went dark on the weekends during the summer session and students had nothing to do, Tess arranged a knockout chess tournament. She offered just the right number of handsome consolation prizes for the losers.

The tournament was held on a sizzling day at the Campus Inn, which was just off campus but not affiliated with the school. Tess had initially rented one of the small meeting rooms, but as word of the prizes spread and enrollments climbed, she upgraded to the pastel blue-and-pink ballroom. The tournament lasted all day Saturday, then continued until just after noon on Sunday.

Now Roger and Tess stood contemplating the silent room, empty but for the lingering odor of nervous sweat and the litter of empty soda cans and torn chip bags. Tess could see that he was uneasy, and she knew it wasn't because of the rubbish.

"What's wrong?" she asked, waving the sheaf of twenty-dollar bills she had just been counting. "We won—*you* won—as planned."

"I don't like exploiting my Syrian ancestry. These guys have enough trouble being Arabs in America these days."

"They're happy," she reassured him. She stuffed their winnings into a blue cloth shopping bag while Roger packed up the chess sets and clocks. "Everyone got a prize, even the losers. They're all asking me when the next tournament will be."

"I suppose," he said, still not appearing very happy himself. "At least it was better than holding up a bank."

"We netted twelve-thousand five-hundred seventy dollars, more or less." It was more cash than either of them had ever touched, and Tess carefully zipped the blue bag and snuggled it up to her chest. "I think we can afford to splurge on a nice lunch— after we tuck this safely away in the bank."

"Are we going to deposit it?"

"Just a token amount. The rest goes into our safe deposit box. If we deposit more than ten thousand dollars in cash, we have to fill out special forms for the IRS."

"Why?"

"Because they think anyone with that much cash must be a drug dealer."

Roger studied the bag, as if he could see its contents. "I guess that would be worse than bank robbing."

He held out his hand to take the bag, but Tess held it back. "I'll carry it. You take the boxes with the chess sets and clocks to your apartment. I have to go talk to Wyatt, then I'll meet you at your place and take you for a shopping lesson."

"So now it begins?"

"What begins?"

"You're going to start dressing me up."

"No, I'm not," she said, taking one last look around the room before looking him over. "I told you it's fine for you to look like a geek." She took him by the hand and led him out into the lobby. "Today, we're going to buy you an engineering notebook and a computer."

When the money was safely banked, Tess jogged to Wyatt's office, barely working up a sweat over the short distance, even in the heat. The exercise felt good after almost two days of chess-watching, and she needed it to prepare for this critical encounter with Wyatt. She didn't want to miss this opportunity, because the news had just hit campus that Wyatt had received a huge new grant from the National Institute of Mental Health.

As Tess had anticipated, Wyatt was in a good mood, leaning back in his office chair with his hands behind his head, fingers interlaced. "I heard about the grant," she said, still catching her breath. She hoped he would interpret her panting as excitement rather than exercise-induced oxygen debt. "How exciting."

She need not have worried. "It's just another validation of my work," he said, sweeping his eyes over his award wall.

Your past work, Tess thought. *Not anything you've done recently. You must have been pretty good, once, so what happened?* But all she said was, "Now they'll have to make you Department Chair, won't they?"

He took the bait. "They should have given me that promotion a long time ago. Now, if they aren't going to recognize my contributions, I can just go somewhere else and take my grant with me."

Tess let her mouth fall partly open and touched her lips. "But surely they have to grant the promotion, with all the money you bring to the University."

He motioned her to a seat, preparing to lecture her on departmental politics. "They're snobs—jealous intellectual snobs. If you have publications, they say you have to get grants, but if you have grants, they say you have to have more publications. The simple fact is that they're looking for excuses to keep good men down," he stared out the window as two professors walked past, deep in conversation, "so they can keep their own privileges scarce."

"Then you should give them more publications." She bent her neck back and threw him a wide-eyed look. "That shouldn't be hard for someone with your abilities."

"No, it wouldn't be difficult at all." He stood up and paced back and forth, slowly, his hands clasped behind his back. "But it's time-consuming. I'm too busy doing my research to write everything down and then jump through all those reviewer hoops. I have more important things to do."

"Of course you have. But I could help you," she said. "I'm a good writer."

He stopped pacing and rubbed his chin. "Hmm. Maybe you could at that. You'd have to do it as part of your regular work. I can't pay you extra."

"Oh, I wouldn't be doing it for the money. My compensation would be seeing more of your work available to the scientific community."

Tess began to worry that she was pouring it on too thick, but Wyatt seemed to be gobbling it all up. He stepped over to his file cabinet and extracted three folders. "These are some of my notes." He handed them to her. "Why don't you see what you can do with them?"

"I'd be honored—"

He held up his palm. "Let's be clear, though. Just because you write up my notes, that won't make you a coauthor."

She clasped the folders to her chest. "Oh, no, Professor, I never imagined *that*."

"Good. Then we're all clear?"

She stood up and turned toward the door. Then, as if she just had a new thought, she turned back to face him. "There is one thing."

"Of course. What can I offer you in compensation? A fancy dinner, perhaps?"

Sure, she thought, *I'd rather have a dinner date with a gorilla. At least he'd keep his hands on the food.* But she put a small smile on her face and held her breath for a moment to generate a flush in her cheeks. "It's the data."

"What's the data?"

"Well, you know that Dr. Fixman and I want to do some research on visual processing—"

"I told you we aren't interested in that."

"Of course. I know. But we would like to explore some ideas—"

"I'm sorry, but you and Fixman have to devote all your time to the grant that's paying you. And that's for verbal processing only."

"Yes, that's exactly my point." Hearing the scorn in Wyatt's voice when he pronounced Roger's last name, she decided to keep the focus on herself. "I'd like to pursue my ideas on my own time, but I lack the data. If you could just allow me to have a copy of the same data we take for verbal processing, I could scan it for possible visual clues, too."

She paused to let the idea sink in, then added, "It wouldn't cost you anything. And if I find anything interesting enough to publish, I'd be glad to list you as coauthor."

He toyed with his watch, but she could see she'd caught his interest. He pursed his lips, then smacked them and said, "Senior author, right? After all, it's my data."

It's the government's data, you smarmy cretin, she thought, but she only said, "Why, of course. You'd be the senior author, if you consider the work worthy of your reputation."

"Yes, that might work." He spread his arms in a magnanimous gesture. "Fine. Take a copy of the data—though I doubt very much you'll be able to do anything interesting with it. Just be sure it's not distributed to anyone else."

"Definitely. In fact, we should have an agreement spelled out in writing so you'll be protected."

"I'm too busy for paperwork."

"Of course you are." She took a step toward him and touched him on the arm. "I'll write it up for you. Then all you'll have to do is sign it."

"Fine. Just remember to put in the part about senior authorship on any publications."

"Of course," she said, smiling and heading for the door. *Do you really think we'd be foolish enough to make any of Roger's inventions public?*

15

The security guard finished disabling the video monitors, changed into street clothes, left his uniform in the locker room, then moved cautiously to the men's room on the next floor of the Merchandise Mart. There, he applied his simple but effective facial disguise. He went to yet another floor, then window-shopped for exactly three minutes before wandering into the chocolate wholesaler's to taste a sample or two—and then slipped into the back room for the *Yom alKhamis* weekly meeting.

The other members of the Thursday Group—Qaaf, Zay, and Jiim—were already seated and waiting. Though Alif confirmed that by his watch he was precisely on time, he was surprised that Qaaf had already begun her report on Dhal's condition. "He's holding on by a thread, perhaps now a string."

Alif remained standing. "Has he talked?"

"He *cannot* talk. We saw to that, as you well know. He will not sacrifice his family under any circumstances."

"And you well know my meaning. Has he revealed anything about his situation?"

"Nothing."

"Are you sure? Perhaps they have deduced something without his cooperation."

"They have deduced exactly what we want them to deduce, neither more nor less."

Alif didn't look satisfied, but he sat down and nodded to Zay. "Everything is ready for our next plan. Do we have your approval to proceed?"

Zay betrayed no emotion whatsoever. "Let's hear first about the public reaction."

"Of course. All three major channels carried prime-time editorials berating the police for their lack of progress."

Qaaf nodded her agreement. "And one of them also mentioned the incompetence of the FBI. It's about time they stuck it to those bastards. If …" She was about to say more, then caught herself. No need to give them more information about her feelings about the FBI.

"*The Tribune* ran two Sunday editorials, one calling for the resignation of the chief of police, the other calling for more federal support. *The Sun-Times* editorial blamed the city council, and *The Daily News* says it's the mayor's fault for not paying the fifty million. We've even hit the suburbs with *The Daily Herald*. They say—"

Zay raised his hand. "Enough. Things are going according to plan. Proceed."

More than you know, thought Qaaf, as she took her time leaving the Mart, still in disguise.

16

When Tess and Roger arrived back at Roger's apartment after a long day in Wyatt's lab, they found that two packages had arrived by overnight delivery, a box and a padded mailer. They brought them to the kitchen.

Knowing these were the results of their Internet shopping, Roger grabbed the box and started to cut it open in his ultra-neat way, using his Swiss Army knife. This purchase would power the pipelined parallel-processing machine he had designed to handle Wyatt's data. But Tess snatched the box out of his hands.

"This one first," she said, handing him the mailer.

"But the box has my CPU chips," he protested, trying to grab it from behind her back. "Now I can start—"

"You can start nothing until you open this one."

He was well acquainted with her *she-who-must-be-obeyed* tone, so he relented and took the mailer. He read the brown label out loud, "Swisher Pens Online Stationery Store," and started to slice the mailer along one seam.

"Hurry up," Tess said. "Just rip it open."

"We might need it for something later."

She grabbed the envelope and tore it open, dumping its contents on the kitchen table. Two notebooks—one black, one burgundy—and one fancy silver box the size of an eyeglasses case. She picked up the burgundy notebook, held it in front of his face, and riffled the blank sheets. "Perfect. A perfect engineering notebook. Individually numbered, square-bound pages of twenty-four pound, acid-free, archive-safe paper sewn in and ruled with a quarter-inch grid—"

He pushed the notebook away. "I know what it is. I read the sales literature. Let's open the other package."

"Look," she said, opening the book to its red placeholder ribbon. "Three hundred and twelve pages, and all of them blank. It cost thirty-five dollars, but of course it's worthless if you don't write in it."

"I can write in my computer. It's more convenient."

To show her frustration, Tess pretended to be pulling out her hair. "The computer has no legal standing—not much, anyway. You write everything in the journals, and you write everything with this." Now she opened the small silver case and removed a fat pen that was color-matched to the notebook. "A hundred-dollar Ancora pen."

She pretended to write with the capped pen. "And, at the end of the day, I witness it—with my own pen."

She used her finger to simulate signing her name. "Then, we have proof of invention that will stand up in court."

"Why court?"

Her voice became sweet and loving. "Because your inventions are so marvelous that everyone will want to copy them. And claim them for their own."

Responding to her tone, his irritation seemed to soften into simple puzzlement. "Won't the patents take care of that?"

"Not if they're contested. You have to prove your patent rights—prior invention and all that."

"Well, my software dates my entries automatically."

He tried again to grab for the other package, but she stepped adroitly aside. "Anybody can fake a computer record. This," she tapped the notebook with the head of the pen, "this can't be forged. Not easily. Not without risk of detection."

"Okay, let's assume you're right. It just seems so far off, so remote. And it's such an interruption to my creative flow."

She put down the book and pen and took hold of his ears. "I see the problem. You need more motivation. Fair enough. Here's my offer."

She pulled his face toward hers, locked her lips on his, and parted his mouth with her tongue. After a moment's exploration, she withdrew. "There. For every page you write, you get one of those."

Roger swallowed hard. "Can I write as big as I want?"

"Uh-uh. No cheating." She waggled a finger at him. "You stay within the ruled lines. And write legibly. But you can start a new page each day—as long as it's dated."

"Darn. Only one kiss a day?" He sounded disappointed, but he was smiling.

"You're allowed to write more than one page every day. As many kisses as you want." She took his hand in hers. "And how about an extra bonus? If you write something every day for a week, you can have some of this. . . ."

She drew his hand to her left breast and rubbed it in a small circle. He blushed furiously, then felt the blush running down to his belly. She said, "Underneath my bra, if you do two weeks in a row."

She left his hand in place for another moment, then pushed it away and handed him the notebook and pen. "Now, get to work. I don't want to be on Social Security before I let you put your hand inside my pants."

The burgundy notebook, it turned out, was for all the work he did away from Wyatt's lab, to keep track of who owned what. In the lab, he used the black notebook, and with all the high-tech equipment at their beck and call, Roger earned an abundance of kisses. But the work itself was five steps forward and three back. Forward when they were alone, even with time out for kissing. Backward when Wyatt was home from his grant-hunting expeditions, sending them backward with his "improvements."

One cloudy, muggy day, it had been three steps back and none forward, though at least Wyatt was in Washington. The only reason they stayed in the lab was the air-conditioning. The University, afraid of animal rights groups, made sure the lab animals kept cool. There was no rights group for summer school students.

That morning, the data analysis software had gone berserk, destroying results that had taken two days to produce. Tess was much better at software, but she set Roger to work locating the bug while she restored the data, which seemed the more difficult task. But neither task was as easy as she thought, and by noon, the database was still a mess. Roger had already followed three false trails in the program, so Tess called a break for a quiet picnic lunch of cheese and chips on the cool banks of the Huron River.

Returning from lunch, Tess discovered that Wyatt had left a phone message from Dulles Airport. "Where are you?" his recorded voice squawked. "You should be back from lunch by now. Well, by now you should have discovered the fruits of my labor last night. I accelerated the Fourier software, and just had to change one line of code. I'll teach you the algorithm when I get back. Enjoy!"

Roger ran over to his keyboard and started typing. "*yIntagh!*"

"Don't speak Arabic. You know I don't understand."

"It's not Arabic. It's Klingon."

"Oh. So what did you say?"

"Dumb as a rock! He hacked the configuration control software so he could change the binary code without changing the source. Dumber than a rock."

"Nobody's perfect. Especially Wyatt. But you always expect them to be."

"He could at least be careful."

"No, that's not the point. Every hacker says he's careful." She thumbed her nose at him. "What you hardware guys need is discipline."

"You don't have to be so careful with software. It's much easier to change than hardware."

She leaned over him, pressing her breasts into his back. "*yIntagh!*" she whispered. "Did I say it right?"

"Why is that so dumb?" he pouted.

"It's *because* software's easier to change that it requires more discipline. One swift bit could destroy a year's worth of work—as we may have just seen."

He was about to touch a key, but she reached over and restrained his hand. "It's always better to work with a partner, especially when things get delicate like this. If you'd hit that key, you'd have erased the history file, so I couldn't reconstruct Wyatt's blunder."

After a moment's thought, he knew she was right, and was embarrassed. "Well, he shouldn't work so hard to bypass all the protection I've built into the development system."

"I think you should have let me check the design of that security system—so he *couldn't* have bypassed it."

She tried to tone down the anger in her voice, since it was for Wyatt—and herself—not for Roger. "You're a more creative hacker than he is, hon, but to beat a hacker, it takes somebody both creative and disciplined. From now on, you stick with your instruments—I'll do the software. You can be my backup and check all my work."

"If he's got so much excess creativity, he should pour some into improving the product, rather than into ruining it."

"You two make a good pair."

Roger looked up from the keyboard. "What do you mean? I'm nothing like him."

"Exactly," she smiled. "You're boring, but with him there's never an end to his surprises. Of course, most of them are destructive surprises."

"So why are we a good pair?"

"Because you balance each other. He forces you to be more creative, to counteract his dumb-rock moves. Like this morning."

"This morning was a total waste, completely unnecessary if he'd only followed the rules."

She kissed the top of his head. "First, it was a lesson for you in the importance of discipline. And second, it wasn't a total waste at all. While you were searching for the bug he introduced, you found three other bugs in his work and two places where you could make the program run faster."

"I'd have found those eventually." He poised his finger over a key, but waited for her to give the nod before he pressed. A new screen came up, filled with nonsense characters. "And now we'll waste the rest of the day cleaning up this mess."

She moved beside him, bent over, blew in his ear, "You could clean it up faster than that . . ." She adjusted her body and rubbed his cheek softly with her breasts, ". . . if you had an incentive waiting for you."

"You're distracting me. I have to get this right, or we'll have the same mess all over again." She drew back, but he reached out and took her arm. "But I'll take a rain check. Just wait until I get this done right."

She formed her lips into a serious *moue*. "Someday, I'd like you to explain to me how you got to be such a law-abiding perfectionist."

He touched the ENTER key and swiveled to face her. She seized the opportunity to drop herself onto his lap. "Now tell me a story."

He hesitated, flustered and unable to think of anything to say.

"Once upon a time—"

She stopped his mouth with a kiss, then drew back. "Four words, and it's boring already. Start some creative way."

"It was a dark and stormy night—"

She kissed him again. "Stop that."

"Why? Boring earns me a kiss every time."

"Oh, so that's it. Well, that's a bit more creative . . . so here's another kiss."

"You mean I get kisses when I'm disciplined, kisses when I'm boring, and kisses when I'm creative?"

"Sure, isn't that a creative way to get what I want?"

"So, what's my incentive for being creative?"

"My tongue." She demonstrated.

"Oh. My mother never taught me about that."

She jumped up from his lap. "I should *hope* not." She stuck out her tongue.

He reddened. "Oh, no, I didn't mean that. Of course my mother never . . . I mean, she never kissed me except when I was neat and tidy and followed all her rules."

She looked skeptical, but sat back on his lap and stuck her tongue in his ear. "Tell me about your mother," she whispered.

"I'd rather not."

"Please."

"How about we pay her a visit in Chicago when we visit Fermilab? You can see for yourself, so you won't be biased by me."

"Fair enough. Now get up and turn that keyboard over to me. You can watch, but only after you record Wyatt's bungling in your notebook. And when I'm finished, we'll go home and try something much more interesting."

17

Don Capitol resented having to eat lunch with Inga Steinman in Washington rather than supervise the crime scene at Wrigley Field. On the other hand, it was an excuse to get away from the Chicago heat—both the weather and the public outcry over the desecration of the Cubbies' shrine.

Maybe he would have been in a better mood if the FBI's forensic lab had been able to extract even one clue from the extortion note or its envelope. No fingerprints, other than those from some postal workers and the mayor's mail clerk. The paper was ordinary laser printer paper from OfficeMax, meticulously cleaned of any trace substances; the envelope, the same. The ink was from a plain-vanilla ink jet cartridge, and the printer was most likely an HP model of which 40,000 had been sold in the Chicago area. The linguistic analyst identified the note writer as a plain, Midwestern, moderately educated, native-speaker of English, which could be any of a hundred million people. Not even any DNA on the stamp or envelope flap.

At least, Don thought, *the lack of clues is a clue. We're definitely dealing with professionals.*

Taking a sip of water, he gazed ironically at his lunch mate, then surveyed his surroundings—thickly shellacked pine tables and benches to match, slippery sawdust on the broad floor planks, country and western reverberating off the knotty pine walls. Everything Easterners could do to simulate the real West.

Watching Inga Steinman put away barbecued sausage with both hands, Don could see why she preferred benches to chairs. And didn't want to travel. Even a first-class airline seat would be a tight fit for her hips, but Don knew her pay grade didn't fly first class. Although he didn't much care for the appearance of obese women, he did enjoy a dining partner who could match him bite for bite. Especially one who shared his appetite for barbecue.

If I didn't run ten miles every morning, I'd soon look like her—fit only for a desk job inside the Beltway. He'd tried to bring up their business several times, but Inga would not shift attention from her full rack of ribs, daintily wiping the sauce from her mouth after each rib, using a fresh red-and-white checkered paper napkin each time. To Don's mind, the ribs were as effete as the restaurant—real ribs were not boiled or microwaved before barbecuing. And certainly not slopped with sauce after cooking. But perhaps this was an Easterner's idea of barbecued ribs.

The thought of pork ribs wrenched his mind back to his Muslim prisoner and the problem that had brought him to Washington. He described the situation while Inga polished off the last of the ribs. And fries. And biscuits. She ate slowly and seemed to enjoy every morsel. He admired that.

She set down the last stripped rib and gave her puffy mouth one last swipe. "I understand your problem, Agent Capitol, but I'm afraid I can't help you. The machine's not available."

"You've seen the letter of authorization from the director."

"It's not that you don't bring the necessary clout. The researchers don't have the device working yet, so it wouldn't do you any good."

"Time is of the essence. Let them bring the device to our clinic where we have the prisoner. He can't be moved. We'll give them whatever they need to continue their research. They can fine-tune it there."

Inga excused herself to grab another double portion of fries from the counter. "Pigs' ribs seem to be smaller these days. And less meaty. Are they starving pigs now?"

Don ignored the distraction. "So what about it?"

"The grant leader doesn't want to bring the device to your clinic. He's got faculty responsibilities in Ann Arbor."

"He can drive back and forth. The clinic's not that far away."

"It's on the other side of the state. Michigan's a big state."

"I've read his progress reports. Between the lines. I suspect he's not actually doing the research himself. His two assistants—"

Her mouth full of fries, she finished the sentence for him, "— wouldn't know what to do without Wyatt's direction. And you might have a security problem with one of them. He's the genius who's really behind this effort, but he's half Syrian."

"He'd be watched."

"It would be simpler if you'd bring your man to Ann Arbor."

"He can't be moved. And we couldn't maintain proper security on a college campus."

"It's a big device, but delicate."

"Our prisoner is more delicate. And he can't just be replaced out of a scientific supply catalog."

"You don't understand. This is a custom device. One of a kind. If we move it at this stage, we could lose what progress we've made." She started in on her apple cobbler. "We should have waited to order dessert. The ice cream is half melted."

"Would you like me to get you another one?"

"That would be sweet. I'll just finish this one in the meantime. And bring me a couple of those almond sugar cookies. They make the most wonderful cookies in this part of D.C."

He hoped the desserts might loosen her position, but she picked up right where she'd left off. "I'll be frank with you, Agent Capitol. You've read the progress reports. The device isn't working yet. It wouldn't do you any good."

"What's holding it up?"

"Quite honestly, I don't have enough in my budget to obtain the equipment they need. . . ."

She paused, and he took the hint. "Tell me how much you need. I'll get it for you. My project's priority is off the scale."

Inga knew enough not to ask why, but based on her research reports, she could understand his interest. She wrote a number on one of the clean napkins. "This should do—until the next request."

Don folded the napkin without looking at the number and stuffed it in his breast pocket. He wanted to look at it, but he needed to impress her that his project's urgency trumped any dollar amount. "You'll have your money. When will I have the device?"

"Nine months, minimum."

"He might be *dead* in nine months. Along with some other people."

She shrugged her huge shoulders. "What can I say? Ideas don't come on schedule. You can't rush research."

"I can try."

18

They were an hour late for dinner by the time they reached West Rogers Park. "Oh, Roger, I didn't know you were famous already," Tess teased. "Is West Rogers Park named after you?"

Roger waved off her comment. "Probably some illustrious ancestor. I'll be so famous, they'll rename the whole city for me."

Tess was surprised to see that the quiet neighborhood was typically Midwestern, with all-brick, tile-roofed, single-family homes on small lots. Knowing that some of the 400,000 Chicago-area Muslims lived here, she had half-imagined she would see camels hitched out front of gaudy tents in a noisy bazaar.

Inside the yellow-brick Fixman house, however, some of Tess's prejudices would be confirmed. There was a profusion of Oriental rugs layered one upon another, from the midst of which stared Roger's mother, Kamilah, stooping down to relieve the carpet of a small leaf apparently tracked in from outside. Tess noticed that Roger's five uncles, all of whom had turned out with their families and dogs for their first view of Roger's Christian girlfriend, were dressed in Western business suits and ties. Tess wondered to herself, *Maybe this is the first time Roger has brought a girlfriend home.*

After the initial introductions had been made and the group moved toward the dining room, Tess excused herself to freshen up, dragging Roger with her so she could write down phonetic spellings of the uncles' and aunts' names. A dozen or so siblings and cousins sitting at one table hadn't been introduced, but one of them, Adara, still in her nurse's uniform, introduced herself, shaking hands and begging Tess to call her "Addie." Tess noticed the disapproving look Nazim's wife tossed at her daughter, but Addie just shrugged her shoulders and slipped into a chair next to Tess at the second table.

Roger's mother said something in Arabic to Addie and motioned toward the children's table, but Addie shook her head at Kamilah and grabbed onto Tess's arm. Kamilah turned to Nazim and raised her eyebrows, but he simply shrugged his shoulders. Giving up, Kamilah fetched an extra chair as Nazim's wife hurried to set another place at the adults' table. Tess remembered that Addie was older than Roger, and she wondered why they wanted to put her with the children. Did they just want to separate her from the Christian girlfriend? And why did they give in when she'd refused? Tess decided that Roger's family was at least as messed up as her own.

The dinner seemed to be a potluck, with each woman serving her own dishes from her place at the table while the men sat at the table and conversed about politics and work. They addressed all questions about work to Roger, leaving Tess to spend most of the time in sisterly conversation with Addie. Though Addie spoke fluent Arabic with her uncles and aunts, her speech, Tess thought, was a hundred-percent genuine Midwestern American. The meal, however, was anything but.

Tess didn't recognize half the dishes, but Addie dutifully explained each one's name and ingredients. First came a tasty lentil soup—*shorbit Adas*—served lukewarm, though Roger explained that in winter it would be served hot. After the soup was finished and the bowls cleared, Tess recognized the next dish, *taboule*—cracked wheat salad served cold with cucumbers and tomatoes. Then came loaves of *kibbeh nayeh*, a mixture of raw ground meat, pine nuts, spices, and other fillings, drizzled with olive oil and served with warm pita bread, spring onions, and radishes. Roger whispered to Tess that all she needed to do was have a taste, but she gobbled down two of the tiny football-shaped loaves, much to the delight of Nazim's wife.

Next on the table were stuffed vine leaves; then *shish kabob*, though, unlike her father's barbecues, this was lamb, not beef.

Then *falafel*, to which Roger had already introduced her. And, finally, an upside-down eggplant dish with rice and ground beef whose name Tess didn't catch. All of this was accompanied, of course, by an ever-filled bowl of *hummus.* And no alcohol.

Dessert was strong coffee, which Tess declined, and *baklava*— made with walnuts, not the pistachios Tess was used to. Then Tess thought the meal was over, but she could see that the children were anticipating more. And more there was, with three kinds of dates, baskets of fresh fruit and nuts in the shell, followed by dark chocolates, Jordan almonds, and sesame *halwah.* Tess thought it was a good thing she was eating for two.

After dinner, while the other women cleaned up and tended to the children, Tess joined the men in the living room for more discussion, more coffee, and, for some of them, cigarettes. Tess declined all but the discussion, the one offering she was apparently supposed to decline. Others might have been intimidated by the ambiance, but it wasn't in Tess's nature to be intimidated by anyone. After a while, the men seemed to switch modes and began talking as if she were an American, rather than an American *woman*.

Marid, a chemical engineer, was the only uncle who expressed real interest in and understanding of what she and Roger were trying to accomplish. After a while, Zahid got up from his seat, motioning Marid to take his place beside Tess. After that, the discussion broke in two—four brothers and three engineers.

Marid, who'd been quiet when his older brothers were in the conversation, seemed to come alive when he was talking to other engineers. Tess noticed that he was closer to Roger's age than Nazim's, and thought that might be the reason. "Is business all they ever talk about?" she asked him in a whisper.

"Don't have to whisper. They don't listen when women talk anyway."

"I noticed. Except their women don't talk."

"Rasha says they do talk, when men aren't around. I wouldn't know, of course, but Rasha talks to me. I don't think the other wives talk much to their husbands. But I married Rasha here. She was born in America."

"And the other wives weren't?"

"No. They all married in Syria. I think all of them were arranged, mostly for commercial reasons, though my brothers are Americanized enough that they won't talk about that."

"Then how did they happen to come to the States?"

Roger joined in. "My mother came first. She came to college, on a scholarship, then returned home to do her doctoral field work at excavations out near Palmyra—"

Marid lowered his voice. "A really bleak place. Fascinating ruins, but now it's most famous for torture—in the military prison there."

"Mother says there's not much to do there if you're not involved with the prison. And if you're not, you'd better not say anything about the prison that might be misinterpreted—"

"Which means you'd better not say anything at all."

Roger set down his coffee and glanced at the others to see if anyone was listening. "Anyway, that's where she met Dad. He was digging, too. Probably the only one she could talk to. So when the family objected to an American boyfriend, they got married and he brought her back here."

"Then, when things got a little hot in Syria, Kamilah started bringing us over," Marid continued. "I was first, actually, because I wasn't married."

Roger had never talked to Tess about these subjects, and she was fascinated. "So, were they dissidents?"

"Qasim, certainly," said Marid. "But their hearts are still there—and so are their wives' families—so they're pretty careful about what they say, even here. They're quietly active, raising money for Middle East causes, like hospitals and schools, trying to be as apolitical as they can."

"I think they've come to partially approve of my mother marrying an American, since he was fluent in the culture and very sympathetic." Roger poured himself more coffee and stirred it with a cinnamon stick. "And because he's dead now, and they don't have to deal with him."

Marid touched his nephew on the arm. "But they definitely don't approve of you marrying Tess. Is that what you're planning?"

"Well, they'll get used to me," Tess sighed. "Or they won't. Which would be their loss. Besides, my family is worse. My father is a big patriot, and he hates all Middle Easterners."

"Well, we're a new generation," Marid said, "and I guess we'll have to put up with crap like that. It's getting worse now, with these bombings, but our family has always been rather insular. They even hassled me over Rasha, because she was born here."

"So how come you're an engineer, not a businessman like your brothers?"

"Partly my stubbornness. Partly their respect for education—for men, anyway. I'm like Roger. I wasn't expected to join the businesses because I'm very smart," he threw Tess a self-effacing grin. "So, they figured I should go to college. Roger had an easier time of it."

"Because you paved the way?"

"His mother actually paved the way. But what I meant is that he's on the female side of the family, so it's not that important."

"He's not considered an important part of the family?"

"It's not that so much. Sure, they'd have to be in real trouble to call on Roger to help them, but if they did, they'd invoke family ties and expect them to be honored."

Rasha came out of the kitchen, went down to the basement, and fetched her small children. Marid stood up to leave, and Tess told Roger, "You stay with your uncles. I think I'd better go join the women. The real reason I'm here is to get to know your mother. She's the important one for me."

By the time Tess reached the kitchen, the remaining women were seated around the table, speaking Arabic. Before Tess could join them, Kamilah jumped up and led her by the arm to the back of the house. "Let's sit in my office. It will be more comfortable than the kitchen—and more private. I've had enough of baby talk for one evening."

Every available niche in the office was filled with archaeological objects—pots, potsherds with intriguing fragments of designs, grotesque masks, metal and stone weapons, semiprecious jewelry, distorted clay human figurines, and bones and skulls. Kamilah watched Tess scanning her treasures. "To the trained eye," she said, picking up a tiny statue from her desk, "every piece tells a story. This one, for example, is a fertility doll. Notice the bulging abdomen."

"That one's rather obvious, even to the untrained eye."

"Unlike your own abdomen. Have you told Roger yet?"

Suddenly flushed, Tess took a minute to recover from her surprise and decide what to say. She shook her head, hooking behind her ear a loose strand of her apricot hair. "No. I wanted to wait until everything was sure."

"That's wise. I lost five in the first two years. I learned not to say anything. My husband got too upset. Arab men wouldn't, but he was very American. The family never forgave him for giving our only child an American name, but he wanted Roger to be American." She opened her hands in a shrug. "I did, too, but it wasn't that important to me, either way."

"I understand your reluctance. My mother lost at least two pregnancies, maybe more, before me." Tess pointed to her flat belly. "But how did you know?"

"I've had lots of practice. You'll notice that, unlike me, my sisters-in-law are rather fecund. But, specifically, I noticed a certain rosy glow the moment you arrived. That was only a clue, of course, but I overheard some of your conversation with Adara. And I saw you refusing coffee. Then I watched how you kept your eyes on the little ones. That was the giveaway."

"I suspect you don't miss much. Roger seems to have inherited your ability to notice the critical detail. It's one of the things that make him a great inventor." Tess held out her hand for the doll, asking for permission with her eyes.

Kamilah handed her the doll. "Oh, I don't think it's genetic. You've seen my brothers. Except for Marid, they move through life with their eyes, well, not closed, exactly, but focused on a very narrow range of things."

"That's probably a good thing in business—"

"But not in science. Not in archaeology. And, I presume, not in engineering."

Tess ran her fingers over the doll's distended belly. "No, you also need some creative imagination—"

"—which Roger didn't inherit. Not from me or my husband. Archaeologists are not the most imaginative of people. We're probably right up there—or down there—with actuaries."

"You're being too modest." Tess indicated the shelves full of reprints. "Roger was just telling me about your findings in Palmyra. You must have turned a few uncreative archaeologists' heads."

"Just a goat among the sheep, I'm afraid. But you're different, full of wild ideas, and some of it is rubbing off on Roger."

"And that's good? Or bad?"

"We'll have to wait and see, won't we? Do you plan to get married? I want to start thinking about gifts."

19

On her way to the meeting, Qaaf noticed that the Merchandise Mart was gaily festooned, promoting the next season's handcrafted gifts. In the Thursday Group's somber, under-decorated back room, Alif was anything but somber as Zay and Jiim passively allowed him to taunt Qaaf. "Did you notice the crowds when you came in?"

"It didn't seem all that crowded to me."

"Exactly. Retail business is down more than eight percent since we removed the bathrooms from Wrigley. People are afraid to come to public places." He smirked at Qaaf. "And nobody was killed."

"But some people were hurt exploring the wreckage—"

Zay held up one finger. "Even so, it was worth it. When they feel it in their pocketbooks, the merchants will put more pressure on the mayor. We need to keep up the pressure."

"There's one problem," Jiim said.

"You're too modest, Jiim," Zay said. "You did a fine job."

"But I used up the last of our explosives. Our stockpile is depleted."

Zay's brow wrinkled. "That is serious. I can get more, but it's going to take time."

"We can make more ourselves," Alif proposed. "One of my group has had all the basic training."

"That's not smart," Qaaf warned. "It's not a job for amateurs."

Alif hesitated, which Qaaf took as a sign of uncertainty about his amateur chemist. "Perhaps it *would* be good to wait a few weeks," Alif acknowledged. "Give them a chance to pay."

Zay shook his head. "A few more weeks with no attacks and the public will forget about us. We need to keep up the pressure. To escalate."

Rather than respond, Qaaf let Alif pick up the argument. "Perhaps it's good that they forget about us for a while. They'll become careless."

Now Qaaf answered. "Perhaps we will become careless first. It's always some little thing—something you never expect—that trips you up. Perhaps you're becoming cowardly, Alif. Perhaps you've forgotten what we're trying to accomplish."

Alif did not respond. Everyone turned to Zay for a decision.

Zay sat silent, meditating, then looked directly at Alif. "Bring in your amateur. I will probe the market for more ready-made material, but in the meantime, we can't wait. I'm raising our price, so we must raise the pressure."

20

The damp, misty weather on the way back to Ann Arbor couldn't dampen their spirits. All the way back along Interstate 94, Tess and Roger chatted incessantly about the ideas they were bringing back to Ann Arbor from Fermilab. The visit had been a success on all counts. Tess had spent a gratifying day with three analysts, exchanging techniques for storing and massaging vast databases. The Fermilab databases, derived from subnuclear high-energy Tevatron collisions, were enormous, just like Tess's databases derived from Roger's noninvasive probes into animal brains. So, despite the analysts' different fields of expertise, Tess felt she was among colleagues, bright men and women dedicated to their work of wrestling with floods of data.

Roger had found his own colleagues, as well, and happily shared information on his new miniature room-temperature super-conducting magnetic detection equipment in return for information on generating strange particles to be used in mental probes. But most intriguing were the new superstrong magnets, which Roger thought he could use to activate subatomic microprobes.

The day had passed much too quickly—ending with several promises of return visits. Before leaving Fermilab's spacious grounds, they stopped to enjoy the lab's thousand-acre nature preserve, with its diversity of native grasses, prairie flowers, birds, and mammals. Roger's favorite was the flock of Canada geese, especially when they took off from the pond in formation and circled overhead until disappearing on the horizon. Tess had a hard time tearing herself away from watching the buffalo calves nursing, but, in far too short a time, she and Roger were driving out under a tripod arch with thick, flat, silvery metal legs, each penetrated by three large circular holes.

The legs did not quite meet evenly at the top, which Roger found upsetting. "It's supposed to be that way, darling," Tess explained. "That's why it's called 'Broken Symmetry.' It's a symbol of Nature as the physicists have discovered it to be."

"Well, I suppose it's okay then, but it would be better if Nature were more symmetrical."

Tess could only sigh at the memory as they pulled onto the off-ramp in Jackson. Over bowls of hot vegetable soup, in a corner booth at Bob Evans Farm Restaurant, they planned their strategy. The important thing was to present a united front to Wyatt. The new probes would provide a quantum boost to progress, but would bend the budget. Tess couldn't wait to get her hands on the sheer quantity of data she would be able to extract from a dog's brain, but Roger thought the added precision of the data was more important. It was only a lovers' quarrel, and they left the restaurant holding hands, kissing, and agreeing to disagree.

Roger risked driving five miles above the speed limit so they could catch Wyatt before he left for the day. Every other vehicle was driving ten miles over the limit, but Tess couldn't convince him to be *that* daring. They caught up with Wyatt in the vestibule of Haven Hall, where the pelting rain had trapped him into talking to some students from his just-completed lecture. By offering him one of their two umbrellas, Tess induced him to listen to their new idea as they walked to the parking area.

Despite their ardor, Wyatt wasn't convinced. "I doubt that it will work. Even if it did exactly what you say, it would produce far too much data. Terabytes. Where would we store it all?"

Tess had to shout over the clatter of the rain on their umbrellas. "We'd just buy some more storage. Storage is cheap."

Wyatt stepped gingerly around a shallow puddle on the concrete sidewalk. "You're not the one paying the bills," he said.

"You're not either." She reached out and jabbed him playfully in the arm, drawing her arm back wet. "Come on, Professor Wyatt, you're always bragging about how your grants will buy you anything you need."

"Well, even if we needed that much data, we don't need that kind of precision."

"But we do," Roger said, looking up from tiptoeing around wet spots in a vain attempt to keep his shoes dry. "We're only beginning to approach the level we need to really see the patterns we want."

"We were better off with the old probes. All that noise just obscures the patterns. If we can't find patterns, we can't publish," said Wyatt.

"I believe everyone processes pictures in idiosyncratic ways. What you call 'noise' is the data," Roger said.

The rain picked up. Wyatt ducked under the canopy of a bus stop. "We've been through this before, Roger. We don't need that kind of precision for audio processing, and audio processing is what our grant is for."

"But visual processing would be so much better. We could see the same pictures that the subjects remember, and it would be harder to fake than just the words they remember."

"If you believe that so strongly, then put your arguments in your own grant application. We're going for audio. Remember your Bible: 'In the beginning was the Word.'"

While Wyatt laughed at his own little joke, Tess stepped between the two men. "You're right, Harvey." She had started calling him Harvey and telling him he was right whenever she wanted something from him. Now she wanted to get back on track toward the new equipment. "Hey, the rain is letting up. Let's get moving before it starts again."

She took his arm and walked under his umbrella. "I brought back some new processing ideas. They'll mean we don't have to process nearly as much data, and they're perfectly suited to audio information." *They're even better for video*, she thought, but she kept that to herself.

"Yes, well, that may be. But there's still cost to consider. I'm the principal investigator, and it's my responsibility to spend the grant money wisely."

"You're absolutely right, Harvey. Neither of us is really very good at the money side of the research, so we'll leave it to you to get the best deals possible."

She had timed her little speech so she'd have the last word as they arrived at Wyatt's parking space, easily recognized by his '98 red Ferrari 550 Maranello two-seater—"Wyatt's pick-up car" was what they called it behind his back. He offered Tess a ride home, but she pleaded errands on campus.

He opened the driver's door, but Tess held his arm for a moment. "I know you can get us the money, Harvey. When you go to Washington tomorrow, wine them and dine them." She patted him on his little pot belly. "But go easy on the dining part," she glanced inside the sports car, "or you'll have to buy a bigger car."

Roger watched the Ferrari roar off, splashing unwary students who happened to be standing nearby. "I notice he didn't offer *me* a ride."

"It's just a two-seater."

"You could have sat on my lap. We were going to the same place."

Tess laughed and kissed him on the mouth. "Let's go. I'll sit on your lap when we get home. He doesn't even know we live together."

"You'll get me all wet."

"I'll take off my clothes first, silly. And so will you."

"I don't like to get wet."

She snatched away his umbrella and collapsed it. "Oh, come on. Let's get thoroughly soaked. Besides, you were born wet."

When they reached the shelter of their front porch, Roger shook himself and wiped the water off his face. "Do you think he'll get us the equipment?"

"Of course, darling." Roger tried to extract the key from his pocket, but Tess was already undoing his belt. "The idiot still thinks that if he gives me what I ask for, he can get into my pants."

21

Wyatt studied the celebrity caricatures covering the walls of The Palm's bar. That way, he didn't have to watch Inga Steinman slurping down her lobster bisque. She'd already devoured a jumbo lump crabmeat cocktail and two martinis, while he— thinking of the comment Tess had made about his waistline—had picked at a simple mixed green salad and washed it down with iced Evian water. He was impatient, but he knew from experience that it wasn't wise to bring up business before she'd taken the edge off her prodigious appetite. *Especially now,* he thought, *when, in spite of the excellent lunch I am buying (with grant money, of course), Inga Steinman is furious.*

She tore off a ragged chunk of bread and mopped the last bisque from her bowl. When she finished, she waved for the waiter to bring the next course, then turned her wrath on Wyatt. "You may think I'm not a real scientist, Harvey, but I know what a fifteen-tesla supercooled magnet costs. This is no off-the-shelf item."

"I have assurances from the Fermilab people that they know how to raise the magnetic field strength of a commercial five-tesla model. And increase the usable magnetic field to the size of a basketball."

"Don't pussyfoot with me. You mean the size of a human head. That's our goal, and don't you forget it."

Two waiters arrived, set out the side orders, and with synchronized flourishes, lifted gleaming silver half-domes from the entrees—broiled salmon for him, filet mignon for her. As soon as Steinman started digging into the enormous side of deep fried onions, Wyatt resumed their argument. "Well, we're not going to do anything with humans until we're absolutely sure it's safe. That's why we have lab animals."

She chose an asparagus spear from her other side order and dipped it into the béarnaise.

"I'm not interested in interrogating lab animals." She pointed the spear at him like an accusing finger. "If you can't use human subjects, I can't support this acquisition."

"Of course. We will use human subjects—eventually."

She glanced around at the other tables to see if anyone was listening in. "Eventually? The man who appointed me won't be reelected if we don't do something spectacular about terrorism."

"Terrorism?"

"Yes. What do you think this grant is about?" She herself didn't know for sure, but she wasn't about to let Harvey Wyatt know the limits of her power.

"I didn't know."

She looked at the now-empty asparagus plate and wished she'd ordered two. "Well, you still don't know—officially. But, yes, it's about terrorism. Now. Not eventually. How long before you can try this new approach with human subjects?"

"If we interpret the guidelines in our favor, I'd say twenty-four months."

She didn't wait to swallow her half-chewed mouthful of steak. "Totally unacceptable, Harvey. Don't you want to play ball for our team?" She washed the steak down with a gulp of her third martini. "How about you say six months? I have to have a working model to show in six months—or less. And a demonstration before that."

"You know I couldn't do that without seriously violating the rules for ethical experiments on human—"

"That's just an excuse, and you know it. You know that's not a problem, Harvey. I can supply you with all the human subjects you could ever use. No rules."

"But if someone finds out—"

"Nobody will find out. Nobody knows the government is even holding these people, and nobody will miss them if something goes wrong. Nobody that counts. So when can I get some human results?"

She's like a damned alligator, Wyatt thought, *and she has me in her jaws. I don't have to like it, but I have to put up with it.* "When can I get my money?"

"First, you have to cut this budget." She extracted his rough budget from her purse, unfolded it, laid it facing him on the white tablecloth, and tapped her claw-like nail on one line item. "This quote for refurbishing and customization is way out of line." She laid a business card on top of the budget. "Have these people take care of all the magnet work. They owe me, and they're politically correct."

Wyatt examined the card. "I know these people, from personal experience and their reputation. They wouldn't be my first choice for this job."

"Perhaps, but they're *my* first choice." She waved over the waiter and ordered coffee, black. When it arrived, she heaped in three packages of noncaloric sweetener. "I never use sugar," she told Wyatt. "It's just extra calories, like your budget. You use my vendor, or you won't get your magnet."

Wyatt knew the conversation was over. He would get the magnet, and no one would have to know about his concession. Relieved that lunchtime was over, he managed to depart as Inga dug into her first dessert.

Once Wyatt was out of sight, Inga took out her cell phone. As the second scoop of mousse slid down her throat, she hit the speed dial.

"He bought it," she said. "Be sure it's ready. And properly prepared, if you want the information."

22

A week after Wyatt returned from D.C., his magnet arrived. It was almost as if Inga's vendor had anticipated the order. Even so, the vendor's modifications overran the budget, forcing Wyatt to short-change other equipment and activities—especially testing. Although Tess was told their priority was human subjects, she started her tests with rats, then puppies. She fitted the animals with Roger's brain-wave-detecting skullcaps and placed them under the magnet. The animals were subjected to perception tests at the highest power Roger thought the magnet could sustain—bypassing tests at lower levels of magnetic flux. Fortunately, the animals didn't seem to mind, and willingly provided mountains of deep-brain data in exchange for yummy treats.

The flood of additional data proved both a bounty and a burden for Tess's data reduction software. Although the data surely contained more information, the information was more deeply sunk within oceans of meaningless noise. *At least*, Tess thought, *it's meaningless to me and my software—up until now. It's up to me to build algorithms that separate the wheat of brain processing from the chaff of brain noise. I just wish my hormones weren't kicking my own brain around. I didn't know pregnancy could do this to my ability to concentrate.*

She decided to inform Wyatt that their present computer power was inadequate for the task ahead. Her first opportunity came when she was in the midst of tending to the laboratory animals. She knew he didn't like the squeaks and smells of the animal room, and hoped that he would be eager to concede what she wanted just to escape the head-high stacks of cages. But all Wyatt could say was, "We don't need to spend money on more processing power. Work with what you have."

She held one of the white rats, checked the identity code on its embedded ISO transponder with the handheld reader, locked the rat back in its cage with a fresh food dish, and wrote a note on its chart. "If I had just twice the speed, I could process higher frequencies, so I could get at some brain patterns that are just below the surface. I know they're there."

Wyatt scrambled backward when the next rat she extracted from the cage started to squirm and squeal. "Then just think harder. Don't solve every problem with brute force."

"Sometimes brute force works."

"All right, if you want brute force, why don't you make the signals stronger by boosting the strength of that magnet? You're not operating it at rated design capacity."

Finished with the rats, she lifted one of the beagle puppies from its pen. "Roger says it's not safe. He says the refurbishing work was shoddy. He wants to redo some of it before we try boosting to max power."

The puppy was so excited to be handled, it peed on Tess's lab smock. Dabbing at the damp spot with a towel, she offered the pup to Wyatt to hold, but he held up both palms. "I don't have time to mess with it."

"Do you mean Fido here, or the computer?"

"The computer, of course. We need results."

"If you're in such a hurry, Harvey, help me multitask. The puppies need exercise, so you play with this one while I fetch another." She handed him the beagle and lifted another from the same pen.

He took the puppy, but held it at arm's length. "What am I supposed to do with him?"

"Not *him*, Harvey. *Her*." She turned over the one she was holding so he could look underneath. "This one's a 'him.' Can't you tell the difference?"

The color rose in his cheeks. "Of course I know the difference." He put his female puppy back into the pen. She started to whimper. "Look, I don't have time for this."

Tess didn't have to fake her annoyance. "Why do *you* never have enough time to do things right, but we always have enough time to do them over?"

"And why are you so conservative all of a sudden? What's the worst that could happen if we boost the power?"

"We could destroy the magnet."

"Not likely, but if we did, then we'd have an excuse for being late. And Roger could fix it. Right?"

"Maybe." She grabbed up the female so she had a puppy in each arm, both licking her face. "But we might hurt one of our animals."

"They're just animals. We can always get more."

Just then, Roger entered the room carrying a fifty-pound sack of kibble. "More what? If you've got so much money to spend, how about letting me fix up that magnet. They did some shoddy electronic work in there."

"My God," said Wyatt. "You didn't touch the insides, did you?"

"No, I wouldn't do that without asking you first."

"No need to ask me. You're *never* to touch anything inside that machine."

"Why not? It's not safe to use the way it is now."

"Safety is not an issue here. I have explicit orders from our sponsor that nobody's to touch the insides of that machine except the people who refurbished it."

Tess saw the contradiction between this and Wyatt's assurances that Roger could fix the magnet, but she kept quiet and let Roger argue his own cause. He needed the practice.

"But they're the ones who messed it up. I can do a much better job."

"The sponsor says the insides of the machine are off limits to anyone without the proper security clearance—which you don't have. And probably won't get. If you break the seal, you're fired. Period. Just be a good team player for once."

Tess cringed at Wyatt's "team player" comment, but decided she could use his mood to her advantage. "All right. I understand. The team needs to show some victories to satisfy your sponsor. Right?"

Wyatt nodded. "That's right. And it's about time you both took the trouble to see things from my point of view."

Roger started to say something, but Tess waved him back. "I'm sorry we've been so insensitive to your needs, Harvey. We've been too focused on the technical details to fully appreciate how much you're doing for us."

Wyatt swelled visibly. Tess pressed her advantage. "So, if I understand correctly, what you need is to show some human results as soon as possible. Right?"

"That would be nice, yes."

"And when we do, then you'll be able to coax some more funds out of your sponsor? So we can upgrade the magnet?"

While Wyatt thought about that, Tess twice had to shush Roger's eager attempts to break in.

"All right," he said at last, "as soon as you give me some human results—they have to be impressive, though—as soon as you do that, I think I can get the money. Yes."

Tess pressed on. "For now, though, how about the human interface? I'm afraid to use it for human experiments. It's clumsy as hell." As soon as the words were out of her mouth, she saw from Wyatt's reaction that criticizing the interface was a mistake.

"I designed it, and it's state-of-the-art. Don't either of you touch anything." Wyatt pivoted toward the door and stormed out of the animal room before either of them could reply.

23

As soon as Wyatt was out of sight, Roger hugged Tess and gave her a long, passionate kiss. The puppies, bundled with Tess in Roger's arms, joined them in the kissing. Releasing each other at last, Roger sighed, "I'm glad he's gone. I suppose we can work with human subjects, but we're going to have to work with the magnet as it stands, weak as it is. I wouldn't dare raise the power the way it's put together."

"This magnet is stronger than we thought."

"What do you mean?"

"It's attracted my father all the way from California."

"Your father? Your mother, too?"

"Yep."

"Brothers, too?"

"Don't know about that yet. It's the old man that I dread."

"Why are you so down on him? You never talk about him."

She handed him the female puppy. "Here, put a leash on her while I do this little guy."

"Are you avoiding my question?"

"No, just in a hurry to take them out. They just ate, and maybe I can get them to do their business on the lawn instead of in the pen."

They carried the puppies outside and sat down with them under a hundred-year-old maple tree. Tess's puppy wanted to crawl back onto her lap, but she placed him firmly back on the lawn. "It began when my brothers were born. Suddenly, it was like I didn't exist for him. The boys were everything."

"I don't understand."

"Well, your mother understood. She experienced the same thing with your uncles. Nothing she ever achieved was as good as any little thing her brothers did. Even today, when I'm five times the engineer of all of my brothers put together, all my father talks about is *their* work. He just doesn't think girls should be engineers."

"I don't understand. Didn't he support you going to engineering school?"

"Sure. Do you know why?"

"So you could become an engineer?"

She teased the puppies with a twig, playfully, but she wasn't smiling. "It was supposed to be a good place to find an engineer for a husband."

"Oh," he was beginning to see her point. "But you didn't get a husband . . . or is there something you haven't told me?"

"No, silly. You know I didn't get a husband."

"Then you thwarted his plans. You should be proud of yourself, not angry with him."

"Mel's plans are more devious than that. He said that if I got an engineering degree, but then couldn't find a husband, I could always find a *good job* as an engineering secretary."

"Oh, wow. But when you graduated first in your class, he must have changed his mind."

"He did. He said that now I could get a good job as an engineering secretary . . . but now I'd *never* get a husband."

"You're kidding."

"Do I look like I'm kidding?" The male puppy squealed when she inadvertently poked him with the twig.

"No, but don't take it out on that puppy."

"Whoops. Sorry, junior." She picked up the little guy and let him lick her nose. "And that's just part of it. Mel must always get his way with everybody."

"Gee, I wonder which of his kids inherited that trait."

"Touché. But at least I'm not a Christian bigot like Mel."

"That's pretty harsh."

"It's the simple truth." She kissed the puppy, picked the other one up, and stood up. "Time for their nap. And speaking of naps, I'll have to find a place for you to sleep while my father is here. He'll go nuts if he finds me living with an *A-rab*."

Roger laughed at her mockery of Mel's pronunciation. "So what? That's his problem."

"He'll do his darndest to make it my problem. *Our* problem. I don't need the fuss."

He held the door for her as they re-entered the animal room. "Then let's get creative."

"I'd like that," she said. "What do you have in mind? The Bag Bandit?"

"It involves the Bag Bandit, yes."

She took his pup and lowered both beagles into the pen. "So, let's hear it."

Roger fumbled in the microscope drawer and found a retainer ring, which he slipped onto her third finger. "How about you and the Bag Bandit get married before your father gets here?"

She grabbed him and kissed him so fast that all the animals cowered in their cages. "Why, Roger, you sly thing. I thought you'd never ask."

24

The wedding was quick and private, as they both preferred. The day after, the parents' visit was not so private, but quick enough that Tess lost her temper with her father only a dozen times.

She'd known that as soon as Mel met Roger, he would be conflicted about his new son-in-law. He thought Roger was too young for Tess, but he admired his engineering genius. He didn't like Tess marrying an "*A-rab,*" but he was somewhat mollified when he heard that Roger had not been raised as a Muslim.

As Roger said to Tess, after first meeting Mel, "I can see where you learned to talk dirty."

"He learned that from my mother." *In fact,* Tess thought, *Leonora had taught Mel just about everything except engineering—and his prejudices, which she failed to expunge.*

After surviving Mel and Leonora, Tess plunged into her work, soon reporting to Wyatt that her programs were picking up some information that might be from the auditory part of a puppy's brain, perhaps correlated with sounds that alerted the puppy—another puppy barking, a squeaky toy, the food cabinet opening. Hearing of some positive results, Wyatt apparently decided to forgive them for marrying, thinking he could bide his time with Tess, to wait for the opportunity he was certain would come sooner or later.

Wyatt watched patiently as the newlyweds debated endlessly about the puppies' brain-wave patterns. Tess thought the patterns were reactions to the sounds. Roger thought they were encodings of the sounds themselves—which would place them earlier in the aural processing sequence. Tess trained the puppies to recognize several words—"treat," "playtime," and "outside"—all of which signaled something the puppies associated with positive events. Roger tested the brain patterns in response to these words and compared them to similar words that had no canine significance— "treacle," "playground," and "outcome." With these words, the reaction patterns disappeared.

Despite their progress, Tess still wasn't totally comfortable using puppies in their experiments. Experimenting on people would be better, but Roger said the equipment was not ready to test on people. Rats weren't smart enough, and adult dogs had unknown training histories. So she needed to use puppies, but at least Roger's brain-wave monitoring equipment wasn't invasive.

To further salve her conscience, she forced Wyatt to accept humane conditions for the animals' treatment. No puppy would be cut or harmed in any way. Everything would be done to raise the puppies normally. And, when they grew too mature for the experiments, they would all be placed as pets with good families.

When Wyatt left them, to return to his office, Tess stuck her printouts between Roger and his computer screen and flicked them with the backs of her fingers. "This means the patterns are coming from too deep in the brain. It means I'm right, but it also means that your damned instruments are too sensitive."

Roger seemed more optimistic. "I can adjust that. Now that I have a starting place, I can work the surrounding regions, see what's triggering these reactions."

"That could take months." Months were becoming significant for Tess, but Roger didn't know yet. She'd have to tell him soon, because he was beginning to notice her rapidly changing moods.

"We could go faster if you'd do some surgical interventions on the pups. Open them up so I could place some electrodes more accurately—"

Tess clapped her hand over his mouth. "You know I won't do that. Never. I'd do it to myself first."

He pulled her hand away, gently, and kissed her palm. "You know I was just kidding."

"Well, you'd better not say that around Wyatt. He'd like nothing better than to cut open my babies." She was starting to cry, and turned her head so Roger wouldn't see.

"Hey, be fair. He's not that bad. But I'll keep quiet, and we'll take it one step at a time."

"Wyatt isn't going to like that one-step-at-a-time approach." As she blinked away her tears, she was thinking that she wouldn't like it if she had to stop working on the project to have the baby. They had to move faster, even if that happened to please Wyatt.

"Since when are you worried about what Wyatt likes? Give him your 'Harvey' routine."

"I don't think that will work anymore. Not since he knows we're married."

"I think you underestimate the depths of Wyatt's depravity." He laughed, then grabbed her and kissed her deeply.

Though she yearned to be held longer, she pushed him away after a minute. "This is serious, Roger."

"I am serious. Let's take the afternoon off and go home."

"No. Really," she said. "We have to speed things up, and only using the animals just isn't going to do it. By the time we're ready, these puppies will be too old, so we'd have to wait for another litter. We need a human subject—one who can understand speech and talk to us. Then we'll go ten times as fast."

"No way. This equipment hasn't been tested enough to use on a person. I don't even like using the pups. Rats, they're a different story. I don't get too attached to rats."

"Well, I do. They're living things." She glared at him. Everything he said was making her angry, but she couldn't stop. "And I wouldn't have used any of the animals if I thought it wasn't safe for them."

"Maybe you should worry more about people than rats."

"Now you're telling me I'm insensitive? And you think that makes you very sensitive?"

She started to cry, unable to control it this time. She'd been crying a lot lately—the strain of the wedding, the pregnancy, Mel and Leonora's visit, Wyatt's pressure—but never in front of her husband.

Roger didn't know how to react. He attempted to say something, to console her, but no words came out. He tried to hug her, but she pulled away and cried harder.

"Just go away," she sobbed. "Just leave me alone. I've got to feed the animals now."

He packed his things and left, which Tess felt was exactly the wrong thing for him to do. He had left her alone. Trying to busy herself, she splashed her face with cold water, then snacked on a granola bar. That seemed to clear her head—*perhaps the mood swing was just low blood sugar, not hormones,* she thought—so she made some changes to the software. Her mind felt totally clear, which was confirmed when she tested the changes and found no problems. She decided she didn't want Wyatt to see how she had repaired the code he had corrupted—didn't want him to tamper with her code anymore—so she changed the encryption key that locked the code base. *I'll give the new key to Roger at supper.*

Thinking of her argument with Roger depressed her, and she turned to the napping puppies for solace. She climbed over the gate into their pen and sat down on the floor, ignoring the puppy droppings scattered across the newspapers. All the pups woke up and piled on top of her, trying to lick her face.

She spoke to them, sure they could understand at least her tone. "I'd never do anything to hurt you kids. Never. Why should you be different from people? No experimenter would try something new on a person that they hadn't tried on themselves. It's against all ethical codes. And I wouldn't do it, anyway."

In their excitement, two of the puppies peed on her jeans, but she was deep in thought and didn't notice. "What do you think, kids? Should I show him he's being silly? Yes, we'll show him it's safe, then everything will be okay again. After all, I've done it with low power before—just with an earlier version of the software. What could possibly go wrong?"

She carefully placed the puppies on the floor, but when she put one down, another would climb back onto her lap. In desperation, she reached in her bait bag and took out a handful of Charlee Bear treats. She let the puppies smell them, then tossed them into the far corner of the pen. While the puppies competed for their shares, she stood and stepped out of the pen. "You be good, now. I'll be back in five minutes. All I need is a small data sample, to prove it's absolutely safe."

It actually took Tess more than five minutes just to adapt two sets of Roger's puppy sensors so they would stay in place, taped to her head. She set the parameters for her weight and brain size on the control computer—a difficult task because Wyatt's awkward interface required her to translate pounds and inches to kilos and centimeters. Then she set the timer for a one-minute test and, to play it safe, adjusted the magnet to lowest power. *Roger's probes will be sensitive enough,* she thought.

She rolled the examining table closer to the machine. She climbed on top with her legs hanging off one end and her head resting in the magnet's aperture. From that position, she could plug the sensor cables into the computer, but she couldn't reach the power switch. She got up and fetched the poop scoop handle to extend her reach. The puppies thought she was coming back and scrambled over one another to rush the gate. "Not yet, darlings. This is taking a bit more time than I thought."

Tess crawled onto the table and plugged herself in again, assuming the position with her head squarely in the aperture. For a moment, she hesitated, wondering if she was really thinking clearly enough to do this. She remembered her promise to the puppies, her fear of what Wyatt might make her do to them, and Roger's low estimation of her skills. Minimal power would be perfectly safe.

She extended the handle and hit the switch.

25

The day was hot, even for a summer day in Chicago, and the air-conditioning at the Mart couldn't keep up. Odors of unwashed human sweat and Jiim's cigarette smoke mixed with too many exotic spices in the tiny room made Qaaf regret the quiche she had for lunch. Zay, as usual, seemed unperturbed, but Qaaf realized that the heat was worsening Alif's never-mild temper. "There are rumors that the Vice President will be visiting Chicago," he said. "We need to step up our activities, to bring pressure on the city officials to pay us off before he comes."

Qaaf had a different idea. "We should remain quiet until then, to lull them into complacency."

"It won't matter," Alif sneered. "The Secret Service isn't going to become complacent about guarding the Vice President. They won't be affected by anything we do."

"Perhaps not. But then our attack on the Vice President's quarters will be more dramatic. And will embarrass the city officials even more. But if we're too successful with many attacks before his visit, they might change his plans and not come to Chicago at all. His propaganda value is that of dozens of congressmen."

"You have a point," Alif conceded. "But we won't need him if a few more dramatic strikes make them pay before he's scheduled to arrive."

Qaaf decided it was best to agree. "Especially now that we've raised the ante to eighty million."

Alif wasn't put off by the surprise of Qaaf agreeing with him. He turned to Jiim. "You're confident you can handle this?"

Jiim turned to Zay for approval and received a nod. "Yes, I'm sure."

"Then, unless you have objections," Alif looked at Qaaf as if to dare her to object, "I recommend we strike at least twice before the Vice President's scheduled visit."

"I have no objections," Qaaf responded, "as long as Jiim remembers that there's to be no killing."

"I'll take care," Jiim assured her. "Can you provide several possible targets and dates for each?"

"Of course," said Qaaf. "But the trail between us must be broken in several places. And the final choice will be Alif's." *Might as well give this rabid dog a meaningless bone.*

Alif sat a little straighter. "But you'll assist in executing the plans?"

"Of course. But I can't be seen in the neighborhood at the time of an attack."

Alif grunted, as if Qaaf were making cowardly excuses, but said nothing. Qaaf started to protest, but Zay raised his arm signaling a halt. Qaaf could see age spots on his hand—an inexcusable clue to his identity. "It's decided. We will carry out Alif's plan for a series of dramatic attacks as we prepare for the final convincing blow at the Vice President."

Qaaf, not willing to break protocol by saying anything, made a mental note to buy a pair of gloves for Zay before their next meeting. She could buy them right here, today, in the Merchandise Mart. She would, of course, pay cash and dispose of the receipt.

26

I know I'm Tess, and I know I'm awake, but how do I know? Everything is blank. My mind is clear. Six cubed is . . . two-sixteen, but nothing's coming in. Only flat. Only gray.

It must be I'm dreaming, but what a strange dream. I'll test it. If I'm not dreaming, I can sit up. Oh, nothing happens. I can't seem to sit up. I thought it, but it's not happening. Must be a dream. Wake up!

I still can't move. Am I strapped down? I can't feel any straps, nothing binding my body. But nothing moves. No straps. No nothing. I don't feel anything . . . anywhere.

Maybe I can wiggle my toes. . . . No, no toes. Fingers? . . . No fingers either. I must be anesthetized.

Am I in a hospital? Maybe I'm having the baby. I can't remember. Careful, don't panic! Just check it out. Look around. Oh, no, my eyes don't seem to be responding, either. Am I blind? Well, stupid, that's not right. I can see something. Something moved, changed. I think my eyes blinked. But why didn't I feel them blink?

Light. Color? No color. White. White with dots. Aha, it's a ceiling—at least it looks like it's a ceiling. White. Off-white. And full of tiny dots, no pattern. Is there a pattern? No, not an easy pattern. Random? Acoustic tiles? Yes, could be a hospital ceiling. Oh, God, I've been in an accident. I'm losing the baby!

Calm down, silly. It could be just about any place. Every place has a ceiling—check it out. Oh, I can't seem to move my eyes. Just lots and lots of dots and dots.

Oh, that rhymes. Very funny. I must be scared if I'm making bad poetry. Get back to work!

Just lots of dots, oh, and a few lines. Space between tiles, that fits. They must be tiles.

Wait, there's a brown spot on one of the tiles—looks like a coffee stain. But coffee doesn't spill on the ceiling. Am I looking at the floor? Oh God! Am I upside down?

No, don't go nutso on me. Number one: Nobody uses acoustic tiles on the floor, okay? I'm not strapped to the ceiling.

So, where? Be logical! What happened? What was I doing?

Wait a minute—a sound! What sound? Where? Okay, that might help. Close the eyes and just pay attention to the sounds.

Nope, they won't stay closed. Same ceiling. Can I listen with eyes open? Don't look! Okay, look but don't see it. Look right past it, through it. There, I can do that. Now listen!

Someone's breathing. Sounds like white noise. Oh, shit, it must be me.

Wait a minute. Two different sounds, two different rhythms. Two people breathing. Who's here? Roger?

Roger studied Tess's every breath, every eye blink, and twitch, as if each might be her last. Or it could be the first sign of awareness. He saw no change he could positively identify, but it seemed to him that in the last few minutes, her unmoving eyes looked more . . . what was it? Alive? Alert?

An EEG would tell for sure if Tess was still in there, but Roger had refused to allow any instruments to be placed on her head. Now he didn't know if he was more afraid of hurting her or more afraid of finding out the awful truth. The final truth. He thought of the baby—that was the first thing they'd tested when they brought her in. Why hadn't she told him? He started to sob again, but his tear ducts had emptied their reservoirs over the past twenty-four hours.

Someone's there. I can hear, what? Crying? Why would someone be crying?

Over me. They're crying over me. What does that mean? Is this what death feels like—no feeling, but seeing and hearing?

What about my other senses? I can't taste anything, but I can never taste my own mouth. And I certainly can't feel anything. Must be anesthetized. Not dead.

What about smell? Hmm, can't make my nose sniff. Can it smell anyway?

There's something there. Concentrate. Stink. Body odor. Someone who hasn't bathed recently. Can't be Roger. He never misses his shower.

He had been sitting at her bedside for twenty-four hours in the same clothes, with only two quick bathroom breaks. A nurse had offered him food, but he couldn't bear the thought of eating while she lay there like a living corpse. The nurse insisted that he drink water, and he'd been able to do that—ashamed that he could when Tess couldn't. When the nurse had tried to give her some water, Tess had gagged, giving Roger a momentary flash of hope. But after the nurse wiped up the water, he could see that nothing had changed.

Now the IV was dripping, dripping, like a Chinese water torture.

There's another sound. Like dripping. What is it?

Where is it? Focus. Left. And up. Yes, there's something there, at the edge of my vision. But it's just a blur. A blue blur.

A riddle. What's up, left, blue, and goes bloop, bloop? An IV, of course. They're feeding me. Jesus, how long have I been here like this?

Like this? Like what? Don't panic.

Oh, if they're giving me an IV, I can't be dead. That's a relief. I hope it's to counteract the anesthetic. This is really boring. I hope it's over soon, whatever they're doing to me.

But what the hell happened? Is the baby okay?

27

During the next days, Tess overheard enough to know their baby was still okay and that Roger now knew about her pregnancy. From arguments between Roger and several doctors, she deduced that she was indeed in a hospital, immobilized into a locked-in state by some sort of accident when the controls on the superconducting magnet had failed. *I don't remember a thing about the accident—only my argument with Roger.*

She overheard that Roger had examined the lab equipment. Apparently the magnet had logged a thick pulse that exceeded its rated maximum. Roger traced the failure to an error in the software code—Wyatt's, of course—but that was in an old version of the code. The newest version was locked inside the source-code control system, and now Tess remembered changing the password. The doctors wanted to give Tess another magnetic shock, believing it was the best chance for a quick reversal of her condition. But Roger refused, wanting to figure out Tess's password or otherwise access the control system. No human being had ever been hit with such a huge magnetic pulse. Except for Tess.

She heard all of this, but she couldn't respond. *I'm not sure another shock is a good idea, Roger, but let them perform an EEG at least. I know your experience with the sensor embedded in your hand made you afraid of hurting me, and that's sweet—but silly. Even if something goes wrong with the equipment, an EEG is a different matter from your invention. Totally passive. Totally safe. God, I wish you could hear me.*

After each argument with the doctors, Roger returned to her side, breathing quietly, sobbing, and smelling worse and worse. She knew telepathy was bunk, but she wished she was wrong so she could tell Roger what to do. *What other chance do I have? I'll go crazy if I can't get some control. It's okay, Roger. Okay to leave me and clean up. Okay to let the doctors perform the EEG. Damn, I'm not getting through.*

In the end, perhaps it was her mental waves, or perhaps the doctors just wore him out, threatening to use a CAT, MRI, or PET scan to assess any brain damage. They told him those scans were more intrusive, perhaps upsetting some delicate balance in Tess's brain, so he gave permission for an EEG, as a start. In any case, the movement and noises told Tess they were setting up for an EEG. Still, her nose said he hadn't received her telepathic message about cleaning up. He was staying in the room, stink and all, watching to see that everything was done right. Nothing the doctors could say could persuade him to leave.

After three sleepless days and nights at her bedside, Roger had begun to daydream about apples. Perfect apples. Perfect thousand-dollar apples like those he'd seen once, arrayed at a Japanese fruit stand.

At first he tried to brush away these visions as irrelevant delusions. He had no experience with daydreams, with sleeplessness, with problems he couldn't solve in his head. Until Tess's accident, every problem had been easy for him, but the tangle of tubing sustaining her life had snarled his mind in an unfamiliar way. For the first time in his life, his logic had failed him.

Perhaps, now, for Tess, he needed a different logic. Could there be a clue in those perfect apples? He knew the Japanese believed that the more perfect the fruit, the more it helped cure the broken, the sick, whatever imperfections ailed the patient. But Tess had no imperfections—quite the contrary. Her buttermilk skin was unblemished. Not a single apricot hair was out of place. Her breathing was as regular and quiet as a Swiss clock.

But, like a clock, she couldn't move or talk or show the slightest sign of awareness. What good would a perfect apple do to cure that?

In response to these daydreams about apples, his stomach growled, protesting three days and nights without sustenance. He ran his hand over the stubble on his cheek, catching a whiff of his own rancid armpit, sickening, like rotten fruit.

And then he knew. *I'm the apple. I'm the imperfect one who's failing her.*

He rose, stiffly, and walked to her tiny hospital bathroom. He washed his face three times with antibacterial soap, just so he would be pure enough to plant a soft goodbye kiss on her doll-like forehead. "I'll be back," he whispered.

After stopping for a haircut, he visited the drugstore, buying a new three-blade razor, imported English shaving cream, a huge bar of French almond bath soap, blue anti-dandruff shampoo, strong lemony mouthwash, Arid deodorant, Rembrandt toothpaste, a Sonic toothbrush, and new white Jockey shorts and socks. At the checkout counter, he glanced at his shoes and ran back to Aisle 7 to pick up shoe polish and a brush.

Hugging his bundle, he raced home, not wanting to leave Tess alone any longer than necessary. But once at home, he took his time. He borrowed an iron and board from Mrs. Tarkanian upstairs. He'd never ironed anything before, but he found instructions on the Internet. He ironed his best shirt and pants and hung them to air while he cleaned and polished his shoes.

Stripped naked, he lathered and shaved, studied his face, then lathered and shaved again. He searched the medicine cabinet for Tess's tweezers, then plucked a dozen stray black hairs from his unruly eyebrows. He showered with the almond soap, shampooed his hair, and soaped himself again, paying special attention to his body's creases. He dried himself with a fresh towel, sprayed deodorant at his armpits, brushed his teeth through three electric cycles, and dressed.

He checked his hair, spit on his fingers, and plastered down three loose strands. *Now, my beloved, you will awaken.*

Something has changed, Tess thought. Roger had disappeared, then reappeared smelling fresh, conversing calmly with the doctors. She heard the bleeping of the machine, then somebody fussed over her head. She felt nothing. All she could do was listen intently to the verdict. "Your wife's brain patterns are completely normal."

Don't refer to me in the third person, you jerks. I'm here, and I'm not dead yet.

"All her vital signs are normal, even her involuntary reflexes. But we see no voluntary movement at all. She can't tell us what's going on inside."

They must have tested my reflexes, which are apparently normal. But I didn't feel anything. Okay, so I can hear and smell, and see things if they're in front of my eyes. But I can't feel anything—except helplessness. There has to be some way I can communicate. But how?

She focused again, picking up something Roger was saying. "How long will she be like this?"

"Quite frankly, we have no idea. None of us have seen a case like this before . . ."

Now, Tess thought, *I'm a "case."*

". . . but we're only a Student Health Center. We don't see that many unusual cases. We'd like to bring in someone from the med school faculty."

Yes, do it.

"All right," Roger said. His voice was strained and gravelly. "As long as I'm able to watch what they're doing—and veto anything I don't like—I don't see any reason to object."

Good. Way to go, Roger.

"Well, there could be expenses that won't be covered by your student health policy."

"Expenses! I don't care about expenses. She needs the best there is."

"I don't know if they'll come if you can't show proof of ability to pay."

"The goddamned University should pay. It was their equipment that screwed up. Their professor's stupid programming." Anger was not an old acquaintance of Roger's, but Tess could hear they were fast becoming friends.

Call Mel. He'll pay. And stop swearing at them. I know you're taking this hard. If only I could tell you I'm okay—to calm down and be more effective.

"The administration doesn't think it's liable."

"The government, then. They funded the project. Talk to Wyatt."

"Who's Wyatt?"

"Professor Wyatt. He's the lead investigator. He modified the software without proper testing. He didn't even notify us."

"I'll have someone call him."

"He hasn't been here?"

"No, nobody's been here since you brought her in."

It figures.

"That *bIHnuch.*"

Tess had been brushing up on her Klingon. *That coward, indeed.*

28

Wyatt was indeed afraid. Afraid to face Roger. Afraid of saying something that would put him in legal jeopardy. Afraid that when Inga arrived, she would crucify him if he did something wrong. Even if he didn't. More afraid because she'd been strangely calm and pleasant when he called to tell her about the accident. The only thing she said was to stay away from Tess and Roger until she arrived. That was no problem.

Inga had been uncharacteristically quiet on the phone, and Wyatt figured that she, too, was afraid. The politics of this grant must be touchier than he realized—so touchy that, much as Inga hated to travel, she had told him she was coming to handle this mess personally. And the FBI would have to be involved—agents would get to Ann Arbor faster than she could. So, she warned him about keeping his mouth shut about her vendor arrangements— about everything—until she arrived.

When Don and Lucinda knocked on his closed office door, Wyatt hurriedly hid his Scotch in his bottom desk drawer. He was terrified as soon as they entered and flashed their badges—and the icy woman was even more frightening than the steel-eyed man. She introduced herself and Don, confirmed Wyatt's identity, and warned him he faced prison if he didn't stay put. If he didn't cooperate.

Wyatt invited them to sit and saw Don give Lucinda a sign to let him take over. Wyatt had seen enough TV to recognize they were double-teaming him, and Don was taking the good cop role. Wyatt gritted his teeth, then clamped his jaw hard.

"This is a matter of national security," Agent Capitol was saying. "If you talk to anyone—you haven't talked to anybody, have you?"

"No. Just Dr. Steinman."

"That would be Inga Steinman, the one who notified me?"

"Yes. Yes, she's my sponsor, so I had to tell her."

"You did the right thing," Don soothed. "Exactly the right thing. And you didn't talk to anyone else. Right?"

"No. Nobody else."

"So you don't know how she is?"

"Dr. Steinman?"

Don looked at his partner and raised his eyebrows in disbelief. "No. Not Dr. Steinman. The girl. The one who was hurt?"

"No. All I know is that she's at the Student Health Center. One of my colleagues saw her husband carry her over there. That's how I knew."

"So who's this colleague?"

Wyatt told him. "I'll go get him," Lucinda said. Wyatt thought he saw a slightly sadistic gleam in her eye as she checked her holster and stood up.

As soon as Lucinda left, Wyatt spoke up. "Listen, it's not my fault that the mag—"

Don stared at Wyatt and put his finger to his lips. "Not here." He stood up. "Let's go."

"Where are we—"

Don shook his head. "Not now. Just follow me."

Five minutes later, they were sitting in the Speech Pathology Department's acoustic isolation room tucked away in a corner of the basement of the Frieze Building. A minute later, they were joined by Lucinda, who looked pleased with herself when she examined the waffled gray padding of the windowless room. A technician finished checking the room for bugs, set up an electronic device to provide further shielding, and left. Inga arrived a few minutes later. Lucinda double-checked that the video camera was physically disconnected from its cables. As soon as she secured the door, Don opened the conversation. "The first thing we want to know, Professor, is whether this incident will set back your schedule."

Wyatt noticed the eerie lack of reflected sound when he spoke. "Definitely. And it's not my fault." He pointed at Inga. "She made me buy inferior equipment."

Inga started to defend herself, but Don shushed her. "There'll be lots of time for blame later. How long is the delay?"

"That's impossible to know unless I know how long—or if— she's going to be out of commission."

"We can't control that. Assume for the moment that she never revives. What then?"

"Then I think we'll never finish. Apparently, she encrypted all our files before the accident and nobody knows the key. We'll have to start over."

"We'll send in our cryptology people," Lucinda said. "They can crack anything."

Wyatt disagreed, hoping Lucinda wouldn't retaliate. "These kids are clever. I've never been able to crack their encryption."

"Just assume our people can crack it." Lucinda stared at Wyatt and he looked away. "Can't she be replaced?"

"Probably, but that's not the problem. I might be able to replace her—given enough time—but if she, uh, . . . dies, then I don't think he'll ever come near the project."

"By 'he' you mean . . . ?"

"Her husband. Roger Fixman. He's not much of a team player, but I think it would be hard to replace him."

"How hard?" Lucinda's irritation infected her voice, sounding even colder in this echoless room. "Be specific. We don't have time for games here."

"Actually, I don't think I could replace him."

Don turned to Inga. "Is that true?"

She nodded. "Fixman's why we funded this project. It wasn't going anywhere until my review panel read the kid's papers. Then they were ecstatic. He's a goddamn genius. That's why we had to risk him, even though he's half Arab." She stared at Wyatt, daring him to claim otherwise. "Our professor here is basically the administrator. Not totally stupid, but hasn't had a fresh idea since his doctorate. Maybe not even then."

Lucinda wrote something in her black leather notebook. Wyatt hung his chin against his chest, totally whipped. Don studied Wyatt and then Inga. "Then it seems we have two alternatives. First, we need to do everything we can to revive the girl. At the same time, we need to convince her husband that somehow her cure depends on him staying on the project. That will motivate him. The floor is open for new ideas."

Wyatt, still smarting under Inga's put-down, kept his mouth shut. Inga pressed her lips together and shrugged her shoulders. Don turned to his partner. "Any bright ideas, LD?"

She closed her notebook, snapped it shut, then looked around the room as if she thought somebody could be spying on them through the windowless foam. "We have some of the best neurologists in the world up at—you know. And it's a secure facility. I could go along and encourage him."

"Good thinking. If we offer his wife free treatment and move her up there, we could move the whole project, magnet and all, along with her. Actually, from the briefing I've had so far, I suspect we ought to buy a new magnet . . ." he started, fixing his gaze on Inga, ". . . from a different vendor."

Inga blanched, but said nothing.

Lucinda waited a moment for Inga to speak, then said, "And we'd suggest that if he didn't cooperate, we wouldn't be able to convince the higher-ups to pay for her treatment."

Inga looked puzzled. "What higher-ups? I thought Don was in charge."

"Forget what LD said," Don warned. "There are no higher-ups. That's just the story we'll give him."

"It gives us a better negotiating position," Lucinda added. "We'll have to keep him in the dark about a lot of things. Remember that."

"How do I know what I can say and what I can't?" Wyatt squeaked.

Lucinda threw him a stern look. "I think the best thing would be to sever you from the project entirely. If we need your advice, we'll call on you."

"Maybe I was a bit hard on him," Inga countered, laughing nervously. "He can be useful. After all, someone has to clean the animal cages."

"If that's all he does, the clinic has techs who can tend the animals."

"No, I just like to prick his ego from time to time. Keeps him in line. Actually, there are a number of things he can do that you won't easily replace with technicians. You'll just have to keep an eye on him so he doesn't screw things up again."

"I resent that," Wyatt pouted. "This wasn't my screwup."

"I wasn't referring to this incident, but, yes, I suppose this is yet another one. If I've learned one thing about you, it's that you have to be watched."

"I'll be there to keep an eye on him," Lucinda assured her. "I'll keep him on a short leash." Don had to suppress a smile, thinking that Wyatt would probably love that, literally. He had background information on Wyatt's nightly entertainment in D.C.

Apparently Wyatt didn't think it was funny. "You can use your short leash on some other dog. I can't leave in the middle of a semester." He stood up as if to leave.

"Not to worry," said Lucinda, blocking the door with her muscular body. "We've already cleared that with the dean. You're now officially on leave. Now, sit!"

Wyatt sat.

29

The government's secret "neurology" clinic was housed on a nineteenth-century railroad mogul's estate on the Eastern Shore of Lake Michigan, somewhere north of Muskegon and south of Ludington. On the day Roger and Tess arrived, by ambulance, the secrecy was enhanced by a shroud of fog that obscured the lake. He had been told that the view was magnificent, but as far as Roger could tell from peering into the white mist, the lake could have been a hundred miles away.

Through the mist, details of the estate were revealed to Roger one at a time, as the ambulance crept cautiously along the winding gravel road. They approached a wrought-iron electric gate in a high brick wall. The guard had a military bearing in a red uniform that was self-consciously nonmilitary. Don showed the guard his credentials. The gate slid open, noiselessly, and the ambulance proceeded down what appeared to be newly tarred pavement.

Ornate letters on a weathered scroll announced the property as The Edgemoor Estate. The facility's disguise was furthered by a riding stable with four real horses, an exercise ring, and authentic piles of manure. Other than the military bearing of the guard, there was no indication of the true use of the property until the ambulance crested a second barrier hill and a complex of buildings with all the trimmings of a posh residence was revealed.

Roger was impressed by the care that went into the camouflage, but he thought the array of buildings was too extensive to be believed by any but the most casual observer. Perhaps keeping the entire existence of the clinic secret was the government's primary camouflage. Nobody would be looking for it. He'd signed a sheaf of papers that pledged his life should he reveal the clinic's existence. Even so, he was asked to ride with Tess in the windowless back of the ambulance until the last ten minutes, when he'd been invited up front. He still hadn't been told the exact location.

In the eight days since the accident, Tess had shown no signs of awareness or improvement, but also no clear signs that her condition was deteriorating, which gave Roger hope in his darker moments. Her EEG remained normal, and Roger was eager to tap into the deeper electrical waves his instruments could reach. He wanted to find some wave pattern he could use to access Tess's thoughts—something simple at first, but enough to prove to the world that she was conscious inside her passive shell.

First, though, he needed to crack her encryption so he could use his system, and so far the government's experts were baffled. He was proud of Tess's ability to design the security system, but angry with himself because he could not crack her password and discover exactly what had happened. He didn't want to start up the system again until he learned for sure how it had failed.

He had bargained for sole use of the old magnet for this purpose, along with funds and time to put it in the condition it should have been in when they bought it. Without his work, it would be a piece of junk, and, besides, there was a chance that his work with Tess might provide a useful stopgap measure for whatever spy work the team seemed to have in mind for his invention. Not that he cared. It was just a way to keep them supporting Tess's recovery.

He told them he was sure Tess would be a huge help in accelerating the main project, once she could communicate. He could tell they didn't really believe it. They were humoring him. Still, he didn't dislike Don, the FBI agent in charge, but he had to be cautious. Maybe they were playing good-cop/bad-cop with him. Don's sidekick, Lucinda, was certainly the bad cop. As much as Roger enjoyed seeing her handle Wyatt, it gave him chills, but so far, she had largely avoided him. Don told him Lucinda had ample reason to hate Arabs, but didn't elaborate.

The ambulance pulled up in front of one of the two, long five-story buildings facing each other across a trellised rose garden, connected at the far end by a two-story enclosed corridor. Two attendants in green scrubs were waiting on the sidewalk to transport Tess inside. They seemed to know what they were doing, but Roger hovered over them anyway. He and Don stayed close to Tess's gurney as she was wheeled up the ramp, inside the electric doors, and down the long hall to the laboratory suite that would double as the couple's apartment.

A medical team was waiting in the bedroom to transfer Tess to her hospital bed. While they hooked up Tess's IV and instruments, Don explained to Roger that he would have preferred to put them on the top floor, with a view of the lake, but the weight of the magnets made that impossible. The upper floors simply wouldn't support them safely. Besides, he explained, the animals would be easier to care for on the ground floor, and it would save time to have everything in one place. "Time," he said, "is our scarcest commodity."

Once Roger was sure that Tess was as comfortable as circumstances permitted, he toured the laboratory rooms with Don, pointing out some immediate changes that he would like to make. Don watched him with a knowing eye. "You enjoy being in charge, don't you. I gather you weren't too happy working under the professor's thumb."

Roger thought that Don might be trying to flatter him because he thought Roger was the total brains behind this technology. *If so, Roger thought, he won't be so motivated to cure Tess.* Determined to set the record straight, Roger quickly responded, "Tess is the one who likes to be in charge, but I'll take over until she's back on her feet. I'll try to think the way she would—like, I know she'd be happier if we had an adequate staff. We're expected to keep the same schedules, with half the lab staff and with time lost because of the move."

"Wait until you meet our staff here. I'm told they're the best, and you'll have your pick."

Roger liked the way Don endorsed the staff, a sharp contrast to Wyatt's attitude. "I appreciate that, but what I need most is from Tess."

"The encryption key?" Don made a key-turning motion with his hand.

"That, too, but most of the critical ideas are hers."

"You're too modest."

"No, she always pushes the credit onto me. I'm just a plodder."

"Then let's get her back. We both want that. My reasons are national security, but I'll tell you, one human being to another, your reasons are better. With this assignment, I don't see my wife as much as I'd like, but I don't think I could work at all without her—and my kids—backing me up."

Roger smiled at this slight crack in Don's agency armor. "Does Lucinda have a family, too?" He found that hard to imagine.

"No, she lost her fiancé in a car bomb attack when they served in Military Intelligence, in the Middle East. I don't think she's ever gotten over that. She was injured, captured, and tortured before our guys rescued her." Don touched his fingers to his lips, as if hesitating to tell more. "Her fiancé was wounded, too, and captured. But he died during torture. I think she watched him die, but she never talks about it."

That explains a lot, Roger thought. "That's too bad."

"Don't tell her I told you. She left the military because the memories were too harsh. And she likes to keep her private life private, but I thought you might work with her better if you knew."

"Fair enough. Teamwork is going to be critical. So how good is the team here, really?"

"Most of the patients here are agents wounded in the line of duty. So, we've got the best doctors, terrific nurses, physical and occupational therapists, speech therapists, psychologists, and social workers. And they seem to really work as a team. None of that doctor arrogance you see in many hospitals."

In the bedroom of the couple's suite, Roger and Don studied the medical team fussing over Tess's tubes and wires. "I'm worried that they're not keeping her on an IV all the time."

"That's because they know how to feed her liquids orally without her gagging. They thought she'd like that, and it would be one more relatively normal thing. Might help her recovery."

"I hope she can taste them. What about the other tubes? You know . . ."

"They have to stay, for now. The doctors told me they might use a diaper later."

Roger tried to picture Tess in diapers. He knew she wouldn't like that, but maybe it was preferable to tubes. "How are they on prenatal care?"

Don frowned slightly. "Did that come as a surprise, finding out from the doctors?"

Roger knew it had, but he wanted Don to think he was cool. "It was logical. I imagine she didn't want to tell me until the baby was further along—"

Now Don was smiling. "You're going to discover that not much about pregnancy is logical. My wife was like that with both of ours. But I think that under the circumstances, the doctors were right to tell you."

"They said she should be able to carry the baby to term, even the way she is now, but that's hard to believe." A nurse rolled Tess onto her side and smoothed the sheet with her free hand. "She's in enough trouble without the extra strain."

"We're bringing in an OB-GYN just for Tess. We've never had a pregnant patient here before. At least not one who was pregnant in the line of duty." Don buttoned his jacket and gestured toward the medical technicians as they put away their instruments. "They seem to be finished. If that's all, I'll leave you and your wife alone. Just don't be afraid to complain if everything isn't right. We need you working at your best."

Roger pulled off his own jacket and hung it on the back of the door. "Then I'd better get to work. Have my nanowires arrived?" He had no illusions about how long they would take care of Tess if he didn't produce something they wanted. He had to be careful. This high-security situation disturbed him, but in spite of himself, he was glad Don was there.

30

Using the nanowires and a slimmed down, rebuilt version of the old superconducting magnet, within three days of solid, sleepless work, Roger had Tess's light-mesh skullcap ready for a trial. When Don remarked that it looked like a snood his Italian grandmother had crocheted, Roger laughed. "Maybe that's because I crocheted this one. More or less."

Don took it in both hands, feeling the weave between his fingers. "You made it by hand? It's so much finer than Nonna's."

"It's made of nanowires."

"I thought nanowires would be thinner than these threads."

"Oh, those are actually bundles of nanowires. Thousands in a bundle. Otherwise, they'd be impossible to work with."

Don handed the snood back gingerly, as if it were much more fragile than he'd thought. "Nonna's was black. This one looks like a rainbow."

"The wires are color-coded, otherwise I couldn't keep track of which wire picks up which signals."

"It looks harmless enough. Do you need volunteers to test it?"

"No, not yet. Are you volunteering?"

Don raised his eyebrows at the thought. "I guess I should, as the real sponsor of this project. I'll think about it, but I have to admit it scares me somewhere down deep. But you've already tested it on the lab animals, haven't you?"

Roger looked at Tess, deep sadness in his eyes. "There's no way I'd allow anybody but me serve as a guinea pig."

"I'm not happy with the idea of risking my resident genius, but I understand. And I admire you for it." He clapped Roger on the shoulder. "I could supply you with volunteers—real volunteers, and not cowards like me—but I can see that if you don't do it first, nobody will."

When the snood was in place on Roger's head, the first trial began. As soon as the magnetic field clicked on, Roger bit down on his lower lip. He couldn't get Tess's accident out of his mind. At first he felt nothing. By controlling his breathing in a way Tess had taught him, he began to relax. Step by step, the field increased around his head. When it reached 9.5 teslas, his vision began to waver.

He could barely read the instrument panel. All the straight lines were curved. All the colors blurred into rainbows.

Then he couldn't read it at all.

He became so disoriented, he didn't know if he could coordinate his right hand on the magnet's emergency switch.

He held his breath, not knowing if he should stop the experiment before there was no turning back, but he kept ramping up the magnet. When the field passed 10.2 teslas, the disorientation vanished. It seemed to have been some sort of threshold—like crossing the sound barrier. He remained at 10.2 for a few minutes, running through mental exercises to generate data for calibrating the machine. Then he terminated the first experiment.

With human data in hand, Roger scheduled the next few days for thinking and analysis, but he felt disoriented—not by the magnet, but by the pulls and emotions of the world around him. A few months ago, the concept of the project had been simple enough, all worked out in his head. Now that the machine was built, dozens of little glitches were beginning to get on his nerves, delaying every little task. Delaying the moment when he could really communicate again with Tess. Delaying her cure. Or worse. The doctors told him that the longer she remained in a vegetative state, the worse her chances of a complete recovery. Or of a recovery at all.

Today's glitch, as it turned out, was that all the data from his first experiment were useless. At the magnet's maximum, if he moved his head even the tiniest bit, he could actually feel eddy currents in his brain. These currents fouled the measurements. Another delay.

He saved the data anyway and made an appointment for a consultation with the clinic's neurosurgeons. Encouraged by Don, they provided the components of a surgical theater from which Roger could create a jig to hold his head within the magnet's aperture in a precise alignment. But because the magnet would have seized metal components in its gap, he couldn't use the jig. Instead, he had to fabricate his own plastic components to replace the jig's metal ones.

Then he learned he couldn't get useful measurements because he couldn't align the snood precisely from one experiment to the next. The surgeons showed him how to place small markers— fiducials—on his head to provide calibration points for precise, repeatable alignment of the snood. Another delay.

The fiducials improved the situation, but still left minuscule movements that complicated the signal processing. He believed he could control them with a computer feedback system, but that would be another delay. For now, he found a workaround. As long as he shaved his head just before each experiment—the alignment was sufficiently precise for matching the gross patterns of his brain activity. A more precise solution would have to wait until he'd reached Tess.

Once he was finally positioned properly in the jig with the magnet operating above twelve teslas, he was able to capture a consistent pattern every time he thought of a letter. It still took him two days to faithfully produce an A. Then another day to produce a B. At that rate, the entire alphabet might take a month. Roger thought *he* was frustrated until he saw Don's reaction to that schedule. Stopping short of a full-blown seizure, Don calmed himself and led Roger to one of the clinic's small outbuildings, well across the lawn from Roger's lab. There, he introduced Roger to a group of hotshot programmers, warning him not to inquire about their regular assignments.

Roger assigned the team the task of writing software to recognize the patterns and convert them to letters on a monitor—a task that under happier circumstances he would trust only to Tess. But one of the geeks—a very tall, skinny, bearded fellow with thick glasses—surprised him by returning a flawless program before the day was over. His teammates called him "SOS," for Stephen Orem

Spencer, and he wouldn't respond to any other name. He also seemed to speak fluent Klingon, which immediately won Roger's affection. SOS was four years older than Roger, but he seemed like a kid. Roger thought, *I think I'm growing old too fast.*

SOS was not only taller than Roger, he seemed even more of a perfectionist. He insisted that he personally watch the entire system at work until he was sure it was bug-free. Don gave the okay, and within the hour, Roger had put on the snood—the name had stuck—and strapped himself into the machine. He concentrated on A, and instantly a capital A appeared on the screen. Rather than declare the experiment a success, SOS offered a short lecture on the importance of testing. It appeared to Roger that SOS thoroughly enjoyed lecturing Don on software topics. Don cringed as if he'd heard this lecture before, but Roger didn't mind. He was too pleased with the result, though he didn't feel like celebrating yet. There was still a long way to go.

With the program running well and in good hands, Roger was able to train the system to the entire alphabet and a few special characters before they quit at two in the morning. Don had stayed to watch the entire process, enduring a few more of SOS's lectures—and even fetching caffeine drinks and sugary snacks whenever Roger or SOS started to bog down.

Roger demonstrated the finished product by spelling out, mentally, "WHAT HATH GOD WROUGHT?" Although SOS didn't recognize the allusion to Morse's first telegraph, Don did, and Roger's estimation of the FBI agent rose several notches. *I think I'm actually building a team. But we won't be complete until we have Tess.*

Roger wanted to try the device on Tess immediately, but her prior mental profiles were locked under the unbreakable cryptographic key. After some effort, Don persuaded Roger to get some real food in the clinic's all-night cafeteria. Although Roger would have gladly skipped dinner to hurry the project, reason prevailed, and he agreed with Don that it was more logical to get some rest and try again in the morning.

Logic, however, didn't calm his excitement once he'd gone to bed. For two hours, he wrestled with his pillow; then he muttered that logic was useless. He got out of bed, put on a hospital robe, and sat next to Tess's bed. She lay there as always, like an exquisite marble statue. No expression on her face. No eye movement. No wink. Not even a twitch. Only the same irregular blinking she had shown from the first.

Roger was exhausted and emotionally devastated. He spoke to her, feeling that this might be the last time ever. "I'm so sorry. I was such a fool. What did I expect? I was blinded by my hopes. How am I going to live without you?"

He sat for a long time, staring at her lovely face, trying to memorize each and every freckle, stroking her apricot hair. He hardly moved until he became aware that the room was growing lighter. Morning already. All his hopes were exhausted. A beam of sunlight broke through the window, illuminating a tear forming in Tess's eye. But Roger did not see it. He'd already broken down and started to sob.

31

Speaking mostly to Zay, but casting Qaaf and, to a lesser extent, Alif an occasional glance, Jiim reported details of the success of his latest mission. His satchel bombs had leveled both the old Water Tower and the Chicago Avenue Pumping Station—the only public buildings that had survived the Great Chicago Fire of 1871. Qaaf thought it was an excellent choice. No people had occupied the buildings at night, so there was no danger of death, but the two buildings had symbolized Chicago's fierce drive to survive. They hadn't survived Jiim's bombs, and the symbolism had not been lost on the newspapers. *The Tribune* had a front-page editorial suggesting that the mayor resign. Of course, he belonged to the paper's least-favored political party, but even his supporters were beginning to suggest he needed to do something soon.

Jiim filled them in on more than they could read in the papers, and Zay greeted the news by complimenting Jiim and suggesting he was an example for the others to follow.

Alif scowled when Qaaf sounded impatient with Zay's compliment, but Qaaf ignored his stare. "Zay, the bombing was fine—an excellent job—but the news is not so good from the clinic where they hold Dhal."

"He has talked?" Zay asked.

"No, he's still holding out. But they've had some success with their interrogation machine." Qaaf waited for a reaction.

"I thought you said that one of their key researchers had been disabled," Alif snapped. "Was that your doing?"

"You don't need to know the details." It wouldn't hurt Qaaf if Alif thought she'd done the deed. "But, yes, a key person was injured."

"Then why is that bad news?" Alif asked her.

"Because it's given the Agency an excuse to bring the damned machine to Dhal's hospital. To use on him. To get inside his mind, whether he will allow it or not."

"Will it work?" Alif's voice was challenging, with a subtle tinge of fear.

"Not if I can help it."

"And if you can't?" Everyone could hear the doubt in Alif's voice.

"Then I'll see that it has nobody to work upon."

Alif stood as if ready to fight. "Perhaps we should storm the hospital. Kill everyone involved. We can muster all our people. That should be sufficient."

"I admire your audacity, Alif, your courage, but storming the hospital would be stupid and futile. We could not get within a mile of it before setting off alarms. Don't worry. I'll take care of Dhal."

Alif wasn't willing to let the subject drop. "You could disable the alarms."

"Maybe I should disable your mouth. Let me do my job."

They continued to argue childishly for ten minutes, then Zay raised his hand and inclined his head. "Enough. I need quiet to think this through."

After that, they all waited silently until Zay lifted his eyes and nodded toward Qaaf. Dhal's fate had been decided.

32

No part of her condition was more frustrating for Tess than her inability to exercise even the simplest control over her husband, who no longer seemed the genius she had always believed. All she wanted from him now was to interpret one wet tear rolling down the side of her face, but he wasn't getting it.

He sees it. How boring, you big beautiful dolt. Use your brain. Come on! If I can cry, it means I'm . . .

"You've got something in your eye." Something shadowed her eye, but she felt nothing. *Maybe he wiped away the tear.*

No, dummy. Nothing in my eye. But wiping is good. Clears my face for the next question. Watch carefully while I think of something happy. Playing with the puppies.

"I must have gotten it. Did it hurt?"

Not hurt. Think again. Watch.

"They're tearing again. Did I miss it? I wish you could tell me, so I could get it out for you."

You didn't miss it. I am telling you. There's nothing in my eye.

"Maybe it's just natural wetness. I'd better not wipe it away."

No, keep wiping. But watch me after they dry. Damn. Don't leave. Stay here and think.

He turned and started for the door.

Damn. How long does it take for tears to evaporate? One. Two. Three . . .

He had an idea and turned back. "Maybe you're sad, too. Are you?"

Okay, girl. Remember how you felt when the puppy died. That should do it.

"You're crying again. What's going—"

You've got it. Now think!

"—you *are* feeling sad. And it's making you cry. Can you control it?"

Remember how you tried to save the poor little tyke.

"Is that a yes? Or just a coincidence?"

It's not a coincidence, dummy. And please ask just one question at a time while I think of something happy to stop the tears.

"If you *can* control it, I can test it. Okay. Try this. Your mother's name is Rumplestiltskin, right? Cry for yes."

I feel like laughing, but don't make me laugh so hard I cry.

"Okay, no crying. Let me try another. Your father is ten feet tall. Right?"

I used to think he was, and that's sad. But not enough to make me cry.

"Still dry. Okay, let's try a yes. One plus one is two, right?"

Two dying puppies, yes. Forgive me for the thought. God, that's terrible.

Roger jumped up and spun in a circle. "That's it. Tess! You are in there. I knew it. I absolutely knew it." She could see from the shadows that he'd stopped spinning. "Are you okay? Are you . . . no, I'd better keep it simple. Just one question. Are you okay?"

Yes. And I'm sad, sad, sad that you didn't know. Now settle down and ask the key question. Or don't ask anything, just watch.

"Okay, I think it's a yes. So you're okay. Let's play twenty questions. Is there anything you need?"

Yes.

He wiped away the tear. "That's a yes. Animal?"

No.

"Vegetable?"

No.

"Then it must be mineral."

No.

"Oh, I should have asked. Is it mineral?"

No. How can you be so boring? Get creative.

"If it's not animal, vegetable, or mineral, how could that be?"

Don't ask questions. Think.

"Is it something abstract?"

Yes. Yes. Yes. How many virtual puppies will I have to murder?

Her vision shadowed while he wiped away the tears. "I got it. Now, what's abstract. Is it a number?"

Yes.

Wipe. "A number. Of course. The code. I mean, is it the password?"

Yes.

Another wipe. "But I don't have the—oh, you want to give me the password?"

Finally! Yes!

He wiped so vigorously that Tess's field of vision wobbled. "I understand. Okay, let me get some paper—and some dry tissues—then I'll sit here and you give it to me in binary."

She waited for him to return, trying to put her mind in order so she could give him the code. *What's taking you so long? Okay, there's your beautiful face.*

"I'm back. I know it's got to be at least twenty-four decimal digits, right?"

Yes.

Another wipe. "Can you translate it into binary in your head? I mean, I could do it, but can you?"

Yes, idiot. Though I won't do it the same way as you, you stupid genius. Now stop and pay attention. And be patient. Be sure to dry between the digits. First, here comes my high-school locker combination. First number is 23. One, zero, one, one, one—in binary. Tediously, she spelled it out for him in tears.

"I think I got that. Was it twenty-three? Or were there zeros at the end? Forty-six? Ninety-two? How am I going to know?"

One question at a time. Please, before I die of frustration. This is slow enough as it is.

"Okay, here's an idea. How about we use a fixed number of binary digits, and do one decimal digit at a time? Four bits, to make one decimal digit. Okay?"

Yes. Anything to get this done.

"All right. I think I have twenty-three, but let me check with the new system. Is it twenty-three?"

Yes. Thank God I don't have to repeat that. Only twenty-two more digits to go.

33

By the time the sun was fully over the horizon, brightening the wall opposite the window, Roger was exhausted but confident he had figured out the process. All of a sudden, weariness and depression overtook him. He couldn't understand why, partly because he'd never really been depressed in his life, and partly because it wasn't logical. Just when he could see an end in sight, he should have been overjoyed—and he was, but depressed at the same time.

Maybe it was accumulated fatigue. All he wanted to do was put his head under the covers, curl up, and sleep. Or maybe it was that for the first time he allowed himself to glimpse the long road ahead. Whatever it was, he forced himself to keep going. He leaned close to Tess's ear, though apparently she could hear perfectly well. "Wait a minute while I get something better to write on. I don't want to make any more mistakes." He kissed her on the forehead, then disappeared from her limited cone of view.

When Roger returned and began the tedious communication process again, Tess seemed to be crying all the time. It took Roger a few minutes to realize she was "saying" yes to everything. Just about that time, she stopped crying, and he was able to get a few more digits.

He estimated the time remaining, but then she began crying yes to everything again. Roger couldn't figure out what was happening. His focus was so strong that their futile attempts to communicate might have continued for hours but for a nurse's interruption. "Hi, Tess. It's time for our lunch."

"Come back in half an hour," said Roger. "We're doing something important."

The nurse seemed to be speaking to the blanket she was tucking in. "Now, Dr. Fixman, what could be more important than your wife's lunch? She's got to keep up her strength."

"She can wait. We need to do this."

The nurse began to fluff Tess's pillow. "Why, what have you been doing? The poor thing is crying."

"Yes. And that's why you have to go away and come back later."

"But her broth is warm now, and she needs her . . . look how pale she is."

Roger took this as meaningless nurse banter until he actually looked at Tess's face. Her skin color almost matched the pillowcase. "Is she all right?"

"No, actually." She took a quick pulse and her bland tone turned to alarm. "She shouldn't be that pale." She grabbed her pager and punched a few buttons, then shoved Roger out of the way so she could pull back the covers and examine Tess's abdomen. "I know she's pregnant, but she wasn't this far along, was she?"

"I don't know what you mean."

"Her belly. It looks swollen to me." She was feeling around Tess's navel when the obstetrician arrived. She immediately took over the task, a worried look on her face.

As a crowd of medical staff members joined the examination, Roger felt himself pushed helplessly aside. "Is it the baby?" he asked. When they ignored him, he raised his voice. "Can someone tell me what's going on?"

The obstetrician stepped away from the pack. Immediately, the vacant space was filled by other medical people whom Roger had never seen before. "I don't think it's the baby," she explained. "We're going to take her to Radiology and have a look."

Roger trailed the parade, studying Tess's face as she was wheeled into the other wing of the building. Other than her pale skin, he saw no sign of distress or pain. He wanted to stay with her, but he had to stand outside while she was X-rayed. He was, however, allowed to hold her hand while a technician scanned her belly with an ultrasound wand.

After the ultrasound, the doctors played and replayed the recording, then huddled over the developed X-rays, with much shaking of heads and quiet arguing. Sometime during the huddle, Don appeared in the room and began asking questions. "We're not sure," said the male doctor who seemed to have taken charge. "We're going to do a CAT scan. It appears to be some sort of intestinal blockage. I understand she's been immobile for quite some time."

It took Roger a long moment to realize it was a question, to him, followed by a barrage of questions about painkillers, diet, bowel movements, and whether her history contained such diseases as diabetes, scleroderma, amyloidosis, dermatomyositis, muscular dystrophy, and myxedema. As far as Roger knew, Tess had never even mentioned being sick before he knew her.

He watched in a daze while the CAT scan took place behind a thick glass window. The doctors huddled again over the screen, then broke the huddle like a football team that had just decided on the winning play. "It seems she has formed an intussusception," their quarterback told Roger.

"I don't know the term."

"Not surprising. It's extremely rare, especially in adults. One part of her intestine has folded into itself, like a telescope." He illustrated with cupped hands. "Nothing can pass through."

"How serious is it?"

"If she could express her pain, you'd see how serious it was. The nurse said she was crying, so she probably feels it."

Roger wanted to kick himself in the head for not realizing what the continuous crying signified. "Can't you fix it?"

"Sometimes an enema will help, but not here. It's been blocked too long. And too high up. She had no way to communicate, or you would have heard about this much earlier. We're not even sure if she feels anything."

"I think she does feel something. She was crying."

"Then why didn't you report it earlier? It's been going on too long, and now infection is a big risk. We're going to have to operate immediately."

As Roger tried desperately to take it all in, he chewed nervously on his thumb. When he noticed what his thumb was doing, he pulled it out of his mouth, and wiped it on the back of his shirt. "Can't you just treat it with antibiotics?"

"We could if infection was the only risk, but the section of intestine that's folded may not be getting blood. It could tear, and stool could leak into the abdominal cavity. We don't want that to happen."

Roger swallowed hard, thinking none of this would have happened if he'd been paying closer attention to Tess. If he'd never let her become immobilized in the first place. The doctor, seeing his distress, clasped his shoulder in a fatherly way. "But don't worry, though. We use the latest robotic endoscopic equipment, so the procedure is considered minor surgery."

Roger wasn't reassured. He was discovering something about himself. When it came to Tess's welfare, his limitless faith in technology seemed to have limits. "What does that mean, 'minor surgery'?"

One of the doctors laughed. "Any surgery that's done to someone else."

Roger didn't think that was funny at all.

34

For Tess, the surgery seemed minor as promised—quick, painless, and completely successful at relieving the intussusception—though Roger suffered through every moment in the waiting room, unable to even read. As the attendants wheeled her into the recovery room, the surgeon pronounced the malady unlikely to recur as long as the staff adopted a daily routine of exercising Tess's inert body. Roger immediately decided he would take over that task himself, then sat down to keep an eye on Tess in recovery.

For their unborn, unnamed child, however, the surgery proved anything but minor. While she was still in the recovery room, Tess started hemorrhaging. Two minutes after Roger sounded the alarm, Tess was wheeled back into surgery. Twenty minutes later, she lost her baby girl.

When she was finally released from recovery and back in her room, the doctors reassured Roger that Tess would be able to have other children—if her neurological problems were solved. Roger refused to accept the "if." Taking advantage of the clinic's library, he poured himself into studying everything in their stacks concerning the human nervous system, more determined than ever to establish communication and bring Tess back to the world of the living.

Roger felt trapped. The books gave him many ideas, but he couldn't help Tess until he could apply them. But he couldn't apply anything until he could find out more about what had caused Tess's condition. And he couldn't learn that until she was well enough to restart their stressful process of communicating. He agonized through three days of Tess's enforced rest before the doctors accepted his explanation and permitted him to restart their tear-driven communication process. It was just as well. With her crying all the time about having lost the baby, the process would not have worked.

On the fourth day, the doctors, urged by Don, gave the go-ahead. By sheer force of will, Roger put aside all his morbid thoughts about Tess's prognosis and worked through the twenty-two remaining digits of the security code, one at a time, battling boredom and distracting thoughts that might cause him to make a mistake. He checked and rechecked everything as they went along, but that added to the boredom.

Tess began again with her high-school locker combination—23-17-21. Communicating the six digits took more than two hours.

Next, she gave Roger her first telephone number, the number Mel made her memorize in case she got lost. Ten more digits. Two more hours. Sixteen done.

The nurses forced Roger to stop while Tess was fed and bathed and exercised. She resumed with Miss Pinchney's high school biology lab room number. Three more digits. Only half an hour, and only five more to go.

Finally, after the better part of an hour, Roger finished capturing the zip code of Animal Rescue in California, where Tess had often mailed donations. That made twenty-four, but Roger wasn't confident. He knew the computer would allow him only three tries to log onto the system. If he made the slightest mistake, the computer would lock up for twenty-four hours before he could try again. To make sure, he read the entire twenty-four digits back to Tess to check one more time, even though he feared he would drive her insane with boredom. Then he logged in with the code. The computer responded:

WELCOME TO B-WAVE ANALYZER, V5.01.01

Roger stared at the screen for a dozen eye blinks until he realized he had finally reached Tess's operating system. Struggling to control his urge to go too fast, he stood up, walked to the sink, and washed his hands. Then, deliberately, he wheeled Tess's bed into the magnet room. While he fitted the snood to Tess's cranium, he carefully explained every detail, including Don's reaction when he walked in and found Roger lovingly shaving her head.

He felt he had to apologize to Tess for shaving her head. "I know you can hear me. Soon, I'll be able to hear you, too."

He didn't dare try the magnet at high power, fearing to injure her further. In his heart of hearts he hoped that the low magnetic field might actually produce a change for the better, but nothing in his library work had given him any logical reason to hope. Only a large jolt of magnetism had any chance of doing any good, and there was no way he was going to risk that. If he could just hear what she was thinking, he would be satisfied—for today.

He decided to shortcut the process by using data in their files from earlier, low-power experiments they had done in Ann Arbor. There, Tess had been able to spell out, one letter at a time, whole words and sentences. He knew her brain patterns might no longer be exactly the same as they were before her accident, but he was hoping, he told her, "that the old data will be approximately correct. If that's true, it should cut down the training time from weeks to days, maybe much less."

Though she already knew all this—she had designed the software herself—he patiently explained to her motionless body how the software was to be trained for any slight adaptations. He turned her head gently to the side and adjusted the monitor's goose neck so the screen was eighteen inches away, directly in front of her face. He switched on the magnet, watching her for any sign of distress as he gradually raised the power to the effective operating range. When the gauge passed the first threshold, he studied her face, then allowed himself a small breath. Then he raised the power to a full five teslas and stepped to the other side of the table to watch the screen.

Nothing happened.

The screen was blank. Not a flicker.

His shoulders slumped as he walked to the window, trying to think of what he might have overlooked. *Maybe it's not a bug. Maybe it's just too hard. Or maybe she's not all in there at all.*

The sunny day had turned gloomy, and now tiny wet drops were dotting the window. *But she can remember twenty-four digits. And encode them in binary. Has she become an idiot savant?*

He shook off that idea as unacceptable. *I must have screwed up somewhere, but where? Well, we'll just have to start over from step one. Maybe my blood sugar is low. Maybe hers is. I'd better get a nurse.*

The rain was coming down hard now, drumming on the building as the wind blew it off the lake. The drops on the window had become runnels, or maybe the water was in his own eyes. *I won't even be able to take her into the rose garden.* Before fetching the nurse, he walked back to the table to look into her eyes and apologize for his failure. All his failures. "I know you can't feel anything, but you look uncomfortable with your head turned like that. I'll just turn your—"

He moved around the bed to straighten her head and shoulders, but from that position, he could suddenly see the monitor from her dead-on angle. The screen showed a simple message:

"ROGER, COME HERE. I NEED YOU."

35

Even in the new FBI building, Don was having trouble finding space for all the new agents assigned since the Water Tower bombing. Bringing more agents in wasn't going to help much, but throwing more bodies at a problem was the standard Washington approach. It might even hurt the investigation. It was certainly taking more of his time away from the case itself, and few of the new agents knew enough about the Chicago area to be of much help. But he had to at least create the appearance of keeping them busy, which kept him busy thinking of new assignments, no matter how farfetched.

The largest assembly room was almost inadequate to hold the task force now under his command—he had to wait while the last few arrivals found seats in the amphitheater. There might still be a few more, but he impatiently signaled Lucinda to begin her slide show summarizing all the leads so far, mostly dead ends.

The first slide showed a brown suitcase handle with black scorch marks. "Three of these were found in the Wrigley wreckage. This one was in the best condition, and we traced it to a generic brand sold in Wal-Mart, Sears, and several smaller outlets. Some of you will be assigned to check for multiple sales in the past three months—further back if that yields nothing. These people are professionals, and it's doubtful they bought all three in one store, so we've assigned a computer team to cross-correlate sales. Probably cash, though, so it may not be much help."

The screen flashed some shreds of what appeared to be black plastic. "These are from the Water Tower site. Lab analysis suggests they took the place of the suitcases on this job. They're probably from Hefty Lawn and Garbage Bags, of which millions are sold each month, so it's a long shot. But we'll look for multiple sales, possibly correlated with the suitcases."

Scattered groans were heard from the audience. "I know," Lucinda apologized, "but that's why you're here, to check out everything. Everything." The slide changed—stacks of brown, white, and red-white-and-blue envelopes in all shapes and sizes. More groans.

"Evidently some of you recognize what these are. We've had over thirty-five thousand letters since the bombings began. More coming in every day. Naturally, most of them are from cranks turning in their neighbors, but we're going to check them all out. Pardon me. I mean, *you're* going to check them all out."

More groans, mixed with laughter. Lucinda raised her hand for silence. "The good news is that in checking out the first two thousand, we've turned up some actual criminals—though none involved with these bombings. So pay attention. It's not entirely a thankless task."

She turned to the screen, which changed to show what appeared to be a computer listing. "Now we turn to a truly thankless task—the phone calls. There are three times as many calls as letters, and I can't even promise some actual criminals. But we'll— *you'll*—check them all out, individually and with computer cluster analysis."

The screen went blank. "That's basically all the positive leads. As you all know by now, the biggest inferential lead comes from the extortion notes, which only serve to demonstrate that we're dealing with professionals who know police procedures." The auditorium lights gradually brightened, and Lucinda stepped to the front of the stage. "Any questions? Or suggestions?"

"What about the captive?" a voice rose above the clatter of other voices.

"I heard that one, but from now on, please raise your hand, and wait to be recognized. Let me put off the captive for the end, when Agent-in-Charge Capitol will bring you up to date."

She then handled a barrage of other questions, mostly about the explosives (stolen and untraceable), the profiling of the terrorists (nothing useful), and the choice of targets. "Obviously, they've been chosen for symbolic significance, to gain maximum attention, but so far they seem to have avoided situations where people could be killed. That, of course, could change at any time, though we believe that *they* believe they have a better chance of getting their money if nobody's been killed."

A woman in the left front row raised her hand and asked, "Do they? Have a better chance, I mean."

"As you know, that's not up to us. In fact, we're spending more money trying to find the terrorists than they've asked for, but naturally that's not the logic that will decide the question."

"How much are we spending to defend these symbolic targets?"

Lucinda laughed. "You must not be from Cook County. Do you know how many landmarks we have here—just counting identified ones?"

The woman shook her head. Agents were not encouraged to guess about facts. "No idea."

"Over seventy thousand. Does that answer your question?" The woman sat down. Lucinda invited Don to the stage and handed him her laser pen. The auditorium lights dimmed. Don had decided to save the most important lead for the last, to end the presentation on the most optimistic note. His first slide was a photo of the suburban bombing. His laser beam highlighted the driveway. "We found the victim here, though he was removed to the hospital before we could obtain photos."

His next slide was of the victim in his hospital room. "As you can see, he's burned over most of his body, including his fingerprints. We didn't know if he was a victim or one of the terrorists, though we had several clues to suggest he might be the latter. You can find those clues in your file folder. Since nobody came forward to claim him, we weren't able to obtain an identification until his prints grew back enough for us to try IAFIS. But as soon as we did, the system spit out a three-nines identification. One chance in a thousand it was wrong, but it checked out in Cleveland."

A man's head filled the screen—full face and profile—obviously a mug shot, and with obvious Middle Eastern features. "Meet Hamal bin Masruk bin Salman. Born and raised in Syria, in the States on a student visa for Case Western, picked up three months ago in Cleveland on suspicion. He lived in the same dormitory as another suspect, who had shared an apartment with the brother-in-law of one of the 9/11 bombers. Released after being held for ten days. Disappeared a week later and not seen until he showed up on the driveway here."

A hand shot up in the third row, though the agent remained seated. "What has he told you?"

"Nothing yet. He's either unable or unwilling to speak. We believe unwilling, but we will soon be trying a new method of approaching that problem."

"What's that?" the hand continued.

"Sorry, no need to know." Don ignored several other hands. "Let me tell you first what we're doing besides that. The Cleveland branch has rounded up all his known associates, and our friends overseas are trying to check out his family—some in Syria and some in Lebanon. Given the difficulties there, we don't expect much from them. But most of all, I received a call just an hour ago that makes me believe we're finally going to succeed in interrogating him. I hope to have more for you at next week's summary."

36

"ROGER, COME HERE. I NEED YOU."

As he stared at the message, Roger at first wondered whether SOS had played a geek trick on him. *Tess could not possibly have sent me this message,* he thought, as she lay motionless on the table. *It has to be a spoof.*

Then he thought about how SOS brought fresh wildflowers to Tess's room every morning and realized his lanky friend would never play such a cruel trick.

I was so excited, I forgot about the time lag Tess had needed to practice, to train the adaptive software, Roger realized. Vowing not to allow himself to lose his logic to excitement again, Roger spent the next two hours catching up with Tess on so many important matters. Tess spelled out, one letter at a time, that she was feeling no pain, no discomfort at all. She conveyed her grief at the loss of their baby, but she was optimistic they would be able to have another. Many others.

Then, hungry for control after her long starvation, she insisted that she be the one to ask the questions. When she started with, "WHERE ARE WE?" he started to pour out everything that had happened, but she stopped him and explained that she had over-heard the conversations that had taken place in her presence. She knew what had happened to her and she understood that nobody knew if and when she would recover. What she wanted now was information to fill significant holes in her knowledge.

It was slow going, and long before Roger had completely caught Tess up, Don popped into the room to remind Roger he was to meet him for supper. "Shouldn't we wait for Lucinda?" Roger asked.

"WHO IS LUCINDA?" appeared on Tess's screen.

"She's Don's sidekick," Roger explained.

"Don't let her hear you calling her that," Don said.

"Don't worry. I wouldn't want to cross her."

"I DO NOT KNOW HER."

"That's because she never comes into your room," Don said.

"WHY NOT?"

"She's a control freak, and seeing you strapped to the table gives her the creeps."

"I GIVE MYSELF THE CREEPS."

Roger swallowed hard and moved his face out of Tess's line of vision. He was working hard to keep the tears out of his voice each time he spoke.

Don said, "Anyway, you can forget about Lucinda. I just returned by helicopter from Chicago but she's still there and not joining us for supper."

"We've got so much to do," Roger said. "I'd better skip supper, too." Roger shifted position so Tess could again see his face. He invited Don to watch Tess's screen a little longer, to show him the full extent of their breakthrough. Don watched their demonstration with businesslike interest. "This looks like real progress. I'm really happy for you two. Tess, it's great to know you're really in there."

"THANKS."

"Do you have to concentrate to produce messages, or does it pick up letters you happen to be thinking about?"

"CONCENTRATE."

"The computer program filters out stray thoughts from other areas of her brain," Roger explained. "Concentration helps the computer when it's learning to sort out the patterns of a new person, but after a while, it should get easier."

"IT'S ALREADY GETTING EASIER."

Don turned away from the screen and addressed Roger. "Do you think this represents progress on the project, or is it just a sidetrack?"

"Tess wants to help me now. She says she's been saving up lots of ideas."

"I'm sure that will help. Can you speed this thing up?"

"We've both got ideas. Can I have more time with your software guys? Particularly SOS?"

"Well, they're not my guys. And certainly not SOS. He's the best by far—looks like a new-age freak, but he's the most sensible of the lot. But, yes, I think I can borrow him for you—as long as he stays interested. He's like a buffalo. I can get him to do anything I want him to do, as long as he wants to do it."

"I suspect he'll be more than interested in being able to talk to Tess. He brings her flowers every day."

Don raised one eyebrow and looked at the screen. "Speaking of Tess, I think she's been trying to get our attention."

"Damn. I guess one of the things we need is sound output so she can signal us. That's probably the first thing, so she can initiate, rather than wait for us to look." He turned to the screen:

"NEED MIRRORS"

Both men adjusted their positions so they were leaning over into Tess's field of vision. "Sorry," said Don. "I forgot that you can't just turn your head and look at us. I'm sure Roger can rig up something."

"MY CONTROL"

"What does she mean?"

"She wants to be able to control the movement of the mirrors, or whatever we use. For now, it's the only way she can move."

"YES"

Roger noticed that she was already speeding communication by simplifying grammar and dropping punctuation. "If the doctors allow it, maybe we can get her some kind of powered wheelchair."

"WOULD BE A REAL REWARD"

"You deserve it. Both of you. But you didn't really answer my question about progress." He pointed to Tess's screen. "All this is voluntary. What about picking up thoughts that the subject isn't actively trying to reveal? Maybe even trying to conceal?"

"I'm not sure. I still think we have a better chance of that with visual processing."

"AGREE"

"Can you keep both projects going at the same time?"

"I . . . we . . . have nothing else to do."

Don missed the innuendo, but Tess didn't. As soon as Don left, she put another message on the monitor:

"YOU MISS ME? WANT TO MAKE LOVE?"

He bent over and kissed her, first on the lips, then on her neck. "You couldn't feel that, could you?"

"NO" The screen hesitated. "NOTHING"

"That's good."

"WHY GOOD?"

"Because your doctor wants to insert a Groshong catheter for feeding you. Sometimes they can be painful at first."

"WHAT'S A GROSHONG CATHETER?"

Roger held a diagram in front of her eyes, showing how the catheter entered the chest and tunneled under the skin into the superior vena cava. "He was hoping for a quick recovery of your nervous system, but now he thinks we'd better prepare for the long haul."

"IT'S UGLY. WHY WILL IT HELP?"

"Your swallow reflex is pretty good, but he's worried that you can't get all the nutrition you need that way. Or the medications. So you still need your IV, but pretty soon they're going to run out of places to stick you. So they put in this Groshong catheter more or less permanently, and they can use it all the time."

"SO HE'S LOSING HOPE"

That was Roger's fear, but he didn't want Tess to know. "Not losing hope. Just preparing . . . in case."

"DO YOU THINK IT'S BEST?"

"Under the circumstances, yes."

"OKAY. BUT IT'S UGLY. IT'S LIKE A THIRD BREAST."

"You'll still be beautiful."

"SO WILL YOU MAKE LOVE TO ME?"

Roger didn't understand. "What do you mean?"

"YOU KNOW. WHILE I LAY HERE?"

"No," he stammered, horrified. "Not if you can't feel anything. I couldn't. . . ."

"WILL YOU KISS ME ANYWAY? I LIKE IT."

"Sure, lots of kisses. But that's it."

"UNDERSTOOD.   WANT TO TRY ONE OF THOSE NURSES?"

"What?"

"FOR SEX. RELIEF."

"Tess! I would never . . ."

"BET YOU THOUGHT ABOUT IT"

"No. Never."

"WILL WHEN YOU GET HORNY ENOUGH"

Roger was about to speak when Tess resumed spelling out her message.

"GO AHEAD. I WON'T MIND."

"Well, *I* would. The only way those nurses are going to help my sex life is by getting you fixed."

"SWEET. BUT WE'LL SEE."

"There won't be anything to see. I can't imagine even looking at another woman that way."

"PUT A BAG OVER YOUR HEAD"

37

Inga didn't trust the security of cell phones used in public places, but her client assured her the new phone was securely encrypted using the latest technology—and technology was their business. Besides, this news was too good, too positive, to keep. If she delayed important news, she would lose her value—and the generous rewards that allowed her to dine in the style she adored—great food and lots of it.

"This is a real portion, not some nouvelle cuisine nonsense," she muttered to herself as she surveyed the two plates of appetizers she'd carted to a corner table in this vast, dark, anonymous restaurant. She'd already gulped down a dozen fried dumplings to take the edge off her appetite before she made the call. She sniffed the delicious aroma of the spring rolls as she dialed, almost hoping her client wouldn't answer. Maybe she could do a bit more gastronomic preparation before engaging in what might be a long conversation.

To her chagrin, the phone call was picked up after the second ring, but she managed to down two spring rolls while the mono-toned young woman at the other end was finding her boss. Inga already had the third spring roll in her fingers when she heard the familiar but anonymous voice on the other end. "Give me the bottom line. I'm in a meeting."

Inga was happy to oblige. "The woman has awakened." No need to give details. "They're contacting her by machine."

"Is this a machine we can use?"

"Perhaps. I'll deliver the details by the usual method."

"What else?"

"They're making progress toward the machine you really want."

"What about the professor? Is he still an impediment?"

"He's been marginalized, but I'll continue to keep an eye on him. He's unpredictable—or, rather, it's predictable that he'll try to grab some of the glory for himself."

"Don't let that happen. What else?"

"The rest is detail. You'll have it in a few days."

"Any new estimate on a workable machine?"

She licked some sauce off her fingers. "I'll work that up and put it with the rest of the material."

"Fine." He hung up, as usual, without goodbye or compliments on her work. Inga didn't mind. She was already deciding whether she would start the entrees with Kung Pao pork and beef with garlic sauce, or Sha Cha chicken and beef with black bean sauce. She thought the hot-and-sour soup smelled quite wonderful. She would try a bowl or two before she made up her mind about whether to try the pork or beef first.

38

Over the next week, Roger had no time to enjoy the soft lake breezes or the lovely weather at the beach, let alone think about having sex with nurses. He spent most of his time in the library, studying any new subject that might throw light on Tess's condition—and especially a possible cure. Every remaining hour, he spent with his wife, discussing his findings.

"By now," he told her on the third day, "I've searched all the literature for any cases similar to yours. All I could find about magnetism and brain function were numerous articles speculating about the effects of long-term, low-level magnetism on the nervous system."

"WHAT THEY SAY? COULD EXTRAPOLATE"

"Pretty much that small fields don't produce much in the way of effects. As far as the literature shows, nobody in the world has ever subjected their brain to anything near the eddy currents created by a ten- or fifteen-tesla spike. One ten-thousandth of that, maybe, in a few cases."

"EDDY CURRENTS?"

"Sorry. They're circulating currents induced in a conducting material by a varying magnetic field. Like in your head."

"NO CONDUCTOR IN MY HEAD"

"There is if the field is strong enough. Your brain is an electrical and chemical machine. Who knows what extra currents in there could have done."

"YOU"

"Me, what?"

"YOU WILL KNOW. SOON"

And, indeed, he did know more in two more days. Having exhausted the magnetic literature, he turned to the anatomy of brain function, a subject he already knew much more about. Several articles led him to the idea that some area of Tess's brain had been sent into a metastable state.

"METASTABLE?"

"That just means its stability is also stable. In the case of your brain, it's neurons firing other neurons in closed loops."

"LIKE SEIZURES?"

"A lot like that, only it may be just in a small region of the brain. Maybe more than one small region."

"SO WE COULD DO SURGERY. LIKE CUTTING CORPUS CALLOSUM. THAT STOPS SEIZURES"

Roger swallowed hard. "We could, if we knew where the regions were. Severing a few—or many—connections would break the loops. But it stops other things, too. That's why they don't do that surgery anymore."

"SO WE DON'T KNOW WHAT WOULD BE LEFT"

"No, there's no way to know. Not with the current state of brain science. It's more like phrenology."

"HEAD BUMPS. I KNOW. I DON'T WANT CUTTING"

"Good. I don't either. Maybe as a last resort. You can't stay like this forever or bad things will start to happen."

"I KNOW. BAD ALREADY. CAN'T FEEL ANYTHING. CAN'T MOVE ANYTHING. CAN'T TALK"

"Oh, you can talk. You're talking now. It doesn't seem like any of the affected regions are speech centers."

"THEN WHY CAN'T SPEAK?"

"The metastable regions tend to absorb any input without breaking the loops."

"A SIGNAL TRAP?"

"Precisely. So, when you try to activate a muscle, the signal starts out but tries to go through one of these regions and is absorbed. It's not passed on to the muscle, so you can't activate the muscles involved in making sounds."

"SAME WITH PAIN, BUT THE OTHER DIRECTION?"

"I think so. The pain signals coming back from your body try to pass through a metastable region and are stopped."

"PLEASURE, TOO"

Roger instinctively pulled back the hand that was stroking her neck.

"SO HOW CAN I SEE?"

"Apparently some of the other sensory data—taste, smell, sight, and sound—don't pass through any metastable regions. And I think that gives me some clues as to where these regions might be."

"NOT BE"

"Yes, that's more accurate. We know some of the pathways through which those sensory signals pass, and evidently those are clear of metastable regions. But it still leaves many, many places to search."

Tess heard the discouragement in his voice and figured she had to show some optimism, even if she didn't feel it right now. She formed her words carefully, grammatically. "SO, IF YOUR MODEL IS CORRECT, WE HAVE TO LOCATE EACH REGION AND FIND A WAY TO JIGGLE IT WITHOUT DESTROYING MY BRAIN. SOUNDS LIKE A JOB FOR THE BAG BANDIT"

He smiled at that, mostly because he was happy to see she could still make jokes. "Well, to do that, we'll have to know a lot more about brains in general, and your brain in particular. Don't you want to keep some secrets from your husband?"

"THEY'LL GIVE YOU SOMETHING TO MOTIVATE YOUR SEARCH"

"I don't need any more motivation than getting you back."

"SEX FIEND!"

Roger blushed from the truth of the accusation, then tried to change the subject. "Well, whatever my motivation, you're lucky I'm the right one to design probes. Blind jiggling is just as likely to lose more function as to gain any back."

"NOT REALLY"

"I'm serious."

"ME TOO. THERE ARE WAYS TO JIGGLE THE BRAIN WITHOUT SURGERY OR ELECTRIC SHOCK"

"What ways?"

"STROKE VICTIMS OFTEN RECOVER FUNCTION WHEN THEY HAVE A STIMULATING ENVIRONMENT. AFTER A

WHILE, WITH ENOUGH STIMULATION, THE BRAIN FINDS A WAY TO RESTORE THE FUNCTION"

"Okay, but often it's just a workaround of the affected portion."

"I DON'T CARE IF IT'S A WORKAROUND. THIS ISN'T ONE OF MY ELEGANT PROGRAMS. IT'S MY BRAIN. I HAVE TO USE MY MIND OR I'LL LOSE MY MIND"

By the end of the week, they made a rough plan. He would restore as much of her life as possible without messing with her brain until he had gathered all possible data that might reduce the risk of a mistake. Only then would they attempt to break the metastable state. In the meantime, he would build as stimulating an environment as he could for her. He would build, or have built, artificial abilities for Tess—giving her speech, sight, telephone, e-mail, Web access, and movement. These were all stopgap measures, but as Tess said, maybe she would get lucky. At least they would make her condition more tolerable. For the long term, he would exercise her limbs several hours a day, and try to build an automatic exerciser, but he would need to see some robotics people about that.

Putting voice to Tess's words was the easiest project in the plan. After inflicting a mercifully short lecture on Tess and Roger, hailing the benefits of "simplest possible design," SOS cobbled together a system using standard Mac text-to-speech software. The software's selection of voices was quirky, and the pronunciation was odd for some words. None of the voices sounded much like Tess, and Roger wished he had some recordings of her voice to use as the basis for synthesizing another voice. Perhaps her family had some, but for now, the speech was adequate. In the present circumstances, everything else was a frill.

Tess's mirror idea proved more difficult—until SOS suggested they use video cameras instead of mirrors. The clinic's security people had lots of obsolete spares in inventory. Though the cameras were black-and-white with mediocre picture quality, they were easy to mount around Tess's rooms. Linking her mental patterns to the cameras' control mechanisms was another stumbling block. After several dead ends, they compromised on a system where Tess gave commands as strings of letters and control characters, motivating SOS to offer another boring lecture, this time on the advantages and disadvantages of command-line programming. By now, Tess and Roger had come to expect SOS's technical lectures, and though Roger wouldn't admit it to Tess, he had actually come to look forward to what he learned from them.

The response time of the system was poor, so SOS added a voice-activated module that would automatically point at least one of the cameras at anybody speaking—or at any speech-like noise in the room. Tess could override the voice-activated module and point the camera elsewhere, but that took a few seconds and often missed what she wanted to see.

Although Tess was seldom alone in her room, they bought a telephone device for the deaf and attached it to the computer attached to her skullcap. The TDD allowed her to dial calls (only internal, because of security) and send text messages when she was alone. She could also control Internet access, bringing whatever she wanted to the screen over her head when she lay on her back. But the snood tended to irritate her shaved head, so the doctors forbade her to wear it for more than a few hours at a time. Roger vowed to design a new sensor array—when he found some spare time.

Mobility was another matter. Once Tess learned to control a motorized wheelchair by spelling out commands, she wanted to be able to take herself to the rose garden. Her doctors vetoed the idea. Because of the delay required for the commands, they didn't think it was safe.

Roger toured the grounds with Don to see if they could find a safe place for Tess to practice, but everywhere they went, Roger saw obstacles. Strolling among the roses, Don had to agree. "I was hoping we might spin off some military applications—mind-controlled missiles and such—but this just doesn't seem to be a safe way to control what amounts to a motorized vehicle. Not to speak of a flying bomb."

Roger's mind contemplated the incongruity of discussing weapons while bathed in the scent of the roses. "Just one more reason to drop the auditory approach and try to capture visual information."

"Why would that be better?"

"Because, if it works the way it should, Tess should be able to visualize where she wants to go. We could capture those patterns and use them to control the chair."

"Sounds just as complex to me."

"Controlling the chair is complex, but it's already been worked out for rolling robots. All we need to do is port the software to this environment." Roger bent a peach-colored rose toward his face and studied the blossom. "Do you think I'd be allowed to cut some of these for Tess?"

"She seems to have plenty of wildflowers."

"That's SOS's doing. I want to give her something different."

"I'll ask the gardener, but I don't see why not."

"Thanks."

Don stopped walking and looked at Roger. "So how come you suddenly changed the subject? What aren't you telling me?"

"You don't distract easily, do you. All right, I confess. Capturing the visual patterns is the hard part."

"But you already know how to capture brain patterns."

"Only from the auditory regions of her brain. Sure, we have the instruments, but we have to start over again finding the right locations."

"There's more than one?"

"We're not sure, but, yes, probably. So we have to investigate several areas emitting patterns when she sees, for example, this rose." He twisted the stem of a red rose so Don could see it. "What's happening in your head when you see it? Is it a picture of the rose, or a memory of some other rose? Or is it a memory of a red sled you had when you were a kid?"

"So I might be thinking of the *word* 'rose'?"

"But in what language? Are you thinking of 'rose' or *'wardah'*?"

"I probably wouldn't be thinking *'wardah.'* Do you think in Arabic?"

"Sometimes," Roger said. "On some subjects, especially childhood things."

"Funny. I'm fluent, but I don't have an Arabic child's vocabulary. I guess my vocabulary is heavily biased toward espionage and terrorism. But Lucinda told me she often dreams in Arabic. She spent a lot of time in the Middle East. I did, too, but more in the overseas American community. She lived and worked among the people."

"That's another problem with basing the system on language. Not just what language, but what context. We used to have a dog named Rose."

Don scanned the balconies on both buildings facing the rose garden. "So each person here might be thinking of something different when they see a rose."

"Right. Until we learn how to decode the patterns, we won't know which ones contain the information we want."

"Sounds hard. Is this going to detract from your schedule on our project?"

"If it's a dead end, yes. But if it's not, it's going to make everything go faster."

"Then let's get started. What do you need?"

39

Though Tess's new technologies gave her a much more stimulating mental world, her physical world was a different problem. Her doctors were still concerned that she would experience other medical difficulties unless she had some kind of exercise, some movement of her inert body. They also felt that a more varied environment would be beneficial, and encouraged Roger to hurry his work on designing a practical, Tess-controlled wheelchair. In the meantime, they insisted, Tess must have a full-time nurse in attendance, to offer physical therapy for her withering muscles, as well as to watch for any signs of distress.

Don, seeing progress that he liked as Tess became involved in the projects, offered to reward her with her choice of nurses, which would also free Roger from the time-consuming physical therapy. Although she liked most of the men and women who had attended her, they were all a bit too "army" for her taste. Just the thought of having one as a constant companion would have caused her to tear out her hair—if her head hadn't been shaved, and if she could use her hands to tear anything.

"what about cousin addie?" her computer voice said. Roger noticed she was no longer capitalizing words that appeared on the screen as she communicated. He also realized she was avoiding

Adara's Arabic name—probably so as not to arouse any of Don's security concerns.

"Who's Addie?" Don asked.

"My cousin. She's a graduate nurse with a specialty in rehabilitation. Just finished her specialty internship, but I think she must be darn good. Graduated first in her class."

"a family tradition," Tess added. Roger turned crimson.

Don, always the agent, had to know more. "Which side of the family?"

"The tradition? Both, actually."

"I meant the cousin."

"She's my mother's brother's eldest. Yes, the Arab side, if that's what you're worried about."

"Give me some credit. I don't think all Arabs are enemies of the state."

"Well, she's a hundred-percent American. A Cubs' fan who chews Wrigley's gum."

"So she doesn't even speak Arabic?"

"Actually, she can, but she prefers not to. Except with the older generation. Typical first generation—like me. And I don't know what language she dreams in."

"Her language skills could be a plus around here. I'll check her out. If she's a Cubs' fan, she might be all right—or she might be a fanatic devoted to hopeless causes."

"make it fast," Tess's machine said. "i need the exercise"

And Don did make it fast. He wanted to keep Roger happy, but he really wanted to get to work on his captive terrorist, so Addie's low-level clearance went through in record time. Her first impulse was to say yes to the job offer, but she restrained herself, remembering her heritage as daughter of a long line of traders. Coached by Uncle Qasim, she negotiated a number of perks, including one step up the pay ladder and the privilege of bringing her horse to the stables.

Once she was brought to the clinic, Addie quickly settled into a large room across the hall from Tess. Though her badge allowed her to wander in most areas, she spent all her waking time with Tess. Roger hadn't noticed, but after a week, Tess pointed out that since Addie arrived, SOS also spent more time with her. And brought two bunches of wildflowers every morning.

The thought-controlled wheelchair project was going nowhere, but with Adara in attendance, it was no longer a priority. A manual wheelchair was brought over from the Rehab building and adapted for Tess. Because he'd need a large magnet, Roger couldn't rig a portable version of Tess's speech system. Fortunately, Adara seemed adept at anticipating Tess's needs when out on their thrice-daily regime of walks. At least, Roger heard no complaints.

On rainy days, Addie and Tess walked the corridors. Days when the sky over the lake threatened, they stayed within running distance of the buildings, but mostly in the rose garden. When the sun shone, they went to the beach. That's why they missed Wyatt's unpleasant sunny-day visit.

40

To keep his former professor out of his hair—not that his shaved head had any hair to keep out of—Roger had Don assign Wyatt and his graduate assistants to work on the now low-priority thought-driven wheelchair. The tactic was only partially effective, because on paper Wyatt remained principal investigator on the original grant, so he was required to visit the clinic every so often to "check the books."

When Wyatt arrived for this latest visit, escorted by Lucinda and Don, Tess was at the beach. Lucinda showed great interest in Tess's condition, but she refused to be in the same room with her. She wouldn't say more than that Tess's helpless condition was too close to her own experience.

Since Tess was not available, Roger put on the snood himself and demonstrated the speech system using the machine voice of Mickey Mouse. Wyatt didn't appreciate the joke, but he deferred to Lucinda, whose sour expression perfectly reflected how he felt. "Is this how we're spending our time and money?" she asked.

Don punched her playfully in the arm. "Come on, LD. Loosen up. While you've been running to all sorts of exotic places shooting bad guys, we've been slaving our butts off up here."

"I've only shot one bad guy in my life. And that's because I had no other choice. Mostly I've been reading thousands of crank letters."

"Too bad. One of these days we're going to capture one of these bombers alive."

"We already have one. That's what you're slaving for, isn't it? Otherwise, what's the significance of all this crap? Are you getting anywhere with real people, not Mickey Mouse?"

Lucinda scowled when Don tried to make a joke by putting his fingers in his ears. "Okay, Roger. Switch to another voice."

The computer said a few words in a deep, male monotone. Lucinda's frown looked cast in plaster, so Roger played another joke by switching the machine to speak Arabic with a Syrian accent. "*Shoo beddak? Ana la tet kalam al Arabiyah.*"

"Very funny," Lucinda said sternly, but her plaster face had cracked a tiny smile.

Wyatt didn't understand, and didn't get the joke. "What did it say?"

Lucinda looked at Wyatt with contempt. He was the only one in the room who knew no Arabic. "It asked what I wanted. In Arabic. Then it said he didn't speak Arabic. But if he's actually driving the machine, obviously he does." She looked at Wyatt with an expression of cold contempt. "And, apparently, you don't."

Finished with Wyatt, she turned to Don before Wyatt could answer. "Okay, that's something that might be useful. At least it gives me something to put in our report, though I don't know why I get stuck with all the paperwork."

Don, not wanting to go there, chose a diversion. "Show her the cameras, Roger."

Considering their sluggish control delays, Roger didn't think Tess's cameras were that great an achievement, but he kept quiet because he knew that Don wanted to impress Lucinda. She, in turn, would impress their superiors in Washington, so he gave her a visual tour of the room on the monitor.

She did seem to be impressed. "And you're controlling that with your mind. Very nice. That's a little off our course, but the weapons potential will make a nice frosting on the cake. I'll want the schematics and the program design documents to append to my report."

"And a copy of the source code, too," said Wyatt. "I'll need all that so I can add this system to my patent applications."

Don reached over Roger and switched off the monitor as if to hide something from Wyatt. "Slow down, Professor. All this is classified for the duration."

"What duration?"

"Whatever duration I say."

"You can't classify my own ideas."

"In the first place, I can, and will. But in the second place, these aren't your ideas. They're Roger's."

"And Tess's." Roger had removed the snood and stood up so his eyes were level with Wyatt's—several inches above, in fact. "He's right. You had nothing to do with these."

"But I'm your post-doc chairman. That automatically makes me the principal investigator as far as patents are concerned."

Don's eyes narrowed. "Let me repeat myself, Professor. No source code. No design documents. No schematics. No patents. If you still don't understand, I'll repeat it in Arabic."

Wyatt looked away, but sounded defiant. "Fine. I'm forming my own company, based on *my* work. Let's see if you can stop that."

"Depends on what you use from this project."

"It's all my own work. The visual track you're taking is just a rabbit trail anyway. I'll work on sound, the way it should be done. And you'll still be here on this godforsaken beach, groping in the dark, when I'm enjoying my yacht out on the lake."

Before anyone could respond, Wyatt flung himself out the door, slamming it behind him. Don pointed to the Arabic writing on the screen. "When did you do that?"

"In my vast spare time," Roger laughed. "Actually, SOS did most of the work. Apparently he's done some work in Arabic before. In fact, he was about to give me a lecture on Arabic grammar until I told him it was one of my mother tongues."

Lucinda frowned at Don. "He wasn't supposed to tell that he'd worked in Arabic. I told you those freaks couldn't be controlled."

"If you can stop SOS from giving boring lectures at the drop of a hat, you'll earn my undying gratitude. But in this case, no harm, no foul. Besides," said Don, "I think we've now got something to try on our friend in the other building."

41

Don and Roger were passing by the rose garden on their way to fetch the prisoner for interrogation when Lucinda caught up with them. She told Don she'd grabbed Wyatt before he could go wandering around the estate and escorted him off the premises. She suggested that Roger take a break and visit his wife and cousin, who were sitting just out of sight on the sunny side, enjoying the fine weather.

"What do you think you're doing?" she whispered to Don, once Roger was well out of hearing range. They entered the west building and pressed for the elevator.

"If the doctors aren't busy trying to repair the prisoner, we're going to fetch him and try interrogating him on the machine. In Arabic."

"That's exactly what I meant. Why are you taking Roger with you?"

"Because I need him. He has to customize the snood, then adjust the program's parameters as he interprets responses. Who else would you suggest for the job?"

The elevator door opened, and Don waved Lucinda in, but she defiantly stood still. "He doesn't have adequate clearance."

Don gave up their Alphonse-Gaston game and preceded her into the elevator. "He has all the clearance he needs. We can't wait for anything higher. Or for him to train somebody else."

"There must be someone else."

"Okay, look in your database for, let's see, 'electronic genius, programming wizard, fluent in Arabic, recently polished up on psycholinguistics and neurology,'" he watched the floor numbers click by. "What else should we ask for? Besides Q-clearance, of course."

"I won't be responsible when this gets you in trouble."

"Instead of playing CYA, LD, why don't you play CYA?"

"What?"

"Instead of 'Cover Your Ass,' try playing 'Consider Your Alternatives.' There aren't any."

"Shit."

"What's that an acronym for?" Don smiled, but Lucinda kept scowling.

"It means 'I can tell from that look on your face that you're going to do this, no matter what I say.'"

"Clever acronym, LD. I hadn't heard that one before."

"Well, I've seen that expression before. All right, I'd better go along with you—just to see that Roger doesn't make more trouble than necessary."

42

As Roger approached Tess and Addie, unseen, his pager received a message to have them remain outside. He paused behind a rose bush to allow Addie some privacy to finish her "girl talk" to Tess. "SOS took pictures of me this morning," she concluded, not bothered at all that Tess could show no reaction to what she was saying. "He said he wanted one to send to his mother. I think that's a good sign."

Roger stepped out from behind the bush and pretended he hadn't heard. After telling Addie to wait outside with Tess, he returned to the apartment. Don had interrogated the prisoner there once before, telling Roger only that he was the sole survivor of a bombing, and they hoped to glean eyewitness information.

In the previous test, they had used English without much success, so Roger reset the machine for Arabic. The subject was wheeled in. Most of his body was still bandaged for his slow-healing burns and fractures. His head bandage had to be carefully removed by the attending physician before Roger could mount and calibrate the snood. Although he'd worked with Tess's and his own shaved heads before, Roger shuddered when the prisoner's splotchy pink grafted skin was exposed before him.

To recalibrate the software for Arabic, Don asked the subject simple questions while Lucinda monitored his body and Roger studied the brain patterns. After four questions, Don asked Roger, "Are you getting anything?"

"Definitely, but the patterns are different from when we tested him in English."

"Different how?" Lucinda asked.

"Hard to explain, but the computer knows they're different."

"So, is that important?"

"I think it's because English must not be his native language. That makes it more intellectual than emotional, so it's processed by different parts of the brain."

"Should I change the questions?" Don asked.

"Well, we know he definitely understands Arabic, because each response is different. If it was just a jumble to him, all the response patterns would be more or less the same. Kind of an emotional 'huh?'" Roger keyed in a rapid string of commands. "Let's see if we can build an alphabet—Alif, Baa, Taa, and all that."

Don began to read the alphabet while Roger catalogued which response patterns were tied to which letters. After half an hour, they hadn't gotten anywhere. The subject's response pattern for each letter was more or less the same.

Don motioned Roger outside, leaving Lucinda to keep an eye on the subject. "Turn the screen so he can't see it," Don whispered, "and keep the sound off. I don't want him to know what we're getting from his mind."

"Why not? It will help him correct our interpretations."

"That's exactly what we don't want him to do."

"I don't get it. How's he going to answer our questions if he doesn't know how to produce the alphabet?"

"Let's just say he may have reasons for not wanting to answer our questions."

"I still don't get it. Why wouldn't he want—" Roger stopped dead, just outside the door. "Oh, you think he might have been involved in the bombing? That he can answer, but won't?"

"I can't say one way or the other. Let's just keep it clean, okay?"

"It would help me calibrate him if I knew."

"It would help us even more if we knew. That's one thing I hope to find out today. Is there anything in your responses that would indicate whether he's lying, or trying to avoid answering?"

"I don't know. I always assumed the subject would be trying to communicate. Like Tess."

"All right," said Don. "I do have something I can try."

They reentered the room and took their positions. Roger asked the subject to think of the letter Alif. Same old response pattern. Roger shook his head. Don stepped closer to the gurney and pinched the subject's bandaged nose between his fingers. The subject's entire body stiffened with pain. Lucinda watched, expressionless.

"What are you—" Roger began, but Don shushed him with a finger to his lips.

Then Don said, in Arabic, "I can make this as painful as you want, if you refuse to cooperate." He twisted the nose again, harder. Roger gagged. Putting his hand over his mouth, he raced from the room. Don followed.

"What's wrong?"

"You're torturing him."

"It's just standard interrogation technique for an uncooperative subject."

"Not for me it isn't. If that's what you're going to do, I can't be part of it."

"This man is suspected of bombing a congressman's home."

"That doesn't matter. He's still a human being."

"Believe me, I don't enjoy this any more than you do. But I have to get to the bottom of this, and I've run out of ideas. If you've got a better idea, spill it."

Roger's brain scrambled ahead. "Isn't there some sort of truth serum? At least that wouldn't be torture."

"It's not reliable. Besides, the doctors think it might kill him."

"So torture's okay, but killing isn't."

"Killing won't get us any answers. And your machine isn't working, either."

"Maybe it could. Maybe if you asked some questions we knew he wouldn't want to answer. Then we could tell."

Don waited in silence for a moment, considering the idea. "All right, it's a theory. But nothing comes to mind. Nothing we can be sure of."

"Then how about questions you could be reasonably sure you'd know his true answer to?"

"Like what?"

"I don't know. I guess if I were in his condition, I'd want to get well. Not be in pain. Be free. Stuff like that."

Don made a few notes, then agreed to try. They reentered the room. Roger turned off the sound and moved the monitor. Lucinda wanted to know what they were doing, but Don shook his head. Then he consulted his list and resumed the questioning in Arabic. "Do you want to live? ... Would you like to feel less pain? ... Do you want to be released?"

Roger signaled a time-out. This time all three stepped outside.

"What are you doing?" Lucinda asked, glaring at Don.

He explained.

She turned her fiery eyes on Roger. "And what are you getting?"

"He shows an interesting pattern. First, there's a quick response, about thirty milliseconds. Then, there's a quick switch to a different pattern."

"You mean different each time?"

"No, different from the first. The second pattern is always pretty much identical. I think the first response is the true answer, yes or no, but the second shows his attempt to hide."

Lucinda dismissed the idea with a shrug. "That's pretty farfetched."

"Makes sense to me," said Don, "since it's always the same. I think I'd show a pattern like that if an enemy were questioning me."

"Why?" Roger asked.

"I was trained in ways to beat interrogations and lie detectors. He's thinking of something to focus his mind away from the question's true answer."

"So what's he thinking about when he gives that second pattern?"

"Impossible to say. You just learn to pick a neutral image to focus on—in my case, it's an elephant. What's yours, LD? You've got actual experience being interrogated."

Lucinda waved off the question. "This is all speculation. It assumes he's been given anti-interrogation training, but we don't even know if he's one of the bombers."

"I'm sure enough. Let's take it as a working assumption. Roger, I'm going to ask him directly if he's a terrorist, so you look for a yes or no."

Roger wasn't sure. "That won't work if he doesn't think of himself as a terrorist. Do you know the name of the group he belongs to? I mean, supposedly belongs to?"

"We think it's the Thursday Group."

"Better use Arabic. *Yom alKhamis*, or just *alKhamis*. He probably won't respond the same way to the English name."

Lucinda threw up her hands in disgust. "Come on, boys. This is wasting our time."

Roger checked his watch. "How much time do we have?"

"According to his chart, it's time for his next pain shot," Lucinda said.

Don snatched the chart out of Lucinda's hand. "Excellent. He won't be getting any pain relief until I get what I want. I'll tell him that he can suffer until he cooperates. Roger, watch his reaction to that idea."

Don started back into the room, but Roger grabbed his arm, noticing Don's biceps. He was going to ask if this wasn't a form of torture, too, but decided Don wouldn't welcome contradiction at this late hour. "Never mind," he said in response to Don's querying expression. He dropped the arm and went inside. Lucinda disappeared down the hallway.

They started the interrogation. Don had just begun to probe more deeply when Lucinda returned with two doctors, a man and a woman. Both of them insisted on giving their patient a pain shot and that they stop for the day. Before Don could answer, Roger's pager delivered a note from Addie asking if he was almost ready to join Tess for supper. "Can I tell her we're finished for the day?"

Don objected. "We need ten more minutes. We were just making progress."

The female doctor had one bony hand on the subject's pulse. The other hand held a large hypodermic needle. "It won't help you much if he's dead."

Lucinda took the doctors' side, telling Don to cool off. Roger figured these two had argued over the same issue before, because Lucinda seemed to know just what would convince Don.

When Don gave in, the prisoner was taken off Tess's machine and wheeled back to his room. Roger sent Addie a message to wait ten minutes while he straightened up the room, and Lucinda excused herself to pack for her drive back to Chicago. Roger wanted to wait for Tess, but Don insisted they go to a private corner of the cafeteria to discuss their results over coffee. "I think we're getting somewhere. I want you to concentrate on this subject until further notice."

"I'm not sure how useful it will be if he doesn't want to cooperate."

"I can get what I need if I can play twenty questions with him about his collaborators. I've watched you do that with Tess. And why shouldn't you help me? You should be proud of your work."

"I'm not proud of torturing people."

"Come on. Don't be so squeamish. We didn't do anything to him. Besides, if your method works, I won't have to . . . *persuade* him."

Roger drained the last of his coffee, crumpled the cup, and tossed it out. He left Don at the table, to look for Tess.

43

Once outside, Roger stopped, remembering that Tess always chided him for never noticing the world around him. He tried to take in the weather, but to his mind, there didn't seem to be any weather to notice. Others would have said it was a beautiful day—clear with an ideal temperature and a slight breeze—but to Roger it was just an ordinary day.

Once he stopped hurrying, though, he was struck by the contrast between the austere, rectangular confines of the magnet room and the richness of nature in the rose garden. Surrounded by soft, sweet breezes and the songs of birds hidden in the arbors, Roger found it painful to contemplate the torture he'd witnessed just minutes before. Painful and impossible to put out of his mind. This whole situation was wrong.

He found Tess sitting in her wheelchair in the last sunlit corner of the garden. Addie wasn't with her. *Probably checking that the room is really clean,* he guessed. *She must regret leaving Tess alone, but she must know it's perfectly safe here. The worst that could ever happen has already happened.*

At the moment, Tess's most serious problem was a black-and-orange butterfly perched on the tip of her nose. Without her talking machine, Roger had no clue whether it bothered or delighted her. But he was willing to bet she'd already identified the species.

He blew the delicate miracle gently away, then kissed Tess's forehead. Her nose twitched from his breath. He no longer imagined, as he had in those first days, that this was anything but an involuntary reflex. Still, he was sure she enjoyed the sun. He decided to enjoy it with her while waiting for Addie to return. He sat down on the bench with his hand resting on hers, just being with her until he finally noticed a change in temperature. The sun was still high in the summer sky, but had disappeared behind the square corner of the tall building across the way, to the west.

He spoke to her, knowing, now, that she could hear and understand. He didn't want to trouble her, but he had to unburden himself, so he chose his first words carefully. "The Arabic system worked better than we'd hoped. But they . . . we . . . had to . . ." He sucked in a lungful of the soft air and started over. "Don thinks his patient is a terrorist. He's willing to torture him to make the machine work."

He leaned away from her field of view so she wouldn't see him crying. *This isn't working. I need to leave this place, but if we leave, Tess would lose her ability to communicate. If I had the money, I could build the equipment she needs. But I don't, so we have to stay. But if she knew the price I'm paying, she'd insist we leave anyway.*

He made up his mind, wiped his eyes, and stood. "Well, Don's happy, but there's still a lot of work to do. Let's get back and hook you up so I can hear about your day."

They met Addie coming out, and she told them that Tess's room was ready and that their supper had arrived from the cafeteria, including Tess's liquid delicacies. She assured them the food was excellent on the scale of hospital cuisine. Because the snood made feeding Tess rather awkward, Roger was glad to have an excuse to dine with his wife before hooking her up. He was afraid of what she might say about the torture—afraid that he'd already told her too much.

The night before, Tess had told him she always pretended they were dining in a fine lakeside restaurant. But pretending wasn't Roger's strong suit. He couldn't understand how she could interpret bland pureed pumpkin or bilious-green pureed spinach as *haute cuisine*. And tonight his stomach was churning from the afternoon's events.

Addie had just finished spooning the last of the spinach puree into Tess's slack mouth when Don entered without knocking. He quietly asked Addie to come with him for a moment. As they left, Roger glimpsed two uniforms outside the door, and mused, "I wonder what that was about?"

Roger wiped the last greenish stains from Tess's lips, then finished the job with a wet, warm washcloth. He disposed of her waste bags and replaced them with fresh ones, then grabbed her snood, adjusted it on her head, and moved her to the magnet. "I'll have you hooked up in a minute. Then you can tell me about all the exciting things you saw outside on this gorgeous day."

An instant after the last cable was attached, the computer voice announced, "she killed him"

It was hard to relate the significance of this statement with the voice's lack of emotion. "Oh, you were watching TV?"

"no. in the rose garden"

"Addie killed an insect? Not a butterfly, I hope."

"be quiet. this is serious <dead serious>"

Seeing the angle brackets on the screen caused the spoken words to be stressed and Roger understood she wasn't kidding, so he shut up and the voice continued. "man thrown off balcony. top floor. into bushes. must be dead"

When Tess was in a hurry, she dropped even more unnecessary words. As a result, sometimes Roger couldn't be sure of her meaning. "What man?"

"patient"

"How do you know it was a patient?"

"bandages"

"You saw this?"

"yes"

"Why didn't Addie tell someone?"

"addie did not see. was here. cleaning room"

"Wait a minute. I'll page Don."

He pressed the emergency button on the room's pager. An orderly surprised Roger by sticking his head in the door two seconds later. Usually they were minutes in coming. "What's wrong? Is Miss Tess okay?"

"She's fine. We need Agent Capitol. He's with Addie. Bring her, too. Right away."

"I'll find him." The orderly's head disappeared. The door closed without a sound.

"When did this happen, baby?"

"just before you came"

"Oh, God. And I sat there jabbering away. I should have brought you in here immediately."

"you could not know"

"What's taking them so long? Sorry. What else can you tell me?"

"nurse did it"

"A nurse threw a patient off the balcony?"

"yes"

"Did you recognize the nurse?"

"woman. never saw her before"

"This place is starting to give me the creeps." He told her again about the torture, this time in more detail. "If we didn't need all this machinery, I would take you away from here."

"go anyway <really>"

"We can't. You need to be here."

"NO I DON'T!" With SOS's latest version of the software, the machine shouted when Tess used all capitals. "take me away <please>"

"How am I going to talk to you?"

"you will figure it out. you are bag bandit. remember?"

"Your best chance to . . . recover . . . is here."

"other hospitals. better ones"

"But they don't have the equipment, and we don't have the money."

"i can be quiet. will do me good"

"But—" The door opened. "Oh, Don. Finally. Where's Addie?"

"Adara's under arrest."

"Arrest? For what?"

"She murdered our subject. Threw him off the balcony."

44

The Merchandise Mart was relatively quiet, with most of the activity being carried out by the workers tearing down the old displays and putting new ones in their place. But the permanent stores were open for business, and though the crowds were too thin to provide the usual cover for their arrivals, Qaaf's report could not be delayed. Zay and Jiim would have been patient, but Alif chafed in his wicker chair. "Is it done?"

She was prepared for the question, and her answer was brief. "It's done. Dhal is no longer a problem."

"Excellent," said Zay.

After a silent period, Alif looked for Zay's permission. When their leader gave him the slightest nod, Alif asked, "Qaaf, any difficulties?"

"I had hoped to make it look like suicide, but someone saw me."

Jiim gasped, but Alif ignored him and pressed Qaaf. "Did you eliminate him? The witness?"

"Her," she scowled. "She's the damaged one, and she can't identify me. But she's told them it was a murder, so I have to lie low. They've taken a Muslim nurse into custody, though they have no proof against her."

"So they'll release her?" Zay asked.

"Probably not. They'll soon discover she has a background of being involved in protests."

"Another martyr to our cause."

Zay fell silent, but Alif's patience had run out. "We can't waste any more time. With the Dhal problem solved, we're free to concentrate on our preparations for the Vice President."

"I would feel better if the witness were eliminated first, so she can never identify me," Qaaf spoke quickly. "I think she'll soon quit their protection, so I've made plans for her elimination."

Alif wanted to know Qaaf's plans, but Zay cut his questions short. "You won't be involved, so the less you know, the better."

As she wove her way out to Mart Plaza Drive to disappear among the tourists, Qaaf noticed that most of the new displays were already in place. That seemed fitting.

45

Roger sounded shaken to his roots, but Tess's mechanical voice was as calm as ever, with no stress or shouts to reveal her true feelings. "a mistake, don. i saw the murder. it was not addie"

"You *saw* the murder?" Don's eyes widened.

One of Tess's cameras swiveled to point at him. Another aimed itself at Roger. She spoke deliberately, in full sentences. "roger, sit down before you fall down. don, i saw someone in nurse's uniform throw a patient off top floor balcony. i assume that's the murder you're talking about. or was there more than one?"

"That's the one, and Addie was the nurse."

"certainly was not addie. i saw whole thing"

"Did you recognize the nurse?"

"it was not one of those i know, but definitely not addie"

Don looked at Tess directly, not at her camera. "Of course you'd say it wasn't Addie. That's very noble of you, Tess, but you don't want to become an accessory to this crime."

"show me all nurses"

"I can't parade all the nurses in here."

"show pictures"

Don slapped his head. "Of course. We have everyone's badge picture in the database. If you're telling the truth, you can pick out the one you saw."

Roger accessed the network, but was asked for a password when he tried to access the personnel records. Don called an internal number, identified himself, and asked for the password to the personnel database. After a brief discussion and a short wait, he hung up the phone. "Did you get the password?" Roger asked.

Don pointed to his temple, then bent over Roger's shoulder and typed into the password box. Roger dutifully looked the other way until Don finished typing, then turned back and performed a search for all the women who might be wearing a nurse's uniform. One by one, he presented them to Tess, but she kept saying no.

When the list was exhausted, Don shook his head. "I'm sorry, Tess. That eliminates them all. But thanks for not accusing some innocent party."

"i am not making it up. why do you not believe me?"

"Because the last person to be seen leaving his room was a nurse, and Addie's the only nurse who wasn't accounted for."

"so whoever saw the nurse did not say it was addie?"

"Not positively, but he was positive it was a nurse, and it couldn't have been anyone else."

"it could NOT have been her, because i SAW murderer." Tess regretted the limits of her mechanical voice. She could approximate shouting, but spelling out curses just didn't give the same sense of release.

"You could have been mistaken. You were far away."

"then i could have been mistaken about the murder, too. maybe the man jumped"

Roger winced, anticipating Don's answer.

"Both his legs had been amputated. He couldn't possibly have jumped."

"okay, so maybe i was mistaken about the pictures"

Don ignored the question. "Where was Addie at the time?"

Roger had managed to get his mouth back in gear. "She was in here, cleaning the room before she brought Tess back."

"Is there any way to prove that?"

"Not unless someone saw her."

"We've questioned everyone in this corridor. Nobody saw her."

Roger banged his fist on the arm of his chair. "Damn. It can't be Addie. Why would she do something like that?"

"We know she's been active in some Arab causes, and she knew we were questioning a terrorist. Someone was trying to silence him. Who else around here had a motive?"

"Can I talk to her? Maybe I can find something that will convince you."

"That's not possible. It's out of my hands now, and it wouldn't be a good idea anyway. The less you're involved with her now, the better. Otherwise, someone will think you might be involved—"

"What?"

"I know you're not, but just the suspicion will put you off the project for the duration. That wouldn't be good for me," Don placed his hand on Tess's magnet, "or for you. Tess would have to leave the premises. And, of course, you couldn't take this hunk of metal with you."

Tess told herself to stay calm and think. Roger said nothing. Don interpreted their silence as a signal that they had no more to say. As he left, he turned for one more warning. "Stay in your apartment until tomorrow. Don't try to see Addie. You won't find her anyway."

Tess heard the lock click.

Roger stared at the door. "I guess that decides it for us. I think we're locked in for the night. But we should get out of here."

"i agree <angry>." Tess had decided it was better to spell out her anger, rather than bury it inside.

"So, we'll just do the best we can. I have an idea—a long shot—for a portable system. If I can work it out, and raise a little money . . . more than a little . . . then we'll be able to leave and try to help Addie."

"what are you talking about? we agreed to get out of here"

"We did. And we'll only stay as long as we have to, I promise you that."

"i thought we agreed we had to leave, NOW"

Roger flinched. "Is that what you meant? But it's obvious that we can't leave until—"

"obvious we cannot stay"

He stalked back and forth from one wall to its opposite. "If we left here, we couldn't communicate."

"if we stay here, i will STOP communicating. we have to help addie"

"I won't let you be out of touch again. You'll go crazy. I'll go crazy."

"if i can deal with it, so can you. only way to free addie is develop aremac"

Hearing the last word, Roger stooped to examine the computer. Tess stopped him. "it is working fine"

"No it isn't. It's speaking gobbledygook."

"not gobble. just backwards. look"

Roger was about to ask what to look at when Tess's machine voice shouted "AREMAC" and the word appeared on the monitor. He read it in reverse and understood.

"addie needs aremac so i can show pictures of real murderer in the act. picture is in my mind"

46

Inga squirmed in her office chair, interviewing a principal investigator whose grant wasn't being renewed, when the cell phone in her purse rang. This was the phone that never rang, the one person in the world who held real power over her, power because of one indiscretion that nobody else remembered.

She excused herself, picked up the purse, and headed for the executive women's washroom. The outer door had no lock, so she leaned her back against it before answering.

"I hear they're leaving the clinic," said the feared voice, the only voice she expected to hear on this private phone.

"I was going to call you as soon as I finished my meeting."

She anticipated an angry response, but all he said was, "That should make them more accessible."

"I'm not sure they'll even continue the work. They have no money, and they can't do anything without a magnet."

"Any chance they'll raise the money?"

Someone pushed on the door, but couldn't budge Inga's huge bulk. When Inga was sure the intruder had moved on, she delivered the bad news. "Their best chance is to sue you—for the previous failure. The one that put her out of commission."

"That can't be allowed to happen." Now she could hear his anger.

"They probably can't win."

"That doesn't matter. We can't be in the news."

Inga had prepared for this, because she shared his corporation's interest in keeping out of the news. If they were exposed, they would expose her. "Maybe you can make a deal with them."

"What sort of deal?"

"I've worked it out. They promise not to sue, and you give them another magnet in compensation."

"Just a minute." There was a long pause, and Inga was about to search her purse for a candy bar when he came back on the line. "They must agree to keep the deal secret."

"That shouldn't be a problem. Besides, you'll make a friend, which should help you later on."

"In this business, we can't depend on friendship. Not when there are other ways. We'll bug the magnet."

47

All it took was one phone call from Roger. Kamilah mobilized the family for the couple's exodus to Chicago and Adara's defense. Uncle Nazim and Uncle Suhayb sent one of their garment trucks up to Michigan to pick up Tess—not at the secret clinic, but in downtown Muskegon. Nazim drove the truck, but wasn't allowed to see his daughter. He was allowed to take all of Addie's possessions—except her horse, which would have to wait for suitable transport. For now, the mare was happily grazing with the government remuda, as apolitical as only a horse can be.

Uncle Qasim's brother-in-law was a partner in the prestigious law firm Foley, Johnson, and Cuddington. He didn't handle criminal cases, but he persuaded another partner, Arnie Danielson, to take Adara's case *pro bono*. After filing a few motions, he was allowed to see the accused, though only with an Arabic-speaking agent present—which was ridiculous because Arnie didn't understand a word of Arabic.

Uncle Zahid owned a gas station property in Chicago, a single-story brick building, north of downtown. The interior, complete with service bays and back offices, had been leased over the years by a Chinese restaurant, then a Mexican restaurant, then a barbecue restaurant. All of them had failed, the owners said, for lack of adequate parking. Whether that was true or not, no other restaurateur would take a chance, and the property had remained vacant—unsalable and generating no rental income—for more than two years. Kamilah convinced Zahid that, with a little work, the property would be ideal as a laboratory and apartment for the newlyweds. As soon as he agreed, Kamilah set her sisters-in-law to work decorating. They also set up a schedule among themselves and their older daughters to take turns tending to Tess's needs.

They didn't have Addie's skill, but they did bring a great deal of enthusiasm to their self-appointed jobs—keeping Tess healthy, exercising her limbs, and teaching her some Arabic. They bathed her, perfumed her, and massaged her with imported almond oil. Though she couldn't feel any of their ministrations, the exotic odors alone made her feel like a princess out of *Arabian Nights.*

Not all the odors were romantic. The garage reeked of its history—diesel fuel, soy sauce, chili, and garlic. Uncle Marid tried to help by swabbing the walls and floors with potent chemicals, but unfortunately, his chemical engineering education fell short on such practical matters, and the stink remained.

Although Marid's efforts had only served to add ammonia to the rainbow of fragrances, Roger was determined to please Tess by not just learning to live with the rainbow, but to enjoy the olfactory history of their abode. He hoped Tess didn't mind the odors, but now that the Aremac was gone, he had no way to know what she felt. Or thought. Not until Qasim's son Bart came to attempt to paint over the odors. Wherever Bart went, he brought along his seizure dog, Howler.

Bart was a darkly handsome, bright nineteen-year-old who had suffered epileptic seizures ever since he was four years old. When he was fourteen, he'd been given a German Shepherd dog that had been trained by an organization called "Paws With a Cause." Howler could detect Bart's seizures moments before they happened, then howl in a distinctive way. The advance warning allowed Bart to lie down safely so he wouldn't injure himself falling. Howler could also brace Bart so he could let himself gently drop to the ground. If Bart lay on the ground in public, Howler would stand guard against "good samaritans" who might try to take advantage and rob him. If they were home alone, Howler would press a phone pedal that called 911 with a prerecorded message.

While Bart was stripping the myriad layers of paint off the walls in the huge kitchen, Howler gave his warning, and Bart quickly dropped his brush and lay down on the concrete floor. It was a small attack, and soon Bart was sitting up, reassuring Roger that he could go on with the stripping job.

"I don't think so," said Roger. "You rest for a while. That stripping gel needs time to work anyway, so let's just sit here. You can explain to me how Howler knew you were going to have a seizure."

Bart threw his arm around Howler's neck and scratched his nose. "I wish I could. He's so good at it, but nobody has any idea how some dogs just know."

Roger was fascinated. "Aren't there any theories?"

"Some people think it's a change in the owner's scent, or body language. Others think the dogs can sense some electrical activity in the brain."

Roger was fascinated. "That's more up my line. But how did they train him?"

Howler put his muzzle on his owner's lap, and Bart scratched his back under his orange service-dog backpack. "They paired him with a person who had frequent seizures—more frequent than mine. Then they rewarded him—they used a clicker and food treats—every time his partner had a seizure. After a while, he started looking for his reward *before* the seizure happened. Then they trained him to howl when he alerted."

"Didn't he learn to howl just to get a reward?"

"They ignored those howls that weren't followed by seizures. It took a long time, and then they had to transfer his skills to me, which took more time."

"Smart dog."

Roger reached out to stroke Howler on the head, but Bart warned him off. "He's a service dog, on duty, so you're not supposed to play with him when he's wearing his vest."

Roger drew back his hand. "Sorry, I didn't know."

"It's okay." Bart unfastened the vest. "Here, you can pet him now. As long as we're in the house, he doesn't really need to wear the vest. He'll still warn me if necessary."

Roger grabbed Howler lightly behind his ears and rubbed, the way Tess always liked to rub the puppies—before her accident. "The training sounds really indirect. Wouldn't it have been faster if they had some other way of knowing in advance when a seizure was about to happen?"

"Sure. That would be a lot easier."

"But I know how to do that. With an EEG."

"Yeah, I know about that. But who wants to have electrodes permanently planted in their skull? Yuck." Bart smoothed his hair with his hand. "It would freak out the chicks."

"Definitely. But I can do it with a mesh skullcap, so a person would only have to wear it when training the dog. In fact, I could rig it directly to one of those pellet feeders, so it would treat the dog automatically whenever a seizure was about to happen."

Bart's eyes widened. "If you could do that, lots of people would be willing to pay a bundle for it."

"That would be nice, but it would take some time. What I really want to do is adapt the technique to train a yes-no dog for Tess."

"A yes-no dog? I never heard of that."

"That's because I just invented it." Roger held out his hand, and Howler licked it. "In fact, maybe I could do that right away. Without equipment. But I need some way to fund development."

Bart thought he had a solution and, over the next ten days, he used the promise of the seizure detector to get Roger two small seed grants. Roger was amazed at how much quicker service-dog organizations could grant money than the government agencies he'd dealt with. Evidently, the service-dog organizations were in fierce competition with one another, so they kept discretionary funds that could be dispensed without a cascade of meetings. Along with the money, one organization supplied Sandy, their Chicago-area field trainer. Another organization wanted to supply a Labrador retriever, but Roger insisted on a German Shepherd. In this neighborhood, it wouldn't hurt for Tess to have some additional security.

The organization yielded to his logic and gave him Heidi, a ninety-pound black-and-tan who had washed out of her training as a wheelchair dog because she was too protective of her handler. That was just fine with Roger, who watched in fascination as Sandy took only two days to shape Heidi into Tess's yes-no dog.

The training was based on Tess's ability to signal yes with tears. Roger would ask Tess a series of yes questions, followed immediately by a perfectly timed reinforcing reward from Sandy.

It was much the same reinforcement method he used to train his computers, but it was all positive reinforcement. Sandy used no punishment, and Heidi required no instruments—only dried liver treats. When she learned to anticipate Tess's yes reliably, she was trained to respond by lifting her right paw. When Roger and Sandy repeated the process with no questions, Heidi quickly mastered the art of raising her left paw to signal Tess's negative answer. The method, once trained, was much faster than crying.

Sandy stayed on to teach Heidi to respond to simple mental commands—*get help; lights* (toggle off if on or on if off); *door* (so she could unlock the door with a special latch if it were someone Tess knew; and *bark* (if it were someone she didn't know).

Heidi already knew basic dog commands—*sit, stay, come,* and *down*—and it was easy to attach those to Tess's mental patterns. She also knew a few tricks—*shake, over, high five.* And, on her own initiative, Heidi learned to jump carefully onto Tess's bed and sleep protectively by her side. The first time she did this, Roger ordered her off, but she sat up and raised her left paw.

"Does that *no* come from you, Tess?" Roger asked.

Heidi raised her right paw, and Roger laughed at the logical impasse. Was he talking to Tess, or was the dog lying? He wasn't sure, but he was too happy to care. "Okay, you clever dog, you can sleep wherever you want."

48

Not everyone could sleep wherever they wanted. Addie's bed was quite comfortable, complete with an attendant to make it up with clean linens every day, but she would have preferred to sleep on the ground in freedom. She knew the attendant was not really there to make the bed, but to search it—along with every nook and cranny of the room as it was cleaned twice a day.

Addie wondered what they imagined they would find. With every corner of the room under 24/7 surveillance by video cameras, when would she have the opportunity to receive any contraband? And the searches weren't confined to the room. Every cavity of her body had received daily attention from a woman who claimed to be a doctor, though Addie had never met her when she was serving at the clinic as Tess's nurse.

The searches had been doubled after Addie was visited by Arnie Danielson, the attorney her uncle Qasim's brother-in-law had asked to handle the case. Arnie had tried to bring her chocolates from Uncle Qasim, but those had been confiscated. Not that she was deprived of chocolate—hers was an upholstered prison, but a prison all the same. And she had done nothing. Nothing at all.

She hadn't even known what they thought she'd done until Arnie told her. How could they imagine she had murdered someone—a patient, no less? It went against her life's dedication, and now they were trying to make her confess. They'd tried just about everything except torture, and now that horrible Lucinda Somebody was hinting that torture wasn't out of the question. Well, she was a trained nurse. Before she confessed to murder, she would find a way to kill herself.

49

Uncle Suhayb happened to be visiting when Roger demonstrated his cheap, portable, seizure-detecting snood to executives from an epilepsy foundation. After they left, Suhayb pointed out their enthusiasm and suggested that Roger earn some money by manufacturing the cap for sale. It would help thousands of people, but Roger wasn't interested in helping thousands. He had helping only two people on his mind, and one of them persuaded him to allow his uncle to undertake the epilepsy project.

As a first step, Suhayb retained intellectual property attorneys, Nate and Sarah Gold, a middle-aged Jewish couple. They were exiles from Iran, but definitely not Zionists. Sarah reminded Roger of Tess, the way she took charge quickly, incorporating Roger as a research and development company. That was the easy part. Next she filed six broad patents, which to Roger involved an enormous amount of distracting paperwork. "Why go through all this trouble?" he complained. "There's still a lot of work to do."

"Like what?" Sarah asked.

"Miniaturization, for one thing. And cost reduction—don't they want a lower price?"

Sarah banged both sides of her head with her palms. "*Oy*, another perfectionist." She reached over, standing on her toes, and shook Roger by the shoulders. "If MIT had this idea—only the idea—they would have publicized the idea seven years before they had a working model. And patented it. And sold it. Just an idea—and you, you have a working model." That ended the debate.

From then on, Sarah took over, starting a chain of events that tumbled forward much too fast for Roger's methodical mind. Sarah organized a bidding contest among more than thirty rival medical instrument firms based solely on the patent applications and an impressive demonstration. The winning company offered an advance of $550,000 plus a substantial royalty on each cap sold, but only $50,000 of the advance would be paid up front until the patents were approved.

Roger should have been delighted with this windfall, but when Sarah delivered the check, he fell into a deep depression. Sarah noticed immediately. "What's wrong, dear? Didn't we get enough?"

"I didn't know it was so easy to get money for my ideas. Don't get me wrong. The money will help, and I'm grateful, but it's still not enough to buy the magnet Tess needs."

"Don't worry. The royalties are sure to be more than you'll need. You could buy a solid-gold magnet."

Roger wondered for a moment how Sarah could be a successful intellectual property attorney if she thought gold could be magnetized, but his amusement faded quickly. "That won't be for several years, at least. The doctors don't think she can wait that long. I know I can't."

"It's not usually so easy," said Nate. "So don't get spoiled. But when you have something original, with a ready market—"

"And a good attorney," Sarah interrupted, smiling.

"—the right parties will be willing to fight over you. And don't worry, they'll make plenty off this. It's not a gift. And if you need more, you can borrow against the contract. At a discount, of course."

Roger did some calculations in his head. "It still won't be enough money for the magnet. And I've wasted so much time with the government. We could have been so much farther along . . . Tess might have been cured by now."

Sarah held him by the forearms. "If I didn't know better, I'd say you had a Jewish mother."

"No, I had a Muslim mother, and I was too proud to ask my family for help. Not until we'd wasted all that time."

"So, what do you want?" Nate asked. "A medal for your suffering? I *did* have a Jewish mother and I had to grow out of it. That's what you need to do now."

"But I wasted so much time."

"So now you want to waste some more, kicking yourself?" Nate took off his alligator shoe and extended it to Roger. "Here. Kick yourself with the best so you get over it quickly."

"Listen to my husband," Sarah said. "He knows. The more time you spend kicking yourself, the less money we make. Stop kicking already and go invent something else."

50

No amount of money could expunge Roger's depression, but the cash advance was sufficient for Roger to fight off the mood long enough to buy and repair a small, broken, low-power MRI machine left over when two local hospitals consolidated. Roger's uncles used the leftover money—and a few dollars they chipped in—to outfit the garage to Roger's specifications. They walled off one of the old service bays with concrete blocks and lined it with copper shielding to produce a Faraday cage that would shield the sensitive equipment from radio frequency waves from ambient sources. Eventually, they would make it a magnetically shielded room, but for now they didn't have the time or money for that refinement.

But Roger was even more depressed when the machine was all ready to run. The magnet was not as powerful as the original and would yield different brain patterns. Limited as she was to responding with a slow yes or no, Tess could offer only limited help reprogramming the pattern recognition and speech synthesis software to produce a fraction of the former capability. Roger would hold a program segment on the monitor in front of her eyes, moving it to keep the key part within her field of focus. In this awkward way, she would study the code, either approving or disapproving. If she disapproved, Roger usually had to play twenty questions to narrow down the bug.

This debugging process proved excruciating, yet he suffered even more from the inability to access her design talent. She had always provided the truly imaginative software brains of their team. Without her designs, Roger simply couldn't focus his mind on the massive job of starting from scratch.

Don called several times, eventually coming in person. He pretended they were social calls, but his true agenda was obvious even to Roger. Don hoped to persuade them to return to the clinic and finish the job there. And, with each offer, Don raised the stakes. As each day passed without Tess's full communication, let alone any sign of recovery, Roger grew increasingly tempted.

On the hottest day of the summer, Bart and his father were finally installing a decent air-conditioning system while Roger sat by Tess's bed, brushing her teeth with her electric toothbrush. "Why not take advantage of Don's desperation? Just until we get you cured."

Heidi raised her left paw. Tess was saying NO.

"He says maybe he can get Addie a better deal."

NO.

"I can't stand this, Tess, being out of touch with you. I need your help."

Heidi jumped off the bed, ran to Roger, and tugged on his sleeve—the GET HELP response.

"I'm right here. What help do you need?"

NO.

"No, what?"

Heidi ran to the door and unlocked it. Then she ran back and tugged on Roger's sleeve again. Then back to the door.

"Do you mean go *out* and get some help?"

Heidi raised her right paw. YES.

"But who?"

Heidi sat down, then rolled over, stood up and sat again.

"Stop it, Heidi. I get the message. Get help."

Heidi stood up and barked, then sat, rolled, and sat again.

"Stop doing tricks, Heidi. I'm trying to understand what Tess is—" Roger hit himself on top of the head with both hands. "You're trying to send a coded message."

YES.

"But what it is? Sit. Roll over. Sit again. Is it binary?"

Heidi raised her left paw—NO—and began to bark. Howler came bounding through the door and licked Heidi's nose. Bart stuck his head in the door. "What's she barking at? Howler's upset."

"I don't know. Tess is trying to send me some kind of code, through Heidi, but I can't figure out what it is."

"What do you have so far?"

"I'm supposed to get help."

YES.

"See, she's confirming that part's right. But I don't get the rest."

"What's the rest?"

"She does a sit, then a rollover, then another sit. What can that be?" Howler watched Heidi's demonstration, tail wagging, ready to play at the slightest invitation. But he was a service dog, and held his position.

"Maybe she's spelling something with the commands? Like the first letters?"

"S R S? That doesn't mean anything."

"But the command isn't ROLL OVER. It's OVER."

"Oh, damn," said Roger, slapping himself on the side of the head. "It's SOS."

51

Though Heidi had never met SOS, she didn't bark when he showed up at their front door two days later carrying a huge bunch of daisies. Roger was concerned about SOS spying on them, but he trusted Heidi's judgment. He led the gawky programmer on a tour of their new facilities, then sat next to Tess's bed and offered a demonstration of how Tess had made Heidi find him when she needed help.

"Ice cool," SOS said.

"Well, it was good of you to come all the way down here. I'm sure Tess appreciates it, too."

Heidi raised her right paw, and Roger explained the signal.

SOS stared at the dog with great respect. "An adaptive system. Absolute zero. When—"

Much to Roger's relief, Heidi put her front paws on SOS's lap, preempting a lecture on adaptive systems. SOS bent over and exchanged sniffs with Heidi. "But, hey, I don't deserve a parade. After this, I'm going to visit my Mom, too. But why the invitation?"

"I was hoping you could suggest someone to help me reconstruct our software. I've got to start from scratch, and I'm just not up to it."

SOS laughed and absentmindedly wiped his nose on the hem of his T-shirt. "I've got something better." He reached in his shirt pocket and took out a compact memory unit. "Here's all the software you'll need."

Roger stared at the unit, but wouldn't take it. "I appreciate the offer, Stephen, but I can't use any of their software."

"It's not theirs. I rewrote everything from scratch, on my own computer on my own time. Refactored it. And don't call me Stephen or I'll give you a lecture on refactoring." He smiled as if he were beginning to understand that his lectures were not always appreciated.

"All right, it's SOS's software then. We'll hear the lecture another time." He took the gift, acknowledging it with a nod of his head. "But I can't let you work with me. Don would never allow it."

"Doesn't matter. I quit yesterday."

"Quit? Why? What did Don do to you?"

"Oh, Don's okay, I guess, but he won't let me visit Addie. It was mostly that Wyatt bozo."

"Wyatt? My old professor? That *Qa'Hom.*"

SOS tossed a concerned glance in Tess's direction.

"That's all right. Tess understands Klingon."

"Rapacious! That describes Wyatt perfectly—'not even worth the trouble to kill.' Personally, I've been calling him the *qoH.*"

Roger spit out a Klingon phrase, laughing. "*Hegh neH chav qoH.*"

"A fool's only achievement is death," SOS translated, completing their Trekkie bonding ritual. "Of course, the *qoH* says you stole all his achievements."

Roger took SOS's bony elbow and guided him closer to Tess so she could hear his gentle voice. "So what's that *qoH* have to do with this?"

"When you left, Don brought him in to lead the project. Can you believe it? That's why I left. He's totally screwed things up."

"So you left?"

"Yeah. You wouldn't believe the crap he's done."

"Oh, I'd believe it. Tess would, too, wouldn't you?"

Heidi raised her right paw.

"What kinds of things did Wyatt manage to do to the project?"

"Well, the first thing he did was chew me out for some sloppy coding. Once I looked at it, I could tell it was Wyatt's code—not mine! Then he insisted on coding stuff himself. What a *p'tahk*. He can't do anything right, but he refuses to have anyone else review his code."

"You're right about his being a *p'tahk*, but how did you know if you couldn't see his code?"

SOS laughed, his curious high-pitched giggle. "You're kidding, right? Do you think he could hide code from me? Anywhere in the system?"

Heidi raised her left paw, while Roger said, "No, I guess not. What else?"

"Isn't that enough? Well, if you insist. We spent a week entering his project plan into some planning software, printed all kinds of charts, but we've never updated any of it as the project has changed. But he still shows those charts to Don, as if everything were right on schedule."

"Typical."

Heidi raised her paw, and SOS reached down and scratched her chest. "The one thing that really pissed me off was when he noticed a bug in the system and never reported it. Then, when I found it after searching for half a day, he just shrugged and claimed he knew about it already. Geez, if he knew about it, why didn't he tell someone? Definitely *qoH*."

"And why did he tell you he knew about it, after you'd spent half a day looking for it? You'd think he'd be ashamed and want to keep it secret."

"Oh, he never keeps anything secret if he can give a lecture about it. What a bore! He's always—" SOS seemed to come out of a trance, staring at Roger. "What are you laughing at?"

"Because you're starting to give us a lecture on how boring lectures are."

SOS clapped his hands. "Glacial! A meta-lecture. Well, that's appropriate, because Professor Wyatt is meta-stupid. He's stupid about how stupid he is. How did he ever get a Ph.D.?"

"Degrees are less about intelligence and more about doing what you're told. He was always good at doing what he was told. At least by that Inga person. Have you seen her?"

"The battleship? You bet! She's been out several times, snooping around. I don't think she understands anything, but she has to have a copy of everything. At least she kept him out of my hair for a few days at a time."

Roger thought that removing anything from SOS's bounteous hair might prove difficult, but he didn't say anything. SOS reflected for a moment, then continued his litany of complaints. "Maybe that's why he orders everyone else around, like the Grand Imperial Khan of the Galaxy. Once, when I told him it would take three days to finish one of his bright ideas, he ordered me to code faster."

"Yep, sounds like Wyatt. I can see why you left."

"That's not *really* why I left."

"Did he fire you?"

"Nope. He wasn't that beetle-headed. He needed me."

"Then why did you leave?"

SOS gazed down at the floor and reddened. "Because of what they're doing to your cousin. To Addie."

Roger suddenly realized he was being the *qoH*. Tess had probably figured this out the minute SOS came in the door with the flowers. He became aware of SOS saying, ". . . raw deal. She could never have done such a thing. They're looking for a scapegoat because their own security broke down. They should have—"

Roger held up both his palms. "Calm down, SOS. You don't have to convince us. Tess saw the murderer, and it wasn't Addie."

"That was the rumor. So who was it? Why are they keeping Addie?"

"It was someone Tess doesn't know. And not one of the nurses, unless one of them wasn't in the database."

SOS combed his scraggly beard with his fingers. "That's entirely possible. The clinic doesn't do a sterling job keeping that file up to date. They had my own personnel record all wrong." He rolled his eyes toward the ceiling. "Not that I have a password into the personnel records, mind you."

"I don't think that would stop you," Roger laughed. "Not if you really wanted to see those records."

SOS's angular face brightened. "Do you want me to get Tess another look at them?"

"Let's not do anything illegal—not just yet." He explained how the Aremac would enable Tess to display the murder scene so the nurse could be identified.

SOS thought that was rather chancy. "And Wyatt sure won't go in that direction. He's stuck on the verbal business."

"Well, they don't believe what Tess *says*. We have to *show* them."

"So what's holding you up?"

"Money. We earned some," he gestured around at all the new and reconditioned equipment, "to get all this. But things would go faster if we had more."

"I'm no lawyer, but you ought to sue the University and the government for what they did to Tess. They ought to pay plenty."

Heidi raised her right paw. Roger shook his head. "The lawyers are still working on an insurance settlement. If we sue, it will only slow that down."

Heidi raised her left paw. "All right," Roger conceded. "I'm outnumbered two to one. Three to one, if you count Heidi. I don't want to waste my time on a lawsuit, but I'll ask Arnie if he's got a partner who can handle a suit."

"Who's Arnie?"

"He's the lawyer defending Addie. Trying to, anyway. The government's not making it easy."

"Is he good?"

"From what I can tell, he's the best. Especially likes to take on the federal government these days. He thinks they're raping the Constitution."

"He must be expensive."

"He's doing it for nothing. *Pro bono.*" Heidi alerted and wagged her tail. "Calm down, Heidi." He turned to SOS. "She doesn't understand Latin. She thinks it means 'for the bone,' not 'for the good.' Anyway, Arnie believes he can make legal history while doing some good."

"Me, too."

"You want to make legal history?"

"No, I mean I'll work for nothing. To do some good. I want to get Addie out of this, and I want to help Tess recover. I'd—"

"No way. I'd have to pay you."

"I don't need the money. Honestly. I'm a single guy, and I can live with Mom in Evanston."

"Everybody needs money."

"I've got stock options from two start-ups I worked for. I was downsized when the big guys bought them out, but they paid off in these options. I've sold some of them, and the rest are worth a pile. How about you pay me by giving me a share in royalties from whatever we invent? I've been thinking about this a lot." He pointed to the compact memory unit still in Roger's hand. "Wait 'til you see. I've got some great ideas."

Roger extended his hand to shake on the deal, wondering if he had been as naive as SOS just a few months ago. "Fair enough. Let's see what you've got."

52

Even on the Eastern Shore of Lake Michigan, the July heat was stifling, but Lucinda had insisted they open the window while they interrogated Adara. Don dabbed at the sweat on his face, but the towel was already far too wet to do any good. "This heat is torture. Even I feel like confessing something."

The heat didn't seem to be bothering Lucinda. "That's precisely the point. We get the benefit of torture, but nobody can accuse us, since we're undergoing the same conditions ourselves."

"You don't seem to be suffering much."

"I learned to take the heat all those years in the desert. And she's an Arab. She should be genetically able to stand the heat."

Don looked at Adara, strapped to the table, moaning softly. "If you thought that she could tolerate the heat, you wouldn't be doing it. And obviously, she can't."

"Her problem. Our solution."

"It won't be a solution if it kills her."

"A little heat is not going to kill her."

"Maybe not, but it's making her responses erratic. Just look at the log. The machine can't make heads or tails out of them."

"That's just Wyatt's asinine device. You never should have let Stephen leave. You could have kept him here."

"I couldn't have made SOS do any work, or stopped him from sabotaging the machine."

Lucinda imitated spitting on the floor. "Wyatt does his own sabotage—without help."

"You don't know that. It's probably the heat that's causing Wyatt's sensors to behave erratically. Anyway, nothing we obtain this way is going to hold up in court."

"We don't need court. What we need is to discover her coconspirators. When she rats them out, we'll finally be able to stop these congressional attacks."

"Maybe Roger was right." Don had long ago removed his tie and jacket. Now he debated stripping to his undershirt. "Maybe the end doesn't justify the means." Addie seemed like a sweet, innocent kid, and he'd been having bad dreams ever since they'd started these interrogations. "Maybe torture doesn't justify what it does to the torturers."

Lucinda turned up the magnetic field strength, even though more power to the magnet meant the heat would grow worse. "It doesn't worry me. And it didn't worry you when you were torturing our previous prisoner."

"We *knew* he was a terrorist. She's just a suspect."

"Don't pussyfoot with me, Don. We have a witness who saw her coming out of that room."

"It could have been someone else. There are plenty of people working here, and you know how reliable eyewitnesses are. Especially since the guard had no reason to suspect any wrongdoing at the time."

Lucinda thought about that for a while. "Not that many people knew our man was here. Addie knew."

"It was in the goddamn newspapers." He wiped the sweat from his neck with the blade of his hand.

"Not that much detail. But Addie would have known more, through her cousin. And everyone else here has a high clearance."

"Anybody's services can be bought, if the price is right."

"Well, anybody can be made to talk, if the price is right," she countered.

"You may be right. What I'd like to do is check all the other women here. Using the machine—but no torture."

"The director won't allow it. You'd destroy morale."

"Dammit, LD, these bombings are destroying morale."

"And are you going to interrogate all the men, too?" Lucinda sneered. "It could have been a guy in drag. Just how farfetched is your investigation going to get because you're a little squeamish?"

Lucinda reached for the controls again, but Don put out a restraining hand. "Don't you think that's enough for one day? Let's break it off and get some iced tea. Some food."

"I'm not hungry. And you're just another pussy who can't stand seeing a woman cry."

Don was used to Lucinda's male-baiting. He let her remark pass. "We also have a witness who says it wasn't Addie."

"A witness with more than a little bias."

"Here's what puzzles me." He toweled some sweat off Addie's face. "If Tess were involved—even if she just wanted to keep her cousin out of trouble—"

"It's not her cousin. It's her husband's cousin."

"Whatever. If she were involved, why would she tell us she saw a murder? She could have said she saw him jump. Without her testimony, we'd have no way to know it wasn't suicide."

"Except for his legs. He wasn't capable of walking to that balcony," Lucinda glanced at the room's thermostat, then ran the magnet up one more notch, "let alone climbing over the railing."

"She didn't know he had no legs."

"So she says."

Don decided it was time to remove his shirt. "Besides, he was a determined man, probably a fanatic. If he was committed to killing himself, he could have done it. And he was committed."

"How do you know that?"

"He had that poison pill in his tooth. He would have used it if we hadn't removed it. The forensic lab says it was put in very recently—"

"Biting into a poison pill is one thing. Hauling yourself out of bed and over a railing without legs is quite another. If you don't believe that, let's bring little Mrs. Fixman back up here and see how she likes the heat."

"That's not going to happen. Besides, in her condition, you could do your worst and she wouldn't feel a thing."

Lucinda shuddered, showing her deep disgust at the thought of being so helpless. "I'd rather have the pain."

53

Much to Roger's surprise, Arnie was able to get the magnet company to settle their part of Tess's damage claims by donating a new high-powered magnet. The claims against the University and the government were still pending, and Arnie thought they would take years to adjudicate, but that wasn't what worried Roger. Tess's new doctors had just confirmed that the longer she was vegetative, the less chance she had of recovering control of her body. He committed himself to reducing Tess's helplessness within a month.

Although SOS's ultimate goal was to free Addie through the Aremac's full visual processing, Roger's plan put him full time on improving Tess's communication. Once that was working, she could add her considerable talents to the Aremac research. Sarah Gold believed that combining audio memories with video might prove a more viable commercial project, but in spite of her urging, money was a secondary goal.

SOS's new software design combined meaningful phrases with improved syntax using a sophisticated algorithm. As the software adapted to her speech patterns, Tess improved her speed and fluency almost every hour. She still had little mobility in her wheelchair, but with Heidi at her side, she could answer simple yes/no questions. By using Tess's ability to vocalize her thoughts under the magnet, Bart trained Heidi to lift first one forefoot, then the other, to mean "MAYBE." And barking rapidly meant "REPHRASE THE QUESTION." But Tess chafed under the choice between mobility with a crude signal versus sophisticated speech lying flat on her back.

To address her frustration, Roger toiled every waking hour— and in his dreams—to improve his sensors. One small step at a time, he was able to pack more sensors into a snood, and more sensors meant it could function with less and less powerful magnets. Less powerful magnets meant a smaller, lighter, and more portable communication system, eventually producing one that could be carried on her electric wheelchair.

After a few trials around the block and to the local park to watch children playing, Tess proclaimed that she was ready for a real field trip—shopping. Using her mind, she could point her chair so she was facing something she wanted to buy, then answer yes/no questions as the clerk picked up the precise selection. Bart rigged a collar so Heidi could carry a small money purse. He trained her to put her paws on a counter to allow a clerk to take money, give change, and place Tess's purchase in a sack. Heidi would take the sack in her mouth and deposit it in Tess's lap.

Although Roger worried about some of the layabouts in the neighborhood, Tess convinced him that nobody would dare attempt to grab Heidi's purse. After three cautious test runs with Roger lurking a safe distance away, daily neighborhood shopping trips became the norm. This was a small triumph, but one that lifted everyone's spirits a thousand percent.

Roger had other ideas for improving Tess's communication and mobility, but she persuaded him that she was fine for the time being. She was actually losing hope that her condition would ever improve, but Addie was rotting in federal custody, so Roger needed to devote his full attention to the Aremac.

The new snood helped immensely. Roger experimented on himself with this more sensitive device, staring at photographs and trying to focus them in his mind. He didn't have much luck. The machine picked up mental patterns, but nothing seemed correlated with the photos.

Tess watched his frustration. "How about letting me try?" her mechanical voice asked, jolting Roger back to the present.

"No way. Your career as guinea pig is over. Isn't one experience enough for you?"

"It can't hurt. You're not getting anywhere."

Roger still wasn't used to her new artificial voice. More realistic though it was, it still wasn't Tess. He was tempted, but shook it off. "No way."

"If you won't let me try, why don't you try something simpler?"

"Photos are already too simple. We need to capture moving pictures. In color."

"Stop being the perfectionist. Black-and-white would be quite adequate for showing them it wasn't Addie."

"All right," he conceded. "Maybe black-and-white, but the pictures have to move. To show the murder."

"I'd be willing to risk it, for lack of anything better. Roger, you've got to work up to this thing in smaller steps. You're not getting anywhere, and you're losing your ability to think clearly."

"Dammit, you keep telling me that Addie doesn't have much time, and that you've given up on improving. Then you tell me to slow down and be patient."

"Look, Arnie can stall her trial if we need him to. And even if she's convicted, there are always appeals if we can show new evidence."

"That's not going to help *you*." Roger tore the snood off his head, banging the cable against the magnet's housing. "And she could get the death penalty for murdering a federal witness. There's no appeal if you're dead."

"She's not going to get the death penalty. And if she did, the appeals would take years."

"And in the meantime, she's rotting in jail. At least you can go to the corner store and buy dog treats."

"OUCH," Tess's machine voice shouted. "That was a low blow."

"Sorry." He didn't sound the least bit sorry.

After a seemingly endless silence, SOS peered in the door and knocked gently. "Is everybody dead in here? How come so quiet?"

"You should talk," Roger snapped. "Why are you creeping around?"

"Woo hoo. What's eating you, buddy?"

"Nothing."

"Well, I've got something." SOS fanned a small sheaf of paper, each page covered with row after row of hexadecimal characters. "Take a look at this dump."

"What? You're wasting paper again? We're not getting paid by the federal government anymore. What's wrong with your—"

Tess cut him off. "Let me see it, sos." The machine voice rhymed "sos" with "close," instead of "gloss." Tess refused to call him SOS because it caused the machine to shout, and she didn't want to bother spelling out the individual letters "ess oh ess" every time. Roger had promised to fix it "when he had time," but lately, he never had time.

SOS peeled back the first few pages of the dump until he found the one he wanted. He conspicuously held it in front of the nearest camera, as if he were afraid to come too close to Roger. "This is the one you want to see. The rest I can transfer to the server."

The camera's lens changed focus to catch the entire page in a close-up. "What am I seeing?" Tess asked.

"It's a coded form of the information generated by Roger's brain while he was scanning a photo. You won't understand it unless you look at it in relation to the photo. Bring E-14 up on your screen."

She mentally accessed the photo file and saw a picture she recognized as a black-and-white, frontal view of the Parthenon. "Okay, I have it. Now what am I supposed to notice about it?"

"Count the Parthenon's columns. There's eight of them, and seven shadowy spaces between them."

"I see that. So what?"

"Now look at the printout."

"All I see is random garbage. A typical hex dump."

"Not totally random. Focus on the middle of the page— starting about ten lines down and a little left of center. What do you see?"

"Hold on. . . . OH."

While they'd been talking, Roger had pulled up the same picture on his own screen. "Don't shout. 'Oh' what?"

"The sequence of characters repeats itself."

"I don't see it."

"Look for the letters BAFECF. It starts there and continues for a long string. Almost identical for a hundred digits or more."

"Okay, I see those letters. So?"

"Isn't it obvious?" SOS asked.

"Not to me." Too late, Roger realized that he'd just invited SOS to deliver a lecture.

"The BAFECF pattern repeats seven times, then the eighth time, it starts out the same, but cuts off into something entirely different." He pulled the paper away from the camera and turned to the last page. "Here. I've reformatted the printout so each of those lines starts with the BAFECF. The patterns are easier to see when they're lined up. They start—"

"I see it," Tess interrupted. "It definitely repeats."

Roger looked away from the screen and rubbed his eyes. "Not in what I see, it doesn't. There's lots of little differences between the first few lines. And at line five, there's a huge difference. And more on line six."

"Exactly," said SOS. "Take a look again at the photo of the Parthenon. See the shadow between column five and column six?" He grabbed a screwdriver and began using it as a pointer. "See that big patch of sunlight here at the top of the shadow? And between six and seven, look at this big patch at the bottom. I think it's because of holes in the roof. Something like that."

"And you think the patterns are what Roger's mind sees as he scans the columns?"

Roger slapped himself on the forehead.

"Hey pal. Watch it," SOS teased. "One day you're going to hurt yourself like that."

"Very funny. I'm just hitting myself for being so stupid."

"Good. So now you see that those shadows correspond to the breaks in the BAFECF pattern."

"Yes, of course. We've got it! Our first hook!" He jumped up and hugged Tess's inert body. "You were right. I should have started with simpler pictures."

"Be careful you don't injure me, dear. I won't feel it if you do. How about you let up a bit and go find some line drawings."

"Try searching the Web for clip art," SOS suggested.

"And plaid patterns," Roger said.

The two men argued for several minutes over where they could find the best pictures to try next. They stopped when they saw Tess had filled their screens with a pattern of subtle earthen pinks, yellows, and browns, highlighted by bands of black, white, and gray. "You guys have no imagination," she said. "Here, look at what I found on the Web."

"What is it?" they asked almost simultaneously.

"It's a picture of a Navajo rug. This particular pattern is called Wide Ruins. It's one of the simplest. Once you've deciphered this one, boys, I'll find you a bright red, white, and black Klagetoh, with a double-diamond center. Or maybe an Eye Dazzler. That should keep your little brains humming."

54

It was neither the kind of day nor the kind of setting Nazim Halabi wished for. The weather was oppressively hot and humid, and the air-conditioning Qasim and Bart had installed in the converted garage was turned down low to protect the thought-controlled wheelchair he was trying to sell to his venture capitalist friends. The entire situation didn't look good, and it didn't feel good, even to Roger.

As the two venture capitalists came inside, they wrinkled their noses at the Spartan surroundings. Roger was already sweating from walking about forty steps from their silver Rolls limo in the penetrating sun. As Roger followed the VCs inside, he thought, *Their sweat must be turning clammy under their designer wool blazer and cashmere sport coat. Conditions might be ideal for selling temperature-control systems, but not for selling a thought-controlled wheelchair for paraplegics.* Even if conditions were perfect, Roger would rather not have been here. He had work to do to meet his commitment to himself, but the VCs always insisted on meeting the inventor.

"What's the total market?" the taller VC asked. Roger estimated that the man's haircut—hairstyling, they called it—must have cost $150.

Nazim had done his research. "There are about twelve thousand spinal cord injuries in the United States each year. Perhaps half of them could put this device to good use."

"So, six thousand a year. With a market penetration of twenty percent, that would be twelve hundred systems a year. What's the cost of goods?"

"About eighteen-thousand five-hundred dollars at present prices. With volume, that would go down."

"Then there's assembly and testing, marketing, liability insurance—that would be high for a device like this—"

"We figure total cost at twenty-five to thirty thousand, depending on marketing."

As Nazim answered, the shorter VC scribed something in his fashion-statement PDA, and then said, "Okay. So, what's the competition?"

Roger knew that discussion of the competition was Sarah Gold's territory. She'd been staying in the background, letting the men run the show, but now her courtroom voice commanded their attention. "We've got fourteen patents locked up. I know you've researched competing technology, so you know there's nothing this advanced. It will be at least five years before someone can work around our patents and build something comparable."

While Sarah spoke, Roger glared at the shorter VC. *Your hairpiece looks obscenely expensive, probably custom-built.*

Turning to face his partner, Shorty smiled slowly, "Given the five-year horizon, we can set gross margin at any level we wish." He keyed a figure in his PDA, "Let's say seventy percent."

Nazim had warned Roger not to say anything unless asked a direct question, but his young nephew was no trader. Like most inventors in the presence of venture capitalists, he simply couldn't keep his mouth shut. "That sounds kind of high. I'd hoped this would be available to the masses."

"We're not underwriting a charity here, sonny," Shorty lectured. "You take what you can get, as much as you can get, while you can still get it. As soon as this product hits the shows, we'll have imitators up the wazoo. Seventy percent is the minimum we can afford, and that's cutting it close. Remember, it's only gross margin."

Longlegs finished doing his own calculation. "That makes a nice round hundred thou selling price—ninety-nine, to sound more charitable. So, how many of these cripples can afford that much?"

Roger winced and almost spoke out again, but Nazim was ready for the question. "We figure insurance will pay for most of them. Also, there are federal programs."

"They're going to drag their feet on a high-ticket item like this," Shorty said. "Figure four years, maybe five, to get the device on their approved list. That's a long time before we see significant cash flow. And maybe never. I don't like the risks."

"On the other hand, you have to figure in follow-on income. Parts replacement. Service. Training. That's all gravy," Nazim said.

"But the gravy doesn't flow unless—and until—you've got product out in the field," said Longlegs. "Then, even more delay. I can spreadsheet this, but I can tell you right now, it's not going to be cost-effective. Even at a thousand chairs annually, that's only a gross margin of seventy mil. By the time we recover expenses and our return on investment, most of that will be . . ." he flicked closed the platinum cover of his PDA, ". . . gone."

"But it is interesting," said Shorty. "What else can you do?"

"Nothing, really," Roger said. "Everything else is in rough prototype."

"We love rough prototypes," Shorty beamed, showing some real interest for the first time.

Sure you do, thought Roger. *You can demand a bigger share for your money.* When Nazim asked him to demonstrate the Aremac, Roger had to respond. "It's not just rough. It's vulgar. I'd really rather not show it."

"Show it anyway," Tess's machine voice said. Even though they'd seen Tess demonstrate the wheelchair before she was moved to her table to rest, the two VCs startled at the sound of her voice. Regaining their cool exteriors, they demanded an explanation of Tess's device.

"My master's voice," said Roger. "She's using the voice-only version. Step over here by the big magnet." Taking the snood off Tess, he began pulling it onto his own head. "I have to warn you again, this is the Aremac.0.3, a long way from release to the public."

Roger handed the shorter VC a stack of photos. "Pick one, then show it to me for an instant, then put it back." He lay down on the table and inserted his head in the magnet's aperture.

The VC riffled through the pack and chose a picture of a jet-black spider with distinct bright-yellow spots on its thorax and on the joints of its long legs. He held it up as instructed, then placed it face down on the pack. Roger pointed to the 1.5-meter flat panel on the near wall. "Now look at the screen. What you're seeing is from my head."

On the screen, many times life-size, was the spider, not quite as sharp as the photo, but with clearly delineated black and yellow areas, plus a small brown spot on the anterior of the thorax. Shorty checked the photo, then the screen. His mask of indifference cracked a bit, and he actually seemed impressed. "I didn't notice the brown spot before, but it's really in the photo."

Longlegs stepped forward to examine the screen more carefully, tracing details with his index finger. "Look at these faint lines. It's the web."

"Some are missing from the picture," said his partner.

"I warned you that it is only a prototype. And moving pictures are even worse."

"You can do movies?" Longlegs asked.

"Not well enough to show you," Roger glanced at Tess, "regardless of what my lord and master says."

The VCs tried a few more photos—a bear, a pair of lemurs, the Taj Mahal, and a World War II cannon. Then they huddled around their PDAs for what seemed like an eternity. After fifteen minutes, Shorty turned to Nazim. "We'll take two thirds, for a million up front, with a reserve of two mil more if the pictures improve and you can do movies."

Roger was about to speak, but Nazim told him sharply in Arabic to be silent. Then Nazim spoke English to their guests. "Thank you. We'll consider it and get back to you."

Roger remained quiet until the VCs walked out of sight on the way to their silver Rolls. Then he turned to Nazim. "If I understood that correctly, they offered us three million dollars."

"For two thirds of your company."

"Shouldn't we take it? With that kind of money, I could refine the Aremac to the point where we could easily clear Addie."

"That's only their first offer. And they're the first people who've seen it."

"How can you be so calm? It's your daughter we're talking about."

"And it's Adara I'm thinking about. Never show them your bottom line."

"But we need the money."

"Perhaps, but you don't need them controlling your research. They will let you develop the quality just far enough to get a marketable product. The Aremac has many possible applications—military intelligence is only one—and as soon as one becomes commercially viable, they'll go for the cash flow, not further development. That would probably be well short of the quality we need to free Adara."

Roger was ashamed of himself for acting like such a novice. "I didn't think of that, Uncle. I'm sorry."

"Not to worry. Negotiation is my job. Inventing is yours. Let's go back inside and discuss this further. This heat is too much. Perhaps I've been away from the desert too long. And, I think your lovely wife and your—well, not-so-lovely lawyer—will want to participate."

55

Sarah Gold may not have been lovely, but Roger had already learned that this short, stubby, middle-aged Iranian Jewish lady had a mind that cut through problems like hot piano wire cut through ice. With a tongue to match. "My mother says I was born at night, but I wasn't born last night. Who did they think we are— ignorant Arabs living in tents?"

Nazim laughed at the insult. Sarah reached way up and clasped Roger on the shoulder. "Young man, you have a fortune here, and they thought they could steal it for twenty rials. You were very smart to have kept your mouth shut."

"It was a lot of money. I would have said something, but Uncle Nazim told me to shut up."

"I know, but you listened to him. And now I want you to listen to me. Whatever you do, don't sell even a fraction of your rights in this invention. Not for any price. Sleep on a rock and eat sand, but raise the money you need by yourself."

"So you think it will be valuable someday?"

"Someday? Someday?" She cupped her gray hair in both hands as if she were holding her brain from flying out. "I can use it tomorrow, and I'll pay you a pretty sum just for one use." She straightened her ivory-colored linen skirt over her adequate hips.

"Actually, my *client* will pay you a pretty sum. Out of her settlement."

Sarah explained that her case involved a disputed contract over motion picture rights to her client's short story, "The Philosopher Pooch." The author, Constance Runemaker Ackely, had sold the story twenty years ago to a college literary magazine, long defunct. The only payment she received was five free copies of the magazine, and in the excitement over her successful career as a novelist, she had forgotten about the story until the movie came out and topped the charts for six weeks in a row. The producer had read a reprint of the story in his dentist's office, liked the possibilities, and purchased the movie rights from the college for a share of the movie's profits. That share was now worth more than forty million dollars. Connie believed that at least some of that money belonged to her.

Unfortunately, she couldn't find her contract for the story. The college's attorney claimed he couldn't locate the college's copy, either, but that it surely was their standard contract, one which reserved all rights to the college. Connie knew she had signed away only first North American   rights, but she had no way to prove it, so it was her word against the college's. When the college accused her of lying, Connie engaged Sarah's services to sue for her share.

"It's one of those he-said-she-said cases," Sarah explained. "A form of financial rape. But I believe Connie, and she says she has a clear memory of being in the editor's office and making him strike the 'all rights' clause. If you can display that memory with your machine, and convince the jury that it's real, she'll be a rich lady. She deserves it—and so do I." She lowered her head modestly.

"But she could fake the memory, couldn't she?" Nazim asked.

"Roger has a way of detecting the difference between a real memory and a manufactured one," Sarah answered. "If you want a technical explanation, though, you'll have to ask Roger."

"Not needed. If Roger says so, I believe him." Nazim rubbed his thumb and forefinger together. "Okay, what's your fee?"

"Nothing if we don't win. It's a contingency."

"You didn't answer my question."

"Well, if you must know, after expenses are taken out, our firm would get one third of the royalties, plus any punitive damages. My own share comes out of that. It was a long-shot case."

"Your firm?" Roger asked. "I thought it was just Gold and Gold. Just you and Nate."

"It is, but my husband always insists on his half."

"You're really a piece of work, Sarah. I'm glad you're on my side."

"I like to think I'm on the side of justice. Let's see if your machine . . . your Aremac . . . can help my poor author."

56

Inga Steinman had just finished her first *gâteau Saint-Honoré* and dug her spoon into the quart of marshmallow chocolate fudge ice cream when the cell phone rang. The special phone. She would never have interrupted her nightly delight for any other call. She wiped her hands on a roll of paper towels before she dug into her purse for the phone. She hated interrupting her snack. Other people wouldn't interrupt sex for a phone call, so why should she have to delay her greatest pleasure? She hoped her caller would appreciate her sacrifice.

The familiar voice spoke before the phone was at her ear. Inga heard "—refused our offer."

As the voice filled in the details of the offer, Inga looked down at the street from her fourteenth floor condo. Though the rain had stopped for the moment, Connecticut Avenue reflected the head-lights of the never-ending evening traffic. She absent-mindedly spooned marshmallow chocolate fudge while she waited for the caller to finish. "—so I want you to get Wyatt signed up. Yesterday."

She embedded the spoon in the ice cream, still holding the handle. "What good will that do? He's incompetent."

"It's his patent claims we want."

She tested a spoonful of the ice cream while she thought. It was beginning to soften. "Okay, I have an idea how to do that. I'll have to go to Michigan."

"Then go to Michigan," he said. "Whatever it takes. They're about to go public. Time is of the essence." He hung up.

Inga finished her feast, adding a second quart of ice cream to fortify her for the rigors of her trip. Then she phoned the home number of her travel agent.

57

According to Sarah, the judge in "The Philosopher Pooch" copyright infringement case was about as fair-minded and open to innovation as anyone they were likely to draw. True to Sarah's word, Judge Clara Christensen said she would consider evidence from the Aremac before proceeding to trial. Since the Aremac couldn't be moved to the courtroom, the courtroom came to the Aremac.

Roger was ready to proceed with the demonstration, but had to wait for what seemed to him to be a million legal motions by the defense. The judge swept them all away, some outright, some to be decided by the jury—if the case went that far—and some to be saved for a possible appeal. It seemed quite clear to Roger that she preferred to settle a case like this without a trial.

When the legal maneuvering was cleared away, Roger presented more or less the same demonstration he'd given the VCs. The judge beat the defense to the punch by asking how she could know if the pictures were actually seen and the sounds actually heard, rather than made up. "The easiest way to show that, Judge, is to have you try it yourself, if you're willing."

Roger caught her looking dubiously at the snood with all its wires. "It's absolutely safe. You saw me use it on myself, and we actually developed it so my wife could communicate. I wouldn't have done that if it weren't absolutely safe." He crossed his fingers ever so slightly, hoping she wouldn't ask how Tess came to be immobilized in the first place.

"Do I have to shave my head? This isn't England, you know. We don't wear those silly wigs."

"No shaving. We used to need that, with the earlier versions, and we got in the habit of shaving our heads. It's actually very convenient—no hair in the shower drain, and—"

Sarah yanked his elbow. "I don't think Judge Christensen wants to hear about hair in the drain."

"Thank you," the judge said. "I'm willing to give it a try." The defense attorney started to object, but the judge waved him aside and sat down in the special seat.

Roger placed the snood gingerly on her head and made a small adjustment to the strap. "Is that comfortable?"

The judge nodded.

"It's okay to talk," Roger explained. "And you shouldn't feel anything once I start the machine. If you want to stop for any reason, just hit this red button. Don't worry, the button's been tested, though we've never actually had to use it."

The first test was verbal, with Roger instructing the judge, "I want you to remember some things you've heard someone say, then say them out loud. And I want you to make up some things you've never heard anyone say, and say them, too. Mix them up, so I don't know which things are made up and which ones are remembered."

Then Roger turned to the court reporter. "Please write down each thing she says, and watch me for a signal as to whether it's made up or remembered. When she's done enough, she can check your list and see if the machine got it right."

The test ran smoothly. After a dozen statements, Judge Christensen said she'd done enough. The court reporter read back the list and the machine's decisions. The judge nodded. "Very impressive. You got them all right."

"Not me, Judge. It was the Aremac that got them all right."

"How does it work?"

"Remembered information comes from one area of the brain. Composed information comes from another. Their patterns are completely different. It's impressive, but it's actually quite easy for the Aremac to distinguish the two." He started to step toward a brain diagram Sarah had asked him to mount on the wall. "I can show you on a map of the brain."

"That won't be necessary. I'd just like to see the visual part."

The defense attorney was visibly agitated, and asked the judge for permission to speak. "Go ahead," she replied. "What's your objection this time?"

"What if a witness made up a statement, but had someone read it out loud to him in advance? How would the machine know when he heard it. Or whom he heard it from?"

"That's a fair question," the judge said. "Dr. Fixman?"

"The Aremac turns out to be a fine lie detector, too. So all we have to do is ask you who said what you heard. And when. It will know if you're lying. Would you like to test it?"

The judge agreed, and Roger and Sarah left the room while the defense attorney and the court reporter made up sentences and read them aloud to the judge. They also read sentences she made up herself. Then Roger returned and had the judge repeat all the sentences. After each one, he asked, "Did the court reporter say that to you? Are those the defense attorney's words? Is that something you made up for someone to say to you?"

Once again, when they finished checking which yes/no answers had been true and which were false, the Aremac had classified them all correctly. It had even identified whose words they had been. "I'm convinced," said the judge, raising her hand to quash any further objections from the defense attorney. "Now I'd like to hear Miss Ackely's testimony."

"But what about the pictures?" Roger asked, eager to show off the full powers of the Aremac.

"From what I've seen, that won't be necessary."

Sarah objected. "Does that mean we won't be able to use it at the trial?"

"Not at all, Ms. Gold. If the case goes to trial—" she scrutinized the face of each attorney in turn, "which I sincerely hope it won't—you may present to the jury any form of evidence you feel will be convincing. Miss Ackely, are you willing to wear that cap?"

Constance Ackely, thin and wrinkled but erect and smartly dressed in a gray cotton pants suit, sat down and submitted with pronounced dignity to the fitting of the snood. Roger performed a few calibrations, relieved in a way that he was only doing the verbal test. The calibrations were much simpler than for the visual test.

When he signaled that everything was ready, Sarah started to ask her client a question, but Judge Christensen interrupted. "I would like to question Miss Ackely myself. When I'm finished, each attorney may ask anything additional that strikes you as pertinent."

The judge then turned to the court reporter and asked her if she'd seen how Roger had determined whether a statement was true or false. "Yes, Ma'am," the reporter said. "It's very simple. The screen shows the word TRUE or the word FALSE. I don't think I could make a mistake."

"Good. Now, Dr. Fixman, if you would please step back to the wall, we can all see that you're not in contact with the device in any way."

Roger wasn't prepared for this request, but he stepped back as instructed, folding his hands in full view in front of him, confident in the simplicity of the Aremac's human interface. Judge Christensen rolled her chair closer to the Aremac and said, "Miss Ackely, this is an informal procedure. You are not under oath, but I believe you saw how well this device can detect any untruths. Are you still willing to tell your story?"

"Yes, I am."

"Excellent. Please answer yes or no to each question. First, did you have a contract with the College covering the sale of your story," the judge glanced at her notes and continued, "'The Philosopher Pooch'?"

"Yes." The screen read TRUE.

"And did that contract have a clause granting movie rights to the College?"

"No." Her voice was strong and firm, but the screen read TRUE AND FALSE.

"Judge," said the reporter, "I don't know what to make of this."

The judge studied the screen. "Dr. Fixman, what does this mean?"

"It means that part of the answer is true, and part is false. Something about your question is confusing her."

"I see. Well, Miss Ackely, were you aware that you were confused?"

"Yes." TRUE.

"Can you explain why?"

"Yes." TRUE.

"I'm sorry," said the judge. "This device takes some getting used to. I didn't mean to ask a yes/no question there. What I wanted you to do was explain why you were confused."

"Because the contract they presented to me *did* have a clause granting them movie rights. But I made them cross it out—I kept all rights except first North American print rights." TRUE.

"And why did you do that?"

"I was an unknown writer then. I wrote the story in a writers' workshop in Lincoln City—that's in Oregon—and I was eager to see my words in print. But the instructors emphasized that we should never, ever, give away rights just to sell a story." She paused. The Aremac read TRUE. The reporter informed the judge.

Miss Ackely went on. "I mean, we weren't supposed to *give* them away. If they offered compensation, then it could be okay." TRUE.

"So, did they offer you compensation?"

"No, they said the rights were worthless anyway, so they just crossed them out." TRUE.

"Whom are you referring to when you say 'they'?"

"The editor. Mr. Wallace." TRUE.

The judge turned to the defense attorney. "Mr. Mayfair, was Mr. Wallace the editor at that time?"

"Yes, he was."

"Can you make him available for questioning?"

"Yes, Judge. He retired to California several years ago, but I have his deposition. He's rather old, and I wouldn't like to have him make this long trip."

"In that case, Mr. Mayfair, was anyone else present at this signing?"

"Not to my knowledge, Judge."

"Miss Ackely, were any others present?"

"No. Just the two of us." TRUE. "Mr. Wallace said our two signatures were enough, since there wasn't much involved—just some free copies of the magazine." TRUE.

"And what were his exact words when he struck out the rights clause."

"He said—"

"No, please. Don't say 'he said' or anything else. Just say the words he said to you."

"'If it will make you happy, I'll just cross this out.'" TRUE.

"And that's all he said at that time?"

"After he crossed it out, he said—"

"Just his words."

"'There. That will do it. If they make a movie out of this, all the royalties will go to you.'" TRUE.

"And that's all he said?"

"Well, he laughed when he said it." TRUE. "He seemed to think the idea of a movie about a philosopher dog was ridiculous." TRUE AND FALSE.

"Why are you ambiguous about that, Miss Ackely?"

"Well, because he didn't actually say it was ridiculous. Just the way he laughed when he said it made me think so. Actually, I thought so, too, but my teachers were very clear about not signing away my rights." TRUE.

"All right, Dr. Fixman. I've heard enough. You can come disconnect her from the device."

Roger started forward, but the defense attorney wanted to cross-examine the witness. The judge stopped him. "Mr. Mayfair, you can cross-examine Miss Ackely at the trial—if there is one. Let me remind you, however, that Mr. Wallace's deposition will not be sufficient. He will have to be subject to the same sort of questioning as Miss Ackely. And, if you go before a jury and it turns out that Mr. Wallace is lying, the jury is likely to consider that fact in rendering the size of the award."

"Yes, Your Honor. In that case, I'll hold my questions for the trial."

"Then we are finished here. I'll leave you now in case the two sides have anything they'd like to discuss before I set the court date." Even Roger could see what Judge Christensen wanted them to discuss.

The court reporter packed up her machine and left with the judge. In twenty minutes, Ms. Gold and Mr. Mayfair had worked out a settlement, with half the royalties going to Miss Ackely. There would be no trial.

58

Although the settlement was supposed to be confidential, word of the Aremac somehow spread through the city's legal community like The Great Chicago Fire. Roger learned about this news conflagration indirectly when he began to receive offers from attorneys. The offers sorted themselves into two broad categories. Some attorneys wanted to use the Aremac to support their cases. Others wanted to retain the Aremac for their side to suppress its use by the other side.

Roger had no trouble refusing offers of the second type, even though they generally involved more money. He believed they were made by sleazy lawyers who didn't want their clients' lies refuted, though Arnie explained that the lawyers were simply doing their job for their clients. Given the money paid for the Aremac's use during the Ackely case, Roger felt he could afford to ignore the legitimate requests, too, but Arnie took him to lunch so he could argue his own case for selecting at least a few.

As they entered Lipinski's Deli, the restaurant was redolent with smells of garlic and spices. Roger immediately noticed that the skinny, black-bearded man slicing corned beef behind the display case wasn't wearing a *yarmulke*. Roger didn't have much experience with Jewish food—at least not European Jewish food—

but he knew enough to see that Lipinski's was kosher-style, not kosher. Arnie, despite his Norwegian ancestry, seemed to know quite a bit more than that. "If your stomach's feeling a bit light, start with some soup. The *matzo* balls are like cannonballs, but they're *gooooood*."

"Do we order here, or take a table first?"

"If they were full, we'd wait for a table, but there's lots of places this late, so we'll order here. When it's ready, they'll bring it to us." He pointed to the slanted glass front of the display case. "This way, you can see what you're getting, and tell Gershom what you want by pointing. He doesn't speak English, unless it's Yiddish, like, '*blintzes*.'"

"I feel as if I'd like to sniff each item in the case!" Roger looked around him. "Lots of new aromas for me."

"You might not like the way the pickled tongue smells. You have to be brought up with it to appreciate some of this stuff." Arnie patted his more-than-adequate belly, "Me, I love everything that anybody eats. Jewish, Armenian, Chinese. If I ever go to the North Pole, I'm sure I'll love whale blubber. But I especially do love the lox. And potatoes—*latkes*, *kugel*, whatever. You can't have too many potatoes. That's my Norwegian blood showing through. For you, I recommend their special triple-header—three *challah* rolls, one of each stuffed with corned beef, pastrami, and chopped liver."

"Sounds like an adventure."

"If you don't like one of them, it won't go to waste. I suppose, if you want to be safe, order the rare roast beef on white bread. They probably have a loaf of white bread somewhere back there. But it would be a wasted opportunity."

Roger ordered the triple-header and *matzo*-ball soup. Arnie chose the lox plate special and a Ringnes beer, but passed on the soup—"because I'm on a diet." As an afterthought, he added a double order of potato *kugel*—"because I had a small breakfast. We'll order dessert later, after we see how much room we have left."

Arnie led the way to a booth all the way in the back of the narrow restaurant. He set his briefcase in the corner of the booth, on the red vinyl bench, slid in beside it, placed his cell phone on the gray Formica table, and grabbed a pale, whitish-green pickle out of the bowl. "You start with a young one," he advised, and pointed to the dark-green pickles. He offered the pickles to Roger. "The aged ones take some getting used to."

Roger sampled a crunchy dark-green pickle that seemed only a few days older than a cucumber. Arnie started making his case. "There are many reasons for taking some of these court contracts, but I'll start with the one that you'll understand the easiest, being an engineer."

Roger thought of himself as more of an engineer-scientist, but he didn't object to Arnie's image of him, so he let him continue. "I know enough about engineering to know that you can't really make a solid product without some field testing. Am I right?"

"You're right. Testing in real situations can produce incremental improvements—new algorithms, new features, and such. But we just tested the system with a real judge, and we're doing a lot of testing with Tess."

"Ah, but you haven't tried the pictures yet in court, and that's critical to my defense. We don't know how a judge—let alone a jury—will react to that. They're used to verbal evidence."

Before Arnie could continue, a motherly waitress arrived with their meals. Roger's soup held two apple-sized *matzo* balls. Arnie's lox was served on both halves of an open-faced bagel smeared with half an inch of cream cheese and surrounded by sliced onions, cucumbers, lettuce, and tomatoes that hung over the sides of the oval platter. After the waitress greeted Arnie by name, he introduced her to Roger as Hedva.

Hedva leaned close to study Roger's face, almost hitting him in the neck with her more-than-ample bosom. Then she cupped his chin in her hand and said in a loud, throaty voice, "Not your usual *shiksa* companion, this one. You like boys now, Arnie? Looks like a nice Jewish boy."

Roger thought it was a good idea not to correct her, and simply smiled.

Hedva amused herself with a few more laughing remarks about Roger needing to find a "nice Jewish girl," then left when another customer rang a glass with his fork. While Roger tested the first *matzo* ball, Arnie continued his brief. "If I understand correctly, using new algorithms means you can use a less-powerful magnet. And that's good. Am I right?"

The soup was hot. Roger had to wait for it to cool in his mouth before swallowing. "Yes, a less-powerful fixed magnet would be cheaper."

"And smaller? More mobile? That's important, because what you've got right now isn't easy to move into a courtroom. And criminal-case judges will tend to be a lot less accommodating than Clara was in a civil case. Much less."

"I didn't know that."

"No, Judge Clara's a pearl among swine. And that brings me to my second reason—your own lack of courtroom experience."

Appearing at the table with Roger's triple-header, Hedva promised Arnie that the *kugel* would arrive soon, explaining that it needed just a few more minutes to heat. Roger wasn't even half finished with his soup, but Arnie's lox must have magically leapt from the plate to his stomach while he was talking, so Roger let him continue. Besides, Arnie was right about the need for experience.

"We have a little more leeway introducing new technology on the defense, but at the very least you're going to have to demonstrate and explain the Aremac to a packed courtroom. You have to do it so the judge and jury—even the reporters—can understand. No technical mumbo jumbo. And I've seen expert witnesses freeze up on much simpler issues, like explaining how a valve works. And that's what the prosecution will try to make you do."

Roger decided his own stomach couldn't support a second *matzo* ball, so he pushed the rest of his soup aside and started on what he thought was the *challah* with pastrami.

"You can tell it's the corned beef, not pastrami—pastrami has the little black peppercorns," Arnie explained when Roger admitted his mistake. "But let me proceed to my next reason. Money."

"I don't see how money is a problem. We've got enough for now, and soon we'll get a big payment from the insurance company for Tess's accident."

"Soon? Hah! Soon? Like my *kugel* was supposed to be soon?" He looked around, but Hedva was nowhere in sight. "They're going to delay and stall and postpone and delay some more, trying to make you settle for less. More money means you can be in a better negotiating position. Hold out against their tactics."

"Maybe, but I think we can scrape by."

"Maybe. I'll come back to that. From my point of view, the most important thing—"

Hedva arrived with the *kugel* and, noticing that Roger hadn't finished his soup, asked Arnie in a concerned voice whether Roger was sick. When Roger replied he just wasn't all that hungry, she shook her head and left the soup, urging him to give it another try—"for the starving children in Israel."

While Hedva was mothering Roger, Arnie was digging out huge forkfuls of *kugel*. By the time she finished her mothering, Arnie was almost half done with the double portion. "As I was saying, the most important thing from my point of view is to establish precedents. Even if they're civil cases, enough of them will increase the chance that Addie's judge will accept the Aremac for a test, at least."

Roger set down what he'd thought was the corned beef, which his taste buds and the presence of bits of black peppercorn told him was indeed the pastrami. "Why only increase the chance? Wouldn't the precedents determine the issue?"

"Ah, the law in its majesty is not that simple. Otherwise, we shysters couldn't charge such ridiculous fees. What's good enough for a human like Tess to communicate may be good enough for a civil case. It may even be good enough for police work in a criminal case, but that's no guarantee it will stand up in court. Civil evidence need not meet criminal legal standards."

Arnie let Roger ponder that idea while he polished off the *kugel* and washed it down with swigs from his wavy brown bottle of Ringnes. Roger finished the second *challah*, stuffed with thin-sliced pastrami, but as liver wasn't his favorite, he pushed the plate away without touching the liver. He'd never actually tasted kosher-style chopped liver, but he was already more than full. Arnie pushed the plate back. "You've got to at least *taste* the chopped liver. Otherwise, Lipinski won't let us leave. Just take a bite or two, and I'll finish the rest. But save room for dessert."

When Hedva reappeared, Arnie ordered cheesecake for himself. Then he and Hedva conspired to order rice pudding for Roger. Over Roger's protests, Arnie said, "Don't worry. I'm paying. Which brings me back to the subject of money. More money would mean you could hire better doctors for Tess. I don't think she's getting all the help she might get."

That was the clinching argument for Roger. He was so busy worrying about Tess's deteriorating condition, he ate the entire rice pudding without noticing the taste.

59

As soon as Qaaf opened the storeroom's hidden door, she saw the furious expression on Alif's face. He attempted to start their meeting, but Zay prevailed, cautioning him to have patience. When Jiim finally arrived, completing their group, Alif, chastised but still angry, held up the day's *Tribune* and appealed to Zay.

"The machine works. They'll use it on the woman and Qaaf will be exposed." He jabbed at the headline for emphasis. "Qaaf should leave our group, and we should change our meeting place."

Qaaf said nothing, but Jiim, who now seemed more confident of his place in *Yom alKhamis*, protested. "The machine could be valuable to us, and Qaaf is essential for my plans for the Vice President. We have to find another way to eliminate this threat."

"Qaaf failed to do that as promised."

Zay looked to Qaaf for a response. Qaaf spoke quietly, in contrast to Alif's tone. "She's well watched. A direct attack is proving difficult."

"Obviously, we need a fresh approach," said Alif.

Qaaf knew he meant a fresh leader, but Jiim avoided the implication by turning the debate. "The bomb is a mighty weapon, but perhaps not for killing flies. Perhaps we can catch this one small fly with honey."

"Fine," said Alif, his tone suggesting it was not fine at all. "And who will provide the honey?"

Zay answered. "God will provide."

Alif was still furious, but the meeting was over.

60

Arnie spread the word that Roger would accept certain types of legal work for the Aremac. Arnie and Sarah would screen all offers, leaving only the most promising for Roger. Roger was amazed at the amount of money Arnie was asking—a nice round thousand dollars an hour, plus expenses—but both lawyers assured him that anything less would signal that he wasn't much of an expert witness. They assured him that after Roger had been the tipping factor in a couple of cases, his price would go up to two thousand. Maybe more. Much more.

Under the circumstances, Roger felt they could afford a van to give Tess more mobility. Besides, from time to time he would need a van to transport the new, lighter Aremac to court. A van with a lift and some special outfitting would be more convenient than removing the racks from one of his uncle's large garment trucks.

Uncle Suhayb introduced Roger to a former neighbor who now owned a Ford dealership in Skokie, and soon Roger was the proud owner of an orange-and-white, six-year-old Ford Econoline High Top with a handicap conversion. Tess was so excited she insisted he put his work aside for the day and take her out for a drive, saying she wanted to go to the Art Institute. Although Tess didn't have her handicap tag yet, Roger thought he could talk someone at the museum into letting them park in a handicap space anyway, close to the museum's entrance.

As the weather was cool but clear, with a fresh breeze off of Lake Michigan, Tess indicated she wanted to enjoy a longer wheel-chair ride, so they took a walkway along the Lake, going the long way from the van to the museum. Heidi daintily marked near bushes as they walked, taking ownership outside the museum, as if she knew there would be no doggy toilets inside.

Roger was eager to get inside the museum. As a teenager, he had often accompanied his mother to the Art Institute, and while Kamilah worked with the curators on Middle Eastern artifacts, he had become well acquainted with the museum's many permanent collections. Earlier, Tess had told him that she wanted to see the Chinese bronzes, so Roger, concerned about overtaxing her, resisted the many tempting exhibits and steered her directly to the white-walled Asian Art section.

They were admiring an eighteen-inch-tall Shang Dynasty bronze wine vessel when a well-dressed Asian man stepped along-side them, bowed slightly, and extended a white business card. "Please excuse me for interrupting your visit, but I know some-thing of these bronzes and would be happy to answer any ques-tions, if I may."

"Thank you," said Roger, taking the card and noticing that the man, a Mr. Tsang, was president of something called The Sunshine Bank of Hong Kong and Chicago. "I have no questions about the bronzes . . . do you, dear?" Heidi raised her left paw. "But perhaps you could answer a question about the stone bodhisattva back there." He gestured to one of the rooms they had passed through. "Do you know it?"

"Of course. Tang Dynasty. Quite famous. What would you like to know?"

"I read somewhere that a leaning bodhisattva indicates thinking. But this one leans to the left, not to the right as is usual. And he looks amused. Is he thinking of a joke?"

"I am impressed. You seem well informed. And correct. In that period—much earlier even—leaning to the right did mean that the figure was in thought. This one . . . frankly, nobody knows what it means. Perhaps the sculptor was dyslexic."

Roger laughed. "Thank you. Now I'm free to speculate as much as anybody."

Mr. Tsang bowed again, then looked at Tess. "Given your wife's condition, I imagine you have become quite adept at watching for body language. Or do you not require that skill, given your amazing machine—the Aremac, I believe you call it."

Roger did a double take. "You know about the Aremac?"

"Yes, of course. You are quite famous—in certain circles."

"I think you exaggerate. I didn't think anybody would recognize us. There have been no photographs, as far as I know."

Mr. Tsang bowed yet again. "You must forgive me. I saw no picture, but actually came here intentionally to see you as soon as possible. One of my clients wants to offer a business proposition. He did not want to take a chance of one of his competitors reaching you first."

"But how did you know we would be here?"

Tsang sidestepped the question. "Perhaps I could offer you a refreshment in the Garden Restaurant, if you would be willing to join me in enjoying this rather lovely weather. We could have more privacy there, and I could explain many things."

Roger could see that the old gentleman carried a cane, which was probably why he wanted to sit if they were going to talk. He was curious enough to ask Tess if she wanted to go, and Heidi pawed a YES. Mr. Tsang remained silent all the way to the restaurant, seeming to concentrate on his labored walking. The restaurant was largely unoccupied, but he chose a table as far from the other patrons as possible. They ordered drinks, and Roger carefully spooned lemonade into Tess's mouth as Mr. Tsang began his pitch.

"My client wishes to buy your company."

"Unfortunately, it's not for sale. But first tell me how you knew we were here."

"Oh, I'm sorry. I went to your building, but just missed you. A tall young man," he made a gesture imitating SOS's long flowing hair with his hands, "told me you had come here to view the bronzes. So, rather than wait another day, I followed."

"I'm sorry you went to all that trouble. But, as I said, the company is not for sale."

"Perhaps you should read my client's offer first." Putting on thick, tortoiseshell glasses, he extracted an envelope from his inner jacket pocket, removed a single sheet of embossed letterhead, and laid it on the table in front of Roger. "They are offering you forty million dollars."

He studied Roger's face as he read the note, but Roger did his best not to show what he was feeling. When Roger said nothing, Mr. Tsang raised the ante. "I suppose I shouldn't tell you this, but I'm sure they would be willing to consider a much more generous figure."

This time, Roger couldn't help but let out a whistle, loud enough that it evidently annoyed three nuns several tables distant.

"They thought you would be impressed with their generosity. For that price, they would require all rights to your invention, including the right to decide who may and may not use its services."

"You're right. It is generous, but I could never accept. My wife needs the machine to communicate."

"Of course." Mr. Tsang took the paper and pointed to a short paragraph near the bottom. "They have anticipated that. They will allow you to build a machine for her personal use. It would belong to you, but it would be for her personal use only."

Roger couldn't avoid thinking of how much medical care he could buy for Tess with forty million, including robotic prosthetics. Mr. Tsang seemed to be reading his mind. "They would also retain your exclusive services—both of you—for an annual retainer of one hundred and fifty thousand dollars. Each," he clarified. "In return, you would provide services exclusively to the company and designated customers. You would also be covered by a private medical policy that would carry all her expenses—yours, too, of course."

"There must be limits. Restrictions on preexisting conditions."

"No, no such limits. Or restrictions. They wish you to have at your disposal whatever medical care you think might improve your wife's condition."

Roger spooned more lemonade into Tess's mouth. "That's a very tempting offer, Mr. Tsang. I'm inclined—" Under the table, Heidi had sat up and was tapping her left paw frantically up and down. "As I was saying, I'm inclined to *consider* the offer, but I must of course consult my colleagues." Heidi raised her right paw, and Roger reached across the table to retrieve the paper.

"Of course," said Mr. Tsang. "This is not a matter to be decided rashly. Naturally, I hope that upon careful reflection, you will decide to accept. And, if you would be so kind, please notify me before you accept any other offers."

61

The news of the Aremac's success didn't waste any time spreading out from Chicago into northern Michigan, sending Harvey Wyatt into a fury. Harvey didn't waste any time before he spread his own fury all over the clinic staff. "You're all going to lose your jobs if we don't come up with something quick and dirty. My sponsor is coming for a demonstration of progress."

His new lead programmer, a rather attractive young lady with a lisp, wanted to know about his plan.

"We don't have time to make a plan. Just work harder. You'll be working weekends and overtime until our sponsor gets here. No more days off, either. No personal time. No sick leave. I'm doubling the staff so things will go faster."

"But what about Brooks's Law?" she asked. She pronounced "Brooks" as "Brookth."

Wyatt had never heard of Brooks or his law, but of course he couldn't show that in front of a mere programmer. A *female* programmer. "What does Brooks have to do with it?"

"I don't know. Brooks says if you add people late in a project, it slows things down. The new people pester the old people, so they stop them from getting work done. But if we tell new people not to bother us, they won't understand the system and they'll make mistakes. Either way it will slow us down."

Wyatt was annoyed by the difficulty he had understanding her. She must be stupid. *Thtupid*, he laughed to himself. Then aloud, "Your Mr. Brooks doesn't know what he's talking about. You're just looking for excuses."

Wyatt thought that would shut up the presumptuous programmer, but as she walked away, she said over her shoulder, "You really need to think carefully about the steps you plan to take."

Wyatt grabbed her arm and turned her around, flushed with rage at the insubordination, but noticing how firm her flesh was. "Thinking is a luxury this project can no longer afford. Just put your nose to the grindstone and grind out more lines of code."

That shut her up, and she must have told all the other programmers, too. But grinding out code didn't seem to produce anything but piles of software that didn't work. Don hadn't visited the project in two weeks, but Wyatt knew he was scheduled to bring that Steinman woman—and, even worse, Lucinda Dukes—to pay him a visit. They would demand to see results.

According to an e-mail from Don, the most important feature of the system was its ability to distinguish truth from lies. The system Roger had left at the clinic could do that, but after Wyatt hacked the software, that feature no longer worked reliably. Even worse, Wyatt had managed to lose the original code, so he couldn't even restore Roger's old system. When none of the programmers could understand Wyatt's undocumented code well enough to fix it, he became desperate. Two days before the visit, he sent all the programmers home and locked himself in the lab.

Forty-eight hours later, he emerged and went to the front entrance to meet his sponsor and the two agents, exhausted but confident in the success of his work. The weather had cleared. The sun was shining hot over Lake Michigan, increasing the humidity and matching his mood. He led them inside and offered them coffee and the pastries he'd had specially made to Inga's taste, but she surprised him by insisting she didn't have time to waste on frivolities. *This demonstration must be really important.*

"Very well," he said, positioning himself in the interrogation seat. When the snood was in place, he switched on the machine. He began making a series of statements, some obviously true, others obviously false, indicating they should pay careful attention to the screen.

"My name is Professor Harvey Wyatt."

TRUE, the screen said.

"Two plus two equals five."

FALSE.

"I am the best programmer in this installation."

TRUE.

After a few more statements, he noticed Inga was eating a cream puff—a good sign. He then directed them to ask him true/false questions—questions they knew the answers to. His confident smile grew as the machine unerringly classified all his answers correctly.

"I think that's enough," said Inga. "Very impressive."

"Yes," said Lucinda. "You've shown us a lot. Now let me try it."

Wyatt's brow knitted. "What do you mean?"

"Let me sit in the chair and see if it can tell when I'm lying."

Wyatt thought fast, trying not to show his anxiety. "We'd first have to calibrate it to you. That would take some time, and Ms. Steinman is in a hurry."

"Okay, so calibrate it. I can wait. Ms. Steinman can leave if she wants to." She winked at Inga and shoved him out of the seat and snatched the snood off his head. She was a lot stronger than she looked—hard as a diamond, and just as cold.

"We . . . uh . . . weren't set up to do a calibration today." He was losing his nerve.

"I think I can calibrate it."

"What?"

"I said, 'I think I can calibrate it.'"

"I heard what you said. I just didn't understand what you were talking about."

She pulled the snood onto her head. "Just turn it on. I'll show you."

Unable to resist the commanding tone in her voice, he flipped the power switch.

"Now," she said to Inga and Don, "I'm going to make a series of obviously true or false statements. We'll see if the machine can tell what's the truth and what's false. Ready, Professor?"

Wyatt didn't know whether he was ready or not, but nodded his head. "All right," she said. "Here goes." She looked at Don and said, "My name is Lucinda Dukes."

The screen showed TRUE, and Wyatt relaxed a notch. Sometimes the software did work. Maybe he would get lucky.

"I am a terrorist agent."

FALSE.

Wyatt started to breathe more easily. Then she repeated the first statement, "My name is Lucinda Dukes."

FALSE.

"I am a terrorist agent."

TRUE.

"What's going on?" Inga demanded, but she didn't sound surprised.

Wyatt jumped in quickly. "I suppose she's using her agent training to fool the machine. I'm sure we can compensate for that, with a little more time."

"Good guess, Professor. I *am* using my agent training. Let me demonstrate. Ms. Steinman, tell me whether you would like to see TRUE or FALSE on the screen."

"Try false."

Lucinda didn't say anything, but the screen showed FALSE.

"Now TRUE."

Again, she was quiet, but the screen changed to TRUE.

Don raised one eyebrow. "I'm impressed, LD. I don't know if I could do that, training or no training."

"Sure you could, Don. Here, try it." She took off the cap. He reached for it, but instead of handing it to him and yielding her seat, she remained seated and placed the cap on the floor. "Go ahead, make a statement."

"Huh? I'm not wearing the snood."

"Oh, the Professor's machine is advanced way beyond the need for such props. Go ahead." She winked at Inga again.

"Okay. My name is Marilyn Monroe."

The screen changed to FALSE. Don's eyes widened, and he tried again. "One plus one equals two."

TRUE.

"See," said Lucinda, "isn't it marvelous?"

Wyatt cringed, and Inga, finishing another cream puff, noticed. "What's the problem, Harvey Boy?"

"Ah, Ms. Steinman," Lucinda said, "why don't you try it yourself?"

"But I don't have any agent training." She was having trouble concealing her smile.

"Oh, I'll give you some agent training right now." Lucinda stood up and faced the chair. "When you want the machine to say FALSE, you press here." She jammed her hand on the cushion of the left arm rest. The screen changed to FALSE.

Inga Steinman's eyebrows rose. She started to say something to Wyatt, but Lucinda interrupted. "Excuse me, Ms. Steinman, but you're only half finished with your agent training. You see, if you want the machine to say TRUE, you push the right arm rest. Like this." She pressed down, and the screen changed to TRUE.

"Let me try that." Inga reached around Lucinda and activated the two arm rests in turn, checking the screen. Then she turned again to Wyatt, who looked as if he were trying to shrink himself to the size of a peanut. Slowly, deliberately, Inga extended her index finger so it pointed at his nose from an inch away. Wyatt's nose was now white, as if all blood had been drained away. "You're finished, Professor Wyatt. Your grant is canceled, and you will never do business with any government agent again. In fact, I will ask the dean to have you removed from your chair."

"And that's the least of it," said Don. "You're also under arrest."

Wyatt opened his mouth, but Don held up his hand. "You have the right to remain silent. Anything you say . . ." Wyatt fainted and never heard the rest.

62

The next morning, the weather along Lake Michigan's Eastern Shore remained clear, though growing hotter. By the time Don reached the outskirts of Gary, though, south of the lake, clouds were forming, hinting at a storm to come. Don had driven to Chicago hoping to pay Roger a visit. He hadn't called ahead because he anticipated Roger would not greet him warmly, perhaps refusing to see him at all. As he endured the traffic on Lake Shore Drive, the clouds grew more threatening, and he debated whether to use the power of his office to force Roger to grant him a hearing.

When he ran from his car to the door of the converted garage, the rain was hammering down like nails. As he knocked, standing under the canopy, he still hadn't decided about using his badge. Fortunately, it seemed unnecessary. Roger not only instructed the guard dog to let him enter, but extended his hand warmly. "That was fast. I only sent you the e-mail this morning."

Don shook his hand. "What e-mail?"

"You didn't get it? I asked you if you would come."

"No, I was driving down here. Haven't checked my e-mail today at all."

Roger became suspicious. "Then why are you here? Is Addie okay?"

"She's fine," he said, which was not exactly true.

"Has something changed in her case? Did you find the real killer?"

"No, we still think she's the real killer. Look, it's not personal. I like her." He raised his palms in apology. "She seems really sweet and innocent, and nothing would make me happier than learning that she didn't do it. But the case against her is solid. She'd be convicted already if not for that slick lawyer of hers. You've got to reconcile yourself to the fact that she's guilty. You can't be responsible for the political views of every member of your family."

"No way. Never. My Aremac here is going to let Tess prove it was somebody else."

"Well, good luck to you, then, but you're wasting your time. After what Wyatt pulled, even if you get it working, you'll never convince a judge or jury to trust what it says."

"Not says. Shows. The Aremac will show a full motion picture of what happened on—wait a minute. What did Wyatt pull?"

"He faked a demonstration of his machine's lie-detecting ability. Fooled me, too. But LD picked it up. I think you would have enjoyed seeing his face when she exposed his fake."

"Fake? What would he have to fake? It worked just fine."

"When you left it did. I know that. Apparently he messed with the software and couldn't get it working again."

Roger turned to Tess, who was lying down, but not connected to the Aremac. "Did you hear that, sweetie?"

Heidi raised her right paw.

"Do you want me to hook you up so you can join the conversation?"

Heidi raised her left paw. "Okay," Roger said. "She just wants to listen. Heidi will let us know if she changes her mind."

"That's something new, isn't it? The dog, I mean."

"She's had her for a while. But get back to Wyatt. He really tried to flimflam you? And why couldn't he wait until he had it working again?"

"Steinman was pressing him. And I don't think he *could* get it working again. We spoke to the programmers, and apparently it's beyond repair. We arrested him—"

"You arrested Wyatt?"

"Yes, but it's a long story." Don wiped his brow with his palm. "Listen, do you have a towel I could use?"

Roger fetched a towel from the bathroom, while Heidi sniffed Don's cuffs. When Don's thick hair was partly dry, he took a seat and continued. "We arrested Wyatt, yes, but he's been released, and we're probably not going to press charges. Wouldn't make the Agency look good. But the project has been canceled."

"Well, lucky for you, you don't need it anymore."

"But we do. The Museum of Science and Industry was bombed last night. Didn't you see the news?"

Roger shook his head. "I'm too busy for news. But I think the Museum of Science and Industry is sacred—like a cathedral. Was it badly damaged?"

"Pretty bad. Fortunately, it was closed—that's the pattern—but several visiting bigwigs were being given an after-hours tour. Four of them were hospitalized, and the President has raised the pressure. And the temperature. We have a couple of suspects—witnesses, at least—who may know something about it, but nobody's talking. If we had the machine, we might have gotten something useful."

"But I thought you said it wouldn't hold up in court."

"Probably not, but right now, I don't care about court. I need leads, and I could have gotten them from these suspects. If I'd had the machine."

"I'm sorry to hear that, then. You know, I don't like what they're doing any more than you do. Less, probably, because in addition to hurting our country, they're giving all Muslims a bad name. My family is beginning to fear for their safety."

"Then is there any way I can persuade you to work with us again?"

Roger didn't know what do say, and stood silently until he felt Heidi tugging at his pants leg. "Oh, Tess wants to say something now."

He moved Tess into the Aremac in a seated position and put on her snood. "Looks like you've simplified the procedure," Don said. "No calibration."

"We've made lots of progress, no thanks to you," Tess's machine voice contributed.

Don heard his chances fading, but listened as Tess's machine voice went on. "But we would be willing to cooperate with you . . . on one condition."

"Really. That's great. Let's hear your condition."

"You drop the charges against Addie and release her."

Don's face drooped. "You know I can't do that."

"I know no such thing. You have no case, anyway, and if you don't want to look bad in court, your best bet would be to drop the charges now."

"I couldn't even get her released on bail."

"You could question her with our machine. Then you'd know she's telling the truth."

"I've been fooled once in the past twenty-four hours. I'm afraid you couldn't make me believe the machine wasn't rigged."

"I resent that," said Roger. "I'm not like Wyatt. I've never been like Wyatt."

"In this case, I can't afford to trust anyone. As much as I'd like to believe you, you have to remember that I trusted you about Addie. That's put me in deep trouble."

Tess's voice came over the speakers. "Then I guess we have nothing to discuss. Maybe when you get more desperate."

"Okay. Maybe we both need time to think it over. Come up with something creative." He turned toward the door, then heard the rain and halted, turning back. "What was that e-mail about?"

"I wanted to ask you something. Maybe we can help you in another way. Maybe help Addie, too."

"What's the question?"

"What kind of cover company would terrorists use if they wanted to do legitimate business? Or business that looked legitimate?"

"Is this a theoretical question, or is there something more behind it?"

"I guess I can tell you this much. A bank president came around with an offer from one of his clients to buy our company, lock, stock, and patents. It was a very generous offer, but it would prevent anyone from using the Aremac without their permission. Tess thought this looked suspicious. Addie's attorney thought it smelled like rotten whitefish."

Don stepped back into the center of the room. "Like they're hiding something?"

"Exactly. But it could be just another one of these corporate scandals. It seems that everybody in Chicago has heard about the Aremac now, and anyone with something to hide wants to buy us off in some way. And the ACLU would like to do business with us. But maybe there's more to it. Something more serious than yet another corporate crook who won't be convicted anyway."

"Well, if it's a front, then there's sure to be a tangled web of legitimate companies."

Tess's machine voice broke in, "That's all I've found so far. A tangled web. I haven't got much else to occupy my time, but all I've found in my searches is a giant hair ball, with lots of cut ends."

Roger kissed Tess on the forehead. "You've done a great job." He turned to Don. "That's what made us suspicious. If there was something legitimate behind this, Tess would have found it. We thought your agency might have access to resources we can't reach."

"I'm sure we do. But what are you offering in exchange?"

"Come on, Don," Roger said. "I may not have gone into the family business, but I'm a better trader than that. If we want to be safe, all we have to do is turn down the banker's offer. We weren't planning to sell anyway. For you, though, it's a possible new lead to some bad people."

"I could threaten to get a court order to take away the Aremac. That would put something on my side."

"You could do that, but you wouldn't be able to make it work. Believe me. And we could always make another one."

Don grinned. "I know that. You know, my ancestors were all government employees, so I'm no good at this bluffing game. And I can see that threatening you would never get me what I want. So maybe if I show some good faith, you'll reconsider letting me use your machine."

"Do you really want to show good faith?" Roger said.

"Yes, I do. But I can't do anything about Addie. I mean it."

"I was thinking of something else."

"All right. What is it this time?"

"Do you have access to advanced military technology?" Tess interjected.

"Yes, certain things. But I'm not going to outfit you for a war on the government. What do you want?"

Roger answered for her. "There's a joint robotics prosthetics project between the Army and UC Berkeley. We want one of their exoskeletons to help Tess's recovery."

Don was surprised. "How will that help? They only augment a soldier's movement, and Tess can't move at all. Or can she now?"

"No," Roger sighed, "not at all. How much theory do you want? It's neurophysiology, something Tess found on the Web."

"Just give me the outline."

"We want to use the exoskeleton to move Tess's limbs for her—"

"Oh, I get it. To exercise her muscles."

"Well, that, too, but that's not the main reason. I can do that myself. I'm going to try coupling the exoskeleton controls to Tess's brain signals—"

"So she can move herself mentally, like the way she moves the cameras or accesses the Web?"

"Not exactly. We're aiming a little higher. A lot higher. She's going to visualize a movement—something simple, like raising a finger—at the same time she tries to order her finger to make the movement."

"What will that do?"

"Well, the theory is that if the exoskeleton moves her finger at the same time she's giving signals to her nervous system to move it, then it creates a kind of rehearsal for her body-mind connection. It's been successful on a small scale—moving a nerve-dead thumb, for example—but for a case like Tess's, it's purely speculative. And the equipment is expensive—"

"So that's the favor you want. To get you a robot?"

"Yes. At least for a trial."

"And what are you offering in return?"

"We would share any findings with the government."

"That's it? I'm supposed to count on your good will?"

"Don't get your hopes up," the machine voice said.

"We'll talk about it." Roger led Don to the front door, then outside, under the canopy. "Tess doesn't want to give you anything, and it's her body. But I'll be honest with you. I would do anything to give her a chance. If you get this exoskeleton for us, I'll find a way to help you catch the terrorists. That's a promise."

63

The sun had not given Ann Arbor residents a peek at its face for a full week now, with no end to the depressing grayness in sight. From his corner-office window, Wyatt had seen no change in the sky for the past four hours—just gray, grayer, and ominous black, much like the expression of the campus security guard who'd been watching him pack his belongings for the same period. Since the pursed-lipped biddy from the auditor's office had finished taking away all his financial records, none of his former students or colleagues had even come to ask him if he needed help moving out. Not even his graduate assistants. *Ingrates, all,* he thought.

All the books were packed. He'd saved his framed degrees for last, to put into the final box reserved for breakable things and last-minute items. Little good the degrees were going to do him now. Whatever one university knew, all the others knew five minutes later. It was like a national calling tree—international, actually. Academics were gossips in a hundred languages. *Just one little slip and your name gets passed around the world like the latest computer worm.*

He taped the last box shut, then added the identification label. The only thing the University was paying for was storing the boxes until he decided where he was going next. *Storing them because I have no prospects. Then shipping them because they are so eager to get rid of me. Oh, they kept all the valuable equipment, as if the administration had won those grants.* They wouldn't even let him keep one of the computers for his personal use. Well, he'd off-loaded all the valuable data and erased the files—and their backup. *They owe me that much.* They would have tried to stop him if they'd known what he was going to do. *So smart, but they didn't think of everything.*

The guard made Wyatt stand and wait while he surveyed the contents of the office, checking the equipment against his inventory list. Wyatt would have walked away, but he wasn't quite sure what the guard might do with his pistol. *You can't predict what low-level employees might do once you give them a little power.*

Finally, the guard gave him a thumbs up, then a thumbs out. Wyatt held his tongue and started across campus toward the parking lot. He was so carefully avoiding puddles—they never would put in a new sidewalk—that he didn't notice an elderly Asian man hurriedly limping up to intercept him. The man caught up with him just as he reached his car, gave a little bow, and said, "Professor Wyatt. Please excuse me for interrupting your busy day." He handed Wyatt a white card. "Allow me to introduce myself. I am Mr. Tsang, of Sunshine Bank. One of my clients has a business proposition that may be of interest to you."

64

"Someone else has recruited the Professor." Qaaf knew Wyatt was a bungler, and that nothing was sure, but she had to sound confident among these alpha males. She could see that Zay, Jiim, and especially Alif were ready to pounce on any sign of weakness. "But we need not worry. We will watch these people who hired the Professor, and if necessary, gain possession of his machine."

"Don't count your chickens," Alif warned. "Too many things are left to chance."

"I stand corrected. But the plan's a good one, and chance favors the prudent planner."

"Prudent? Is that all you think of? You think like a woman. If we want to be prudent, we shouldn't tie all our horses to the same rope."

Qaaf lowered her voice, trying to sound more assertive, more masculine. "And what rope did you bring, Alif? One with which to hang yourself?"

"One that will hang more of the bastards." He pulled a newspaper clipping from his inner pocket and handed it to Zay, who studied it for a moment, then handed it to Qaaf.

Qaaf gave the clipping the merest glance. "Yes, I already told you the Missouri congressman is coming. And that he'll be heavily guarded."

"I have a plan to avoid the guard."

"You know we have nobody to spare for a minor congressman. The Vice President's visit is—"

"—a long way off. And my plan involves no great effort. Read the underlined sentence."

Qaaf didn't like taking orders from Alif, but she knew that Zay was almost blind. He mustn't be embarrassed in front of the others, so she was trapped. She gave the clipping another glance. "Fine. It says that he's on the Select Committee on Homeland Security. So what?"

"Finish reading."

"He chairs the Subcommittee on Emergency Preparedness and Response. Again, so what?"

"He's on tour to examine the security of mass-transit systems. I propose we teach him something about how unprepared Chicago's Finest really are."

"And how do you propose to do that?"

"With God's help," Jiim said, with earnest piety, "and a small contribution from you."

Here it comes, Qaaf thought. "A small contribution?"

"I figured he would use the El," Alif boasted. "He's studying mass transit, right? But we don't know which line, and when."

"That's a small contribution indeed—from someone who has my sources. He'll certainly take the Blue Line from O'Hare. As you could have discovered from any tourist map."

"You have to find out when he arrives, and which train he will be taking."

"You are an idiot, Alif. You won't be able to get anywhere near that train with explosives."

"Maybe I am a fool, but I am supported by a skilled technician." He nodded toward Jiim, who lowered his head modestly before explaining his plan. Qaaf had to admit—to herself—that it was a clever plan, with no risk to her and a substantial chance of success even if the timing wasn't perfect.

When Jiim finished, Alif looked at Qaaf and raised both eyebrows in triumph. "Now I suppose you'll find fault with my plan."

"No, it's a good plan. Bringing down the El will cause major traffic problems and put that much more pressure on the mayor. But we'll need the assistance of a structural engineer. Not from here. Otherwise a lot of people could be hurt."

"That would be difficult."

"But essential."

"I don't think so," Alif said. "Jiim will simply use more powerful explosives."

Qaaf looked to Zay for permission to pursue her objection. He shook his head. There was no further discussion.

65

Tess's wheelchair, with its simple portable speech mechanism, was working reliably now, and, in spite of the sudden chill in the air, she wanted to conduct their busy schedule of meetings with Don somewhere outdoors, away from their garage home. Roger wanted her to continue practice sessions with their newly acquired exoskeleton, but Tess didn't like to have people watch her exercising, so they agreed to meet Don at the Skokie Northshore Sculpture Park. It was open and outdoors, so they could speak in private, without fear of bugs—the electronic kind, anyway. Tess had become a bit paranoid since Roger was served notice that a company they'd never heard of was suing for patent infringement.

Sarah, who seemed to know everybody's business in Chicago, informed Roger that the company was represented by Mr. Tsang and that Wyatt was on its payroll. Sarah assured them that, in the end, there wasn't much chance Wyatt's company would win, but that the end could be far in the future. She warned that the court proceedings might prevent them from using the Aremac in Addie's trial.

Roger wondered if the true objective of the suit might be to muffle Tess's evidence, so Tess had decided to discuss the matter with Don, who was still researching Sunshine Bank's ownership.

Don was waiting in the parking lot in his nondescript agency car when they arrived. Roger wheeled Tess out of the van, leashed up Heidi, grabbed a tour booklet, and then gave a nod to let Don know they were ready to set off through the park.

Don immediately asked about any progress with the exoskeleton, and showed genuine disappointment when told there had been no sign of improvement so far. He remained pensive until they reached the first sculpture, called "Trunnion II." It appeared to be a giant aluminum octopus tipped onto one side.

Don watched as Roger attempted to discourage Heidi from marking too close to the sculpture. "I think she wants to make a critical statement," he laughed, as Roger tightened up the leash. "What's a trunnion?"

"I learned about trunnions in my M.E. class," Roger said. "They support cannons and other things that have to pivot."

"Looks like a spider," added Tess through her device.

"Looks like Sunshine Bank," said Don. "Tentacles reaching in all directions, supporting the devil knows what."

"What have you figured out?" Roger asked.

"Not a whole lot, though if it's this complicated, I figure they must be hiding something. For a while, I thought it was related to a Sunshine State Bank down in Florida—the Sunshine State, get it? But it turns out it's some sort of translation from the Chinese—"

"I looked it up," said Tess. "'A flower cannot blossom without sunshine, nor a garden without love.' It's from 'The Book of Songs.' Wonderful saying for a bank."

"Inscrutable," said Don as they approached a large, abstract steel structure. "Not like this statue. Clearly one of those oil pumps you see in Southern California. Though I never saw one painted red."

"Some of the new ones are," Tess said. "The better to show oil leaks. But the oil soon makes them all black."

Don agreed. "More like Sunshine Bank. Everything they touch soon becomes hidden under a dark slippery coating."

"Like their client," Tess added. "I can't find out much about it, except for them suing us."

"Yes, they've gone underground, though it's hard to see how they think they can get anything useful out of hiring that charlatan Wyatt."

"Sarah thinks that they're not trying to get anything out of him except control of us through patent litigation," said Roger. "She says they might prevent us from using the Aremac at Addie's trial."

"I hope not," Don hesitated briefly and then added, "I do think she's guilty, but I'd like to see her get the best defense you can mount. If she doesn't, then the liberal politicians will be all over us, like . . ."

"Like jackals on a wounded camel. That's what my Uncle Zahid would say."

They came upon a vaguely human cast-bronze figure.

"What's this one?" Tess asked. "It looks like a pinhead person sitting on a white bench."

"It reminds me of those three-legged pots in the Art Institute. That's where we were when Mr. Tsang approached us."

"Really? So it was a coincidence?"

"No. He said he followed us from our office. Had a letter ready, with the proposal all typed up."

"Definitely a sign of careful preparation. He's got resources behind him." A few yards farther down the path, Don stopped in front of a tall structure. "What's this? Looks like a Tinkertoy structure on stilts."

"It's also three-legged," Tess's speaker said. "Like the pots."

"Are the three guy-wires part of the sculpture? Or are they just there to stabilize the structure?"

Roger consulted the tour brochure. "Who knows? But it says here they found the materials in the alleys of Rogers Park."

Tess said, "That's your old neighborhood. Maybe we could save some money by building the Aremacs that way."

"It's called 'New Hope Ris'n.'"

"So if I found some new parts, it would give me some new hope?"

The three were silent for a while, then Roger said, "Actually, Don, we do have some new hope. Not for Tess yet, but for the Aremac. The quality of our pictures is getting much more refined. Soon you'll be able to recognize whoever threw your man off the balcony. If she's someone in your files."

"Or someone in my agency." Don squinted, then rubbed his lower lip. "It's always possible that there's a mole somewhere, buried deep. They seem to know the mayor is wavering, and their price has gone up now to a cool hundred million. Kind of like the way *you* negotiate."

"But I give you something in return. If the murderer is your mole, the Aremac will bring her out of her hole, into the light."

"Well, good luck to you then. I know you hope it doesn't show us Addie. But if it does, you'd better not try to hide it. It's evidence."

"If she did it, we'd be the first to come forward. But she didn't. I can already see that much in Tess's rough pictures."

"I want to see those pictures."

"Sorry, but Arnie says no. Not until they're ready and his legal case is in place." Roger looked down at the tour booklet. "But don't worry. Like it says here, it's just a matter of time before we can prove it to the world."

Don looked over Roger's shoulder. "It says that in the guide-book?"

"Well, that's the name of the sculpture—'A Matter of Time.'"

It was a tall abstract sculpture, forged out of some kind of gray metal. Tess commented, "It looks like the Greek *pi*. How is that supposed to make me think of time?"

"I think the sculptor had a different idea," said Don. "To me, it looks like part of an iron Stonehenge."

"Yep. Says here that it's designed to act as a solar observatory. Doesn't say Stonehenge, but that's what Stonehenge was."

Tess spoke up. "Speaking of time, let's go home. I can see you guys shivering, and think my body must be getting cold."

"I can see goose bumps on your arm. Want my jacket?"

"No, thanks. Maybe I can use goose bumps as a backup communication path. All I have to do is put them under mental control, then I can code messages in goose-bump binary. GBB. All good things have TLAs." Don looked puzzled, so she explained. "Three-Letter Acronyms."

"Oh. Well, you know, FBI is also a three-letter acronym." Don paused while that sunk in. "Before you leave, I want to warn you. Maybe it will give you a different kind of goose bumps. I know you turned down Sunshine's offer, and I know you don't believe they're a threat anymore. I haven't pinned down the whole . . . trunnion . . . but I've run across enough unfortunate 'accidents' to know that Sunshine's people aren't going to stop at patent infringement."

"Aren't you exaggerating a bit?" Tess's speaker said.

"I don't think so. They seem to be going to a great deal of expense to keep you from using that machine in Addie's trial. It might have nothing to do with Addie. Perhaps they just have a commercial reason for wanting to keep you from having a public success. But it might mean they have something they want hidden—like the identity of the murderer, if it really isn't Addie."

"It isn't," Tess said.

They had reached the van, and Roger put Heidi back in her crate. "So what do you want us to do? Buy a couple more German Shepherd dogs?"

"Let's get some puppies," said Tess.

"This is serious, folks. Tess is a key witness. Just in case she really did see someone else, I'm putting a guard on your place until the trial is over. This case is too important to screw up."

66

Wyatt's patent injunction was distracting enough to Roger's work, but his next move was an attempt to hire away SOS. Though SOS was never going to work for the *qoH*, Wyatt's attempt proved to Roger that the hassle was never going to stop. The offer was for three times what Roger had just begun to pay, with lots of perks thrown in—including an initial month's fully paid vacation in a place of SOS's choosing. Clearly, Wyatt or his backers wanted SOS out of the way until after the scheduled trial. SOS turned down the offer, but this was only the opening volley in what was to become an all-out war.

Wyatt's next shot was more subtle. When Roger complained about his paperwork load from the mounting stack of court cases, Sarah told him to hire an assistant. Then she wrote a job description that was so constraining—paralegal experience, sales experience, and administrative experience—that Roger predicted they wouldn't find even one qualified applicant. He was wrong. Out of more than forty eager applicants, two survived the tough screening to which Sarah and Arnie subjected all the candidates, thoroughly testing them on their legal knowledge. So Tess could talk to them and Roger could watch their reaction to Tess, the applicants were interviewed successively, while Tess was strapped into the full Aremac.

First of the two was Rebecca Solomon, a mid-forties proper Englishwoman, too reserved for Tess's taste and too conservatively dressed for Roger's. She was polite, friendly—though not effusively so—and had impeccable references, with a stunning job history, including unspecified work with a private security company.

Bonnie Harmon, the other candidate, also had impeccable references. She was younger than Rebecca by about twenty years, so her job history wasn't as stunning, but she was charming, pretty, very friendly, and a good listener, if a bit nervous. Her eyes kept flitting away from Tess to the painted walls, where Tess's delicate pastel Navajo rugs failed to cover all the drips and scars, serving instead to highlight the converted garage's shabbiness.

As Bonnie described her work experience, she became more assertive, looking deep into Roger's eyes. He quickly looked away, staring down at her application. He thought, *Surely, the International Bank of Trade didn't have gouges in its walls from flying car parts. Nor would the legal firm of Grant, Warner, Mullen and Duchamp have reeked of garlic, chili peppers, and used transmission oil. At least her purple blouse matches the color of the sofa,* he thought, when he dared to look up again.

Roger struggled to divert his attention from that blouse, which probably was worth ten times the cost of the ancient sofa—in fact, ten times what all the threadbare furniture in the reception area cost. When Bonnie fingered and then opened the third button at her neck, he reddened. He had been imagining what the semi-sheer material promised underneath, and now there was much less left to imagine.

Why is she unbuttoning her blouse? Is she too warm? He wanted to adjust the air-conditioning, but standing would reveal his dilemma. Instead, he shifted her application down to his lap and called SOS over to listen in as she described her experience with electronics and software.

When Roger and Tess were finished with the candidates and Tess's wheelchair had been moved away from the Aremac, Roger gathered SOS's impressions—favorable to both applicants—and wheeled Tess to the nearby park to hash out a decision. They had both become adept at spotting the late-model Fords or Mercurys favored by FBI agents assigned to them for protection—and sure enough, the car that had been parked in front of the garage all day trailed their stroll at a discrete distance. When Roger locked the wheelchair brake, put Heidi in a down-stay, and settled onto a painted wooden bench next to Tess's chair, the Ford parked where its occupant had a clear view of anyone who might approach them.

"I'm beginning to feel like a flea under a microscope," Tess said. "I think we should ask Don to call off his pack. Heidi is all the protection we need."

"I'll speak to him about it. Right now, we have a decision to make." He decided to kick off the discussion with a show of neutrality. "I'm sure we'd be okay with either one, but I do prefer Bonnie. I like her energy and enthusiasm."

"Well, my choice is Rebecca. The job requires competence. And wisdom."

"You think she's wiser? Because she's older, or because her name is Solomon?"

"Because she's had more experience. Deeper. And she knows about security. I think she could be a real asset if things get tough. Bonnie came across as a bit flighty for my taste."

"You call it flighty. I call it enthusiasm. Maybe nervousness, which is to be expected when applying for a great job."

"Roger, you old goat. What you call enthusiasm is sex appeal. And big boobs."

Roger blushed bright red, but quickly turned the focus back to Tess. "You're against her because she's got big boobs—bigger than yours?"

"That's only because I'm flat on my back most of the time. If you want to sleep with her, go ahead. You don't have to hire her for that."

"You know me better than that."

"Underneath, you're still a man."

"And underneath, you're jealous."

"You're being irrational. If you want a reliable assistant that you can delegate to, someone who will guard our interests, hire Rebecca. That's all I have to say to you now. Take me home, please."

The mechanical voice revealed no emotion, so Roger missed how much he'd hurt Tess. All he felt was his own embarrassment, at having been so transparent to his wife. He made no move to leave the bench.

"We haven't made a decision."

"<I need more time to think about it>," Tess's machine voice said, this time with emphasis. "I want to look something up. Take me back now and connect me to the Aremac."

"Fine," Roger said, though his tone didn't match the word. "Just don't think about it too long. Candidates like Bonnie are not going to be on the market long."

For hours following their return to the garage, Tess refused to talk to her husband. She lay on the table, perfectly still as usual, hooked to the Aremac, staring at the monitor directly over her face. Roger couldn't see the screen or her face from where he was sitting and he didn't dare move closer. He had no way to tell whether she was sleeping or doing something with her computer.

He went to his desk and tried to concentrate on a simple program modification, but he kept making beginner mistakes. Feeling sorry for himself, he wondered if there were any other wife in the world who could cut herself off so utterly from her husband. Every fifteen minutes, he would get up and sit by Tess, attempting to apologize if he'd said something to hurt her. He tried to explain that he didn't think he favored Bonnie because of her sex appeal, but supposed that maybe that had been a subconscious influence. Babbling on, he acknowledged that Tess was better at seeing these things and that in her condition, she was probably justified in feeling insecure about his devotion. He wished out loud that they'd seen some progress from their work with the exoskeleton.

Their usual dinner hour came and went without any word from Tess. He tried to write her a poem of apology, but tore up three attempts before giving up on that approach. He was hungry and miserable and wanted to order a pizza, but he knew that she hated to smell things she couldn't eat. Instead, he took some pretzels and cheese into the other room and washed the snack down with a bottle of Double Diamond. Then another—and another.

The creamy ale loosened his mind. Before long, he came up with what he thought was a brilliant idea of resolving the argument by hiring both Rebecca and Bonnie. He went back and suggested his idea to Tess, but she just lay there. No response. He finished the last cold Double Diamond—way over his usual limit—then debated between drinking warm ale and helping himself to one of SOS's Bud Lites.

He was still standing in front of the open refrigerator when Heidi came to fetch him. He raced to Tess's bedside. "Roger. I'm ready. I've got something that will interest you, if you're not too drunk."

Roger teetered closer to her. "Whad makes you thig I'b drungk?"

"I heard what you had for dinner. Mostly liquid. Maybe you should sleep it off. This can wait."

The idea of waiting longer jolted him to stone-cold sobriety. "I've been waiting long enough." He tried to keep the resentment he felt out of his voice, but the last effects of the alcohol let it leak out. "Let's hear what you have."

"Check the wall monitor. I've slaved it to mine."

"Just tell me."

"I checked Bonnie's work history. Something about her credentials caught my attention, but I couldn't pin it down. I looked at it up and down, checked the time sequence of her promotions against the employers' stated personnel policies, everything I could think of."

"And what did you find?"

"Nothing. Except that she was a fast-tracker. Outstanding performer. I even cracked a couple of personnel files—I've learned some useful stuff from SOS. I found she had always received top-of-the-scale reviews."

"Did you check Rebecca's, too?"

"Of course. I may be a jealous wife, but I'm still a scientist."

He ignored her self-deprecation. "And . . . ?"

"And it was the same. Maybe not such a fast riser, but never anything but good things to say about her. And I found out what she did at the security company. It's a plus."

Roger refused to be distracted. "So, should we flip a coin?"

"Wait. I'm not done."

"What else could you possibly want to know?"

"I pondered that for a long time, and almost decided I was indeed just reacting like a jealous wife. I think I napped for a few minutes, and then it came to me. I was looking at the wrong level. Here, you have to look at the screen to see this."

The large monitor flickered for a moment, then displayed three columns, with lists of company names, aligned side by side. "What's this?" he asked.

"On the left are the companies that Bonnie worked for. On the right are Rebecca's."

Roger squinted at the screen. "And the middle? I don't recognize the names listed there."

"That's a list Don provided—Sunshine Bank's commercial banking clients. Now watch. I'm going to eliminate the ones that aren't relevant for this purpose." The middle list shortened to four names.

"What makes those relevant?"

"Look on the left." Four out of five of Bonnie's former employers matched the four companies on the center list. Roger's mouth formed a large O.

"Now the right." None of Rebecca's longer list matched. Roger nodded slowly as he double-checked.

"I know you're going to say that it's a coincidence and doesn't prove anything—"

Roger shook his head, as if not quite able to believe the implications of what he was seeing. "No, I wasn't going to say that."

"—but I think Don will be very interested in knowing the names of those four companies. I think Bonnie is a plant. A spy. Maybe even a saboteur."

"Jesus," he said. "If they can do such a perfect job of faking all these records, do you realize what that implies about the organization behind this?"

"I do. And now I'm glad that the Ford is still parked outside."

67

Tess's guards had barely established a satisfactory routine for her local shopping trips when she declared that it was finally time to buy something better than the ancient purple sofa to hide the steel floor plates covering the old gas-station service pit. It seemed that no local rug merchant would do, and, besides, Tess argued, Uncle Qasim had connections with several rug merchants at the Merchandise Mart, making it an ideal place to shop. Roger tried to argue that carpets would interfere with her wheelchair mobility, but Qasim brought in one of his own carpets and demonstrated how it could be taped down—if they indeed wanted to place such a valuable carpet on the floor. That whetted Tess's appetite for even more carpets to add to her collection of Navajo rugs they'd already put on the walls. Roger's resistance collapsed. He let her go.

Qasim identified Thursday as the best day for rug shopping. "The new shipments from overseas arrive on Tuesday, but it usually takes all day Wednesday to inventory them, so on Thursday you get the best selection. Friday isn't bad, but by then the weekend shopping has begun. Best to go on Thursday."

Don worried that the trip to the Merchandise Mart posed an increased security threat to Tess, and decided to augment Tess's regular guard. With Lucinda away on other business, Don took the task himself. Before letting Tess out of the van, he sent two agents as scouts ahead to the floor she proposed visiting. They returned with reports of "Arabs swarming all over the place," but Tess argued they were just being paranoid and insisted on proceeding with her shopping.

"You're harder to guard than the Vice President," Agent One quipped. "And preparing for his trip is nuisance enough." Tess took the comment as a compliment, and asked to be taken inside.

Qasim had urged them to visit his shop first. He didn't specialize in rugs, but had said he had "a few of museum quality" in his back room. When Tess saw an exquisite antique Persian Cheleberd rug in the display window, she wondered just how good "museum quality" might be. She started to roll her wheelchair toward the door when a large man dressed in camouflage jeans and a black T-shirt stepped in front of her, blocking her way.

"You don't want to go in there, lady," the man said angrily.

"Why not?" she asked through her machine, just before noticing that the placard he carried announced a Christian boycott of Arab goods.

"Aren't you a loyal American? You don't want to support our enemies, do you?"

Don didn't want trouble, so before Tess could construct an answer, he slipped between her and the man while one of her other guards backed the man away. "I don't like crossing picket lines," he said tersely to Tess. "You never know what they'll do. Let's try another place."

"They'll be picketing everywhere," Tess said.

He checked Qasim's list of rug merchants. "Not all these places are Arab-owned."

"So we're just going to give in to these bigots? I don't think so." She started forward, but Don quickly flipped the emergency shut-off switch, immobilizing her chair. She was helpless to move, but she could still shout through her machine. "LET ME GO! HELP!"

Don cast a glance at the crowd of picketers she was attracting. "For God's sake, Tess, let's think about this for a minute."

"I don't want to give them the satisfaction of turning us away. Why reward racism?"

"This crowd looks angry. Why invite trouble?"

"That's ridiculous. Let me talk to them. I want to see those rugs."

Against his better judgment, Don turned her power back on. Tess swung the chair around to face the picketers. There were more of them than she'd realized, but most of them looked less threatening than the man who'd confronted her. "LISTEN UP," her machine shouted. "I can't move without my chair. I can't talk except through this machine. I'm one-hundred percent a patriotic American, and I got into the condition I'm in while serving my country. How about letting me go about my business?"

The crowd hesitated. She hoped they hadn't noticed that she hadn't said anything about Christianity. A couple of the more tentative ones started backing away, but the man in camouflage who'd blocked her passage held his ground. Was he going to dare to ask her just how she had served her country? He opened his mouth to say something—then thought better of it and reached an arm across his chest, rolled up his sleeve, and pointed proudly to the eagle, the globe, and the words, "*Semper fi.*" Then, with a hasty salute, he quietly stepped back and allowed Tess to roll past him into Qasim's store.

Once inside, Tess confessed to Don, "I feel a little bit ashamed. I think he thinks I am a disabled veteran."

"You have nothing to be ashamed of. You *are* serving your country, in your own way. In fact, you should get a purple heart."

"Sure. Even so, let's get this over with quickly."

Qasim hurried toward them. The tension on his expression revealed his fear as he explained that the rugs were locked in his vault in the back room. He didn't want to bring any out front with the protesters right outside. "It's a very small room. Just space enough for you and me and your chair. Your companions will have to wait here."

"Uncle Qasim, I want to see your rugs, but I don't want to get my chair caught in a confined space. Please bring the rugs out here."

"No," he looked again at the crowd out front, "those people. The rugs are priceless. It's not safe."

"Uncle, no disrespect, but do you know who my companions are?"

"I don't know them."

"I'm forbidden to tell you who exactly, but they're top agents in one of our government's top security agencies. Nobody—nobody at all—is going to bother your rugs while they are around."

Qasim hesitated again, and then acquiesced. "If that is the case, I will bring my rugs out so your companions can see them, too. Perhaps such Americans can learn to appreciate the culture of the Middle East." He disappeared into the back room, reappearing a long minute later with a small, pure-wool, hand-woven, nineteenth-century Caucasian Kilim, which he carefully draped over a glass display case next to Tess's chair.

Qasim returned to the back room again and again, until an astonishing collection of richly colored geometric Kilims, Sumaks, tapestries, and, finally, the prize of his collection, a delicate, seventeenth-century floral Aubusson was added to the pile of rugs. Tess praised the rugs as effusively as her limited vocal apparatus would allow, leaving Qasim beaming with pride.

"Of course," she said, terminating the visit, "Roger and I could never put such fine works of art on our floor, let alone anywhere in our garage home. But, someday, when we have a proper home of our own, I'm going to be back here begging."

"But you, blessed wife of my sister's son, will never have to beg from Qasim. What's mine is yours, the moment you say the word." He helped her move the chair to the door as he spoke.

Once Tess and her escorts were out of the store and safely past the picketers, she questioned Don, "Did you like the rugs? Qasim wanted you to appreciate them."

"They were incredible—very beautiful—though I have no idea of their value. They didn't have price tags. How much do you think they cost?"

"You have to bargain for them. Price tags would be offensive. To the owner, and to the rugs."

"I see."

"Of course, it's mostly a matter of personal taste. Read the list of shops again. I remember there was a Navajo rug dealer. The Orientals were beautiful but I can see now that I'd only want Navajos in my home. I hope Qasim will understand."

"What is so special about—" Don stopped walking and grabbed his cell. "Where?" was all he said before snapping the phone shut. "Tess, you'll have to teach me about Navajo rugs some other time. There's been an explosion on the El, near the Damen station. I've got to get over there now." He turned to the older of the two agents. "Conner, you'll have to get her home. Be careful. This may be a diversion."

68

Even from a distance, Don could see this was no diversion. Unable to drive any further because of billowing shrouds of smoke and throngs of rescue workers, he made the last two hundred yards to the site on foot, growing more and more distraught with each step forward. If this was a diversion, he didn't want to see the main attraction. Every step of the way, the anguished screams of people trapped in the wreckage pounded more heavily in his skull. He tried to comfort himself with the thought that screams meant some people were still alive. That hopeful rationalization was refuted when the smoke from two burning cars started blowing in the other direction, giving him his first clear view of the ghastly site. Now he could see the rounded silver corners of an El car, which hung from the twisted track above like a giant coffin about to be lowered into a grave.

Before he had time to wonder how many people might be on board, his eye was drawn to the colorful clothing of trapped passengers pressed against the window glass. The car seemed full. Probably was, at this time of day. If the car broke loose, the impact would probably kill everyone on board—but he could see that they had no way to escape. He had never witnessed a scene like this and felt unqualified to estimate how stable the car might be in its hanging position.

The only possible means of escape seemed to be a bright red fire truck just now extending its ladder toward a window that had popped out. As he watched, the ladder stopped, just short of contact with the car. He wanted to rush forward and tell the ladder operator to hurry, but a uniformed cop ordered him to stand back. He flashed his identification and waited a second until the same officer motioned him to move closer. Then he saw the problem. The people at the windows were fighting off other passengers to be the first rescued.

Someone started throwing out luggage, and Don remembered that the Blue Line came from O'Hare. If they were thinking first of their possessions, the fireman on the ladder was wise to want them to calm down before he risked coming within reach. "I want the children first," he shouted, but Don doubted the combatants could make out what he was saying over their own shouts and the cries of the wounded.

Someone touched his shoulder. "It's the fire department's problem." Lucinda's voice was cold and calm—professional. "We have other work to do."

He stopped brooding over how he could help. He calmed his voice, but his insides still churned. "Sorry, LD. It's hard to watch this and not do something."

"I've seen worse," she said. "Try cluster bombs in the market square of an Iraqi village. Unless you like playing jigsaw with the arms and legs. And heads."

"What are the casualties here?"

"No way to tell yet. Some dead on the ground, but most of the people are still trapped on the train."

"How many on the ground?"

Lucinda started walking under the silver car, showing no fear that it would fall any time soon. "Too many body parts so far. Impossible to count. Come on, I'll show you."

Don searched for signs of the primary explosion among the twisted brown beams. "Have you identified the pattern? There might be some unexploded bombs."

"Pattern? I'd say the pattern was to try to blast everything they could reach. A crude job."

"Seems to have done the job, though."

"It could have been much worse. There were some bombs duct-taped on the support pillars, but none, apparently, high up."

She picked up a red metal fragment. "There were quite a few of these. Looks like at least one bomb was in a newspaper vending machine."

For the first time, Don noticed the newspaper litter blowing around the site. Definitely more than a typical Chicago trash cyclone. "Anything else?"

"Oh, yes. At least two car bombs. Trucks, actually."

"Suicides?"

"More likely parked in key places in advance. It's a fixed target."

Don glanced back at the still-hanging car. "Maybe not. Wouldn't the train have stopped automatically when the track lost integrity? Maybe it was timed to the train. Or triggered by something on the track."

"When we can get people up there, we'll study the track, but perhaps the train did slow down, so the timing wasn't perfect. If it had been at full speed, I think it would have come off the track entirely."

"So it could have been worse?"

"Yes, much worse."

The passengers at the open window had apparently calmed down. Don watched a small child being relayed down the ladder. Another fire engine moved into position to raise some sort of sling with its turret. A third engine disgorged firefighters who began spraying retardant on the burning cars. Further back, he saw a mobile command post strategically parked. It had somehow pushed its way through the stalled traffic and seemed to be coordinating the clearing of passage for ambulances. "We'd better go offer our services."

"You go," said Lucinda. "I'm going to look for clues before the site is trampled beyond usefulness."

"Okay. I'll follow you as soon as I check in." But as he neared the command post, he forgot his promise. Already, there were more than a dozen bodies lined up on the sidewalk awaiting body bags. Four of them were children, and all of them were missing significant body parts.

He grabbed the door handle of a crushed car, clutched his belly, and bent over. *I'm an agent*, he thought. *I shouldn't be vomiting.*

69

Qaaf didn't want Zay or Jiim to hear any hint of gloating in her voice, but she wasn't in full control of all the undertones of disgust and anger. "A total screwup, Alif. Total."

"We brought down the El. The Blue Line will be inoperative for months. Millions will feel the traffic confusion and—"

"Idiot! People were killed. Nobody was supposed to die."

"We couldn't know the train's safety mechanism would fail."

"It wasn't the safety mechanism. It was the timing," Qaaf said. "The safeties worked, but there wasn't enough time for the train to come to a complete stop before reaching the break."

Alif shrugged. "What's the difference? We've accomplished our purpose. We've made Chicago's Finest look like the fools they are. You have to expect a little collateral damage."

Qaaf knew Alif talked like this when he was trying to convince Zay, but she had his number this time. "This wasn't collateral. It was central. You could have disabled the Blue Line with one tenth the explosives, had they been properly placed. And timed. Instead, you used enough to bring down the Blue Line, Red Line, Brown Line, Purple Line, Orange Line, Green Line—the Rainbow Line, if they had one." She stopped to breathe, daring Alif to respond.

"The El structure is a difficult one. Heavily over-engineered." Alif's tone was now clearly defensive. Jiim should have been making this argument, but had the sense to remain quietly ashamed.

Qaaf pressed her advantage. "Any competent structural engineer could have told you that, while explaining how to bring it down with one tenth the explosives. It's not as if we have an infinite supply of explosives, and the more we use, the more clues we leave."

"We get your point, Qaaf," Zay said calmly. "And we remember who suggested the structural engineer. We've made the mistake, and it cannot be undone. So, what's the lesson?"

"I suppose you're going to say we should always do what Qaaf tells us," Alif said.

"Not at all. The point is that we should all use all our brains, not our balls, in making decisions. Work with finesse, not force. So, Alif, what progress can you report on the viruses?"

70

When Don reached Roosevelt and Damen and saw the rain-wet facade of the new FBI building, he thought he was finally free to relax for a moment and gather his thoughts. After three hours of grisly on-site work, he needed some gym time, a shower, and a change into dry clothes before facing any of the higher-ups, not to speak of the press corps vultures. But it was not to be. As he drove by the dramatic two-level entryway, he spotted the broad rear of a familiar and unwelcome shape. Inga Steinman had come to pay a visit.

By the time he'd parked in the secure garage and reached his eighth-floor office, Inga was already waiting. She wasn't alone, and her arrival with the deputy attorney general so soon after the bombing was no coincidence.

"Hello, Agent Capitol," Inga said, attempting to take control of the situation. "I believe you know Deputy Tempkins."

Don extended his hand to the bony, Beltway-pale government official, not failing to notice Inga's formality. "Yes, though I doubt he remembers me."

Reggie Tempkins' hand felt flaccid and weak. "I know your work. It's been exemplary—up until now. I know it's only been four or five hours, but what have you got on the Blue Line bombing?"

"Let's go inside, Sir," said Don as he unlocked his office door. "The Agency discourages hallway conversations."

A quick 360-degree check of his office confirmed that he'd left it orderly. Don offered his own chair to Inga, realizing that she might not be able to squeeze into either of his guest chairs. Seating himself facing the deputy, he got right down to business.

"The Blue Line bombing missed the congressman from Missouri. That's the good news."

"And the bad?"

"Twenty-three other human beings were not so lucky."

"I understand there were two Polish diplomats on the train."

"Yes, on a goodwill visit. Chicago is the second-largest Polish city in the world—after Warsaw."

"I know that, Agent Capitol. Let's cut to the chase. Are they okay?"

Don swallowed hard. "No. They were among the dead. Along with one of their aides. Two other aides survived, but are currently hospitalized."

Tempkins drew a black leather notepad from his breast pocket and jotted a few words. "So now your little nuisance bombings have become an international incident. Any other notables?"

"Just ordinary people, as far as we know. But I wouldn't call them nuisance bombings."

Tempkins ignored Don's correction. "What do you mean, as far as you know?"

"Most of the people on that train were coming from O'Hare. Not locals, most of them. So we don't know yet who some of them are."

"Any leads?"

"Just the usual physical evidence."

"Nothing on the bombers? Was it a suicide?"

"Not likely. Evidently the bombs were placed well in advance, to bring down the tracks when the train approached."

Tempkins lifted the silver pen set from Don's desk and turned it around in his hands. "But somebody must have triggered it, if it was targeting the congressman. Was it?"

"Was it what? Triggered? Or targeting the congressman?"

Tempkins didn't look up from studying the inscription. "Both."

"We have no way to be sure, but both are likely. They could have been targeting someone else on the train, but we won't know more about that until we identify everybody."

"Could it have been the Poles?"

"You would know more about that than I, Sir. Is there any reason someone might have a grudge against the current Polish government?"

Tempkins lowered the heavy pen set back down onto the desk. "There are always people who have grudges against governments, Agent Capitol."

"I understand. From what I've seen so far, though, this attack has the earmarks of the other attacks."

Inga Steinman rolled forward, then stopped her momentum with both pudgy hands against Don's desk. "But it's not the same pattern as the others. They were all attacks on empty buildings."

"Mostly empty, but, yes. And we thought we'd done a good job of stopping those with increased security. Perhaps the bombers decided they needed to change their pattern. To escalate. They seem to want their money."

The deputy pointed a bony finger at Don. "In that case, your security backfired. We have to protect the Congress, of course, but not in a way that leads to murdering ordinary citizens. Or diplomats."

"I agree, Sir. Absolutely. But unless the congressmen—" he paused and glanced at Inga, "—or congresswomen—are willing to authorize money for twenty-four hour security of their homes and offices, there's not much we can do to prevent this sort of thing. There are just too many places to secure at once."

Tempkins made a note. "Are all the bombings part of the same pattern?"

"We believe so."

"No copycats?"

"The forensic evidence doesn't indicate any."

"So, it's spreading all over. Even more places to watch."

"I'm afraid so, Sir."

The deputy put down his notebook and pen and fixed Don unblinkingly with a stare. "Then you have to do more to catch these people. That's the only way it's going to stop. Have you made any progress at all?"

Don summarized the situation—the Sunshine Bank connections, the loss of the suspect at the clinic, Adara Halabi's capture and interrogation—while the deputy resumed note-taking, finally interrupting with a question to Inga. "This Halabi woman. She seems their best lead, so why haven't they used your new interrogation device on her? Why aren't you cooperating?"

Don's chair didn't leave Inga Steinman much room in which to squirm, but her fleshy body made a defiant effort. "We've had some setbacks. Our best version was produced by Halabi's cousin. Of course, we can't have him working with us on any of this."

The deputy was no fool. "Can't? I thought he refused."

Inga still wasn't ready to take the blame. "No, it was a security issue." She stared at Don as if daring him to challenge her fib. "He was eager to continue working on the project, but we had to dismiss him."

Don grunted his support of Inga's version, but the deputy wasn't finished. "So you're really sure Halabi is the murderer?"

"I'm growing less and less confident every day," Don said. "We've questioned her, using—"

Tempkins raised his hand. "I don't want to hear the methods. That's your business, not mine. Just give me the results."

"She keeps breaking down, but she won't admit to anything. She doesn't act like a trained agent."

"Perhaps she was just paid for this one job."

"We've tracked all her financial records—and her family's. If she was paid, the money hasn't shown up anywhere."

"There are other motives," said Inga. "They might have threatened a member of her family."

Don shook his head. "Possibly, but in that case, everybody is a suspect."

"Then check everybody," said the deputy. "Inga, you arrange to get Dr. Fixman back on the team. I'll take responsibility for any security problem."

"Don should do it. I think Fixman trusts him, somewhat."

"Fine." Tempkins turned his attention to Don. "Then you get him back. I don't care how you do it."

Don assured them he would give it a try, but he knew there was no way Roger would come back on the project. There was no arguing with Tempkins, so he said nothing more. Tempkins then returned to hounding Steinman. "Your job is to see that there is no security problem. And to clear all the paperwork and the scientific details."

She hesitated. "We have another alternative."

"What's that?"

"Fixman's former professor, Harvey Wyatt."

"I thought he was a fraud?"

"He wasn't making fast progress, so he rigged a phony demonstration. It's been done before. In fact, everybody does it."

"So how do we know he won't do it again?"

"He's working for a large corporation now. They have controls against such hanky panky."

Tempkins looked doubtful. "You have more faith in corporations than I do, but I'll look into it."

71

Roger didn't want to talk to Don unless Tess showed some progress with the exoskeleton, but Tess took a softer, more rational approach. "Let's hear what they have to offer. But let's meet on neutral ground." Neutral ground turned out to be an early supper at Poznan Polish Restaurant. Tess thought it was Don's choice for tactical reasons, since it was only three blocks from the Blue Line Massacre, as the *Tribune* was already calling it. He probably hoped to nettle Roger's conscience by emphasizing the loss of Polish diplomats. As they came in out of the drizzle and entered the restaurant, she saw she'd been right. A rough black wreath containing white calla lilies—usually seen only at Polish funerals—greeted them at the front door. Inside, the polished dark wood and glass furnishings were draped from every possible surface with black crepe. Every table held a small pot of yellow chrysanthemums, another funereal tradition.

The headwaiter greeted them with a muted, *"Dobry wieczor,"* but when Don apologized, explaining that they didn't speak Polish, the man looked surprised for a moment, then recovered quickly and seated them where Tess would have a full view of the somber interior.

Once at the table, Don revealed that his original family surname was Czapiewski on his grandfather's side, though his mother's side was one-hundred percent Italian. He didn't speak Polish with the waitress, but he did know what the menu selections meant. Inga let him choose their dinner items, but not the quantities. She started with a triple order of potato pancakes served with double sour cream and applesauce. Roger and Don shared one regular order. Roger was able to spoon a few tastes of the applesauce into Tess's mouth, letting her automatic peristalsis handle the swallowing. He, or she, was getting better at this, and only two or three blobs of applesauce dropped to the napkin he'd placed around her neck.

Shortly after the waitress brought their three orders into the kitchen, the owner came out and introduced himself as Maksymilian Wierzchleyski. He was concerned that Tess hadn't ordered any food. Although Roger explained that she couldn't eat anything but liquids, after some persuasion, Maksymilian convinced her that he could purée his famous *zurek*—white *borscht*—for her. He assured Roger that the potatoes, sausage, carrots, parsnips, and the like would be reduced to minuscule bits that could not possibly cause her trouble.

When the platters of food arrived along with a brimming bowl of purée, Maksymilian came out to confirm that he had been true to his word. Tess thanked him, and then allowed Roger to feed her one spoonful of *zurek* at a time. While Inga polished off tripe soup and pork tenderloin with extra dumplings, Don turned the conversation to business.

"I spent today in the neighborhood interviewing people who were near ground zero over the past few days, to see if they saw anything suspicious. Nobody could remember anything, but I suspect they saw things they didn't register consciously at the time."

Roger knew where this was leading, but kept still, concentrating on feeding Tess. Don took a bite of his stuffed cabbage, staying quiet in hopes Roger would respond. Instead, it was Tess who ended their game of silence by naming Don's point aloud. "You want us to process their memories with the Aremac, don't you?"

"Would you do that?" Don asked, gesturing with his fork toward the other people in the restaurant. "For these people. For the Poles, who lost several of their own to these monsters."

Roger was about to say no, but Tess's mechanical voice was faster, indicating that she'd already known the answer she was going to give. "We'll do it for Maksymilian, and people like him, but only if the people volunteer."

Don looked to Roger, but he refused to agree. "First of all, the pictures we're getting so far wouldn't be worth much to you. They're not sufficiently refined."

"We may not need much detail," Don countered. "We might be able to identify a truck, or some characteristics of the bomber. We have nothing now. Nothing."

"Well, even supposing the resolution was adequate, what are we getting in exchange? You're asking a lot, but offer nothing."

"We'll pay, of course," said Inga. "Name your price."

Tess was offended by the offer of money and was surprised that Inga didn't anticipate that. "My price is that you release Addie."

"Be reasonable," said Don. "You know I can't do that."

"No," said Tess. "We don't know that."

"Then you'll just have to believe me. I can't get her released."

"Inga?"

Inga stopped mopping up gravy with a huge hunk of dark rye bread. "If he can't, I certainly can't. Money is my currency. Unlike Don, I don't trade in bodies."

"In other words, neither of you has the authority to release her until her trial. Not even if we put up bail money?"

Inga and Don exchanged looks. "That's correct," said Inga. "So that's off the table. What do you want instead?"

Before Tess could answer, the waiter began to clear away some of the finished dishes. Inga was still eating, but she ordered a dessert of *szarlotka*, *pontshki*, and *sernik*. Then she persuaded Don to order *makowiec*, "Just so I can taste their famous poppy-seed rolls."

Tess refused to be sidetracked by dessert, even puréed. "We want to speak to the person who does have the authority." The cold mechanical quality of Tess's voice was never more evident. When neither Don nor Inga responded, Tess gave the verdict. "Come on, Roger. Take me home. We're finished here."

"Aren't you even going to have a bit of dessert?" Inga pleaded, but to no avail. Once Roger had wheeled Tess safely out of hearing range, Inga gloated at Don. "Well, we seem to have maneuvered them exactly where we want them. Now your job is to stay on friendly terms with them. Make them think you're on their side."

Inga knew that Tess had lost the use of her body. What she didn't know was how her hearing had compensated for that loss.

72

The next day broke bright and sunny, and spirits at the Aremac headquarters, already improving with the recent hiring of the English administrator Rebecca Solomon, soon followed the weather. On a conference call with the deputy attorney general, Tess's mechanical voice successfully negotiated Addie's release. Uncle Zahid and Uncle Qasim both put their homes up as bail bond, and Addie was free. Not completely free, of course—she was restricted to certain Chicago neighborhoods and required to wear a GPS locator ankle bracelet so her movements could be tracked. She was not to visit the Aremac but otherwise had the freedom of movement that the deputy attorney general's office secretly hoped would lead to her coconspirators.

To fulfill his side of the bargain, Roger used the Aremac to "interview" three people who'd been working outside in the neighborhood the week before the Blue Line Massacre—a sign painter, a window washer, and a panhandler. Though they didn't consciously remember anything useful, Roger was able to extract sequences of rough still pictures of neighborhood activities. From these, Don identified three suspicious vehicles by color and size.

A two-tone green-and-white car turned out to belong to the visiting cousin of an apartment dweller. A blue truck belonged to a decorator who was remodeling an insurance agent's office. But a dark-gray panel truck could not be identified by anyone in the neighborhood. By soliciting three different mental views of that truck, Roger was able to give Don a partial license plate, and from there, Don's junior agents took up the search.

Rebecca had been on board long enough now that her help was becoming really valuable. Roger had a hard time imagining how he had ever gotten along without her. Bonnie, he knew, had been detained for intensive questioning, but he had not heard anything further. All was going well.

One week later, the Aremac battled its first virus.

"Actually," said SOS, visibly agitated, "it didn't touch the Aremac itself, which is physically isolated from the other systems except when we put it online. But if I'd downloaded a new version of the software, we'd have been in trouble."

Roger didn't understand. "But you didn't experience any problems on the other systems, and they were the ones containing the virus."

"That's the tip-off, actually." SOS plucked a stray hair from his chin. "Those systems run on conventional CPUs, but the Aremac is built on a custom chip set."

"Right. So what?"

"The virus was designed for the Aremac chips. It was meaningless junk bits to the other machines. It had to be aimed at the Aremac. Someone specifically designed it to attack us." He studied the plucked hair as if it held some clue to the identity of the attackers.

"So that's why we didn't hear about this virus from anywhere else?"

"Precisely. There's one and only one machine in the world that would have been affected by it."

Tess joined the discussion. "But it was propagated through the conventional systems. They were like carriers. They spread the virus to any system they connected to, but weren't affected themselves. Like echinococcus *granulosus*."

"I love it when you talk dirty," said SOS. "What's that mean?"

"It's the dog tapeworm. Latin. Heidi had them when we got her."

Rebecca had been following the discussion up to this point, but now she was puzzled. "So what does that have to do with our virus? Is it carried by another virus?" Without taking her eyes off Tess's passive face, she picked up the wastebasket and extended it to SOS. He looked baffled for a moment, then dropped his loose hair into it. Rebecca nodded her approval.

"We're talking about worms, flatworms," Tess said. "I'll spare you the dirty language. Part of its life cycle takes place in rodents, or pigs, or sheep, but it doesn't really affect them in any serious way. But when dogs, or humans, eat undercooked meat containing tapeworm cysts, they get infected and it becomes serious."

"So, it was actually a kind of computer worm, not a virus."

"Well, if it's self-contained, yes. But you geeks aren't known for your care about precise definitions."

"Me, a geek?" SOS took off his thick glasses and leaned over to glare in Tess's face. "Look who's talking, ubergeek. Who taught me the Vienna Formal Definition Language?"

Roger scratched the table with his nails. "If you two are finished playing geekier than thou, how about getting to work squashing this worm?"

"Oh, that's already done." SOS and Tess spoke the same words, almost in harmony. SOS deferred to Tess's machine, and she explained. "It never really had a chance against Dr. Geek's layers of defense. He caught it before it was fully downloaded into our outer systems."

"She's giving me too much credit, Roger. Ms.—or Mrs.—" He interrupted himself. "Did you know that in Austria, you would be Frau Doktor Doktor Ubergeek?"

"Stick to the subject," Roger said.

"Okay. Okay. Frau Doktor Doktor designed more than half of it. I thought I'd done a pretty good job, then she took my Maginot Line apart and rebuilt it into an Iron Curtain. I thought she was being paranoid. Not anymore."

Rebecca groaned. "Well, the Iron Curtain came down, too, if I remember my history."

"Don't worry," said Tess. "We haven't stopped trying to improve. This was a rather crude attempt, but I'm guessing whoever it is will keep trying to improve, too." She paused. "And I doubt that there's anything you don't remember, Rebecca. I wish I had seen and done one tenth of what you've experienced."

Roger silently added, *before you lost your body.*

Rebecca didn't acknowledge Tess's compliment. "Maybe we should put out some disinformation, to let them think they really hurt us. We did that at, well, at one of my former employers. If they think we're damaged, maybe they'll stop bothering us."

SOS held up his hands in protest. "No, no. We want them to continue. Each attack gives us more chances to pinpoint exactly where this is coming from."

"Don't get too cocky, young man," Rebecca chastised him. "They might get lucky and beat you. Besides, you already said you know it's coming from Professor Wyatt. Why take chances?"

Tess raised her volume a notch. "There's a good reason, Rebecca. Knowing *who* it's coming from is not the same as knowing from *where*. I think Don would like to know what facilities are being used."

"Do we want to help the FBI?"

"Of course. For one thing, it's a federal crime to transmit such stuff, so if we can give him evidence, he might be able to get a warrant to search some premises. Slow them down, at least."

"I guess that might help Adara," Rebecca conceded. "Search warrants turn up all sorts of interesting items. But Don doesn't need a warrant, does he? These are terrorists."

"We don't know if Wyatt's working for the terrorists," Tess explained. "If he is, he probably doesn't know either. It may be plain old industrial espionage. Don's pretty careful about not tainting an investigation, so he'd rather have a warrant. If he can get one."

"Anyway," said SOS, "what's he going to get a warrant for? All the computers in the world? We have to pin it down for him."

"All right," said Roger, standing up. "Let's keep working on defenses—but let's not lose sight of our main objectives. We've got to clear Addie and get Tess up and running again. After that, if you want, you can save the world for democracy. Or whatever."

73

Jiim had the good sense to look ashamed, but Qaaf knew Alif wouldn't admit to another blunder so easily in front of Zay. "A five-year-old could construct a better virus," she said. "They disarmed it in minutes."

This news seemed to surprise Zay. "Is that true? I thought our man knew what he was doing. What damage did it do?"

"Nothing," said Qaaf. "Not even a flea on a dog's belly."

"Alif?" Zay asked.

"I have no information one way or the other."

"Of course you don't," said Qaaf. "That's my job, and nothing was harmed. Believe me, the only result is increased caution."

"Can you do better?" Zay asked. "I know nothing about computers."

"I can write instructions to our programmer," Qaaf said. "Whether he does his job or not is another matter. I think we're wasting resources."

Alif wasn't satisfied with her answer. "Then you should instruct him personally. Are you afraid of the man?"

"I can't allow him to see me in this context," she said. "It'll have to be in writing."

Alif was adamant. "Then instruct him to double his efforts. We're running out of time."

"Of course." She stared hard at Alif. "I assume you know how to put pressure on him. I'm sure he's a coward, so even you should succeed."

Alif swallowed his first answer, then broke eye contact with Qaaf and looked at Zay. "With God's help, I will succeed."

"That's an admirable sentiment," said Zay, "but perhaps it's time we learned from experience and brought in another expert."

74

As the weather grew cooler, the virus attacks continued. For a while, the attacks grew more and more sophisticated—but Tess and SOS managed to stay ahead, with just one close call. They soon realized that Wyatt's viruses were crafted even more clumsily than his other code, but even so, combatting them slowed down their project by wasting valuable time. Then the coding style abruptly changed, raising the virus's level of sophistication a notch. That's when their defenses were almost breached.

Tess thought she had an explanation. "The style of this coding is completely different. I think we have a second cracker. And this one's better."

SOS nodded agreement, and Tess flashed a section of virus code on the large monitor. "And there's something else. Take a look at this." She mentally highlighted three lines of code. "Here, this is the key to the backdoor the virus was using."

"I see that it's different from the other viruses," Roger said. "That's just what I would expect if it was written by a different person."

"We didn't expect this," SOS said. "If this little bugger gets through one of the many holes in the firewall security—"

Roger banged the table. "Why are there still holes in our firewall?"

SOS made a raspberry, but Tess explained the problem simply. "It's a commercial product, made by a large software company. It came packaged with the hardware, and we haven't had time to root it out and replace it with a better one."

Roger wrote a note in his PDA. "Okay—well, not okay—but for now, what happens after it gets past the firewall?"

"It would have exploited a glitch in our code, if it got that far." SOS illustrated with an obscene gesture using his fingers. "Fortunately, the glitch was in the previous release, not the current one. If we were still using the previous release, the virus would have gotten through our barriers and done damage."

"Lots of damage," said Tess.

"But the new version doesn't have this glitch, so nothing happened that we couldn't handle."

"So," Roger shrugged, "what's the problem? You guys don't have to lecture me about every problem you solve. I already know you're good."

"Thanks," said Tess, "but you're missing the point. The previous viruses were based either on the chip structure or on the old code sections that Wyatt would have known about. This one is based on code I wrote since we moved down here. There's no way Wyatt could have known about this glitch."

"But," said SOS, "there obviously is a way. We've got a leak somewhere."

"Damn," Roger swore. "I don't have time to deal with this. I need to get ready to go to lunch with Arnie at Lipinski's. Take everything off-line until we find the leak. Then go over everybody who's been in and out of here since . . ."

"Just since yesterday," Tess filled in.

"Why yesterday?"

"Because we do a daily build, and that code glitch was only there for one day. If someone snatched it, it had to have been after yesterday's build and before today's."

"But nobody's been in here since yesterday. Just us."

"Nobody that we know of."

Before Roger had a chance to fully process the implications of this mystery, he heard the sound of Arnie's Cadillac pulling up. He hurried out, leaving his wife and friend to solve the seemingly impossible problem.

Sliding onto the passenger's seat of the Cadillac, Roger told Arnie that he had compiled such a long list of questions that his sticky notes were falling out of his book. He held up his copy of *The Expert Expert Witness,* and waved it about to make his point.

When the two men arrived at Lipinski's, they sat at their usual table, where Roger hoped to get answers along with the pickled tongue and Swiss on rye he ordered—a combination that had turned out to be his favorite. Instead, he ran into their first big legal roadblock.

As soon as Hedva delivered their appetizers of gefilte fish and cheese blintzes, Arnie took the initiative. "I want to thank you for getting Addie released. It's very helpful," he paused long enough to bite into a blintz. "But I have to know if you compromised our case in any way to do it."

"Tess did it. I didn't think we compromised our case, but maybe we were snookered."

Arnie's attention perked up. "How so?"

"At first, all we had to do was agree to use the Aremac to help the FBI process memories of Blue Line witnesses. That was okay because they all volunteered."

"And did it help?"

"It did. Even though the pictures were rough, we were able to identify a truck that didn't have any business being in the neighborhood."

Arnie licked a bit of cheese from his lips. "That's good. If they used the Aremac pictures to help their investigation, it establishes something of a precedent out of their own mouths."

"That's what Tess thought, which is why she wanted to make the deal. I wanted Addie out of custody, sure, but I didn't want to compromise us."

"No, you did good."

Roger toyed with one of the gefilte fish balls on his plate. "I think maybe we did too good."

"Too good? How?"

"We were able to extract a partial license plate from the pictures, and the FBI made an arrest."

"Sounds good to me. If they catch the terrorists, it will clear Addie." Arnie hesitated, and a worried look spread across his face. "Or won't it?"

"No, no. It's not that. Addie's innocent. There's no doubt about that."

"So what could be wrong?"

"Now they want to use the Aremac to interrogate their new prisoner."

"Good. Great, in fact. The more they use the Aremac, the more it establishes its authenticity."

Still holding his fork, Roger pushed the side plate away. He discovered he wasn't hungry for gefilte fish at all. "But this is a forced interrogation. That's why I left in the first place. They were torturing people. Well, one person. But I spoke to that ACLU guy the other day—"

"That wasn't wise—"

"I let him do all the talking. But he made a good case. The Aremac could be the worst thing for civil liberties since the Ku Klux Klan."

"That's a reasonable argument, but not if there's a way to use the Aremac without the torture. You may not believe this coming from a lawyer, but I don't want you to compromise anybody's civil rights. Why do you think I took this case?"

"There's certainly a way to do true-false testing without torture," Roger flicked a few fish crumbs off his fork, "but I don't trust them."

"Fair enough. So, don't agree for now. I'll work with you and maybe we can come up with some protection. It would definitely help us in the trial if we seemed to be cooperative."

"Speaking of the trial . . ." Roger opened his book to the first pink note.

Arnie dug into another of his cheese blintzes before looking up. "Put your book away. You aren't going to be an expert witness."

Roger kept the book open. "Why not? Do you think I can't handle it? I'm well prepared." He waved the book and a pink note fluttered out, "Just a few questions."

Arnie caught the note. "It's not me. The prosecution objected, saying you have a double conflict of interest in the case. Do you understand?"

Roger's shoulders sagged. "Okay, I suppose they're right. So SOS will have to handle it. He doesn't have a Ph.D., but he's sharper than I am."

Arnie finished the second blintz. "No, not SOS."

"Then who can handle the Aremac? Not you?"

"Maybe nobody. First, we'd have to get the judge to accept the Aremac."

Roger pushed the football-shaped fish balls around on the side plate. "How can we do that if neither of us can be an expert witness? Do you want me to train Rebecca? She really knows court procedure."

"That she does, but I don't think it will be necessary." Arnie scraped the last few morsels of blintz onto his fork. "I should have taken a double order."

"Come on, Arnie. What's wrong?"

"There won't be *any* expert witnesses. The judge will not allow any use of the Aremac at all. Even for pretrial disclosures. Because of the injunction over patents."

Roger had plenty of time to ponder this setback while Hedva delivered their sandwiches along with an elaborate spiel about today's special dessert—coconut cream pie. After Arnie yielded and ordered a piece of the special for each of them, Roger waited while Hedva cleared all the starter plates away except his fish plate, and then asked, "What's it going to take to lift the injunction?"

"If we had your engineering notebooks from your time at the University, and if they show what you say they show, the injunction would evaporate."

"But you know I don't have them. Can't you make Wyatt give them up?"

"I might . . . if he had them. He says he doesn't. Says the University took all his papers when they kicked him out—though he claims he resigned."

"If he resigned, they wouldn't have taken his papers."

"Of course! Hey, if you're not going to finish that fish, push it over here. The bouquet is too much to resist."

Roger slid the gefilte fish plate across the table. "How come you never gain weight?"

Arnie patted his flat belly. "Arguing with prosecutors burns lots of calories."

"So you think the University still has the papers?"

"Maybe. I had my assistant call, but they claimed they didn't have time to go through his papers. They're all sealed in boxes somewhere in Rackley Hall—"

"You probably mean 'Rackham.' The graduate school offices."

"I'll check my notes. It could have been Rackham. All I'm sure of is the rack part. Figured that's where they tortured the grad students."

Roger laughed. "Not too far from wrong. It must be Rackham. So can't you force them to let us at those boxes?"

"Not at this stage. They're not a party to the suit—at least not yet—so I can't force discovery at this early stage. Besides, they claim they're willing, but they have to follow procedures in cases like this, and that can take months."

"Yep, that's Rackham all right. Damn."

"Well, we'll think of something." Arnie pointed to Roger's sandwich plate. "Are you going to finish your tongue?"

"I thought you didn't like pickled tongue."

"Hey, to a starving man . . . I'll get a doggie bag."

"You know what?" said Roger. "I've just thought of a way to get those notebooks." He shoved his dessert plate across the table. "Have you got room for another piece of pie?"

75

It was just after two, in the middle of preregistration for the Fall semester, precisely at the time Rackham was at its busiest, when the Bag Bandit showed up amidst the crowd of students, seemingly out of nowhere. Some of the newer grad students didn't recognize him, but even they soon picked up the chant. "Bag Bandit, Bag Ban-dit. Bag the bu-reau-crats."

The Bag Bandit held up his hands to quiet the chanting. "This time, mighty Bag Bandit is here to save a fellow student, one who is powerless to save himself from the clutches of the dreaded Bureaucratic Swamp Thing. But the Bag Bandit needs your help. Who will help?"

Cries of "Yes, yes—we'll help" arose from the crowd, soon making the cry a new chant.

The Bag Bandit raised his hands again. "This poor student, fired from his job by a rogue professor—" boos swelled from the crowd "—this poor student has been doubly injured by Rackham. They stole his lab notes so they could claim a patent that was rightfully his."

The boos swelled to a roar, driving two middle-aged women to emerge from their offices to see what the ruckus was all about. "There they are," cried the Bag Bandit, pointing an accusing finger over the crowd. "Don't hurt them, but don't let them get away."

The students surrounded the two now-cowering clerks. "Don't hurt them," the Bag Bandit ordered again. "But make them show you where they've hidden the papers of the evil Professor Wyatt."

The older of the two women squeaked that she didn't know anything about any papers, but the other woman was conspicuously silent. "She knows," said the Bag Bandit, stepping up to the frightened clerk and pointing the feared finger of blame. "You know, don't you?"

"D-don't hurt me, p-please," she stammered.

"Just show us the boxes and nobody gets hurt."

"B-but everything's in s-storage in the b-basement."

"No problem. Is the door to the storage area locked?"

"I d-don't know. D-don't hurt me."

The Bag Bandit walked around to face the other clerk. "Is there a master key?" She nodded and pointed into her office. "Escort her back there," he ordered two hefty students. "See that she gets the key and doesn't make any mischief." He nodded his bagged head at the first clerk. "Then everyone will be fine, just fine."

The two students returned with the clerk and the key in less than a minute, and the crowd rushed down the stairs to the basement, the Bag Bandit in the lead, followed by the hoard flanking the hostage clerks. At the storage room door, the student holding the key unlocked it, and the first flood of students into the room fanned out to search for the boxes. Within seconds, a coed wearing a purple-flowered peasant blouse and mini-skirt found them stacked next to a structural column.

"Split them up among you," commanded the Bag Bandit. "No, wait, you four stay here and guard our Rackham lovelies. We're looking for lab notebooks with 'Property of Roger Fixman' marked on them."

"Hey," shouted a pudgy, bearded student wearing scarcely more than sandals and a tie-dyed T-shirt. "I knew him. He was an odd dude. But he got all our grades raised, or we all would have flunked Wyatt's class. Wyatt was a real prick."

His words seemed to motivate the melee, and before long, all of the boxes had been ripped open, searched, and four notebooks were laid at the feet of the Bag Bandit. He held each notebook close to his eyeholes to confirm its contents, then turned to address the crowd.

"You've done a superb job here today." He stepped between the clerks and raised their hands in the air. "Especially these two brave stalwarts. Let's give them a round of applause!"

The students stamped their feet and applauded, laughing and shouting congratulations to the clerks. When the revelry died down, the Bag Bandit—and the notebooks—were nowhere to be seen.

76

Arnie said, "Thank you, Your Honor," and swept Roger out of the judge's chambers before Roger and Wyatt had any chance for an interaction. When they were in the corridor, he whispered to Roger, "Now, will you tell me how you pulled that Bag Bandit stunt?"

Roger merely put his finger to his lips and said, "No-talk rule, remember? Just keep quiet and savor our victory."

That morning, Arnie had turned Roger's engineering notebooks over to the judge, asking that the injunction on the Aremac be lifted. Wyatt's attorneys had protested, saying that Roger had stolen the notebooks from the University's locked storage space in Ann Arbor. Arnie then brought forth Hedva and Gershom from Lipinski's to testify that he and Roger had been in Chicago enjoying a long lunch that afternoon, so that Roger couldn't possibly be the so-called Bag Bandit. Although Gershom couldn't testify in English, there was a rabbi in the court building performing a marriage, and the judge brought him in to interpret.

After Gershom's testimony, Arnie had further offered to find some of the dozen or so regular Lipinski customers who had seen them at lunch, but the judge said that wouldn't be necessary. Instead, he asked Hedva if Lipinski's *latkes* were as good as their reputation. She assured him they were even better and invited him to come in for a sample. He said he just might take her up on the offer, and then he dismissed Hedva and Gershom, and rendered his judgment on the spot: Roger was innocent of any wrongdoing. The judge then called a recess and retired to his chambers to examine the notebooks.

After an hour-long break, the judge returned. Before he could speak, Wyatt's attorneys objected that regardless of their provenance, the notebooks were Wyatt's property, not Roger's. The judge waved that one off without even hearing arguments from Arnie, saying, "I've looked at the notebooks, and though I don't understand a single word or diagram, it's apparent that these were written by Dr. Fixman, not by Dr. Wyatt. Therefore, the contents of the notebooks are unquestionably Dr. Fixman's legal property, regardless of how they came back to him."

He squashed a halfhearted objection from Wyatt, who couldn't seem to obey his lawyers' instructions to keep his mouth shut. He then announced to Wyatt's attorneys that he was lifting the injunction. "You can contest the patents in full trial, but in the meantime, Dr. Fixman is free to use his invention as he sees fit."

Then he turned to Arnie. "Unless and until you seek injunctive relief, Dr. Wyatt may use *his* invention as he sees fit. I believe that closes the matter before me. Good luck to both of you inventors. In times like these, our country certainly needs the services of agile minds such as yours."

Remembering that final compliment, Roger kept a big smile on his face all the way to the parking garage, into Arnie's Cadillac, out the exit, and onto Lake Shore Drive. "Okay," said Arnie. "We can talk now. Why the big smile?"

"For our victory, of course."

Arnie had the disconcerting driver's habit of looking at his passenger while he talked. "That grin looks like it's about more than that."

"I guess I'm remembering how Tess taught me to keep an engineering notebook, something she learned from Mel. I wonder if he'd be pleased to know what happened today."

"Who's Mel?"

"Her dad. She always thought he favored her brothers, but I still think she owes him a lot. I certainly do."

"Well, don't tell him. Not for now. Just keep up the no-talk rule until this thing is over. And maybe after, if the judge says so."

Arnie braked to avoid a motorcycle cutting in front of him. "But you're still smiling. And avoiding my question. How about that Bag Bandit?"

"Just keep up the no-talk rule until this thing is over," said Roger, imitating Arnie's words and voice. "It's better if you don't know, so if they appeal or something, you can be that rare bird, an honest attorney."

Arnie grunted and concentrated on his driving. Roger watched a sailboat executing a sloppy tack on Lake Michigan, then focused on a boy and girl tossing a Frisbee in the park alongside the Drive. He wondered whether Tess would ever play Frisbee again, and in the optimism of the moment, he convinced himself she would. He remained joyful within himself until they approached Aremac headquarters and were blocked by a police barricade. Ahead, Roger could see police cars, ambulances, and a black armored truck labeled BOMB SQUAD in large white letters.

As Arnie slowed the Cadillac, Roger jumped out and started to run for the building, only to be gruffly halted by a police officer in uniform. It took him what seemed like hours to convince the cop to send for Don, whom he could see through the crowd up ahead, trying to coordinate the chaos. When Don got the message and spotted Roger, he ran back to meet him and grabbed his elbow. "You're just in time. Come with me."

"Is Tess okay? Tell me quickly!"

"As far as we know."

"What do you mean, 'as far as we know'?"

"Just come with me. We need you to help us."

As they got close to the building, Roger heard barking from inside. "What's wrong? That's Heidi."

"We know that. She's why my bomb-squad boys won't go inside. They would have shot her already, but they're afraid they might set something off. They're losing patience."

"I'll get her out of there," Roger said, and rushed forward.

Don shouted, attempting to restrain him. "Wait! You need to hear the risks."

Heidi was barking even more frantically now. Roger called over his shoulder, "I know the risks. Don't kill our dog."

"There might be a bomb inside. It could go off at any minute. Do you still want to go in?"

"More than ever." Roger bolted for the door. "Heidi. It's me. It's okay. Hush, now. I'm going to open the door."

The loud barking changed to soft, whiney yelps. Roger turned the knob, but the door didn't budge. A huge man in a padded suit and helmet grabbed his shoulder and pulled him away. Except for the helmet, Roger thought the man looked like Heidi's Schutzhund trainer in protection pants and jacket. Roger knew that Heidi wouldn't know the difference and would seize the man's padded arm when she emerged, and would wrestle him down to the ground. He was about to shout a warning when the man spoke. "The bomb could be triggered by the door. Stand back and let me do it. I'm with the Bomb Squad. Just keep the dog quiet."

"It's locked," said Roger. "I have the key. Let me unlock it. You shouldn't risk your life for me. Besides, she might attack you. She's trained to go after someone in a suit like yours."

The man held out his gloved hand. "Give me the key. It's my job, not one for an amateur. You just keep the dog from jumping me . . . and keep her quiet. I need to listen when I start on the door. There could be something very sensitive in there."

Roger handed over the key and stepped back, noticing for the first time that two windows were shattered. He could see a wide spray of holes in the cinder-block wall, with none apparently going all the way through. The bomb-squad man motioned him to step further back, but when Roger backed up, Heidi started barking ferociously again. Roger moved cautiously forward and spoke to Heidi in a calming voice.

The bomb-squad man bent his ear to the lock. He inserted the key.

He paused for a few seconds, continuing to listen. Then, ever so slowly, his gloved fingertips turned the key.

Roger suddenly became aware that the crowd voices had stopped. He held his breath. The gloved hand twisted the door-knob deliberately, pausing every ten degrees. When the latch clicked, Roger jumped as if he had heard an explosion. Nothing happened.

The bomb-squad man opened the door a crack, but before he could push it all the way open, a black nose shoved through, followed by the whole dog. Heidi paused just for an instant to sniff the stranger, then bounded to Roger, her tail beating furiously. When her huge paws hit his shoulders, he staggered backward half a step, then regained his balance. "Heidi, go find Tess."

The bomb-squad man tried to block the door opening, but Heidi shot between his legs before he could react, pushing him off balance. He started to say something, but Roger swept past him so fast he didn't hear what was said. Inside the room, Roger immediately saw SOS on the floor, flat on his back in a spreading pool of blood, eyes closed. Rebecca crouched on the floor next to him, hissing angrily in his ear. Heidi was standing on hind legs with her front paws on the table, licking Tess's face. Roger could see that Tess was hooked to the Aremac, but she didn't answer when he called her name.

Then he understood why. Something, probably a bullet, had punched a nickel-sized hole right through the Aremac's CPU.

77

Don came rushing in just behind the bomb-squad man. "Don't be crazy, Roger, there could still be a bomb in here. They often leave one to catch rescuers."

Roger was trying to wrestle Tess into her wheelchair. "There's no bomb in here."

"Don't move her. You might set if off." Don threw both arms around Roger, restraining him from moving Tess any further.

"I told you. There's no bomb."

Don held fast. "You can't possibly know that."

"Look, Don. If an intruder had tried to force his way in, either he'd be dead or Heidi would be dead."

Roger's calm logic stopped Don. Releasing Roger, he waved off his men. "All right. What did happen in here?"

"I won't know until I get Tess in her chair and hooked to its voice mechanism. I think she's awake, but the Aremac is wrecked."

"Give me a minute and I'll help you. Let me check on these two first."

"They're okay. I already checked. Rebecca is so angry she wants to kill somebody. SOS seems to have hit his head on something—he's stunned, and he's lost some blood, but no one has any bullet wounds as far as I can see."

Don pulled out his cell phone. "Hang on another minute. I'll get the medics in here."

Four medics rushed in just as Roger finished harnessing Tess into her talking wheelchair. As soon as he'd pulled the wired cap onto her head, she spoke hurriedly through the automated voice. "I'm fine. Stop fussing over me. Take care of them."

"The medics will do that," said Don. "If you're sure you're okay, tell us what happened."

"I'm as okay as ever. In other words, not okay. But not hurt, as far as I can tell. But how would I know?"

Don signaled to one of the medics to inspect Tess for wounds while she told her story. "First sign of trouble was Heidi barking. Someone was trying to open the door. Then the shooting started. That's all I know for sure. I guess they did something to the Aremac, because first I couldn't move my cameras, and then they blanked out entirely. What happened outside?"

"I have no idea," said Roger. "Don?"

"Here's what I've been able to piece together," Don said. "When your dog started barking, my agent who was surveying the house from out front saw somebody with a package at the front door and went to investigate. Someone in a parked car started shooting and my agent shot back. The person at the door ran back to the car, jumped in, and the car drove off, but not before they'd sprayed the house with bullets."

Don nodded when Tess asked whether anyone else was hurt. "My agent was wounded, but he managed to shoot back, which is probably why they sped away. The medics say he got a nasty flesh wound but he'll be okay."

"Does he have any idea who the people were?" Roger asked.

"No. He got their license plate, and we've already checked it. Stolen. Naturally."

While Don was talking, two medics carried SOS out on a stretcher. Arnie quietly slipped inside as they left. Standing to the side, next to Rebecca, he asked, "What's that about the package?"

"It was a bomb, but the bomb squad found that it hadn't been armed yet. They're looking for other bombs now. It's a break for us to find an intact bomb—if it was *alKhamis*, we should be able to identify it."

Arnie stiffened and exhaled a long quiet whistle. "Should we evacuate?"

"I don't think it's necessary. If my bomb-squad boys didn't believe it was safe, they wouldn't have let you in. The one bomb was big enough to flatten this entire building, so there probably won't be another. Anyway, it looks like the same kind of bomb used by *alKhamis*, and so far they've never used two when one would do the job."

"What about the El?" Tess asked.

"You're right. Except on the El, but that was a bigger job. They usually like to get in and out fast, ever since one of their people got caught in his own blast."

Arnie's gaze surveyed the room. "Arguing from the physical evidence, they apparently don't want Tess or the Aremac to testify—"

"I'm afraid I'm beginning to agree with you," said Don.

"—and from that it follows that they know Tess will be able to identify the true killer. And thus exonerate my innocent client."

Don nodded. "If I were on a jury, I'd have to agree—but if you tell anyone I said that, you'll be on my most-wanted list. I still have to pursue evidence with due diligence—"

"I don't fault you for that."

"—which means I'm going to want to see Tess's picture of the murderer. Now."

Roger put his finger in the bullet hole in the Aremac. "You're not serious. The Aremac is ruined. Kaput!"

"I'm not blind. That's why I want the pictures. Now. Whatever you have."

"But that's just it, Don. We don't have any pictures."

Don snapped. He grabbed Roger by the lapels of his suit and started shaking him back and forth. "You're kidding! You're no better than Wyatt. All this time, you've been faking—"

"HOLD IT, boys," Tess's machine voice shouted. Though Tess's wheelchair voice wasn't as loud as the Aremac's, Heidi alerted and the remaining two medics flinched. "Arnie, explain to Don before he breaks Roger's neck."

"It's simple," said Arnie. "I instructed Roger not to let Tess do that scene yet—not until they're before the judge. The judge—or your prosecutor, certainly—will ask them whether they've seen any of the pictures before, trying to prove, or at least imply, that they faked it."

Don dropped Roger's lapels and let his own arms hang, defeated, to his sides. "So there's nothing? Nothing at all?"

Roger and Arnie exchanged looks, then Roger whispered something in Arnie's ear. "No," said Arnie, "we have no pictures of the murder from the Aremac."

Don raised one eyebrow, frowning. "Why do I get the feeling you're not telling the whole story? Other than the fact that you're a lawyer."

"Caught me. Okay, Roger has said he might be able to extract some crude stills from some of the data that's stored on the backups. He hasn't tried it because I told him not to. But I still can't let you have any, even if he can extract them."

Don brightened. "What if I get the judge and prosecutor to agree on using the Aremac?"

"In writing?"

"What other way is there, with you lawyers?"

"I'll help you draft an agreement stating that they won't challenge the Aremac because of this. Then, when it's signed, Roger will start working on extracting some pictures."

"How about you start now, Roger? These attacks are escalating, so we don't have much time before they strike again." Don started for the door. "And, oh yes, how soon will the Aremac be able to help me with true-false testing of our new witnesses?"

Arnie turned on Roger. "You agreed to that? What witnesses?"

Roger studied the ceiling. "It was a trade."

"We think we have the brother of the bomber who died. We're holding him in Cleveland, but we can bring him here. And we also have a mechanic connected with the truck used in the El bombing."

"I want to be there when you interrogate them." Arnie didn't wait for a response before he turned on Roger again. "What did you trade for?"

Don was smiling. "Never mind that, Arnie. For now, you can just believe I promise to triple the guard on this place. More, if I can get the manpower. You just make sure Roger fixes his invention. We might need it to clear your client."

When Don and Arnie had both departed, Rebecca, at Tess's request, also left the room so that Tess could speak with Roger alone. "How long will it take to repair the Aremac, sweetheart?"

"I'll have to assess the damage, but I think we'll just need to replace the CPU. Maybe some other hardware as well. If we can find the CPU in stock somewhere soon, and don't run into hardware problems, we can probably have everything up and tested within the week. Depends a little on when SOS can come back to work."

"Shoot."

He took both her limp hands in his. "It'll be okay. We can still talk, and Don will just have to wait for his pictures."

"It's not that."

"Oh?"

"This morning, when you were in court and I was doing my exercises with the exoskeleton, I think I felt something in my finger. But I'm not sure, and now I have to wait a week to try again. It was easy to be patient when I'd given up hope, but can't you fix the Aremac any faster?"

78

Although the bullet hole in the Aremac tested Tess's patience, it turned out to be a blessing in disguise. When Roger opened the casing to study the damage, he discovered a small electronic device attached to the magnet's internal computer. He didn't have the equipment to identify it properly, so he turned it over to Don. The FBI lab confirmed that it was a transmitter sucking copies of the Aremac's code and sending them somewhere in the neighborhood. From what the technician could tell, it had probably been attached to the magnet when it arrived. Somewhere within a thousand yards of the garage, someone was picking up the stolen code.

As promised, Don had immediately tripled the guard although Roger, visually scanning the area, couldn't see many of the FBI agents guarding the garage. Don also put a team to work scouring the neighborhood for the clandestine receiver. The search team found nothing, but Don was quite sure the receiver had scrammed as soon as the device stopped transmitting.

Despite the tripled security, Rebecca, who had insisted on staying at work to clean up the mess, asked Roger whether she could bring a gun to work. When Roger hesitated, the petite Englishwoman anticipated his first question. "And, yes," she said, "I have one, a legal one, and I know how to use it." When she finally left, escorted home by one of Don's agents, she had Roger's permission to bring in her gun.

The medics had taken SOS to the nearest emergency clinic, where he remained guarded by two more of Don's agents until he'd been fully stabilized. Once released, he returned to the garage, to process the old data. Upon SOS's return, Roger was driven around town by the two agents to hustle up replacement parts for the Aremac, leaving Tess to work on the software from her wheelchair, with Heidi on watch by her side. Arnie fed Heidi some lamb-lung treats in addition to her regular food before setting off to work on his favorite prey—judges and prosecutors.

The following Monday, in the Federal Court Building, Addie's trial judge didn't put up much of a fight over Arnie's draft proposal to allow the use of the Aremac. Arnie was initially disappointed by the judge's accommodating response, but Deputy Attorney General Reggie Tempkins provided plenty of the kind of opposition Arnie relished. He'd learned through some Republican Party connections that Tempkins had been approached by Wyatt's team in an attempt to convince Tempkins that their thought-reading machine was more reliable than the Aremac and should be used as a control on Tess's evidence. Further, they had no conflict of interest, so Tempkins convinced the judge that Tess's evidence should be processed on Wyatt's latest machine before the Aremac data could be introduced at Addie's trial.

Both Roger and Don, each for his own reasons, objected to putting Tess into Wyatt's hands under any circumstances, but Tempkins wouldn't budge. To break the deadlock, Arnie proposed a compromise: Wyatt's team would first have to produce other evidence that their machine worked, after which the judge would subject Tess to a trial with both machines.

After extended private consultation with Wyatt's boss, Tempkins agreed to this arrangement and promised to show evidence from Wyatt's machine on Friday. The judge, probably to protect his golf weekend, moved the demonstration to Thursday, and both parties returned to their offices for three days of preparation.

When they appeared in court on Thursday morning, Tempkins had brought a short, chunky man who looked slightly familiar to Roger. "He's the guard who saw the nurse coming out of the victim's room at the clinic," Arnie whispered.

Tempkins introduced the guard, who testified that his memories of the day in question had been recorded by Wyatt's machine.

He further testified that the video they were about to see was an accurate recording of what he had seen at the time of the murder. Then Roger watched in horror as someone in a nurse's uniform emerged from the victim's room, looked the other way, then turned to face the "camera" full on. It was Addie.

Roger didn't want to show any reaction, but he couldn't help himself. He turned his face away so the judge wouldn't see his tears.

When the show ended, the judge reminded the guard that he was under oath and asked him to repeat his statement that this was a faithful picture of what he'd seen. Then the judge dismissed him, turned to Arnie, and said, "It looks as if their machine works. If yours works as well, I will admit both of them as sources of evidence."

Arnie was about to speak, but Roger grabbed his arm and pulled him closer so he could whisper. "It's got to be a fake."

"I know you believe your cousin is innocent, but that's not going to stand as evidence."

"It's not that. It's the machine. There's no way Wyatt could produce such clear images. He doesn't have the sensitive input capacity. Ask the judge for permission to inspect the video. And their code."

Arnie nodded and rose. "We're not ready to accept their evidence, Your Honor. We request the opportunity to contest the reality of the show they just put on."

"That's your right, Mr. Danielson. I'll give you until Monday to prepare your rebuttal."

"Thank you, Your Honor. To perform our investigations, we'll need a copy of the video."

The judge looked at Reggie. "Mr. Tempkins?"

Tempkins looked at Wyatt, who shrugged. "We agree, Your Honor. We have other copies."

He extended the recording to Arnie, who turned once again to the judge. "And, Your Honor, we also need a copy of the computer code that produced this recording."

"Mr. Tempkins?"

Reggie quickly conferred with Wyatt. "Dr. Wyatt cannot provide that, Your Honor, without losing intellectual property protection. That, he is unwilling to do."

Wyatt whispered something to Reggie. "However, Your Honor, he is willing to exchange computer codes with the defendants, so he can make the same inspection of their claims."

"Mr. Danielson?"

Arnie bent over and huddled with Roger. "No way," whispered Roger. "He'd steal everything. Can't you get his code? It has to be fake."

"We'll just have to do the best we can without it."

Roger wanted to say more, but Arnie shushed him and turned to the judge. "That's not acceptable to my expert, Your Honor. We'll work with the video itself, but I reserve the right to exchange computer codes at some later time."

"Agreed. If there are no more issues about this, I have other business to attend to."

Roger was dejected, but Arnie dragged him quickly out of sight of the prosecutor. "You're showing too much emotion. Defeat is written all over your face. Very bad in poker. Worse in the courtroom."

"But we needed that code. It has to be fake."

"Then you'll have to give up your code to Wyatt."

"He'll steal it. We know that."

"You'll have to decide what's more important to you, your cousin or your code. But for now, all we've got is the video."

They left the courthouse and were halfway north on Lake Shore Drive when Roger spoke again. "I made a mistake."

"What mistake?"

"I should have agreed to give them the code. Addie's more important than any patents could ever be. Let's go back and tell the judge."

"It's too late for that. He's on the first tee by now. We're stuck with the video."

"But can't you make some sort of motion to reconsider?"

"We'd have to find him, and I'm sure he doesn't want to be found for the weekend. I've seen that look on judges' faces too many times."

"So? We'll find him anyway."

"It would probably be worse if we did. Judges take their golf very seriously."

Roger pounded his fist on the dashboard. "But it's Addie's *life* we're talking about. Surely that's more important than making tee time."

"Maybe to us, but, unfortunately, in this instance, it's not more important to the judge. Just calm down and start thinking about what you can do with that video."

79

It was a miserable day. Cold, wet fog billowed off the lake, causing pileups on the Drive. Just the kind of day that would have been perfect for sitting beside a warm fire, with popcorn to eat, and a good comedy to watch. Rebecca made the popcorn—real popcorn, not the microwave kind. But the only fire burning was in Roger's chest—and the video they were watching wasn't exactly a comedy. No, not funny at all.

Roger had propped Tess up in her chair and Arnie, SOS, and Rebecca had seated themselves alongside her. After they watched the two-minute segment, they shared a single reaction—a depressed, and depressing, silence.

Arnie cautioned that they should watch it again, more carefully, but it was no better the second time. "It certainly looks real," Rebecca said. "Don't be angry with me, but is there any possibility that she really did kill him?"

Tess struggled to control her temper, though her mechanical voice showed nothing. "Rebecca, I saw the murder. It wasn't Addie."

"So instead of he-said-she-said, all we've got is he-saw-she-saw," Rebecca answered, shaking her head. "But isn't Addie innocent until proved guilty?"

"Not in these terrorist cases," Arnie explained. "She should be, of course, but she isn't when the whole city's in a panic."

Roger stood and began to pace back and forth. "Damn, I know it's a fake. I should have given them our code. Then I could prove it."

"Stop beating yourself up, darling. It's not helpful. It shuts off your analytical mind."

"That's just the problem. There's nothing to analyze."

"Maybe we should take a closer look," said SOS. "Maybe we can find some distinctive pattern in the digitizing. Something that will show it's a fake."

"We already know it's a fake," said Roger.

"That's not the point. We need something to prove it's a fake. To the judge. Come on, we're good at patterns. Let's focus in and take a look."

"Good idea," said Tess. "We'll each take a third and see what we find."

SOS started to prepare the computer to divide up the visuals, then stopped and looked at the others. "How about we all concentrate on the middle frames, the ones that show Addie the clearest?"

"All right," said Tess. "If that doesn't show anything, we'll check the rest."

"Be careful," Rebecca said. "At—well, you know, at my former employer, we had a case involving an art forger. I learned that in forged paintings, the clues sometimes come in the parts the forger thought were not so important."

"All right," said Roger. "Why don't I concentrate on the background. I've been in that same corridor many times, so maybe I can see some discrepancies."

"I'll take her face," SOS said, smiling shyly. "I guess I've studied that pretty carefully. What about you, Tess?"

"You study all the pretty girls' faces carefully, sos." Tess's humor was lost in the machine voice. "I'm going to look at the movement patterns, rather than any particular objects."

"What should I take?" Rebecca asked.

"You and Arnie don't have the kind of experience the three of us have looking at digital patterns," Roger answered. "Why don't you just wait for us? If we find something, you and Arnie can be our guinea pigs, to see if it's convincing to the nontechnical mind."

"You should know me better than that, Roger. I'm constitutionally incapable of sitting and waiting. What about you, Arnie?"

"Me, neither, but I'll occupy my mind with dreaming up legal arguments in case you don't find anything."

"Thanks, Mr. Optimist," said Tess.

"I'm paid to think of the worst that can happen. And to do damage control. Besides, we're out of popcorn. I'll make some more. No more beer, though. We need to stay fully focused for this job."

"I might think better if I were a little juiced," Tess retorted, then fell silent as she set to work.

Popcorn popped, tantalizing them with its buttery aroma, and somehow disappeared as each of them concentrated on the task at hand. Tess was too absorbed to complain about having to satisfy herself only with the smell of the popcorn. She could feel something wrong with Addie's movement on the video, but couldn't pin it down. Minutes, then hours, went by. Nothing.

When an alarm bleeped on one of Tess's monitors, Roger checked it and announced that her blood sugar was low. "It's time to take a break. We all need to eat something besides popcorn. Rebecca, could you call out for some Chinese while I feed Tess?"

"Order me some egg-drop soup, Rebecca," Tess interjected. "I can eat that. Much better than that glop in the fridge. And order Heidi some Mongolian beef. She's been very patient with us."

Rebecca started for the phone, but turned her head and looked back at the sound of concern in Roger's voice as he spoke to Tess. "Your blood sugar is down now. It will take at least forty-five minutes before—"

"Do that again," Tess interrupted.

"Your blood sugar is—"

"Not you, sweetie. Rebecca, can you do that again?"

"Do what again? I haven't done anything yet."

"Yes, you did. You started for the other room, then you turned to look at Roger when he was playing mother hen."

"I . . . I didn't do anything special."

"Never mind. I've got the recording. Too bad I didn't have that feature when I saw the murder." The Hawaiian surf screensaver disappeared from the big monitor, replaced by a video clip of Rebecca starting to leave, then turning her head back. "See!"

"See what?" they said as one voice.

"The way she turns her head. Here. Wait until I spell out the coordinates. I'll put a tracer dot on the screen that will help." The clip returned to the beginning and froze on a frame showing the back of Rebecca's head. After a moment, a bright crimson dot appeared on the tip of Rebecca's chin. The clip started moving, and the dot traced a gentle curve as it followed the motion of her head.

"I see your point," Roger said, "the red one. But I don't see the point you're trying to make."

"Give me a minute and I'll program a trace." The picture and the dot returned to their starting positions, then repeated the movement. This time, however, the dot left a crimson trail on the screen, marking its path. "Now do you see?"

"No."

"All right. Just a minute." After a short delay, Wyatt's clip of Addie emerging from the murder room replaced Rebecca's picture, but the crimson curve remained. A lime green dot appeared on Addie's chin, which was slightly above the crimson line. Then the dot traced its own line as Addie turned to face the guard.

"I see it now," shouted SOS, beating Roger by a fraction of a second. "Rebecca's line dips at the end," he tested his idea by turning his head, "like mine. Because it's sort of pulled down by my shoulder muscle—"

"Supraspinatus and trapezius, mostly," said Tess's machine voice. "They restrain the movement as you try to look over your shoulder—"

Roger twisted his neck. "So they pull it down. But Addie's chin doesn't dip. In fact, it traces a straight line."

"Perfectly straight, in fact," said Tess. "It's horizontal down to the last pixel. The human body just doesn't move in straight lines. Anywhere. Except mine, which doesn't move at all."

"So this has to be a synthesized picture. We've got it!"

Arnie's face showed no excitement. "Sit down, everybody. Better order the Chinese, Rebecca. We're not there yet. Not even close."

Resisting all pleadings to postpone the food and keep working, Arnie held back questions while Rebecca took orders. While she used the phone at SOS's desk, Arnie explained to the others, "I'm sure you've found something that impresses you nerdy types, but I could see that Rebecca didn't really follow what you were saying. And I'm sure she's smarter than the judge. Heck, even I'm smarter than the judge, and you haven't convinced me."

Roger couldn't restrain himself. "But it's totally logical. Or, I should say that Wyatt's fake picture is totally illogical."

"You're overrating logic in the courtroom. This angle is too technical."

"But—"

Before Roger could object further, Rebecca returned to announce that the food was on the way. "I ordered chopsticks for everyone. If you'd rather, I'll set up some silverware."

"Rebecca," Roger asked, not ready to give up, "Did you understand about the head movements?"

"Well, sort of. But I'm not really—"

"What did I tell you?" said Arnie. "This might be part of what we need, but you've got to find something else."

That started a three-way argument among the techies, until Rebecca spoke up. "I know I wasn't there, up at the clinic, so this is probably a stupid question, but I saw something at SOS's desk."

"What?" asked Roger.

"SOS, is Addie the same woman whose picture is on your screensaver?"

"Yep. That's Addie."

"You have a personal interest in this?"

SOS blushed, which was all the answer Rebecca needed. "Can we compare those two pictures? There's something different about them."

"Give me a minute," SOS said as he went to his desk and started typing. "I'll take a still clip from Wyatt's video and split-screen it with my photo of Addie on the big monitor."

The two still pictures appeared side by side. Although the faces were at slightly different angles, the comparison made it obvious that Addie's obsidian hair was more than an inch shorter in Wyatt's clip.

"When did you take that picture on your screensaver?" Rebecca asked.

"The morning of the murder. I was going to send it to my mother," he reddened again, "but under the circumstances, I decided to wait . . . until Addie's free."

Rebecca reached out and squeezed his hand. "And she will be free, Stephen." SOS reacted to the use of his real name by turning an even deeper red. Rebecca kept his hand in her motherly grasp. "Have we got any other pictures of Addie?"

"Lots," said Roger, "but nothing from around that time."

"Could she have cut her hair after the picture was taken?"

"No way," said Tess. "She told me she was letting it grow out. For . . . well, let's just say she thought it was more attractive longer.

So it was longer that day than it was at any other time while she was at the clinic."

"Hey," said SOS, snapping out of his reverie. "She had to have her picture taken when she got her badge, and that was long before the murder."

"Do you have that picture?" Rebecca asked.

"No," he said, rushing to his keyboard. "But I sure know how to get it. I've done it before, so it should be an easy hack."

A minute later, he mumbled, "The idiots didn't even change their passwords."

Less than five minutes later, he looked up in triumph and pointed to Wyatt's picture of Addie up on the split screen. "Oh, my," said Tess. "It's the *same* picture."

"Of course it's the same," said Roger. "They're both Addie."

"No," Tess corrected. "They're both *pictures* of Addie. But notice the hair—men never notice those things. Wait a minute while I run a comparison." They all stared at the two pictures for a moment, watching Wyatt's video oscillate back and forth among two dozen frames, finally stopping at one of them. "There. These two are identical, bit for bit. This frame in the video is identical to that first photo taken for Addie's badge. That means that—"

"—one is a computer copy of the other," Roger said, smiling for the first time that day. "We've got it!"

"Got what?" Arnie asked. "It's probably just a coincidence."

"Not likely. Not likely at all. How many pixels in that face, darling?"

"A little more than 40K, not including the hair. Which is exactly the same length, if you'd noticed."

"And, Arnie," Roger said, "suppose you had a plagiarism case where, say, ten thousand words of text in two independent manuscripts were identical. What's the chance that was a coincidence?"

"Sounds unlikely, but if you want a legal opinion, you'd have to ask Sarah. Copyright infringement is more in her line."

"We had a case once," said Rebecca, "where maybe seventy-five words were identical and the plaintiff won the infringement case."

"But these aren't words," said Arnie. "Just pixels. And they're two pictures of the same woman, after all."

"Don't worry," said Tess. "I think you could throw a rock in any university's math department and hit ten expert witnesses who would testify that this couldn't happen by coincidence in a billion trillion years."

"I still think the hair length will be more convincing to a judge," Arnie grumbled. "But we'll use all the evidence you've found."

Heidi stood, stretched, and walked to the door, tail wagging. A moment later, a delivery boy knocked with their order. "But," said Arnie, as he went to open the door and tip the delivery boy, "it couldn't hurt if you found some more evidence before Monday."

80

By Monday, they had found other flaws in the video, but in the end, Arnie's legal instincts proved correct: The hair length was the last straw for the judge. Wyatt maintained his innocence, but was severely reprimanded and was dismissed from the trial. The deputy attorney general was furious, thinking the judge too lenient. As Wyatt slunk out of the room, Tempkins looked menacingly at him, and threatened to bring charges of obstruction of justice.

Unfortunately for Addie, Tempkins wasn't furious enough to drop the case. "The other evidence is more than adequate," he said, refusing to discuss the matter further.

To make matters worse, the judge announced that, in light of all the fakery, he would not trust any machine that purported to capture memories. No amount of Arnie's logic—that the fake was a video, not the Aremac—would change the judge's decision.

As they walked out of the courtroom and through the huge wooden doors of the courthouse, Roger cursed, telling Arnie, "I took Addie out of the frying pan and thrust her into the fire."

"It's not your fault, Roger. He's a cowardly judge. He lacks the courage to make any ruling that looks like new law of such wide-sweeping consequences. And, he surely doesn't want to be accused of acquitting a suspected terrorist on the basis of faked evidence, no matter how unlikely that is."

Don caught up with them on the courthouse steps and overheard their last remarks. He tried to sound upbeat, "The judge may not be convinced, but I've seen more than enough. If you show me Tess's pictures and can convince me that your machine isn't a fake, I'll see that this fiasco is put to rest."

"Even if you can't identify the person Tess saw that day?" Arnie asked.

"That would help, sure. But, yes, even if we never find out who really did it. It may be old-fashioned these days, but I still believe in our Constitution."

"You'll forgive me if I don't believe you, Don," Arnie replied. "It's my lawyer's mind."

"You can trust me, Arnie. Tell him, Roger."

Arnie stopped short, his brow furrowed. "Tell me what?"

Roger looked around, but few people were out braving the needles of cold rain, and those that were, were rushing past, more than fifty feet away. "It's what you asked me about the other day and I wouldn't tell you."

"I don't remember asking you anything you didn't answer."

"About the Bag Bandit."

"Okay—what about the Bag Bandit?"

Roger checked around once again, but lowered his voice anyway. "Don was doing me a favor—"

"*You* were the Bag Bandit?"

"Shhh. No, of course I wasn't." Don winked. "Why would I ever do such a thing? I'm a federal agent. Just don't ask me any more silly questions, okay?"

"I understand. Just hypothetically, what reason would a federal agent have for doing such a thing when he could get a warrant?"

"Maybe warrants against a university take too much time to get. Maybe they attract too much attention from the wrong people. Maybe he—or she—would want to do a little misdirection so the bad guys wouldn't know it was the FBI. Who knows what evil lurks in the hearts of federal agents trying to get a new angle on terrorists who've already maimed or murdered dozens of people?"

Arnie took in a deep breath and then slowly let it out as he aimed his remote key at a car parked just ahead of them. "Well, here we are." He pulled open the unlocked door. "I guess you can't ever rely on the answers to hypothetical questions."

"No, I guess not," said Don. "So, here's a real one. Are you ready to trust me to see Tess's pictures?"

Roger rubbed his forehead and then walked around Arnie's car to the passenger side. "I guess now that the Aremac is ruled out of the trial, there's no harm in it. Arnie?"

"No harm, but we'll set certain conditions. Do you both want to go now?"

"I'll follow you," Don replied. "I've done that before."

"You have?"

Don just smiled like a cat with cream on its whiskers, and got into the car parked directly behind the Cadillac.

81

Alif, to say the least, was not pleased with Qaaf's report. "So, none of the viruses worked, and the bomb didn't go off."

Qaaf folded her hands in her lap and waited for Alif to calm down. Zay and Jiim put their fingers to their lips, but Alif took no notice. "Maybe viruses are complicated, but how can something as simple as a bomb not go off. It's a total blunder."

"You're right," Qaaf said. "You're absolutely correct. I have another—"

"No more." He punched the wall so hard that Jiim stuck his head out the door to see if anyone in the store had heard. "I'm fed up with all this female conniving and scheming. It's time for an all-out attack."

"The guard's been tripled. Direct action didn't work before, and now it would be a foolish risk of everybody's lives," said Qaaf.

"Better to die a hero tomorrow than live a hundred years as a coward."

"You're right, Alif," Jiim said, "but the Vice President arrives in six days. Can't we postpone this other action until the more important target is bombed?"

"It takes only one person to set off a bomb near the Vice President, and our person has already begun his work."

Surprisingly, Jiim didn't drop his argument. "Still, we could use backup. Besides, if the guard on Mrs. Fixman is tripled, perhaps the security around the Vice President will be less. And less vigilant if nothing has happened recently."

"And," said Qaaf, "an all-out attack will blow my valuable cover—unless I don't participate."

"More cowardly talk. Talk, talk, talk. It's long past time for talking. It's time for action. And you will be with us," Alif said.

Zay, agreeing, bowed his head for a moment, then rose and, surprisingly, added, "God willing, by our next meeting, both acts will have been accomplished."

And, thought Qaaf, leaving first, *I may have a way to do it and still keep my cover. We're so close to what we want. Men are such fools!*

82

The Windy City was once again earning its name. A traffic light had been blown into the street, knocking out signals in the neighborhood near the courthouse, causing an impossible snarl of cars, trucks, and pedestrians. Don, wanting to use the Aremac before Roger changed his mind, set his red bubble flasher on the dashboard and pulled ahead of Arnie's car to lead him through the chaos. Even so, by the time they arrived at the Aremac headquarters and Roger had led them to the living quarters, it was past four.

"That was fun," said Roger. "I always wanted to do that—in a car, of course, not in an ambulance. But what's the big hurry?"

"I need to see those pictures. Once the trial starts, I'm not going to have time to follow up new leads."

"You have new leads?"

"Let's say, I have new suspicions."

Roger's eyes fell on the bullet holes in the wall close to the front door. "Couldn't be that you want the information before we're killed, could it?"

"Give me some credit, Rog. I'm not planning on getting you killed, but I do need this information to do my job."

Roger opened the door and greeted Heidi, who accepted Don with a long sniff, then jumped up to plant paws on Arnie's chest. "We're here," Roger called. "With Don."

If Don thought this last phrase might be a warning to hide something from him, he said nothing. He greeted Tess, who was working out her right index finger with the exoskeleton. She stopped the machine. "How did it go? Did you discredit that fool?"

"We did," said Roger, "but it backfired. We discredited ourselves, too."

"And just how did you manage that?"

"It wasn't anyone's fault," said Arnie. "The judge was too cowardly to allow any machine data into the trial."

"So, I'm out of the picture?"

"Well, maybe I exaggerated. He will allow your spoken testimony, using your chair, but no pictures."

"So my picture is out of the picture. Then it's just my word against the guard's."

"Maybe not," said Don. "I've come to look at your pictures. If you can convince me it's not Addie, I think I can persuade the prosecutor."

"Can I do that, Arnie?"

"Now that the Aremac has been banned from the courtroom, I don't see why not."

Roger held up his palm. "I'd like to take this in stages. Let's not put all our eggs in one basket."

"Let's not put all our sentences in clichés, darling. It's too boring."

Arnie guffawed. "Good thing you didn't hear him say we were out of the frying pan and into the fire."

"Did he say that? Roger, I think the stress is making you regress back to infancy."

"Can we stick to the subject?" Don said. "I haven't got a lot of time if I'm going to help Adara."

Roger, hearing Don switch to Addie's formal given name, was eager to change the subject. "Fortunately, this shouldn't take long. Tess, can you bring up that old still of the murderer?"

While they waited for Tess to locate the picture in the archives, Roger explained what they'd be looking at. "We took this single frame before Arnie told us not to practice with the actual memory of the event. It's low quality, because that's the best we could do back then."

A picture appeared on the large monitor, filling it with a more than life-sized image. It showed an indistinct face looking back over her shoulder at the camera. Or perhaps it was *his* shoulder—they couldn't be sure because the face wasn't that clear and the hair was cropped quite short. And quite blonde. "As you can see from the hair," said Roger, "that can't be Addie. Wrong length. Wrong color."

"It could be a wig," Don countered.

"There's no way Addie could get all her hair under a wig," Tess said. "We tested one of my wigs on SOS, and his hair stuck out from under the wig. He's got the longest hair here, but it's still shorter than Addie's was at the time. And it's thinner than hers was before your people shaved her head when you had her in prison."

"Come on, they did cut her hair, but we're not barbarians." Don glanced at SOS—who had stopped working to watch the proceedings—then stepped over and felt his hair. "Okay, so it couldn't be someone wearing a wig. But Tess could have digitally changed the color—"

"Arnie warned me that the lawyers would accuse me of lying. Now you're doing it."

"I was about to say 'unconsciously.' I'm not accusing you of outright lying."

"I suppose that, coming from an insensitive FBI man, is as much of an apology as I'm going to get. Fine, apology accepted. Such as it is."

"Now you sound like Lucinda."

"I don't know the woman, so what do you mean when you say I sound like her?"

"She's a bit self-righteous and huffy, that's all. Stubborn." He held up his hand. "But she had to be stubborn to survive what she's been through."

"I'm not stubborn. I'm stuck—I just can't move even if I wanted to."

"All right, I'm sorry. Forget what I said about you sounding like Lucinda. But I still have to be sure it's not a faked image. Is there a way to prove these are real memories, not edited . . . unconsciously? Is there a way to improve the quality of the picture?"

"There's no point improving the quality if you don't believe the pictures are real."

"Fine, so let's work on that first."

Roger looked at Arnie for approval, then said, "You start by telling us what it would take for you to believe. That way you won't keep raising spurious objections."

"That's easy," Don laughed. "But seriously, I want to try the Aremac myself."

"That's going to take a while. We've just finished repairing it, and it's been at least a month since we calibrated for anyone except Tess."

"Is that an excuse?"

"No, it's just to tell you that it's going to take a few hours— assuming we can even make it work for you."

"Then let's get started. Do I have to shave my head?"

"We're not barbarians," Tess mocked, showing more anger than humor in the words.

83

Roger took longer than he'd expected to calibrate the Aremac for Don, mostly because the software code had relied too much on generalizations from one specific set of brain patterns—Tess's. It was after eight when they figured out what the problem was. They set SOS and Tess to work repairing the code while the rest of them foraged for a snack of cold leftovers. By unspoken agreement, the snackers talked about everything but the Aremac as they ate.

When Roger, Tess, and SOS were finished repairing the code, SOS turned up his nose at the remaining leftovers, arguing that he needed a hot meal if he was going to be effective working all night. Don offered to treat them to Italian takeout from his cousin's restaurant, then called to be sure the restaurant could make some strained *zuppa de pesca* thin enough for Tess to have. "They don't usually do takeout," Don said, hanging up the phone. "But they'll do pretty much anything for family."

Arnie stretched quickly and then volunteered to go to pick up the meal, but Don insisted that one of his guarding agents go along with him. While they waited for Arnie and the guard to return with the food, Roger took over the job of running some independent tests, then resumed training the updated Aremac to Don's characteristics.

Arnie and the agent came back with the soup, gnocchi, pasta, and assorted hot antipasti while Roger was still fixing an interface problem. He wolfed down just a few olives as he continued to work, but Tess insisted he stop and eat a full meal. "The Alfredo sauce won't do well reheated," she said.

Finally, with everyone fed, Tess was moved to her chair and Don was capped into the Aremac. Soon, he was able to produce some rough pictures and wanted to begin his tests. "These look good—like what's in my mind—but I'm no software expert. I'd like to do this more or less the way we tested it up at the clinic."

"Fine," said Roger. "Anything you want."

"I'm going to put up a sequence of pictures. Some as I remember them. Some altered. Can you set the machine to tell the difference, like we did before?"

SOS wiped cheesecake crumbs from his mouth. "No problem—unless someone touches my cheesecake while I'm working."

"Do you want me to shoot to kill?" Rebecca asked, getting in the spirit. "Or just wound the culprit?"

"Just make him eat cold pasta. Unless that's too cruel and unusual. I truly wouldn't feed cold pasta to a dog—no offense, Heidi." Heidi heard her name and came to SOS. He gave her a chunk of cheesecake, let her lick his fingers, and set to work. Three minutes later, his computer emitted the piano sounds of the first few bars of a Mozart piece. "'Rondo in D' means it's a true memory." Then they heard the distinctive but monotonous theme of Ravel's "Bolero." "That's false—of course."

"Very nice," said Roger. "But a simple 'REAL' or 'FAKE' on the screen would be sufficient."

"Now you're getting boring again," teased Tess. "You really have to get out more."

"I can't stand it when you two lovers fight," SOS said. "Here, you can have both." A few key strokes and the screen flipped between REAL and FAKE in synch with the music.

"All right, children," Don said in his parental voice. "Can I try it now?"

"Be my guest."

Don closed his eyes. A moment later, the face of an elderly, but handsome, woman appeared on the screen. Don opened his eyes to check the picture, and a moment later, FAKE appeared in a window in the bottom-right corner.

After a few bars of Ravel, Don closed his eyes again. The picture remained the same, but the hair color changed from bluish-white to chestnut. REAL appeared, and Mozart sounded, with no noticeable delay.

Don made several changes to the picture, all FAKE, then switched to a picture of a fat man in a tuxedo and red bow tie. He was so fat and the red bow tie so unlikely that Roger was sure this was FAKE, but the screen said REAL. Then what looked like the same man appeared, but he was in a bikini swimsuit posed like a bodybuilder and looking two-hundred pounds lighter. Obviously a fake, but the machine said REAL.

Roger angrily snapped off the Aremac. "So, you were able to fool it. How did you do it?"

"Yeah," said SOS, more curious than angry. "Inquiring minds want to know."

Don scrunched up his forehead. "What are you two talking about?"

"Obviously, at least one of those last two was fake," said Roger. "How did you do it?"

"But they weren't fake. That's my Uncle Jake. Giovanni. Arnie, didn't you see him when you picked up the food?"

"I did," said Arnie. "Red bow tie and all."

"Then how did you fake the second picture? He had the same face, but he looked like Mr. Universe."

"Not Mr. Universe. Mr. Clifton, New Jersey. That was a hundred and fifty pounds before he moved to Chicago and bought the restaurant."

"Oh," said Roger, unable to think of anything less boring to say.

84

"All right," said Don, as Roger removed his snood. "I now know your machine—the Aremac, I guess I can start calling it—I now know that it can faithfully capture pictures from my memory. And that it can distinguish between remembered pictures and constructed ones. What I still don't know is whether you've rigged it to let Tess's constructed pictures slip by the REAL/FAKE mechanism."

Roger sighed. "Don, you should have been a software tester. You have the knack."

"It comes from dealing with too many crooks. Ask Arnie." Arnie smiled, and Don went on. "I'm sorry I seem to be suspicious, and I don't really doubt Tess. But I have too many recent examples that confirm my suspicions of fraud, like your Professor Wyatt, to take just one."

"Sometimes even *I* hate testers," said SOS, "but just for a moment. Then I get over it—because I'm proud of my work, and wouldn't want anything embarrassing to go out the door. I actually love them for helping me. It's called 'egoless programming.' There's—"

Roger's guffaw cut off SOS's lecture before it reached full steam. "You're telling us you're egoless? In a lecture?"

327

By this time, Roger had put Tess back in the Aremac, and she was practicing with her exoskeleton. "Leave him alone, Roger. But lecture or no, Don, there's absolutely no way we can prove to you that the program isn't rigged—"

"No way? Then where do we go from here?"

"You should have let me finish what Roger called my 'lecture,'" SOS said, recovering quickly from any hurt feelings. "There's no way you can trust our program unless you can find a programmer whom you trust—in both senses of the word. You have to trust his or her competence, and you have to trust his or her honesty."

Don's face brightened. "I know just the person. Denise Yao. From our security division. Do you know her, Stephen?"

SOS winced at the sound of his given name. "I never met her, but the guys up at the clinic were always talking about her. They say she's the geek goddess to end all geekesses. I'd love to meet her."

Don checked his watch. "It's really late, but we've got to keep going." He pulled out his cell phone. "I'll call LD. She'll know how to find Denise, and she can be very convincing. Not that Denise will need any convincing. Not if the problem is challenging enough."

He connected with Lucinda on the first ring, told her about their progress, and explained how she needed to find Denise and bring her over to finish the programming job. When he hung up, he announced that Denise would be there within the half-hour. "Now, how about we spend the time productively?"

"What did you have in mind?" asked Tess, continuing to exercise.

"I'm virtually certain that Denise will give you the thumbs up, so let's plan for that. When she does, that will put the last peg in the board as far as clearing Adara is concerned. So my next question will be obvious—if not your cousin, then who?"

"You want to see refined pictures?"

"Right."

"Unfortunately," said Roger, "what you've already seen is the best we've gotten so far. We figured our big job was to clear Addie—and our picture was good enough for that. We didn't recognize the murderer in Tess's pictures, but it definitely wasn't Addie. You'll be able to see that, but you may not be able to identify the person."

"I've got some new algorithms," said SOS. "It's just that we've never really tested them."

"Then how about testing them now?"

"I don't want to mess up the machine before Denise gets here. Roger was going to install a new floating-point accelerator chip, and it's not backward compatible."

"Do you want to translate that into English for me?"

"He means," said Tess's machine voice, "that if he speeds up the machine to run his new program, the old program won't work."

"Oh." Don checked his watch again. "What happens if you run the new program on the current machine?"

"Oh, it should be forward compatible," said SOS. "Uh, that means, it will work. . . . But it will probably be too slow. It's optimized for the new chip, which may mean it's pessimized for the old one."

"Again, please. Put that in plain English," Don insisted. "Does that mean it will be too slow to produce pictures?"

"Oh, no. It will produce pictures all right, but not in real time. We might have to wait an hour for one frame."

"Damn. I don't have the time."

Roger spoke up. "Or, we could loosen the convergence criterion—"

"Translate, please?"

"Right. We could make it run faster, but the pictures won't be such good quality."

"Will they be better than the one we have now? Maybe it will be good enough to identify the person?"

"Roger wouldn't think of doing that," said Tess. Her finger was still moving up and down, propelled by the exoskeleton. "He wants it perfect. But yes, we could try that."

Don's cell phone rang. He listened for a minute, then said, "All right. You did the right thing. But I want the full backup contingent. . . . Yes, I know some were just on shift. . . . Everyone." He hung up.

"What was that about?" Tess wanted to know.

"Probably nothing. Just an increase in electronic traffic. Sometimes that suggests impending terrorist activity—"

"Suggests?" Rebecca asked.

"There's only a slight correlation. But I'm not taking any chances now that we're so close."

Rebecca got up and walked away from the group to retrieve something from her locked desk drawer.

Don absentmindedly checked his holster. "Let's get some pictures."

Roger removed Tess's exoskeleton and moved it to the corner of the room while SOS made a quick check on Tess, then booted some software. "It's ready," said SOS, "but let me run a couple of tests first. I'm not sure Tess's old calibration is quite accurate enough for this version. Tess, run through the test patterns."

The large monitor displayed a sequence of geometric figures, then paused. Don kept glancing at his watch, but SOS typed in more numbers, then asked Tess to run the patterns again.

The sequence repeated, and SOS seemed satisfied. "Okay, Don. What do you want to see?"

"The whole enchilada, Tess. Everything you saw on the balcony."

"That will take hours," she said. "I thought you were in a hurry."

"I am. Okay, just give me a picture of the nurse."

The monitor cleared. Colored pixels began to appear, slowly, in seemingly random spots on the screen. Don crept forward to get a better look. Roger stepped up to his side as the outlines of two figures began to emerge above the railing, which was already obvious from its regular pattern.

They were thoroughly immersed in their task when someone knocked at the door.

85

Heidi leapt up and alerted. "I'd better get it," Don said, following Heidi to the door. Pistol drawn, he opened the door a crack, paused to let Heidi sniff the visitor, then opened it wide to admit a tiny Asian woman with straight black hair down to her waist and inch-thick frameless glasses. Wearing a long black skirt, sandals, and a T-shirt with lines of software code and the words "Hackers' Conference" sprawled across her flat chest, the woman stood motionless at the door.

"You must be Denise," said SOS, who shoved Roger out of the way and then pushed past Don to extend his hand. "Do you read machine code for the AX321?"

She squinted silently, as if to say, *Of course I do. What do you think I am?*

Don looked back at the screen, but the picture hadn't changed. "Looks like the program is stalled, and that's not good enough."

"We'll take a look at it," SOS said, taking Denise by the arm and leading her to his desk. "Denise, meet everyone. Everyone, this is Denise."

"Just fix it! I need to see that picture."

"Don't rush them," Roger said. "Telling them to go faster only leads to making mistakes."

"When will they have it fixed?"

"When they have it fixed. You need to learn patience in this—"

Heidi let out a low, long, guttural growl and then barked, violently. Seconds later, an explosion somewhere outside shook the building. A Tiffany-style floor lamp toppled and the shade shattered into multicolored pieces. One of Tess's Navajo rugs fell from the wall and crumpled on the floor.

Roger staggered toward Tess on the Aremac table, then stopped short as they all heard three bursts of gunfire. Shattering the door, back first, a short, fat man with a black beard stormed into the room.

"He's got bombs!" Don shouted. "Run for cover!"

Instead of running away, Roger tackled the man's skinny legs. As the man toppled to the floor, his shirt opened, revealing that he wasn't fat at all. His torso was wrapped with bombs.

Don reversed his course and threw himself on the fallen bomber, pinning him to the ground. "I won't let him touch the trigger. Now you get out of here." Roger kept his grip, but Arnie corralled everyone into the back office—except for Rebecca, who joined Heidi at Tess's side. Her body language told them she would not budge.

The captive was still screaming curses in Arabic, but Roger ignored the words. "Don, knock him out. I'll move Tess, then we all need to get out of here."

"I can't let go."

"Rebecca, hand me that wrench and then go outside with the others."

She snatched the wrench—a big one, for loosening the Aremac's heaviest bolts—and handed it quickly to Roger, who smashed it against their captive's forehead. The cursing stopped and the man's head slumped to one side, but Don wasn't satisfied. "He may be faking. Hit him again. Hard."

Roger thought he wouldn't be able to hit an unconscious man, but one glance at Tess lying helplessly on the table gave him the adrenaline for two more mighty smashes. "Enough, enough!" said Don. "He's out. Now get out of here."

"I won't go without Tess," Roger snapped back.

"Nor will I," said Rebecca defiantly.

"No time. The bomb's sure to have an alternate trigger. It will go off soon from a timer." Don was looking seriously concerned. Machine guns were firing in the street.

"Then I'll disarm it," Roger calmly stood his ground.

"You don't know how. It's got to be booby trapped."

"What kind of trigger?"

"Maybe several. Mechanical, electronic."

"I can handle the electronic stuff, but I don't know about the mechanical. Can we get him away from here?" As if in answer, more sounds of shooting outside rattled the windows. "Okay, stupid idea. What else can we do?"

"Damn," said Don. "They're sure to have an explosion chamber outside, but there's no way we can get there."

"Is an explosion chamber what I think it is?"

"Yes. A shielded room for confining the blast."

Roger stared down at the wrench hanging uselessly in his hand. "How shielded?"

"That depends on the bomb."

"Never mind. We don't have a lot of choices." Roger dropped to the floor and ripped away the Wide Ruins rug.

"What are you doing?"

"There's a service pit under here. From the old gas station. Rebecca, see if you can find another wrench."

Most of the pit had been covered over with the concrete floor, but a small steel trapdoor lay beneath the rug. Roger attacked a bolt with his wrench. Rebecca took a wrench to a second bolt. "Damn," she said. "This wrench doesn't fit."

"Grab another one. Grab them all." Rebecca ran for the tool box while Roger kept tugging at the bolt with his wrench. He almost fell backward as the bolt released. "Okay, three more to go. Rebecca, you get the far one."

She set to work, but couldn't loosen the bolt. Roger took her place and sent her to the bolt he'd already started. "Got it," he yelled, and moved to the fourth one.

"I've got mine," Rebecca said.

"Okay, now get out of here. This one's really stuck. I don't know if I can get it off."

"I'm not leaving," Rebecca said. "Don can help you. Don, I'll watch the bomber."

Don shook his head. "No, he might come to."

"Then give me my gun—from my purse. If he twitches, he's dead."

Don hesitated. "Do you think you could really shoot him? This isn't target practice."

"Give me the gun. I'll show you."

Roger suddenly recalled how impressed he was with her résumé. "It's okay, Don," he said. "She can handle it."

Roger let go of the wrench and fetched the pistol. Rebecca checked the load, switched off the safety, and shot the terrorist in the left elbow. Then the right. "That should keep him from triggering the bomb, even if you still believe I can't shoot to kill the bastard."

Don relinquished his place. "I believe you." He leapt over the sprawled captive to Roger and grabbed his hands on the wrench. "Let's get this damn bolt off."

It still stuck.

"Try some WD-40," Rebecca yelled. Don jumped up and fetched the can from the workbench. "And while you're there," Rebecca shouted again, "grab a length of pipe. Use it to extend the handle."

Don doused the bolt with the penetrating oil, then grabbed the wrench again. "Where did she learn all this stuff?"

Rebecca laughed. "Stop winding me up and put your wimpy muscles to work with that spanner."

Don put his shoulders into the work. More shots rang out, and something thumped against the front wall. A loud cracking sound came from the floor.

"Damn, the head broke off the bolt."

"Too much leverage," said Rebecca. "My fault. Get the drill and drill it out."

Don followed orders, and soon the air was filled with sounds of drilling and the smell of hot oil and metal. "There. That should do it. Now we have to lift the thing."

"Damn, it's heavy," Roger grunted.

"There's a crowbar with the tools," Rebecca reminded him. "All you have to do is lift one corner of the trapdoor, then shove the pipe under it and get one edge over the floor. You should be able to slide the door easier than lifting it."

They followed her instructions and soon the hatch was open about two feet, showing the dark pit beneath. "That's enough. Now toss this rotter down there, bombs and all."

The three of them carefully dragged the man by his legs until his lower body was suspended into the pit. Don ordered the other two to take cover. He sat and used his boots to push the man by his shoulders the rest of the way into the pit. What followed was only a thud—the bombs didn't trigger.

"There. He's in. Let's get the trapdoor back in place," said Don. "Now we need to put as much weight as we can find on that cover. Think we can move the old magnet?"

86

With the pit closed and three corners of the steel trapdoor bolted down, they quickly discovered that the magnet was too heavy for the three of them to move. But then Arnie returned from the back office and added his weight to the push. Rapid fire continued to be exchanged in the street. A bullet whizzed through the shattered door and hit the rug hung on the back wall.

Once the magnet was in place, Don and Arnie started jamming desks and file cabinets on top. Roger helped until the pieces closest to the trapdoor were in place, then ran to fetch a hose. "What's that for?" Don asked.

"I thought we could fill the pit with water, through that bolt hole we drilled out. Maybe we can drown the bomb. Maybe the trigger won't work under water."

"Maybe," Don said. "And maybe not. It might set it off, too."

"I'll wait until we're finished piling on the furniture."

"Okay, but I'm not sure what it will do. Rebecca?"

"Sorry, I don't know. Underwater explosions aren't in my résumé."

"All right, start filling," said Don, "but don't fill it all the way or there won't be any place for the shock to go if it does explode. I think."

"I'll just put enough to put him under water," Roger said.

"Will he float?" Rebecca asked.

Roger squeezed the hose trigger, adjusting the flow so not too much missed the small hole. "Good question. I guess we should have weighted him down."

"Don't even think of going down there to fix that."

"I'm not that dumb, Rebecca. Here, you hold the hose while I check on Tess."

Suddenly remembering, they all looked at the screen. The picture was changing again. SOS and Denise must have been working in the back office through all the commotion.

As the pictures became more and more clear, Roger stepped over to the Aremac controls and began to type. "Don't touch anything yet," Don shouted after him. I want to see this pic—"

He and Roger turned and saw the full picture on the screen at the same time. "Oh, shit."

"It's got to be a fake."

"That's the best I can do," said Tess's mechanical voice. "Do you recognize her?"

"Of course," said Don. "What are you trying to pull?"

"I told you, it's the best I can do."

"You've put the wrong face on her."

"No, that's the face I saw."

"I'm not saying you did it intentionally. You must have remembered her face and seen someone . . . similar. Roger, can you verify that? See if it's a constructed picture, rather than remembered?"

Roger didn't touch the computer. "The machine would have told us if it was constructed. Besides, how could she construct it. I don't think Tess ever saw her anywhere else."

Don pounded his forehead with his fist. "Oh, shit. She's always avoided Tess. I never noticed . . ."

"In that case, Tess couldn't have faked it."

"My God. What a fool—"

Tess's machine voice shouted. "WHAT ARE YOU GUYS TALKING AB—"

Another explosion shook the building. Heidi barked, another rug fell—and Lucinda Dukes jumped through what was left of the shattered door. After scanning the room for threats, she lowered her rifle and removed her combat helmet. "Things are still rough out there, but I think we have enough cover to get you out."

Don sized up Lucinda's H&K assault rifle as Heidi moved toward her, growling, stopping just ten feet away. With one hand, Lucinda swung the barrel so it pointed at Heidi.

Tess's machine voice cried out, "Heidi. DOWN."

Reluctantly, Heidi lowered herself to a down position, growling deep in her throat.

"What's with the dog?" Lucinda said, feigning a laugh. "Let's go. I'm here to pull you out."

"That won't sell, LD," Don said. "Take a look." He turned his head up to the screen.

She followed his gaze. There on the screen was her own face, contorted from hefting a heavily bandaged body over a balcony railing.

"Cancel that," she said, not smiling now. Slowly raising her rifle, she looked at each person in the room, one by one, except Tess. "Apparently I'm a bit too late. How unfortunate . . . for you."

"LD—"

"Shut up, Don." She turned in an arc so the H&K pointed at him. "First thing, Don, remove your weapons—both of them. One at a time. That's right. You know the drill. On the floor, then kick them over in this direction."

Heidi's head tracked the path of the two pistols as they slid across the floor, but she remained fixed in her down position. "Good," said Lucinda, squatting twice to lift the pistols and shove them into her belt. "Since my colleagues may or may not make it through your troops, I'll have to take care of a few matters myself."

As she stood, she nodded toward the screen. "First, that picture. It's not very flattering." She fired a short burst into the Aremac's computer, which responded with a loud sizzle of an electric discharge.

Roger heard the magnet's emergency power switch clack off. Tess's body convulsed twice, then lay still. A strong smell of electrical fire assaulted their nostrils, and the monitor screen went black. In the upper-left corner, a string of white letters announced VIDEO NOT CONNECTED.

Roger instinctively started toward Tess. Lucinda stepped between him and the table, waving him back with the rifle. "Be smart, Dr. Fixman. She's not going anywhere. Or showing any more pictures."

Roger stepped back with the others, moving slightly to his left so he could watch Tess past Lucinda.

More shots sounded outside, louder. Lucinda never shifted her gaze from her captives. "That's a good boy. Now, I may have been a bit hasty. Perhaps I should have saved the machine so I could ask you some questions and find out whether you're telling me the truth." She turned to Don. "Did you have time to show that picture to anyone?"

Don clenched his closed mouth shut and worked his jaw. Lucinda studied them all intently for any reaction. "You," she said, turning to Rebecca. "Answer the question."

Rebecca shook her head, defiance on her face, then regret as she glanced at the drawer where she had replaced her gun. "We only saw it a minute before you—"

Lucinda took two steps and smacked Rebecca, quickly returning her hand to the rifle and stepping back. "You're lying!"

Rebecca gasped sharply, but said nothing, starting to sob. Don stared straight at Lucinda. "No need to get rough. She knows nothing."

"She's seen the picture. That means she knows too much." She shoved Rebecca, who collapsed loosely, as if she had no spine. Or knew how to take a fall.

Another explosion shook the building, harder than the first. Glass broke in the other room. Lucinda stepped back to brace her butt against the Aremac table. Roger saw that Tess's head had fallen to the side. Then he saw her wink.

87

Before she risked the wink, Tess had tested her index finger, the one she had been using the exoskeleton to exercise. It not only moved, but she could feel it move. She wiggled it sideways. She could feel the coarse weave of the sheet.

Not daring to make a larger move, she took a mental inventory of her body. Her forehead was wet. And hot. She couldn't talk through the Aremac, but her cameras and her screen were still working. All except one, leaving her blind to one corner of the room—unless she moved her head.

She didn't dare move her head, but she pressed down to feel it resting against the table. It was still inside the magnet's gap. She wiggled her tongue without opening her mouth, feeling the smooth backs of her teeth. She wiggled her toes inside her slippers. They moved, but the effort exhausted her. She let herself rest for a moment, watching the scene without daring to move her cameras.

Lucinda was looking at Don, but Roger was looking at Tess. She took a chance and tried to wink. Her eyelid felt like lead, but it moved. Then her heart stopped in her chest. Lucinda was looking at her. *Did she see the wink?*

"Ah, now there's an idea." Lucinda put the tip of the rifle barrel against Tess's forehead. Tess's head was still resting between the Aremac's magnetic plates. "I think I can solve my problem quite easily."

Lucinda now looked at Roger, but he was still staring at Tess. She winked again, then slid her right hand an inch to one side. It took an enormous effort, but she wasn't sure he saw it.

Roger looked away from her hand, at Lucinda. "Wait a minute. Don't you want the Aremac? You can have all the software if you leave her alone. I don't care what you do to me, but spare her."

Lucinda turned her head to look at Don, her brow furrowed. "Is your boy genius really going to help me? I don't think so."

Roger looked desperate. "I can prove my sincerity. The password is *baH Hong*. Got it? *baH Hong*."

Tess understood. He *had* seen her hand move.

Lucinda's aim at Tess's head didn't waver. "Very funny," Lucinda said. "What is it? Chinese?"

"No," said Roger. "It's Klingon."

A puzzled look began to form on Lucinda's face. Tess crept her hand along the side of her table. Another inch. She wasn't sure how far away the emergency switch was. She wasn't even sure she could reach it, but Roger seemed to think she could.

Another inch. Lucinda was looking around the room, but Tess could feel the cold metal of the barrel against her forehead. They all could hear gunfire outside.

Another inch. Tess's finger bumped against an obstruction. *Can it be anything but the switch?* She would have only one chance, but after being immobile for so long, she might not have the strength, or the speed.

Roger was starting to explain. "It means . . ."

It is the switch that activates the magnet, Tess was certain of that. *But which way does it move?*

". . . in Klingon . . ."

Tess slipped one finger over the switch. Then another, in case one lacked the strength.

". . . that . . ."

She held her breath and pulled. The switch didn't move. With everything she could muster, she pulled again.

With a mighty clang, the H&K snapped against the magnet, pulling Lucinda off balance. Roger had already started moving, throwing himself wildly at Lucinda.

Tess watched helplessly as Lucinda struck at Roger's neck with her left hand, missing slightly and hammering hard on his ear. He dropped out of Tess's view.

Then Heidi sprang up and chomped onto Lucinda's left arm with the full force of ninety pounds of muscle, bone, and sharp teeth. Lucinda swung her arm, slamming the German Shepherd against the table. Tess felt the shock, but Heidi hung on.

Don's fist muffled Lucinda's openmouthed scream.

Don's second blow knocked her to the floor, with Heidi still attached, shaking her arm violently. The Aremac began to spark, and the gun fell away, hitting Tess squarely on the face before it clattered onto the concrete floor. She felt the pain and closed her eyes. When she opened her eyes, her view screen was blank.

"Get the gun," Don yelled. "And guard the door. There may be others coming in."

Arnie ran forward and picked up the assault rifle, but he didn't seem to know what to do with it. Rebecca ran to retrieve her gun as Don pulled his two pistols from Lucinda's belt. Tess slowly turned her head and saw Roger on the floor. Then the front wall collapsed.

88

A thought flashed through Roger's mind: *In the movies, the bad guys always want to gloat before they kill their victims.* These three real-life bad guys didn't. They climbed in over the rubble, shooting all the way.

They also stumbled all the way. For a minute, the pile of cinder block, mortar, and broken windows rendered their automatic weapons largely ineffective. Arnie, still staring witlessly at the assault rifle in his hands, didn't take advantage of their ineptitude, but Rebecca dropped to one knee and started picking them off, first one, then another, until she'd emptied her clip. Still collapsed on the floor, Roger was distracted by a howl of pain from Heidi, and wasn't sure whether Don or Rebecca got the third one.

A long-haired female head came into view. Don shot her in the face before her weapon was even visible behind the rubble. Then he took advantage of a short delay to grab Arnie's assault rifle and greet the fifth and sixth terrorists. He was watching for a seventh when Lucinda tackled him.

Down they went, wrestling for the weapon. Roger and Rebecca tried to throw themselves on Lucinda. They collided. Both missed their target.

Roger, on the floor, got one hand around the barrel of the rifle. It looked momentarily like a three-way stalemate until Rebecca extracted a weapon from one of the fallen terrorists and pointed it in Lucinda's face, just inches away.

"Don't shoot her," Don gasped. "I need her alive."

"Okay," said Rebecca, her voice quavering just a bit. Picking up a broken concrete block in her free hand, she slammed it against Lucinda's head. Bits of dried mortar flew in all directions. One hit Roger in the eye.

He lost his grip on the gun barrel, but Lucinda was no longer conscious. The gun clattered to the floor. Now they were weaponless, and he could hear someone else coming.

A voice shouted from behind the rubble. "FBI. We're coming in. Drop your weapons."

"Don't shoot," Don yelled. "I'm FBI. Don Capitol. Everything's under control, but there's a bomb under the floor. And a bomber."

A flood of men wearing flak vests and FBI caps streamed over the rubble. Two of them checked the downed terrorists while Don cuffed Lucinda. Two others went searching the premises, emerging from the back office a moment later with SOS, Denise clutching his arm. SOS rubbed his eyes and shaded them from the light. "Guess what we—did we miss something?"

"Nothing we can't tell you about later," said Don, dragging Lucinda to her feet. "For now, just get out of here while the bomb squad takes a look downstairs."

SOS stopped walking. "Downstairs? We don't have a—"

Don shouldered him toward the street. "Just move. I'll explain later."

Outside, all the shrubbery around the building had been shredded by bullets from the attack and counterattack. The cars and vans used as cover by both sides were shot up, crumpled, and smoking. Across the street, firefighters were dousing the shell of what used to be a school bus. Roger, one eye closed, carried Tess to a waiting ambulance. The paramedics took her from Roger and laid her on a gurney. In a weak, squeaky voice, she protested, "I'm not injured. I'm just out of shape. Don't take me away."

One of the paramedics rinsed out Roger's eye and gave him a cold compress. Others tried to examine nicks and scratches on Rebecca, but she pushed them over to Arnie, who had taken a bullet wound in his upper arm.

Don carried Lucinda over to be examined. While the paramedics were bandaging her head wound, she opened her eyes, looked at Don, then closed them again.

"Leave her there," Don ordered. "She has some talking to do. Some unfinished business."

Lucinda laughed bitterly. "No talking. Just read me my rights."

"You gave up your rights when you fell in with terrorists—just check the Patriot Act."

The bomb-squad leader came outside dragging the wet body of the bomb-strapped terrorist. "He's safe now. Still alive, but I can't understand a word he's saying. What the water didn't do to dismantle the bomb, we took care of. But it's a mess down there, all kinds of crap floating in the water."

"Sorry," Don dragged Lucinda off her gurney by the arm, and she staggered groggily to keep up with him, "but if it's safe now, we're taking her back inside."

"I want to go back, too," said Tess. Roger tried to argue, but, as usual, all he won was a small concession. Tess would stay on the gurney and be wheeled in. SOS and Denise helped clear a path through the rubble, then followed them inside. Rebecca followed too, but Arnie elected to follow advice instead and take his wound to the hospital. Later, hearing about what followed, Arnie was glad he left his young clients when he did.

89

When Roger finally succeeded in maneuvering the gurney through the maze of rubble, Tess saw Don moving Lucinda to the Aremac table. She wasn't cooperating. "I think I'll have to resort to the Aremac," Don said.

Lucinda laughed a nasty laugh. "I took care of that."

Roger poked around in the machine. "Maybe not. It looks like only a rheostat was damaged. We have a spare."

"You're bluffing."

"You think so? Okay, SOS. Get the rheostat. We'll strap her down while you're installing it."

Lucinda resisted for a moment, then relaxed. "I still think you're bluffing. Do your worst."

Tess decided she could add to the scam. "Don't do it, Roger." She managed to prop herself up on one elbow. She tried to put conviction in her voice, but her vocal cords hurt from lack of exercise. What came out was wheezy and scratchy. "That isn't the kind of thing the Bag Bandit would do." She figured Lucinda would have heard about the Bag Bandit—the kind of craziness he was known for.

"What's she talking about?" Lucinda asked.

Roger seemed to understand what Tess was up to. "She's worried about the rheostat failing."

"Good," said Lucinda.

"Not good," said Tess. "That's the same model that failed on me."

"Don't worry." Roger made a pretense of inspecting the bullet hole. "It probably won't fail again. But if it does, it's not likely to do the same thing to her that it did to you."

Don was catching on. "Wait a minute. Are you saying there's a chance that this could put my prisoner in a coma for who knows how long, like Tess was?"

Tess pulled herself painfully to a sitting position, and then slid her legs over the side of her gurney. Roger rushed to grab her before her atrophied muscles failed entirely. Half carried, she lurched over to Lucinda's side and turned to speak to Don. "I wasn't in a coma. I was conscious all the time."

"So I could question her with the Aremac, like we did with you?"

"Sure. And she'd be safe from torture, because she wouldn't be able to feel a thing." Tess stroked Lucinda's short hair, as if comforting her. "Actually, that's the good part, Lucinda. You don't have to worry. No matter what anyone does to you, you won't feel it. You can just laugh at their efforts."

As Tess continued her recitation of what it was like to be locked in, unable to feel her body or control it, the blood was draining from Lucinda's face. "Well, I guess that's not the whole truth, Lucinda, because you won't be able to actually laugh. Or talk. But it's really not so bad. You sort of get used to it. You begin to forget what having a body is like."

Tess laid her hand on the captive's belly. "And guess what? I was pregnant, but I lost the baby."

Roger poked around noisily behind the Aremac, where SOS was working with a soldering iron, sending solder smoke into their nostrils. "How's it coming?" Don asked him.

"Almost done, but I think we should ramp the magnet up slowly. I'm not too sure of this thing."

"Not necessary. If it's going to work, it will work at full juice."

"Maybe we should wait until tomorrow, when I can get the proper part."

"No," Tess protested, stroking Lucinda's shoulder. "I don't want Don to start torturing her. This way, whatever happens, she won't experience any pain. Just hurry it up."

"Don't you want us to check it?"

"Waste of time," said Roger. "It doesn't have to be a precision job."

"I think you should check, darling," Tess said. "You should be more of a perfectionist."

"Look, why are you all fretting over this?" Roger asked. "If it knocks her out, we'll have it fixed in a few days and give her another jolt. That's what brought you out, wasn't it? So it ought to work again."

SOS stood up to announce he was done. Roger headed for the control panel. "Get the snood, will you, SOS?"

Don protested, "But it hasn't been calibrated for her."

"That's okay," said Roger. "If it doesn't work right, at most, it will take a couple of hours to get it right. And she won't forget anything in a couple of hours. She's strapped down, so she's not going anywhere."

"This worries me," Don said.

"Okay, we'll shave her head first. That should make it more accurate. Rebecca, go get the razor and give her a haircut."

The snood arrived while Rebecca was making one last pass over Lucinda's now-bald head with the electric razor. Tess had held Lucinda's unwilling hand throughout the entire procedure. Roger brushed away a few more locks of blond hair onto the floor, then fiddled with the cap for a minute, baring two low-voltage wires so they'd touch Lucinda's scalp when the cap was on. He began putting the snood in place. Lucinda's face hardened as she gritted her teeth.

"Just a minute," Tess said. "You're not thinking. If she's going to be on there for a while, you have to rig up the tubes. I know what it's like."

"What tubes?" asked Lucinda.

"Just in case you need to . . ." Tess lowered her voice to a discretely conspiratorial tone, affecting an uncharacteristic prissiness for Lucinda's sake, ". . . you know, tinkle . . . or the other thing. We wouldn't want you to mess up the table." She patted Lucinda's hand and stood up. "Okay, Rebecca, get the tubes. I don't think I'm strong enough to do it myself, but Don can put them in."

"Shouldn't I wash them off first?" Rebecca said. "The medics only took them out of you a few minutes ago."

"Don't worry," Tess said. "I don't think I have any diseases. And they don't hurt as much coming out as they do going in. Don, try to be gentle."

"I don't want any tubes."

"Of course you do, dear. Take it from me. If you have an accident, you'll stink up the whole place. And it sticks to your skin. Even if you get knocked out like I was, you'll still be able to smell it. It's awful lying around in your own mess. It itches something awful."

"I keep telling you she won't get knocked out," Roger snapped. "I built this machine, so I know."

Rebecca handed all the tubing to Don, being sure that Lucinda could see the two transparent plastic bags containing Tess's waste.

Tess held her nose as the bags went past, and then turned slightly to face Roger. "You've made mistakes before, darling. You really ought to test it first."

"Okay. All right. If you'll stop second-guessing me, I'll give it a little test while Don's getting the tubes ready."

"Just the first notch, darling."

Roger reached for the switch. "Okay, here it goes. If it's working, she won't feel a thing."

As Roger had intended, a tiny current tickled across Lucinda's bare scalp from the two exposed wires. She strained against the straps without effect, her face taut in a grimace. Tess put one hand on Lucinda's forehead, gently pushing her head back down. "Now, come on, dear. You didn't really feel anything."

Don, washed tubes in hand, approached the table. "I think she's wet herself."

"Darn," said Roger. "I knew we should have put in the tubes first. Okay, take off her wet pants and insert the tubes before I give her the full jolt. Both tubes."

"Make them stop," said Lucinda, sagging her head to one side to look at Tess. "They weren't supposed to kill anybody."

90

Three weeks after all the excitement, with the repairs just about complete on their converted garage, Tess finally felt strong enough to hold a party, to thank everyone personally for helping her through very dark days. Grateful that the building had remained surprisingly sound structurally, despite the collapse of the front wall, she pulled down the shades to hide the picketers still circling the property to protest the Aremac, claiming it was an instrument for the invasion of privacy. She had re-hung Navajo rugs over the patched walls, and draped sheets over all the exercise equipment she was using to restore her atrophied muscles and lost bone mass. Never much of a cook, even at full strength, she had ordered-in a Chinese banquet with everyone's favorite dishes, played hostess until everyone was well fed, and then eased into her real agenda—clearing up a few loose ends.

She turned to Roger. "It still scares me to think that I was so close to where they were meeting—that day Don took me to look for rugs." She hadn't gotten over the delight in Roger's eyes whenever he heard her real voice.

"Well, you were two floors away."

"Even so, it's a scary thought. They were after *me*."

Don put down the remains of his egg roll. "I doubt they knew you were in the building."

"Wouldn't Lucinda have known? She seems to have known pretty much everything else that was going on."

"I'm so, so sorry about that. My fault entirely. I should have figured out that she was the mole. The only one, I hope."

Arnie halted a spare rib on the way to his mouth, scattering a few drops of sauce on his wounded arm's cast. "So how come you never suspected her?"

"First of all, we were looking for Arabs, Muslims at least. Lucinda is Caucasian, a born-again Christian, a so-called all-American. They completely fooled us, which was their intention. They weren't Arabs at all. Most of them wanted to whip up public anger *against* Muslims."

"But the first man you captured, he was a Muslim, wasn't he?" Arnie said, and then pointed at the place on the floor where Tess's new Two Gray Hills rugs covered the steel trapdoor over the pit below. "And the suicide bomber we stuck downstairs?"

"Oh, yes, they were both Arabs." He looked at Roger and quickly checked himself. "Well, the first was Arab-American—"

"An American of Arab ancestry," Roger corrected.

"Right. Of Arab ancestry. This *alKhamis* group—their name was another nice touch—kidnapped the first one in Cleveland, tortured him, threatened his family if he talked, then burned off his tongue and fingers to make sure he didn't. They drugged him and put him near the home they bombed. I think he was supposed to die, with enough clues that we'd know he was . . . of Arab ancestry."

Halfway through this description, Addie had covered her ears. "That's just awful," Tess said, while comforting Addie by stroking her hair, still quite short from her prison experience. "What about his family? Were they harmed? Do they know about his death?"

Don nodded. "We took care of that. They're all right, and they know he's dead, but we didn't tell them exactly how he died. We told them he was a hero, killed while trying to stop a terrorist bomb."

"Well," said Tess, "it seems someone in the FBI has a heart. You could have fooled me. But what about the suicide bomber? Was he one of them? He was quite conscious when he crashed in here."

"He wasn't one of them," said Don. "Just another innocent victim. Another semi-legal ex-student. Quite drugged out of his mind. And running from the threat of being shot in the back. I don't think he knew he was carrying a load of bombs. He doesn't remember."

"Has he recovered from what we did to him?" Roger asked.

"The doctors say he's ninety-percent there, and should be pretty much good as new in a few months. And your heartless FBI is helping him become legal, so he won't be deported."

"But if he wasn't one of the bad guys," Rebecca asked, "how did they expect him to trigger the bombs?"

"They didn't. The only trigger was tied to a cell phone."

Rebecca shivered. "I can't imagine that kind of hatred against any group."

"Well, it wasn't pure racism," Don continued. "They all wanted the money. I don't know if they really thought they were going to get it, because some of their leaders were also desperate to discredit the police establishment. And the city officials. Maybe they would have been satisfied with that. Most of them were former police with a grudge against the city—"

"Except Lucinda," Tess said. "She was federal all the way, wasn't she?"

"She was. She had uncovered the group in one of her investigations and used their resentments for her own purposes."

"So why didn't you spot her?" Roger asked. "She must have slipped up somewhere."

"I listed everyone you knew and eliminated them. I assumed Tess knew LD, but looking back, I can't remember a time when she was in the room with her. That was a mistake."

"Not entirely," said Roger, thinking back. "She was in the room—in the early days. But I guess she wasn't within Tess's line of sight."

Tess looked at the Aremac, covered over with a bedsheet. "I knew there were other people around. But I had no way to know who they were unless someone mentioned their names. And at that stage, I couldn't see anyone who wasn't right in my face. But how did you know they were meeting at the Merchandise Mart?"

"Well, of course, I didn't know that at the time, or we would have shut them down, then and there. But we were closing in on them at the end, mostly from the Aremac clues. We would have shut them down eventually, but I'm glad it was over before the Vice President arrived. Probably saved my job."

"Do you think you've shut them down now?" Rebecca wanted to know. "Or do we still have to worry?"

"Well, would you like to help me on my next case? I need a replacement for a cold-blooded woman."

"Oh, you don't want me. All I ever did was play a little paintball."

"You didn't learn all that from paint guns."

"Okay, so we practiced a little at the range. Just an NRA self-defense class."

"You're too modest," said Roger. "You were the *instructor* in those classes."

"I don't like to exaggerate," she hesitated and then smiled, "like Don."

"I don't exaggerate."

"Yes, you do. That one little old Swedish man who was left didn't seem much of a threat. The one Lucinda called Zay."

"That's because you didn't look in his eyes. He was their charismatic leader. With all sorts of underworld connections." Don leaned back with his hands behind his head. "And, oh yeah, I was wrong before. He was a former federal agent, retired early for some indiscretion involving minors he claimed were consenting." Don rolled his eyes. "Consenting minors. Please. He tried to get a congressional override for his dishonorable discharge. So he could get his pension. He was their money man. The rest of them were more fanatical. But also for revenge."

"Revenge?" Roger asked.

"That's part of it, for Lucinda, at least. It seems she hated the Arabs for torturing her and her boyfriend—and killing him—back when they served in the Middle East. I guess none of us can know what torture might do to us."

Tess looked over at Addie, knowing how Lucinda and Don had tortured her. She decided not to tell Don *I told you so*—he had already made amends with Addie, and she acknowledged that Don had tried to stop Lucinda on that hot day. Tess started clearing the table, but Rebecca jumped up from her chair to clear, telling Tess to enjoy herself and sit back down. "Well, at least we don't have to worry about Lucinda anymore."

"But we'll always have to worry about someone. We capture a few, kill a few, but they're out there somewhere breeding more."

Tess laughed. "Speaking of breeding, why didn't SOS and Denise come to my party?"

"I invited them," said Arnie, "but they've gone on some 'Geek Cruise' somewhere. Does anybody want more of these ribs? You, Tess? We've got to build you back up. Does anyone actually know what a Geek Cruise is?"

Tess gave him thumbs up for the ribs, but she ignored his question. "Addie, I guess SOS got over you in a hurry. Are you okay with that?"

Addie blushed. "I was flattered by the attention, but we never really connected. Now I'm just glad to be out of jail. I can't believe what you guys did for me. And my family. My uncle's still upset that he brought you to the Merchandise Mart."

"Qasim's such a dear man." Tess glared at Don. "I can't imagine why anyone would suspect him—or Addie—of being involved with terrorists." She couldn't resist mentioning Addie after all.

Don held up both hands in surrender. "*Mea culpa.* I'm supposed to suspect everybody—and I didn't even do a very good job at that."

"Well, you suspected Bonnie. Is she in prison, too?"

"On probation."

"Really? How come?"

"She had nothing to do with *Yom alKhamis.* She was hired by Mr. Tsang and that corporate group that wanted to steal the Aremac. She has a very sick little boy, and they offered to pay for his treatment. And she seems genuinely repentant."

"Was that Ms. Steinman's connection?"

"We think she was getting payoffs from one—or more—of the companies in that network. We're still trying to figure that one out, but she's suspended while we're working on it."

"And Wyatt? Was he working for the corporations, or the terrorists?"

"The corporations. But only as a dupe—"

"Nothing new there," said Roger, "but it explains the two different kinds of viruses. Someone at one of the corporations must have taken over the virus programming—someone competent. I hear Wyatt's got a job now at some college in South Dakota."

"North Dakota," Don corrected. "Fargo, or something. No, Jamestown—or maybe Minot."

"Well, he can't do much harm up there," said Roger. "He'll be too busy trying to keep warm."

"You're wrong, darling," Tess corrected. "People like Wyatt can do harm wherever they are. They're parasites who live off other people's inventions."

Don looked over at the Aremac. "Speaking of inventions, Rog, how long is it going to take you to repair the Aremac? How badly damaged is it?"

"One shot went through the control computer. That must have triggered a magnetic spike. The doctors think that's what shocked Tess's nervous system again, but I think it was the exoskeleton exercises."

"So, when?"

"Maybe all we have to do is replace the computer, but right now the system is kaput."

"Then you were just bluffing LD?"

"Of course. The Bag Bandit always bluffs."

"Well, I wasn't quite sure, but you two definitely persuaded her. I always thought she was tougher than that."

"Everybody has a greatest fear," said Tess. "I remembered how disgusted Lucinda was with my condition. Losing control was her greatest fear. I think that's why she never went into our apartment when I was there."

"Could be that," said Rebecca, "but how did she get that way? From her experience, you'd think she'd be one tough woman."

"Like you?" Arnie asked.

"Oh, Arnie, you say the sweetest things. But really, Don, how did she get like that?"

"To be fair, she was held captive as well, along with her boyfriend, by the government in . . . well, somewhere in the Middle East where the U.S. was never supposed to be. You should know that it took a long time to bring her out. She was tortured, brutally, though she would never talk to me about it."

"Now I feel bad," said Tess. "We were just playacting to bluff her into talking. I didn't understand how frightened she would be, even just from the threat of torture. I didn't know her history."

"I knew," said Don, "and maybe it made me too careless with her. I imagined that torture would simply make her a more dedicated agent—if it didn't break her. I see now that torture can do just about anything to the human brain. It's the moral equivalent of blasting a shotgun into a crowd, hoping you'll hit the bad guys and miss the good ones. Maybe the Aremac will make torture obsolete. I'd like to see that."

"That's my hope," said Roger, "but I'm beginning to realize that any technology can be misused."

"Did you know she had been tortured before?" Tess asked.

"I knew," Roger admitted. "Don did say once that she had experienced interrogation. I can understand why she'd fear being tortured, but that doesn't excuse her going against her own country."

"She didn't see it that way. She thought she was a true patriot, giving the rest of us a wake-up call. She was genuinely shaken by the Blue Line Massacre. They weren't supposed to kill any 'real Americans.' She was a terrific agent, but something inside was broken by her experiences."

"You're being awfully generous tonight," Tess laughed. "Want some more wine?"

Don pushed the bottle away. "If it's made me generous, I think I've had enough. But really, you should thank her for doing you a favor or you might still be on that table." He looked over at the Aremac. "Any other damage, Roger?"

"None that I can see. But I've only looked superficially."

"So how long will it take to fix it?"

"You don't give up, do you? We actually do have a spare rheostat. Not exactly the same model, but it should work."

"I don't think we'll need pictures, for now. I want to question the old man. Zay. He's a tough one. I'm sure he's got a lot more to tell about some of his mob friends. I'd be satisfied to play twenty questions for now, but in the future, maybe soon—"

Tess slammed her fist down on the table, rattling the few remaining dishes. "I don't think so, Don. We've got a ton more work to do before we let the Aremac loose on anybody again. Not even on a dog. Right, Heidi?" Heidi, fully recovered from the head blows she suffered from Lucinda, perked up her ears and stood up, wagging her tail. Roger called Heidi over to him and began rubbing her neck behind her ears.

"Maybe," said Don. "But I think that deep down you two are a lot like Heidi—a service dog who's ready to serve if called upon. You won't be able to resist the excitement."

"Don't count on me," Tess said. "I always wanted excitement, but I know now that I can find all the excitement I need in my own mind."

Roger covered his mouth, hiding a smile.

"What did I say that was so funny, darling?"

"You're beginning to sound like me. At least you probably understand me better."

"I still don't see why that's so funny."

"Because at the same time, I'm beginning to sound like you. All I ever wanted was peace and quiet. Isolation. To think. That's why I was so boring. Now I see how much I need outside stimulation."

"You mean you liked all the shooting and bombing?"

"Oh, no, not that. I mean stimulation from real engineering challenges. And, most of all, other people. From now on, I want to devote the Aremac to helping disabled people. People in comas. People with speech problems. That sort of thing. It inspires me to do my best work."

Arnie finished off a morsel of Mongolian beef and licked his lips. "I hope you'll still take on some legal cases—"

"Only when we can help free innocent people." Roger looked pointedly at Don. "And only when it's voluntary. I think I've figured out how to fix the Aremac so it can't be used against someone's will."

"And," said Tess, "we're going to give ten percent of our income from the Aremac to the ACLU. In return, they're going to screen all our applications."

Don smiled. "That's a noble thought, you two. Very liberal. But your nation may need you again one of these days. I know you'll answer the call."

Roger said nothing. After waiting a while, Don decided Roger wasn't going to respond, so he spoke again. "Speaking of answering the call, Roger, I've been wondering for three weeks how you did what you did to LD's rifle."

"I powered up the magnet," Tess said.

"Yes, it looked like the magnet grabbed it, but I thought the field was too weak."

Roger couldn't resist explaining. "Away from the gap, the field falls off rapidly, because the two poles almost cancel each other out. But Lucinda was holding the gun against Tess's head, so it was very close to the gap."

"But LD had crippled the Aremac, so why did the magnet still work?"

"Because she only crippled the computer. The magnet's power runs through a separate circuit. It draws so much current it would mess up the computer every time it switched on or off."

"But weren't you afraid the gun would fire at Tess?"

"Not when it was in the grip of that many teslas." To illustrate his point, Roger grabbed Don's left wrist and pinned it firmly to the table. "Believe me, every metal part of that gun was frozen in place as long as the magnet was on. Pretty funny, wasn't it?"

"Huh?"

"Teslas saving Tesla."

Don tried not to smile. "Did you know that would happen, Tess?"

"I may be named after the great magnetist, but I wasn't sure." She stood and threw her arms around her husband's neck. "I trusted Roger."

"But he didn't say anything."

"Sure he did. He said, '*baH Hong*.'"

"I thought that's what I heard. Is it really Klingon? What does it mean?"

Roger grinned, then looked to Tess to see whether she wanted to answer. When she only repeated, "*baH Hong*," he said, "Yes, it's Klingon. It means, 'Fire the impulse power.'"

A Practical Guide for Everyone Involved in Product and Systems Development

Are Your Lights On?

How to Figure Out What the Problem Really Is

by Donald C. Gause *and* Gerald M. Weinberg

ISBN-13: 978-0-932633-16-3 ©*1990* *176 pages* *softcover*
$19.95 (includes $6 UPS in US)

The fledgling problem solver invariably rushes in with solutions before taking time to define the problem being solved. Even experienced solvers, when subjected to social pressure, yield to this demand for haste. When they do, many solutions are found, but not necessarily to the problem at hand.

Whether you are a novice or a veteran, this powerful little book will make you a more effective problem solver. Anyone involved in product and systems development will appreciate this practical illustrated guide, which was first published in 1982 and has since become a cult classic.

The book playfully instructs the reader first to identify the problem, second to determine the problem's owner, third to identify where the problem came from, and fourth to determine whether or not to solve it.

Delightfully illustrated with 55 line drawings, the book conveys a message that will change the way you think about projects and problems.

> "In a highly readable evolution, the authors present insights on problem identification and practical approaches which will be of immeasurable aid to the manager.
>
> "Although the material is serious, the treatment is neither stodgy nor unnecessarily technical. It is a down-to-earth approach . . ."
> —**Jim Van Speybroeck**
> *Data Processing Digest*

> ". . . serves as a great introduction to problem solving. . . . I highly recommend it."
> —**John S. Rhodes**
> *WebWord.com*

About the Authors

Donald C. Gause and Gerald M. Weinberg bring to this collaboration a combined sixty years' experience helping people in banking, computing, insurance, automotive, and telecommunications industries to identify what the problem really is.

DORSET HOUSE PUBLISHING 353 WEST 12TH STREET NEW YORK, NEW YORK 10014 USA
(800) 342-6657 • (212) 620-4053 • fax (212) 727-1044 • info@dorsethouse.com • www.dorsethouse.com

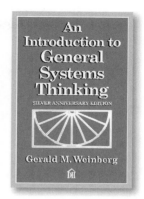

Proven Techniques and Strategies to Help You Succeed As a Consultant

The Secrets of Consulting

A Guide to Giving and Getting Advice Successfully

by Gerald M. Weinberg
foreword by Virginia Satir

ISBN-13: 978-0-932633-01-9   ©1985   248 pages   softcover
$35.95 (includes $6 UPS in US)

If you are a consultant, ever use one, or want to be one, this book will show you how to succeed.

With wit, charm, humor, and wisdom, Weinberg shows you exactly how to become a more effective consultant. He reveals specific techniques and strategies that really work.

Through the use of vividly memorable rules, laws, and principles—such as The Law o f Raspberry Jam, The Potato Chip Principle, and Lessons from the Farm—the author shows you how to price and market your services, avoid traps and find alternative approaches, keep ahead of your clients, create a special "consultant's survival kit," trade improvement for perfection, and much more.

The Secrets of Consulting—techniques, strategies, and first-hand experiences—all that you'll need to set up, run, and be successful at your own consulting business.

> WINNER OF
> *COMPUTER BOOK REVIEW'S*
> MAEVENTEC AWARD FOR
> *"books which are exemplary in style, content, and format."*

"an irreverent, funny, provocative, satirical but true look at those thousands of professionals, as well as con men, who call themselves consultants."
—**Martin A. Goetz**
Applied Data Research, Inc.

"In this book Gerald Weinberg uses entertaining prose littered with humorous paradoxes, dilemmas and contradictions to share his ideas on how to deal with people and organizations to help them change. This book is full of ideas on how to work with people to get them to adopt new ideas."
—**Mary Sakry**
The Process Group

About the Author

Gerald M. Weinberg draws on experiences gained as an author, lecturer, and consultant himself, as well as from a long technical career as a scientist and researcher for IBM, Ethnotech, and Project Mercury.

"outstanding . . . for anyone who has thought of becoming a 'consultant.'"
—*Management Accounting*

DORSET HOUSE PUBLISHING 353 WEST 12TH STREET NEW YORK, NEW YORK 10014 USA
info@dorsethouse.com • www.dorsethouse.com

More Secrets of Consulting

The Consultant's Tool Kit

by Gerald M. Weinberg

ISBN-13: 978-0-932633-52-1   ©2002   *216 pages   softcover*
$39.95 (includes $6 UPS in US)

Widely acclaimed as a consultant's consultant, Gerald M. Weinberg builds on his perennial best-seller *The Secrets of Consulting* with all-new laws, rules, and principles. You'll learn how to fight burnout, stay curious, understand your clients, negotiate effectively, and much, much more.

Consultants need more than technical skills— they need self-awareness and a strong set of personal abilities. Weinberg helps computer consultants identify and strengthen each aspect of their performance using a "consultant's tool kit" of seventeen memorable symbols.

He devotes a chapter to each of these symbolic tools, from The Wisdom Box to The Fish-Eye Lens to The Oxygen Mask and more.

"full of fresh ideas, paradoxes, ironies, and provocativeness. . . . entertaining and concurrently thought provoking."   —**Donald E. Riggs**
The Journal of Academic Librarianship

About the Author

Gerald M. Weinberg is the author of scores of books and articles on consulting and software development, including the 1985 classic, *The Secrets of Consulting*.
Visit www.geraldmweinberg.com.

Weinberg
on Writing

The Fieldstone Method

by Gerald M. Weinberg

FINALIST,
BEST BOOKS 2006
USA BOOK NEWS
~
FINALIST,
JOLT! AWARD

ISBN-13: 978-0-932633-65-1 ©2006 *208 pages* softcover
$30.95 *(includes $6 UPS in US)*

Gerald M. Weinberg, author of more than forty books—including nineteen published by Dorset House—reveals his secrets for collecting and organizing his ideas for writing projects.

Drawing an analogy to the stone-by-stone method of building fieldstone walls, Weinberg shows writers how to construct fiction and nonfiction manuscripts from key insights, stories, and quotes.

The elements, or stones, are collected nonsequentially, over time, and eventually find logical places in larger pieces. The method renders writer's block irrelevant and has proved effective for scores of Weinberg's writing class students.

If you've ever wanted to write a book or article—or need to revitalize your writing career—don't miss this intimate glimpse into the mind behind some the computer industry's best books.

Topics include gathering from literature, decimating your work, discarding stones that don't fit, putting your subconscious to work, knowing when to stop, and much more.

features 40+ exercises for individuals and groups

About the Author

Gerald M. Weinberg reveals the writing method that has propelled him for more than 40 years. He has written on topics ranging from computer systems and programming to education and problem solving.

"Don't write your book—build it with Weinberg's Fieldstone Method. Keep the project moving by breaking the project into easy-to-attack chunks; gather your ideas one at a time. Then stack them as you would stones in a wall."
—**Dan Poynter**
author of *Writing Nonfiction*
and *The Self-Publishing Manual*

"smart, funny, memorable, wise, engaging . . . and, most important, it is all stuff that works . . ."
—**Howard S. Becker**
author of *Writing for Social Scientists*

"It wasn't until I participated in one of Jerry Weinberg's writing workshops that I was able to take my writing to the next level. . . . I'm proof these techniques work."
—**Johanna Rothman**
author of *Hiring the Best Knowledge Workers, Techies & Nerds*

DORSET HOUSE PUBLISHING 353 WEST 12TH STREET NEW YORK, NEW YORK 10014 USA
(800) 342-6657 • (212) 620-4053 • fax (212) 727-1044 • info@dorsethouse.com • www.dorsethouse.com